THE FIFTH SUSPECT

ROBERT MCNEIL

Print ISBN 978-1-913419-46-2

For my wife, Dee, son Stuart, daughter Lucy, and their mother, Heather, who never lived to see this.

1

A sudden gust of wind rattled rain like pellets against the bedroom window. The room flickered briefly as lightning flashed over the city. Thunder rumbled overhead and twelve-year-old Alex Fleming woke up suddenly. He shot up in bed with his eyes wide open. But it wasn't the sound of the rain or the thunder that alarmed him. It was a man's voice downstairs, loud and aggressive. No one had been with his mother when Alex came to bed and she hadn't said she was expecting anyone.

He pulled the bedclothes back and swung his legs over the edge of the bed. The bedroom door was slightly ajar and a dim light shone in from the landing. He crept towards the door and pushed it open. The man's voice was louder.

Alex made his way quietly along the landing and peered down the stairs. He took a deep breath and crept down. At the foot of the stairs, he looked warily along the hallway that ran from the front door to the kitchen. The kitchen door was wide open and he could see his mother trying to wrestle away from the grip of the man. Alex recognised him. It was Jimmy Calder who worked in the small corner-street shop with Alex's mother.

'Let me go!' she was demanding.

Calder ignored her and tightened his grip. 'The police came to see me,' he snarled. 'They seem to think I took the money from the till. You told them it was me, didn't you, Anne?'

'No, I didn't!'

'But you said it wasn't you.'

Anne nodded.

'So, you might just as well have said it was me. Apart from that bitch of an owner, Morag bloody Campbell, there's only the two of us that work in the shop.'

'What else was I supposed to say?' Anne mumbled, trying to pull away from Calder.

'You could have told them the same as me and that a customer could have nicked it from the till when we weren't looking.'

'That's not what happened though.'

'I'll tell you what's going to happen. You're going to say you took it–'

'But I didn't! I can't own up to something I didn't do,' Anne protested.

'I need you to help me out here, Anne.'

'What do you mean?'

'Did you know I was in prison before I came to work in the shop?'

'No, no I didn't.'

'I was and I'm out on parole. If they nick me for this, I'll be back inside.'

'I... I didn't know–'

'No, and there's no way that's going to happen because you're going to say it was you.'

'I can't!'

'Shut up and listen! You don't have a criminal record. You're a single mother with a young son. If you plead guilty, say you only intended to borrow the money to pay the rent and that you're sorry, you won't get a custodial sentence.'

'I won't do it–'

Calder grabbed Anne's hair and pulled her head back, making her scream. He thrust his face close to hers. 'Oh yes you will,' he hissed through clenched teeth. 'I can get some friends of mine to pay you a visit if I go back to prison. They can be nasty pieces of work if I want them to be.' Calder tugged harder on Anne's hair. 'Pity if anything happened to your son. Know what I mean?'

'You bastard!' Anne yelled in a sudden fit of rage. She thrust a knee into Calder's groin. He gasped and staggered backwards, catching his hand against the blade of a carving knife sticking out from a drying rack. He cursed and watched blood seeping out between his fingers.

'Sorry... sorry,' Anne stammered.

'You bitch!' Calder screamed. He grabbed the knife and thrust it upwards into Anne's stomach. A red stain seeped through her white shirt. Her eyes opened wide as she staggered backwards.

Alex screamed, 'Mum!'

Anne looked over Calder's shoulder and saw Alex trembling at the end of the hallway. 'Run, run!' she yelled.

Calder turned and saw Alex, his face twisting into a snarl as he rushed towards the boy.

'Run!' Anne screamed.

Alex turned and ran for the front door. He yanked it open as he heard the harsh thump of feet and heavy breathing behind him.

'Come back here!' Calder shouted. But Alex didn't stop. He ran outside, pulling the front door closed.

Calder cursed as he crashed into it. 'Fuck!'

Alex didn't look back. He was down the steps and across the short path to the pavement. Freezing rain battered his face like shards of ice. Lightning flashed across the dark sky and thunder crashed overhead. Alex tried to blink the rain from his eyes as he turned right, lungs exploding as he ran as fast as his legs would carry him. His bare feet felt as though he was running on broken glass, but he daren't stop.

Calder was catching up with him as Alex reached the end of the street. He was deciding whether to turn right or cross the road when he saw a car coming. Thinking quickly, he thought he might just be able to get across the road in front of the car and that would hold Calder up for a few seconds. He could then turn into the maze of streets on the other side and lose him.

Without giving it another thought, Alex ran straight onto the road. Headlights pierced through the rain. He'd misjudged the speed of the car completely. Alex heard the squeal of tyres and saw the headlights too close. The car skidded and hit Alex, tossing him into the air off the bonnet. He hit the ground and lay still in the middle of the road.

The car doors flew open and the driver and passenger rushed round to Alex. The driver's face was ashen. 'I... I couldn't stop in time,' he stammered. 'He... he appeared from nowhere and ran straight in front of us.'

The passenger had taken control. 'Ambulance! Ring for an ambulance! Quick! I can feel a pulse.'

The driver was hysterical. 'Thank God!' He tried to get his mobile phone out of his pocket, but his hands were shaking so much that he dropped it on the road. The passenger grabbed it and made the call.

Alex could hear voices. His vision was blurred. He could see bright lights and felt nothing but the cold rain falling heavily on his face. Two people were bending over him.

Beyond them he could make out the dark shape of Calder standing on the edge of the pavement, watching. Alex tried to say something, but no words came out. The last thing he saw was Calder turning and melting into the shadows.

2

TWENTY-THREE YEARS LATER

Ronnie Nielson had once joked that Peggy Dobbs was a bit of a psychic. She'd phoned him on more than one occasion to ask if he wanted her to clean his boat just as he was about to call and ask her. And those who knew her well thought she possessed an uncanny sixth sense.

That morning she'd woken up with a sense of foreboding. She'd no idea why. She'd shrugged it off and was making her way from her small terraced house down to the path by the River Thames that led to Bourne End Marina. Nielson had called her the previous night. He'd asked if she could come and clean the boat which he moored near his house when he was up from London.

It was early and the sun was shining with a few white clouds drifting across the clear blue sky. It was eerily quiet as she reached the river. The previous day's heavy rain had left the path muddy with a few puddles and Peggy had to watch her footing. A sudden flapping noise behind her broke the silence. She spun round anxiously with her heart racing, then smiled with relief as two ducks swept in low over the river and came to a noisy splash landing.

Humming a tune to herself, she continued on her way along the path.

Peggy had recently turned sixty, lost her husband five years earlier, and lived on her own apart from her black and white cat, Toby. She wasn't well off by any means, but earned a bit of cash by cleaning for Nielson. Shortly after her husband had died, Peggy had gone to a local pub to drown her sorrows when she'd met Nielson. The pub was quiet and Nielson had bought her a drink. They'd chatted for a while and he'd told her that he'd bought a house near the river, and about the boat. He'd told her he owned a nightclub in London and was looking for someone to look after the house and clean the boat from time to time. Peggy had offered her services and they agreed terms.

Nielson had seemed pleasant enough, but Peggy sensed there was a cold side to him. But, she reminded herself, he was a businessman. *Running a nightclub in London can't be that easy*, she'd thought. That would require a man to have a pretty tough character, wouldn't it? Anyway, he'd been kind to her and that was what mattered. He was a muscular man with receding grey hair. The casual clothes, short ponytail and diamond stud he wore in his left ear gave him a somewhat hippie look. Peggy had admired it and said she would love something like that but could never afford it. Nielson had laughed and told her he'd leave it to her if she did a good job cleaning for him.

Peggy was wondering if he meant it when she heard the sound of heavy breathing and feet thumping on the ground behind her. She turned in alarm, heart skipping a beat. A jogger ran past looking at his watch. 'Sorry,' he panted, 'didn't mean to startle you.' He raced on, glancing at his watch again. Peggy took a deep breath, shook her head and continued on her way.

The *Done Deal* was in sight. It was a beautiful white forty-foot diesel cruiser with three cabins. Peggy couldn't quite put her finger on it, but she had a strange feeling as she approached.

Was it the silence? The only sound was the gentle lapping of water against the hull of the boat and the tap of the open cockpit door swinging in the gentle breeze. There was no sign of Nielson. Peggy felt uneasy. There was no music. Mr Nielson always had music blaring when he was aboard. *Maybe he isn't*, she thought. But why would the cockpit door be open?

Peggy stepped up onto the deck and listened for a second for any sounds from below. There were none. 'Mr Nielson,' she called out anxiously. 'It's Peggy. I'm here.'

No reply.

Her heart pounded as she pulled the cockpit door open and looked down the steps into the saloon. She could hear the buzzing of flies and a sickly smell drifted upwards. Peggy held a hand to her face as she crept down the steps into the saloon. There was blood all over the floor, the white leather seating and the table. She grimaced as flies buzzed round her head.

'Mr Nielson? Are you there?' Peggy called out, dreading what she might find.

The silence was palpable.

Peggy crossed the saloon to the door that led to three steps down to the galley and a small dinette. The door was slightly ajar. She pushed it open and screamed. Nielson was lying face down on the floor in a pool of blood. Peggy staggered backwards and yelled as she tripped and fell into the saloon. She tried to break her fall with her hands and slipped across the floor in the blood.

She pulled herself up, gasping for air, and dashed to the steps leading up to the deck area. Her hands left a smear of blood on the handrail as she steadied herself.

Up on deck, Peggy breathed deeply. She was in shock. Nausea swept over her and she was sick over the side of the boat. She looked at the blood on her hands and screamed again, shaking uncontrollably.

The jogger came back along the towpath, took one look at Peggy and stopped. She was pale and covered in blood. 'Oh my God! Are you all right?'

Peggy looked down at him blankly. 'Mr Nielson... it's Mr Nielson. I think... I think he's dead!'

3

Blue and white tape blocked off the entrance to the path leading down to the Thames. A bored-looking constable was guarding the entry to the outer cordon. He heard a car coming up the road and watched as an old 2003 grey Porsche 911 two-door coupe came to a halt a few yards away. A tall slim man wearing a blue-grey suit and white open-necked shirt got out of the car and walked towards him.

Bloody press, the constable thought. He noted the groomed short dark hair, greying at the edges, the chiselled jawline and hint of a stubble. He half expected the man to pull out a press card as he approached. The constable held up a hand. 'Sorry, sir. This is a crime scene, I'm afraid you can't park there. And I can't talk to the press.'

The man smiled. 'No problem, I'm not press,' he said, fishing into his jacket pocket to hold up a warrant card for the constable to see. 'DCI Fleming. I'm the on-call SIO.'

Colour rose in the constable's cheeks as he shifted his gaze away from the tired red eyes that under normal circumstances would have matched the colour of Fleming's suit. 'Oh... sorry, sir. The car... I thought...'

'Got the call at home so came straight here.'

'Ah, right, well, the boat's down there, sir.' The constable pointed down the path.

'Thanks.'

The constable watched as Fleming returned to the Porsche, opened the boot and kitted himself out with latex gloves, paper shoes and overalls. He nodded at the constable as he ducked under the tape to head off down the path. 'Keep an eye on the car, eh?'

The constable grunted and waited until Fleming was out of earshot. He shook his head. 'Flashy Scots git.'

4

J ust a few yards from the *Done Deal*, Fleming found another officer stationed on the towpath at the entry and exit point of the inner cordon. He showed his warrant card again and the officer noted his name in the log.

'Are Sergeant Logan and the pathologist here yet?' Fleming enquired.

'Yes, arrived about ten minutes ago, sir. Inspector Duggan is here as well... local CID,' he added by way of explanation. 'They're on the boat.'

Fleming nodded and climbed up onto the deck of the *Done Deal* as DS Harry Logan appeared from below. 'Thought I heard your voice, boss. Bit of a mess down there.' He pulled back the elastic hood of his overalls to sweep a hand through his thinning grey hair.

Fleming had taken an instant liking to the ex-army burly sergeant that Superintendent Liz Temple had assigned to him. Logan had joined the Thames Valley Police Major Crime Unit, the MCU, a few weeks earlier at the same time as Fleming. Temple had told him he was a good reliable officer. Recently turned fifty, he had the wrinkled weather-beaten face of a man who had spent most of his life outdoors.

Logan looked from Fleming's bloodshot eyes, to the hint of dark stubble on his chin then the lack of a tie. 'Rough night, boss?' he enquired with a smile.

'Could say that, Harry. Couldn't sleep and had one whisky too many.' Fleming then fell silent. Memories of the day he had to run for his life after seeing Jimmy Calder knife his mother still haunted him. He could vividly recall the horror of Calder behind him and the excruciating pain when the car hit him. His mother had died, but Fleming had been lucky. He'd only suffered a few broken bones, cuts and bruises. There was no permanent damage other than the mental scars. Calder had received a life sentence. Last night had been one of those nights when Fleming had tried to blot it all out with whisky.

Logan seemed to note Fleming's change in mood. 'Oh... right.'

'Where are Duggan and the pathologist?' Fleming asked.

'Down below.'

As Logan spoke, two men emerged on deck. 'Ah, DCI Fleming?' Duggan said. 'This is Dr Kumar, the Home Office registered forensic pathologist. I'm afraid it's a bit crowded down there.' Duggan nodded towards the cockpit door. 'The SOCOs are all over the place.'

Nathan Kumar smiled and shook Fleming's hand. 'Hello, Alex. How's the job in the MCU?'

'Just promoted. This is my first case.'

'Missing the Met?'

'Can't say I am.'

'You two know each other?' Duggan enquired.

'We do,' Fleming replied. He knew Kumar from his time in the Met. Kumar was of Indian descent, a tall slim man of forty-five with dark grey hair. They'd been on first-name terms ever since they first met.

'What have we got here?' Fleming asked, looking at Duggan.

'Chap called Nielson, Ronnie Nielson. Has a house nearby and moors his boat here when he's up from London apparently. Stabbed to death. Body's down in the galley. Local woman found him. Peggy Dobbs. His cleaner.'

'She around for me to speak to?'

'She was in shock. I had her seen by a doctor. One of my men took her to the station in Marlow.'

'Thanks.'

'Oh, and there was a jogger at the scene,' Duggan added. 'He found Mrs Dobbs in a bit of a state after she'd discovered the body. We've got his name and address if you want to speak to him as well.'

'We will.'

Fleming paused. 'Was Nielson married?'

'Cleaner reckons he was divorced last year.'

'Better get someone to trace the ex-wife and any other known relatives. Make sure they're informed.'

Duggan nodded acknowledgement.

Fleming looked at the cockpit door. 'Any sign of a forced entry?'

Duggan shook his head. 'No, the door was open.'

'Lights?'

'Sorry?'

'Were any lights left on, or were they switched off?'

'Er... I didn't ask the cleaner. They were off when I arrived.'

Kumar glanced towards the cabin door. 'I've been waiting for you, before I touched the body. Okay to have a look now?' he asked Fleming.

'Sure, go ahead.'

Fleming turned to Duggan. 'Get the house cordoned off and

put an officer on duty there. And we could do with a sign on the towpath asking for anyone who uses it regularly to come forward. Someone may have seen something.'

'I'll get on to it right away, sir.' Duggan turned to speak into his radio.

Fleming looked at Logan who seemed to be studying the water over the side of the boat. 'See anything?'

'Not a thing. Water's black as night.'

'Let's have a look down below then shall we?'

They made their way down the steps into the saloon area. Four SOCOs were busy there. Two of them were on hands and knees carrying out an inch-by-inch examination of the floor.

Fleming pointed to the door behind them. 'Have a look in there while I check in here,' he said to Logan.

There was a large U-shaped seating area in the saloon with a table fixed to the floor in the middle. The seats and floor were smeared in blood, and some of the wood panelling on the walls bore the signs of a violent struggle.

Opposite the seating area were some storage cupboards and shelves. Fleming walked across and scanned the shelves. There was a postcard on one of them. Fleming picked it up with his gloved hand and sniffed the card. It had the distinct smell of perfume. There was just a brief note. *Looking forward to seeing you next week – need me to bring anything? Call me.* It was signed, Emma.

Fleming stuck his head round the door leading down to the galley. Kumar was kneeling over the body. He looked up at Fleming. 'Looks like he received a severe blow to the head with a blunt instrument. The SOCOs found a large glass ashtray on the floor. Could have been the offending weapon.'

Fleming nodded. 'Anything else?'

'Two stab wounds to the front. One in the stomach and one

in the chest. Two more in his back for good measure. I'd say the murder weapon was a broad-bladed knife.'

'Can you give me an approximate time of death?'

Kumar frowned. 'I'd say he's been dead for over ten hours. Between eight and midnight last night, I'd guess. I can fill you in with more detail once I've done the post-mortem.'

Fleming stepped over the body and went into the galley. He spotted a wooden knife block on the counter that had been knocked on its side. One of the knives was missing. 'Looks like the murderer used one of these,' he said, over his shoulder at Kumar. 'Does this match the width of the stab wounds?' Fleming pointed to the empty slot in the knife block.

Kumar rose to his feet and peered over Fleming's shoulder. 'Don't miss a trick, Alex, do you?' He squinted. 'At first sight, yes, but hard to tell for sure until I've done the post-mortem.'

Logan suddenly appeared. 'Found a couple of things in the aft cabin. Cosy little place. Double bed, en suite toilet, shower. Either Mr Nielson liked to wear perfume, or he had female company. There's a woman's toilet bag and a bottle of perfume there. Calvin Klein Eternity. Can't find any papers, documents, wallet, money, or a mobile phone anywhere. Oh, there's what looks like a laptop case, but no sign of a laptop.'

Fleming nodded. 'There's a postcard on one of the shelves in the saloon. It has a hint of scent on it. Probably the same as the perfume you found. Better put it in an evidence bag.'

'Any sign of the murder weapon?' Logan asked.

'No, but I've a fair guess where it came from. There's a knife missing from the galley. We'll need to get the river dredged to see if it's been thrown overboard.'

Kumar had gathered up his things and made to leave. 'I'll let you have my report as soon as I can, Alex. Good luck with the investigation.'

Fleming smiled. 'Thanks. I'll be in touch.'

Back up on deck, Fleming noticed some dried mud on the decking. 'Better make sure the SOCOs take a sample of that,' he said to Logan. 'Just in case.'

'Okay.'

'Any thoughts?' Fleming asked.

Logan pondered for a moment. 'Could have been a random opportunistic robbery. Door was open, no wallet, money or mobile phone on the boat – possible missing laptop...'

Fleming looked curious. 'I'm not so sure. Seems rather violent for a chance robbery. Maybe someone wanted to make it look like that.'

'Could be.'

'Anyway, I'm going to the station in Marlow to speak to the cleaner. Then I want to have a look round Nielson's house. You go and see the jogger. I'll see you back at HQ later.'

Fleming made his way back to his car. He felt uneasy as he drove off. The last thing he needed was a murder case where the victim had been stabbed to death.

5

P eggy Dobbs was sitting in the witness interview room at Marlow Police Station. Her hands shook as she reached out for the cup of tea Fleming had brought her. Her face was ashen and bloodshot eyes peered at him anxiously.

Fleming sat opposite her and placed his cup on the table. 'Tea okay?' he asked politely. 'I'm afraid it's just from the vending machine.'

'Y... yes,' Peggy stammered.

'I know you've had a bit of a shock. You're here voluntarily as a witness. You can go at any time if you don't feel up to answering any questions. But it is important we do this as soon as we can. Memory tends to fade if we leave things too long.'

Peggy laughed nervously. 'Goodness, my memory isn't brilliant at the best of times. I often wander up the stairs and then ask myself what it is I've come up for. But you go ahead and ask what you want.' Peggy's hands were still shaking when she lifted her cup to take a sip of tea and some spilled onto the table. 'Oh dear, look what I've done now. I can't stop shaking.'

'Don't worry,' Fleming said gently. 'You sure you're all right?'

'Yes... yes, of course. I'm fine.' She blew steam from her cup and took a sip. She seemed to feel more at ease in Fleming's presence.

'Perhaps you could just talk me through what happened – what you saw. Take your time. I know it must all be distressing for you.'

Peggy smiled weakly. 'I set off from home to go to the boat – Mr Nielson's boat. He wanted me to do some cleaning...'

'When did he ask you?'

'Oh, last night. He phoned to ask if I could come this morning before he set off for London.'

'What time was that?'

'Not long before six. Yes, that would be it. I was about to put my dinner on. I always have it around six.'

'How did he sound? I mean – did he sound his usual self?'

'I'm... I'm not sure...'

'Did he sound anxious... in a hurry? Could you sense if anyone was with him? Hear any sounds in the background that might have been caused by another person?'

'No, he sounded perfectly normal. I couldn't say I heard anyone else there.'

'How long had you known Mr Nielson?' Fleming asked.

'About five years. I've cleaned for him all that time. I do his house and the boat.'

'What did he do for a living?'

'He owns a club in London – Nielson's Cellar. He took it on when his father died – it was a car accident. He told me all about it some time back.'

'Did he get many regular visitors to the house or the boat that you know of?'

'People came and went all the time. He had lots of parties at the house.'

'Would you know any of these people?'

'Oh, no. I had no idea who his social contacts were, except...'

'Yes?'

'A couple of weeks ago there was a woman with him on the boat. Now what was it he called her...?' Peggy's eyes looked up at the ceiling as though for inspiration. 'I told you my memory was bad.' She frowned. 'Sorry, I'm not good at remembering names.'

'Was it Emma?' Fleming prompted.

'Yes! Yes, that's it. Emma!'

'Had you seen her before – at the house maybe?'

'No, no I can't say that I did.'

'Can you describe her?'

'Let me see now. She was probably medium height, blonde hair – about shoulder length. Attractive woman, maybe mid-forties. Seemed very classy.'

Fleming formed a mental image in his mind. 'Did you see anyone else on the towpath as you made your way to the boat?'

'Yes. There was a jogger. Startled the life out of me as he came running up behind me.'

'So, he was running towards the boat.'

'Goodness. How did you know that?'

'Because you were walking towards the boat and he came up behind you.'

Peggy nodded. 'I can see why you're a detective, dear.'

Fleming smiled at her naivety. 'And he came back later – saw you just after you'd found the body?'

'Yes, he stopped and asked if I was all right. It was him who phoned the police. I was in too much of a state to do anything.'

'So, when you got to the boat, what did you find?'

'The cabin door was open so I thought Mr Nielson was down below. But it felt strange. There was no sign of life. No music playing. Mr Nielson always had music blaring when he was on the boat. I shouted down to tell him I was there, but there was no answer. I... I went down into the saloon. There were flies everywhere. Blood all over the seats and the floor. It was awful. I

pushed open the door to the galley and... and there he was...'
Peggy shivered and began to cry.

'It's okay, Mrs Dobbs. Take your time. I know this isn't easy for you. But you're doing fine. Can I get you some more tea?'

'Yes... yes, please,' Peggy sobbed.

Fleming put a reassuring hand on Peggy's shoulder as he left to go to the vending machine. He returned shortly after with a fresh cup.

'Thanks,' Peggy whispered. 'You're very kind.'

'So, after you found the body, you came straight back up on deck where the jogger saw you again?'

'That's right... and he rang for the police.'

'Were there any lights on in the boat when you arrived?'

'I'm not sure. It's all such a blur. I don't think so.'

'Mrs Dobbs, you've been really brave and helpful. Thank you. There's one final question. When was the last time you saw Mr Nielson alive?'

'It was a couple of nights ago. I was taking a walk along the towpath and I heard music from the boat. I didn't stay but popped my head in to say hello.'

'Did he have anyone with him?'

'No... he was busy at the table in the saloon working on his laptop. He looked startled when I appeared, a bit distracted. That's why I didn't stay.'

'Thanks. There's one more thing. We need to take your fingerprints and a DNA sample, if you don't mind–'

Peggy's eyes widened in shock. 'My goodness, why? You surely don't think I had anything to do with it?'

'No, no, of course not,' Fleming reassured her. 'It's so we can eliminate them from any other samples we find at the crime scene, that's all.'

'Oh... I see.'

'Once you've finished your tea and we get that done,

someone will run you home. Would you like a WPC to stay with you tonight?'

'That would be nice. If it's not too much trouble...'

'No trouble at all, Mrs Dobbs. You take care now.'

Walking back to his car, Fleming mulled over his priorities. Number one – he needed to trace the woman called Emma.

On her way home, Peggy Dobbs bit her bottom lip and frowned. She wondered if she had done the right thing in not mentioning the other phone call she'd received on the night of the murder...

6

F leming showed his warrant card to the uniformed officer standing outside Nielson's house. Duggan and the SOCOs were already there.

'Nice house,' Duggan observed as he appeared from the kitchen. 'I've had a quick look around, but nothing seems out of the ordinary.'

The house was detached on a small plot, not far from the river. *Expensive*, Fleming thought.

'I gather you've just joined the MCU?' Duggan queried. 'You'll have met Bill Watson no doubt. He's a DCI. Been there a while. I knew him vaguely, years ago, when I was with the Met. He was an inspector then. Bit of a tough cookie by all accounts – old school. Had a reputation for not always playing by the rules. Got results though.'

Fleming did know Bill Watson, and Duggan's description didn't surprise him. He was a bull of a man, about six feet tall. He had close-cropped receding grey hair, a full face and body to match. He always undid his shirt top button and tie to relieve the pressure round his thick neck, and his suits looked too tight on him. He hadn't exactly offered a welcoming hand to Fleming on his arrival in the MCU. Liz Temple had warned Fleming that Watson was not exactly the friendliest of people and that there might be some friction.

There was. Fleming had replaced DCI Anthony Hayden who retired due to ill health. Temple had told Fleming that his appointment had not gone down well with Watson who had expected his friend, DI Frank Jardine, to fill the vacant post and that Watson had exchanged words with her over it.

Fleming didn't want to get into a conversation with Duggan about Watson. 'Yes, I know him,' he said. 'You might as well get back to the station while I have a look around.'

The house was in a quiet setting with private gardens. Fleming noted how tidy and clean all the rooms were. Peggy Dobbs had obviously been at work here. Fleming wandered through the house watching the SOCOs.

There were a couple of photos on top of a bookcase in the living room. One was of a wedding. Fleming picked it up and thought of his late wife. He'd loved Trish dearly. She was pregnant four years after they had married but had caught flu before the baby was born and complications developed. She, and therefore the baby, had died from pneumonia. That was five years earlier.

He took a deep breath and studied the photograph in his hands. There were four people on it, Nielson, his ex-wife, and a man who looked about the same age as Nielson. Maybe the best man, Fleming guessed. There was another man, much older. Nielson's father before the car accident, or his wife's father maybe?

The other was of more interest to Fleming. Six uniformed soldiers in an old army shot. Nielson was one of them. The man he thought was the best man on the wedding photo was on this one as well, together with the four other men. Three men were kneeling on hard-packed sand at the front, three standing behind. Army vehicles were in the background under a clear blue sky. Two of the men had eyes screwed up against the glare of the sun and four wore sunglasses. Iraq or Afghanistan, Fleming guessed. He indicated to one of the SOCOs. 'Make sure these two photos get bagged.'

Upstairs, Fleming found three bedrooms and another room Nielson had converted into an office. A computer sat on an old antique desk with a green leather inlay. The desk drawers contained the usual stuff: bank statements, old bills, utility and insurance documents. Propped up between a pen stand and table lamp were some unpaid bills. Fleming glanced through all of the papers, not really sure what he was looking for. There seemed to be nothing worthy of note. He closed the desk drawers. He'd leave the SOCOs to go through all of this stuff.

There was a photograph of Nielson's club hanging on the wall. Fleming made a mental note. He'd need to speak to people who worked there as a matter of urgency.

Interestingly, there was no sign of anything that might belong to the woman called Emma.

Fleming thought there was nothing more he could do here. He'd leave it all to the crime scene investigators.

He left the house and was about to climb into his car when his mobile rang. It was Freya Nash, his counsellor.

'Alex?'

'Yes?'

'Are you all right? You missed your appointment this morning...'

7

D I Jardine and DCI Watson were off duty. They sat by a window table in the Bear Inn on the corner of Alfred Street and Blue Boar Street in Oxford. The two men were oblivious to the animated shouting and occasional bursts of raucous laughter coming from the bar. They whispered in furtive tones as they leaned over the table.

Watson thumped his glass down and stared at Jardine through his brown bloodshot eyes. His face was flushed and beads of sweat stood out on his forehead. 'Christ, I need a fag,' Watson croaked. His Welsh accent was becoming more pronounced with each drink. 'Get another round in, Frank. I'm going outside for some fresh air and a ciggie.'

Jardine watched Watson haul his large frame up from the table and head for the door before he made his way to the bar. 'Two pints of London Pride,' he demanded, banging the empty glasses down on a soggy beer mat with a scowl. The years had taken their toll on Jardine. He was fifty years old and his thin lanky frame was now somewhat stooped. He still walked with a slight limp from a bullet wound he received to his left leg ten years earlier while with the Met. Any impression of cheerfulness had left the long angular face that seldom offered a smile these days. What was left of his close-cropped hair matched the colour of his pallid face. He wondered if there was anything in what Watson was saying, or if he was just talking through the drink. Watson could be abrasive and belligerent at the best of times, but at least he looked after older officers. He'd had a go at Superintendent Temple when HQ overlooked Jardine for the vacant detective chief inspector post. Mind you, it didn't take much for him to get riled by Temple. He had no time for female officers or, for that matter, younger officers like Fleming.

'Anything else?' the young barman asked as he put two pints in front of Jardine.

Jardine shook his head, paid for the drinks and limped back to the table.

Ten minutes later, Watson returned to find a fresh pint on his beer mat. He flopped into his seat, picked up the glass and took a large swig. He belched and gazed steadily at Jardine. 'Where were we?'

'We were talking about Nielson and Fleming,' Jardine reminded him loudly.

'Fuck's sake, Frank, why don't you let the whole bar know what we're talking about?'

Jardine looked sheepish. 'Sorry, boss.'

Watson shook his head. 'I've told you before you need to keep it down. You've got a voice like a bloody foghorn.' He took another sip of beer and wiped froth from his lips with the back of his hand. 'Anyway... regards Fleming, we need to find a way to convince Temple he's not the man for the job and that you are.'

Jardine frowned. 'Any idea how we might achieve that?'

'I'm working on it.' Watson tapped his forehead with a chubby finger. 'I'm doing a little... shall we say... research...'

'Into what?'

'Into Fleming. A lot of people have skeletons in the cupboard. I need to find out if he does.'

'And if he does? What then?'

'If it could affect his ability to do the job properly, we take it to Temple. But we also need to make sure he gets no help with the investigation. If we get a chance, we point him in the wrong direction. We need to make sure he fouls up – know what I mean?'

'You think there could be problems with Fleming?'

'I know so. We need to get him off the case.'

'You thinking about the investigation into Nielson we were involved in some years back with DCI Hayden?'

Watson ran a finger round the top of his glass. 'Liz Temple is bound to tell Fleming about that.'

'And you think Fleming might stumble across something while he's investigating Nielson's murder?'

'Something like that. I don't want him snooping around over old ground that we'd covered–'

'What if he does find out that Nielson was suspected of dealing in drugs and being behind a gangland killing? That couldn't come back to bite us, could it?'

Watson glared at Jardine. 'You're joking! He finds something Temple thinks we missed. How's that going to make us look, eh?' Watson banged the table with a clenched fist. 'There's no way I'm going to allow a rookie DCI get one over on me, understand?'

∾

Watson's vehemence took Jardine by surprise. 'Sure, boss. I didn't mean to–'

Watson cut him short. 'And you want promotion, don't you?'

'Yes... yes, of course, boss.'

'Then you and I need to work together to make sure our Mr Fleming fails to deliver. You with me on this?'

'Sure. With you all the way.'

Jardine looked over his glass at Watson and wondered what it was he had in mind.

8

There was nothing to suggest what was in the building. It looked like any another block of offices. But inside, it housed the Major Crime Unit.

Fleming was behind his desk making notes. Most of the desks in the open-plan area outside were empty. It was strangely quiet. The normal buzz of activity had died down. Only a few officers were still on phones. The odd telephone rang shrilly to break the silence. The constant hammering on computer keyboards had all but ceased. It was Saturday night, and very late. The detectives assigned to the Nielson murder enquiry sat at their desks. They were waiting for Fleming's first briefing meeting.

Logan and DC Naomi Anderson were outside Fleming's office. Anderson was redoing the bun at the back of her black hair. She was a relatively inexperienced officer in her late twenties, tall and slim with Jamaican roots.

Logan was on the telephone. He looked across to Fleming's office and saw him through the glass partition. He nodded and replaced the handset. He headed for Fleming's door, knocked and popped his head in. 'Super wants to see you, boss. Oh, and

Naomi and I have just finished setting up the briefing room. The incident room is ready too.'

'Thanks, Harry. Briefing in half an hour.' Fleming gathered his notes and made his way to Temple's office at the far end of the open-plan area. The distinct smell of coffee lingered in the air. Some of the team glanced at him as he passed, wondering how much longer it would be before the briefing. Unlike Fleming, some had families to go home to.

Liz Temple's office was more lavish than Fleming's. The furnishings were of a better quality. She sat behind a large desk reading a file through rimless glasses. The door was open.

Fleming coughed gently. 'You wanted to see me, ma'am?'

'Yes, thank you, Alex.' She placed her glasses carefully on the desk and rose to greet Fleming. The black jacket, skirt and white blouse reminded Fleming of funerals. A slight shiver went up his spine at the thought. Her light olive-brown complexion, high cheekbones, and black shoulder length hair suggested possible Indian roots. She had a stern look about her and seldom smiled. Maybe that was the pressure of the job. She was young, mid-forties, Fleming guessed. Tall, slim, and carried an air of authority. 'I wanted you to fill me in on the details,' she said.

'Chap called Nielson was found stabbed to death on his river cruiser near Bourne End Marina. His cleaner found him this morning. There were signs of a violent struggle, but there was no sign of the murder weapon at the scene. The SOCOs have been all over the boat and his house nearby. No witnesses that we know of – just the cleaner who found him. I've got a briefing in a few minutes to set out the initial lines of enquiry I want followed.'

'Good. I'll join you if I may? Save going through it all twice.'

Fleming noted the steady gaze of her brown eyes and took it that it wasn't really a question. 'Of course.'

'There's something you need to be aware of before the meeting. Nielson was suspected of using his London club to front a drugs operation some years back. The Met was handling the case. Bill Watson was working for them at the time. He was one of the investigating officers. They never did find enough evidence to charge Nielson. Bill transferred here the following year. Then, two years after the drugs case, there was a murder in Reading. Bill was the SIO and thought it was drugs related. He suspected Nielson could have been behind it, but never charged him. Chap called Potts eventually pleaded guilty to manslaughter. I suggest you speak to Bill.'

'Thanks, I will.'

'I ought to remind you though that Bill can be a bit tetchy at the best of times and may be a bit guarded over what he tells you. He'll see his personal reputation at stake and may be a little sensitive because Nielson slipped through his fingers twice. So, be careful how you broach the subject, okay?'

Fleming groaned inwardly. He'd already experienced Watson's hostile temperament. 'I'll tread carefully. Thanks for the tip.'

Temple looked thoughtful for a moment. 'Oh, there's one other thing...'

'Yes?'

'I'm afraid you only have a small team, just Logan and Anderson, who are with you full time. I can't let you have an inspector at the moment. We're a bit short-handed. And so you know, DI Jardine wasn't a happy bunny when we didn't select him to fill DCI Hayden's post. I've got him working full time with Bill Watson for now. Didn't seem a good idea to have him reporting to you. Nothing personal, but there could be a bit of resentment that you got the post he thought he was in line for.'

'Okay, no problem.'

Temple looked slightly embarrassed. 'And DS Logan and DC Anderson are new to the unit. I thought it best to team them up with you. Hope you don't feel as though you've been short changed.'

Fleming smiled. 'I'm sure I'll manage.'

~

As they made their way to the briefing room, Fleming was reflecting on what Temple had told him when she casually dropped another bombshell.

'By the way, the chief constable, Matthew Upson, is under a bit of pressure at the moment,' she said. 'Cecil Daubney is pressing him over the thirty-two unsolved murder cases we have.'

Fleming raised a questioning eyebrow.

'The police and crime commissioner,' Temple reminded him.

'Yes, I know who he is, ma'am. I was just surprised at the number of unsolved cases.'

'One of the main objectives in the Police and Crime Plan is to reduce the number. Daubney wants this done in the next two years. Given the current pressure on our budget, that's quite a tall order. He's made it clear that he's holding Upson to account. He'll be measuring his performance against delivery of the plan. The last thing we need is another unsolved murder.'

Great, Fleming thought. *No real pressure on my first case then. Hostile colleagues, small team, all new – and pressure from the start from those in high places.*

9

The few remaining officers in the MCU were in the briefing room. They were tired and wanted to go home.

The buzz of conversation filled the air. There were a few moans about the lateness of the meeting. There were some comments on how small the team was. A few were complaining about the lack of a decent pay rise. One officer cursed the foul-tasting coffee as he poured the remnants into a plant pot. It was pretty much a normal late-night gathering.

The room fell silent when Fleming and Temple entered. There were a few nods, and those present settled themselves into the few chairs scattered around. Temple stood at the back of the room and Fleming strode to the front.

Logan had erected a large whiteboard and there was a noticeboard on the wall. The only thing on the whiteboard was the victim's name. Fleming looked around at the silent sullen faces and felt exposed in his new post.

Logan broke the silence. 'All right, you lot, I know you want to get home. The boss has promised to make this brief so get your notebooks out and pay attention.'

Fleming didn't remember saying that but welcomed the cue.

'Okay, I want to run through what we've got so far and set out the initial lines of enquiry I want followed.' He looked at Anderson. 'Naomi, can you list key points and actions on the whiteboard please?'

Anderson nodded her agreement.

'Not a lot on there yet,' someone shouted from the back.

'We're making good progress then,' someone else commented drily.

There were a few laughs.

Fleming smiled. 'There'll be a lot more on there by the time we're finished, don't worry.' He nodded at Logan. 'Can you put names against the actions so we know who's doing what, Harry?'

Logan lifted a hand to show he had a marker pen ready. 'On the case, boss.'

Fleming smiled and pointed to the whiteboard. 'Ronnie Nielson. London club owner who's had previous brushes with the law. Stabbed to death on his river cruiser on the Thames at Bourne End near Marlow. Approximate time of death was between eight to midnight last night. His cleaner took a phone call from him about six last night and discovered him this morning around nine. The murder weapon hasn't been found, but there is a knife missing from a wooden knife block in the galley. There were signs of a violent struggle so it's reasonable to assume we're looking for a powerful man. We think there's a laptop missing and we didn't find a wallet or any money on the boat. Nor was there a mobile phone there or at his house nearby. Could be a random chance robbery, but we need to keep an open mind on the motive—'

'Excuse me, sir. Was there any sign of a forced entry?' someone asked from the back of the room.

Fleming welcomed the interruption. 'No, and there were no lights on so the murderer must have had the presence of mind to switch them off before he made his escape. Lights burning on a boat all night might have drawn attention quicker than he'd have liked.'

'Any signs that Nielson had a known visitor with him?' another voice asked. 'More than one glass, cup or plate left out – that sort of thing.'

'No, no sign of that. But there was a postcard from a woman called Emma, saying she was looking forward to seeing him. We also found a bottle of perfume and a toilet bag in the en suite cabin. The cleaner saw what could have been her with Nielson on the boat a couple of weeks ago. She described her as being attractive, blonde hair, medium height – maybe in her mid-forties.'

'Did she say how long this Emma's hair was?' an officer called Martins asked.

'Shoulder length,' Fleming replied. He noticed sharp glances between Martins and another officer. 'Does that ring a bell with you?' he asked Martins.

Martins looked uncertain for a moment and glanced furtively at his colleagues before speaking. 'I... I don't know if I should be saying this. There must be lots of blonde women who go by the name Emma...'

'But?' Fleming persisted.

'DCI Hayden's wife is called Emma. Description fits her.' He received some angry glares from around the room. 'But I'm sure it's a coincidence. I mean, how would she know Nielson?' He shrugged and slumped back in his seat. 'Sorry, I should never have mentioned it...'

'You did the right thing. It probably is just a coincidence as you say, but we need to check it out. We need to eliminate her from the search for this woman.'

Fleming drew a deep breath and continued. 'So, here's what we have to do. We need to trace the woman called Emma. I'll go to see DCI Hayden's wife. We need to build a picture of Nielson.

I want everyone on nearby boats interviewed and enquiries made at the nearby marina. Arrange door-to-doors on the streets around his house.' Fleming paused as notes were taken. 'What did people know about him? Did anyone notice anything suspicious or out of the ordinary recently? I'll pay a visit to his club to speak to the manager and staff there.'

Fleming took a sip of water. 'I found a couple of photographs in Nielson's house. One was a wedding photo showing Nielson, his ex-wife, and two other men. One about Nielson's age – maybe the best man, and an older man. We need to find them. The other photograph is of Nielson with five army colleagues – maybe taken in Iraq or Afghanistan. The younger man in the wedding photograph is one of them. I want them all traced. I want everyone who knew him interviewed: relatives, friends, colleagues, associates, enemies – everyone. Who last saw him? When?

'Oh, and I want local hospitals and doctors' surgeries checked to see if anyone turned up with injuries. There was a violent struggle so there's a chance the murderer may have been injured. Also check local custody suites to see if anyone suspicious was taken into custody for any reason.'

There were glances of growing respect from those present. This guy knew his stuff.

Fleming continued. 'We need to find the murder weapon. My guess is that the murderer probably threw it into the river. He's hardly likely to have kept it on him as he made his escape along the towpath, so we need to get the river dredged.'

Fleming looked at Temple standing at the back of the room. 'Anything you want to say, ma'am?'

Temple walked up to join Fleming. 'Only to say the top brass want a quick result on this. The chief constable is under pressure. The police and crime commissioner's chomping at the bit over unsolved murder enquiries. He thinks there are too many, and the last thing we need is another one added to the list. So, let's all pull together and get on with it.'

Fleming thanked Temple. He smiled at the detective who'd joked about progress. 'Bit more on the board now, eh? Thank you all for your time. I know it's late so get yourselves off home and let's start things moving in the morning.'

~

Fleming was last to leave the office. He wondered about Watson and his link to Nielson, and about DCI Hayden who'd been medically retired. Then there was the woman called Emma. Could it really be Hayden's wife?

~

Later that night, in his small Oxford flat, Fleming sipped on his second glass of whisky. The Very Best of The Proclaimers was playing softly in the background. His thoughts drifted from the Nielson case to the call from Freya about his missed appointment.

Ever since he'd witnessed his mother being murdered twenty-three years earlier, he'd seen various social workers, psychologists and psychotherapists. Freya had been recommended to him when he'd transferred to Oxford, but he wasn't sure whether to make another appointment.

He took a last swig of his whisky, put the empty glass on the coffee table by his side and soon drifted off to sleep. He still had nightmares: the knife plunging into his mother's stomach, heavy breathing and footsteps behind him, the car lights, then darkness...

10

'Brought Naomi along for the experience, boss?' Logan asked with a grin.

Fleming looked in the rear-view mirror and smiled. Anderson was sticking her tongue out at Logan's back. They were on their way to the mortuary in Maidenhead. It was Sunday, the day after Peggy Dobbs had found Nielson. Traffic was light and they were making good time from Oxford.

'Thought it would be a good idea to have her present when Mrs Nielson formally identifies the body. She might welcome female company,' Fleming replied.

Logan stretched his long legs in the car. 'As long as she doesn't pass out at the sight of a dead body,' he quipped.

Anderson thumped him on the back. 'Very funny, Sarge,' she retorted with a frown.

Fleming laughed and shook his head. 'You do twitter on, you two. When you're done you can fill me in on how you got on with the jogger, Harry. Get any useful information?'

'Not really, boss. He happened to pass Mrs Dobbs as she was making her way along the towpath to Nielson's boat. He went past the boat but had no reason to suspect anything was wrong.

On his way back, he came across Mrs Dobbs leaning over the side of the boat. She had blood all over her. He thought she'd had an accident, but then she told him that Nielson was dead. He rang for an ambulance anyway – and the police. That's about it.'

'Does he jog along the towpath regularly?'

'Yes, reckons at least once a week. Usually first thing in the morning.'

'Had he seen Nielson before?'

'He'd caught the odd glimpse as he passed, but didn't know the man.'

'And had he ever seen anyone else with him on the boat?'

'Nope.'

'Did he see anyone recently on the towpath acting suspiciously near the boat?'

'Not that he can recall.'

'Oh well, it was worth checking. You asked him to get in touch though... if he remembered anything that might help us?'

'Sure, but somehow I think he's not going to be of much use.'

They remained silent for the rest of the journey and were soon pulling into the mortuary car park.

Sarah Nielson sat next to an older man in the reception area. She was Nielson's only living relative, ex-relative on account that they were divorced. A member of staff had already offered them a cup of tea. Mrs Nielson stood when Fleming and his colleagues arrived. She was an attractive woman with long blonde hair, and bright hazel eyes that showed no sign that she had been crying. Fleming reckoned she was in her forties. Her short slim build fitted snugly into the grey trouser suit she was wearing.

Fleming offered a hand. 'Detective Chief Inspector Fleming.' He nodded his head towards his colleagues. 'And this is DS Logan and DC Anderson.'

Sarah Nielson took Fleming's hand. Her handshake was limp. Her brows were furrowed with anxiety. She put a hand on the arm of the man standing next to her. 'This is my father, Eric Rainer.'

Fleming looked into cold grey eyes and shook Rainer's hand. He was a giant of a man, bald apart from patches of white stubble above his ears. 'Glad you could come,' Fleming said, wincing at the strength of the man's grip.

A few minutes later, the coroner's liaison officer appeared. 'Ah, you're all here.' Smiling weakly, he looked solicitously at Mrs Nielson. 'Ready?'

Sarah nodded.

'I'm Ian Timms. If you'd like to come this way please.'

He led them through the door he'd emerged from, down a short corridor with a polished linoleum floor to swing doors at the bottom. Timms pushed the doors open and led them into a cold clinical room. In the centre was a metal table draped in a green sheet. Timms walked to the side of the table and looked at Sarah. She nodded and he drew the sheet back slowly to expose the head of Ronnie Nielson.

There was no emotional reaction. Sarah Nielson just nodded again. 'That's him. That's Ronnie.' Timms pulled the sheet back to cover Nielson's head. 'Perhaps you'd like another cup of tea?'

'No... no, thank you.'

As they made their way back to the reception area, Anderson walked beside Sarah Nielson who had gone very quiet. 'Are you all right, Mrs Nielson?'

'I'm fine.'

Fleming cleared his throat. 'Mrs Nielson, I need to come and talk to you about your ex-husband, but perhaps now is not the right time. Tomorrow afternoon maybe?'

'Yes, that would be fine. I'll be at home.'

Rainer put an arm around his daughter's shoulders. 'Want me to be there?'

'No, Dad, don't take any time off work. I'll be okay on my own, honestly.'

As they all walked out to the car park, Rainer pulled on Fleming's arm indicating he wanted him to drop back to have a word. 'He was a bastard, Ronnie Nielson,' he whispered in Fleming's ear. 'I'm glad someone got him. He had it coming. He bullied Sarah, you know. Knocked her about on more than one occasion. Sarah used to try to hide it, but I knew how she got those bruises. And he was a womaniser. He had more than one affair. I told Sarah to leave. She finally saw sense and divorced him. Should never have married him. I knew he was rotten from when I first saw him. Bastard!'

Fleming was taken aback by the vehemence of Rainer's sudden outburst. 'You didn't get on with him then?'

'Get on with him! I'd gladly have killed h–'

Rainer stopped suddenly, as if realising it probably wasn't the most tactful thing to say. He walked the rest of the way to the car in silence. He turned before climbing into the driver's seat. 'Wouldn't bust a gut trying to find his killer. Whoever it was did us all a big favour.'

Logan broke the silence on the journey back to Oxford. 'What was Rainer whispering to you when we came out of the mortuary, boss?'

'He called Nielson a bastard. Said he knocked his wife about.'

'Hmm, I'll bet he's knocked a few people about himself in his time,' Logan quipped.

'Sarge!' Anderson protested. 'That's very judgemental.'

Logan turned in the passenger seat to look at Anderson with a smile. 'Show me a big powerful man with a scarred face, crooked nose and cauliflower ears, and I'll show you an ex-boxer.' Logan thrust a hand backwards. 'Bet you.'

'I don't bet,' Anderson retorted, ignoring the hand. 'But I think you might be right for once,' she joked.

Fleming kept his eyes on the road ahead and smiled.

11

The piercing sound of a wailing siren outside woke Fleming. He groaned and pulled himself up from the chair where he'd fallen asleep after drinking too much whisky. God, he felt rough. His head throbbed and his mouth was dry. He staggered to the bathroom and threw up in the toilet. Leaning over the sink, he splashed cold water on his face before showering. There was no time to shave.

The TV was still on from the previous night and, as he went to switch it off, something caught his attention. The prime minister, Oliver Huxley, was under attack again on several fronts. There were rumblings from within the cabinet and widespread discontent amongst backbench Conservative MPs. The foreign secretary, Charles Trenchard, openly continued to voice his support for the PM despite threats of a call for a vote of no confidence. But there were those who believed that Trenchard had plans to realise his ambition for holding the top office. A leadership challenge was looking like a distinct possibility.

Fleming pulled on his jacket, switched the TV off, and took the stairs down from his apartment in Summertown to his parking slot in the street below. He drove his Porsche round to the Banbury Road, turned right towards the A40, then left down to the roundabout where he took a right onto the Woodstock Road. After about four miles, he turned left onto the A4095 towards Long Hanborough.

He felt awful. He was not looking forward to seeing DCI Watson. Fleming somehow knew it was going to be confrontational.

Fleming parked his car and went straight to Watson's office. He could see through the glass window that DI Jardine was with him. He took a deep breath, knocked and popped his head round the door. 'Got a minute, Bill?'

Watson had been expecting him. He looked up and nodded at Jardine to leave. 'Yeah, but make it quick. I've got a busy day.'

So have I, thought Fleming. 'You heard about Ronnie Nielson on Saturday?'

'Yeah, I heard.'

'I'll get straight to the point–'

'That would be good,' Watson broke in sarcastically.

'You were involved in a drugs-related investigation into him some time ago when you were working for the Met...'

'Yeah, what's that got to do with things?'

'Just wondered if you could fill me in on the details.'

'What the fuck for?'

'Want to build a picture of the man. If he was dealing in drugs, chances are he had enemies–'

'Look, I've got my own cases to deal with. Don't expect any help from me in solving yours.' Watson got up from behind his desk and jabbed a finger at Fleming. 'Let me tell you something, mate, so you know where you stand with me. I think they promoted you far too soon. You're too young and inexperienced to be a DCI. You need to have been round the block a few times for this game. Know what I–?'

Fleming cut in sharply. 'I'm not your mate, and I'd like a bit of co-operation here... if that's not too much trouble.'

'Fuck off!'

'Why are you being so difficult, Bill?'

'I'll tell you why. They promoted you in front of Frank Jardine who worked with me and poor old Anthony Hayden before he took medical retirement. He's a good reliable cop, and you've edged him out of a job that should have been his–'

'That's not my problem. I applied for a job and others decided who should fill it. Take your gripes to them. All I want is some answers to a few simple questions, like how come Nielson was never charged.'

'Look on the old Met case files, Fleming... it's all there. Find out for yourself.'

'And Nielson was a suspect in a murder case in Reading two years later. You were the SIO...'

'So?'

'What was that all about and how come there was never enough evidence to charge him?'

Watson's face had turned red and his eyes blazed. 'What the fuck are you getting at?'

'I'm trying to get some background on the man. Paint a picture.'

'Go and paint your fucking pictures somewhere else!' Watson shouted as he slammed a fist onto his desk, making his computer keyboard jump. 'If you must know, a man called Potts pleaded guilty to manslaughter – that's all on the files as well.'

'Is there anything on file about Nielson's army career?'

'What army career?'

'There was a photograph in his house. Nielson's with five

other men in uniform. Looks like it might have been taken in Iraq or Afghanistan.'

'That a fact? Can't remember anything about that.'

'You're not exactly being very helpful, Bill...'

'Like I say. All you need to know is on the files. Read them.'

'DCI Hayden worked with you on the murder case, didn't he?'

'Yes. What's that got to do with anything?'

'Know his wife, Emma?'

Watson looked furtively at Fleming. 'I know his wife, yes. Why do you want to know?'

'There was a postcard on Nielson's boat from a woman called Emma. She wrote to say she was looking forward to seeing him. Nielson's cleaner saw a woman with him a couple of weeks ago. Her name was Emma. Her description fits that of Hayden's wife, apparently–'

Watson lunged at Fleming with surprising agility and speed for a large man. He grabbed Fleming's suit coat by the lapels and spun him round against his desk. His reddened face was inches from Fleming's. 'What the fuck are you getting at? Are you trying to say Hayden's wife was mixed up with Nielson?'

Fleming pushed Watson away and straightened his coat. 'Bit tetchy aren't we, Bill? I'm just following a line of enquiry.'

Watson had regained some composure. 'There must be hundreds of women called Emma with a description that might be similar to Hayden's wife. You want to be careful throwing accusations like that about – accusations involving an old respected colleague and his wife–'

'I wasn't making any accusations,' Fleming pointed out. 'I'm just wondering if there's any possibility that Emma Hayden is the same woman as the one who saw Ronnie Nielson.'

Watson wagged a finger. 'I'm warning you, Fleming. You want to be very careful what you say and whose feathers you ruffle around here. Things could get very nasty if you tread on the wrong toes. Understand?'

Fleming had got nothing from Watson other than the impression that Watson was a dangerous man. A man who had previous dealings with Nielson. A man who had a temper and was not averse to violent conduct.

~

Leo Miller and Charles Trenchard had left a cabinet meeting at 10 Downing Street and were walking down Whitehall deep in conversation.

'This had better work, Leo,' Trenchard growled. 'Your only chance of keeping a ministerial position depends on me becoming leader. You know that, don't you?'

Miller knew it only too well. In his late sixties, all ambition of becoming leader himself had gone. His current position as chancellor of the exchequer was in doubt. The prime minister was threatening a cabinet reshuffle to get rid of those he thought were plotting against him. Miller narrowed his watery blue eyes against the glare of the midday sun and mopped his bald head with a handkerchief. 'Yes, I know, Charles,' he agreed in a wheezy voice.

'You should take more exercise,' Trenchard observed. 'You sound out of breath carrying all that extra weight.'

'My wife nags me about that as well,' Miller agreed, meeting the steady gaze of Trenchard's brown eyes. Miller felt slightly in awe of the man who always seemed to exude confidence and had an aura of authority about him. In his early fifties, Trenchard's upright posture and tall slim frame suggested he had spent time in the military. He was wearing an expensive grey suit, white shirt and blue tie. Trimmed with the utmost care, his cropped white hair and recently grown beard added to his sense of importance.

Trenchard smiled. 'Only looking after your welfare, Leo. We're in for a busy time and I need you fit and well, okay?'

Miller smiled and nodded. 'Sure.'

'Why don't you come over to my house in Henley at the weekend?' Trenchard suggested. 'We can enjoy a gin and tonic, watch the boats go by on the Thames, and take stock of where we are.' He gazed steadily at Miller. 'We need to get this right, Leo. We're both finished if we don't.'

Miller nodded again. There was no mistaking the underlying menace in Trenchard's voice.

12

The black Audi sped along the M4 heading east. Emma Hayden had spent the weekend with an old female friend in Bristol. Saturday night was a drunken haze: pubs, clubs, dancing and sharing secrets with her friend into the early hours of Sunday morning. Sunday was a blur. She'd had a lousy hangover and stayed in bed all day.

It was Monday morning. The sun was shining but heavy grey clouds were drifting in from the north. She was still feeling the effects of Saturday night out and had the windows down. The traffic was heavy and the first spots of rain hit the windscreen.

She put the windows up and brushed strands of her blonde hair from her face. There had been the usual flirting with younger men, but this weekend had been different. She hadn't gone to bed with anyone. True, she'd had a string of affairs in the past, accusing her husband of having no time for her. He was always busy with police work, late shifts, or going to the pub with his mates after work. She liked her material things and good times. Anthony did provide her with new cars, but not the good times she craved.

Thunder rumbled in the distance as Emma's mind drifted.

The steady hum of the engine was making her feel tired. She pulled into a service station and closed her eyes. Heavy rain hammered down on the car roof and she fell asleep dreading the thought of going home to her boring husband. He'd suffered depression, anxiety and migraines for years and had finally accepted an offer of medical retirement. He was fifty-five and burnt out.

She'd been asleep for two hours when she woke to car doors slamming shut next to her. A noisy couple were arguing over how long they'd driven without a break. *Suppose I ought to move,* Emma thought. She turned the ignition on and eased out of the service area car park before accelerating to merge into the motorway traffic.

Soon she was heading up the A34 towards Oxford, then onto the A44 for Woodstock. Their detached house was on a quiet estate and had three bedrooms and an integral garage. She pulled the car into the driveway behind Anthony's car.

Emma unlocked the front door and let herself in. There was no sound in the house. It felt eerie, empty. 'Anthony! I'm home.'

No reply.

Emma frowned. He'd usually have the radio or TV on while he reclined in his chair. She opened the hall door and crept into the living room. Maybe he was asleep. There was no sign of him. There was no newspaper or empty mug on the coffee table. Emma was forever telling him off for not taking empty cups or plates through to the kitchen. 'Anthony!'

Still no answer. The house was silent. She wasn't sure why, but Emma began to feel uneasy. As she opened the kitchen door, she whispered urgently, 'Anthony, where are you?'

The kitchen was empty. There was no sign of unwashed

dishes on the drainer. This was decidedly unusual. Emma made her way along the short hall to the stairs. She looked up to the landing, exasperated. 'Anthony!'

Maybe he was asleep. She made her way slowly up the stairs, not knowing quite what to expect. Their bedroom door was ajar. She carefully pushed it wide open, but Anthony wasn't there. A half-finished bottle of whisky sat on the bedside table. Frowning, she quickly looked in the other two bedrooms. There was no sign of her husband.

Walking back onto the landing, she pulled her mobile out of her bag and tapped in Anthony's number. She heard the phone ringing. The sound seemed to come from under the bed in their room. With her heart pounding, she knelt down and looked under the bed. There, vibrating and ringing on the floor, was Anthony's mobile.

Emma's pulse was racing as she rushed downstairs and into the kitchen where a door led into the back of the garage. She opened the door and looked towards the far end.

Her scream was loud and hysterical. Her hands went to her mouth as she stared in open-eyed disbelief. The rope hanging from a wooden beam in the roof was tight round Anthony's neck. His distorted face and bulging lifeless eyes stared back at her.

13

Temple looked up from DCI Hayden's file as Fleming entered her office. She closed the folder, pulled her reading glasses off and placed them carefully on the desk.

Fleming sensed from her demeanour that something was wrong. 'You wanted to see me, ma'am?'

'Bill Watson tells me you were asking about DCI Hayden and his wife.'

It was a statement not a question, but somehow Fleming knew it demanded an explanation. 'Yes, I was.'

'Why?'

'You were at the briefing. You heard about the postcard we found on Nielson's boat, and that the description of the woman the cleaner had seen with Nielson fitted that of Hayden's wife.'

'So you intend to go and see her?'

'Today.'

Temple frowned. 'You haven't heard then?'

'What?'

'She found her husband hanging in their garage this morning. I got a call after I'd spoken to Bill. It's not a good time to interview her.'

Fleming cursed under his breath. 'Anything suspicious?'

'Local cops found nothing that might suggest foul play. Everything points to suicide. You probably heard he retired on medical grounds. He suffered from depression and anxiety – had a breakdown. He was completely stressed out.'

'I'd still like to go and see her. She's crucial to the investigation into Nielson's murder. You said yourself that the chief constable was under pressure for a quick result on this. How long do you suggest I wait before I speak to her?'

Temple winced. They both knew it couldn't wait. 'Okay, go and see her today, but tread very carefully. The last thing I want is a complaint from the distressed wife of a former colleague saying she's being harassed the very day she found her husband hanging in their garage. This requires the utmost sensitivity, Alex.'

'Understood.'

'And take DC Anderson with you. It might be a good idea to have a female present.'

'Fine. Anything else?'

Temple hesitated and looked closely at Fleming. 'Are you all right, Alex? You seem a bit out of sorts.'

'I'm fine,' Fleming lied. 'Bad night, that's all.' The recurring nightmares was not something he wanted to talk to her about. That was for Freya who he'd made another appointment to see.

Two hours later, Fleming and Anderson were on their way to Emma Hayden's house. Fleming had made sure Anderson was aware of the need for sensitivity.

The house was on a quiet estate on the edge of Woodstock. A black Audi sat on the driveway. Emma came to the door with a glass of white wine in her hand. Her eyes were red.

Fleming wondered whether it was from the effects of the wine or from crying. He gave her the benefit of the doubt. 'Mrs Hayden?'

'Yes.'

'DCI Fleming and DC Anderson. Is it convenient to come in? We won't take long.'

A look of confusion passed over Emma's face. 'I spoke to the police this morning. What–?'

Anderson was quick to respond. 'They would be the local police from Oxford. We're from the Major Crime Unit, where your husband used to work.'

'Oh, I see. You'd better come in then.'

Emma showed them into a large living room. 'Sorry everywhere's such a mess. It's just... oh, I don't really know.' Tears flowed.

Anderson intervened. 'Why don't you sit down and I'll make you a cup of strong tea.'

Emma nodded and sniffed. 'Okay. You'll find everything in the kitchen.'

'Want one, sir?' Anderson asked Fleming.

He nodded and Anderson disappeared into the kitchen.

Emma put her wine glass down on a coffee table. 'Probably wasn't a good idea to start on this so early.'

Fleming smiled. 'I can't say I blame you under the circumstances, Mrs Hayden. We've come to say how sorry we were to hear what happened to your husband. It must have been a terrible shock.'

Emma ran a shaky hand through her long blonde hair. 'Yes, a terrible shock. I'd been away to see an old friend in Bristol. I went on Friday night. Anthony seemed fine. I mean... he was his usual self. There didn't seem to be anything...' Emma's voice trailed away. She paused and wiped tears from her eyes with the back of her hand.

'Take your time,' Fleming said.

'I came home this morning and he didn't seem to be here. I looked everywhere but he wasn't in the house. I began to suspect something was wrong and went into the... Oh, God, it was awful.' Emma took a deep breath and continued, 'I went into the garage and that's where I found him.'

Fleming glanced across the room to a photograph sitting on top of a bookcase. 'Is that you with your husband?'

Emma followed his gaze. 'Yes. It was taken after he retired.'

Anderson returned with three cups of tea on a tray. She bent down next to Emma to put her cup on the coffee table. 'What's that perfume you've got on, Mrs Hayden? It's very nice.'

Emma seemed surprised. 'Oh, it's Eternity. Calvin Klein.'

Anderson smiled. 'I should try some.'

Emma seemed relieved with the distraction. 'I've got some upstairs that's almost finished. I bought a new bottle when I was away for the weekend so you can have the old one if you like.'

'No, I couldn't take–'

'It's fine, honestly. Please, I'll go and get it for you...'

Anderson was about to protest but saw the warning look in Fleming's eyes and the imperceptible shake of his head. She wasn't sure what was going on, but caught on quickly. 'If you're sure. That's really very kind of you.'

Emma got to her feet rather unsteadily. 'Back in a minute.'

As soon as Emma left the room, Fleming got up and walked over to the photograph he'd noticed. 'Can you get decent photos on your mobile?' he asked Anderson.

She frowned. 'Yes, why?'

Fleming nodded at the photograph. 'Take a photo of that. It's Mrs Hayden and her husband.'

Anderson understood why he wanted the photograph. She quickly pulled her mobile out of her bag and took four snaps.

Emma returned and handed over the bottle of perfume. 'There you are. There's probably enough left for a few days.'

Anderson took the bottle. 'Thanks. That's really very kind of you.'

They finished their tea and Fleming made to leave. 'Sorry to intrude, Mrs Hayden. We wanted to offer our condolences on behalf of the office.' He turned at the door. 'By the way, did your husband ever mention a man by the name of Nielson... Ronnie Nielson?'

He saw Emma stiffen, but there was no look of shock. Maybe she didn't know that he was dead.

Emma shook her head. 'No... not that I can remember. Why?'

'Oh, it's just that your husband was investigating him some years back. Nielson was found dead on his river boat on Saturday morning...'

Emma gasped.

Fleming could see the pain in her eyes. He was pretty certain Emma was the woman who'd been on Nielson's boat. And she wore the same perfume.

14

Fleming, Logan and Anderson were back at the mortuary. Anderson was not her usual self. She looked serious and subdued. Fleming guessed she was not looking forward to seeing the results of Dr Kumar's autopsy. Fleming had some sympathy, but she would need to face this sort of thing if she was to stay in CID.

Kumar smiled at Fleming and his two colleagues as they entered. 'Morning all, you're right on time,' Kumar said as he placed a scalpel on the metal table beside him and pulled a sheet over Nielson's body.

Anderson looked open-eyed at the instruments on the table and shuddered.

Fleming had noticed Anderson's unease and hoped she was going to be okay. He shook hands with Kumar. 'Morning, Nathan. What's the verdict?'

Kumar smiled then looked at Anderson as he joked, 'He's dead.'

Fleming grinned. 'Nathan, your powers of observation never cease to amaze me. I trust he was dead before you started on him?'

Fleming looked at Anderson and thought he detected the hint of a smile crossing her face.

Kumar laughed. 'I think so. Anyway, enough of the frivolities, I'll talk you through what I've found and let you have a full written report later.' He drew back the green sheet exposing Nielson's body and pointed to Nielson's head. 'Here, high up on the left side of the forehead, you can see heavy bruising, broken skin, and a depressed skull fracture in the frontal cranial bone which caused a subdural haematoma–'

Logan coughed gently. 'What's that, Dr Kumar?'

'It's when blood collects between the skull and the surface of the brain – more often than not caused by a head injury. The nature of the wound suggests a blow from a heavy blunt instrument. It could have been from the glass ashtray found on the floor at the murder scene.'

Anderson looked pale. 'Was that the cause of death?'

Kumar shook his head. 'Good question, but no – that was the knife wounds. My guess is that the assailant struck the blow to the head first, and then found the knife to stab Mr Nielson. There would be no point in hitting him on the head after stabbing him. From the position of the head injury, I'd say he was struck while facing his assailant, and from the angle of impact it's almost certain the murderer was right-handed.'

Fleming looked thoughtful. 'Two scenarios. One, a chance intruder thinks there's no one on the boat, climbs aboard and comes across Nielson. A struggle breaks out and the intruder sees the ashtray, picks it up and strikes Nielson on the head. He can't afford Nielson being able to identify him so he stabs him with a knife found in the galley. Or someone could have been with Nielson. Someone he invited maybe. An argument breaks out. The murderer picks up the ashtray and swings it at Nielson's head, knocking him out. But this is more than a fallout and sudden fit of temper. The man intends to kill Nielson. But why...?'

Logan scratched his head. 'Doesn't get us very far at this stage though. We still don't know if the killer was known to Nielson or knew of him. We're also no nearer to knowing whether it was planned or not.'

'But,' Anderson mused, 'why would a chance intruder risk going onto the boat to see if there was anything worth stealing if the door was open? Isn't it likely that he would have assumed someone was there? If that's the case, it would seem to point to Nielson inviting someone to visit him, in which case we're looking for someone known to him.'

'Good point, Naomi,' Logan said. 'Except you're assuming the door was open before the murder took place. We don't know it was. All we know for sure is that it was open when the cleaner found it. It could have been closed when the murderer arrived and left open in his rush to get away. We need to keep an open mind on everything other than known facts.'

'I admit it's all speculation at this stage,' Fleming agreed. 'What else have you got, Nathan?'

'The knife wounds. Two to the front and two to the back. The length of the wounds is broadly consistent with the breadth of the empty slot in the wooden knife block. But you should be aware that skin elasticity and angle of the cut can make estimates vary by a few millimetres. It's hard to say which blows the murderer struck first, but my guess is the ones to the stomach and chest. The angle of entry of the blade to both areas suggests upwards thrusts from the right side. This is consistent with my view that the murderer was right-handed.

'It also suggests that the victim was in a crouched position when the murderer stabbed him. He was possibly recovering from the blow to the head and was trying to get up when he received the wounds to the stomach and chest. My guess is he had slumped forwards when his attacker stabbed him in the back. Again, the angle of entry of the blade suggests the attacker was standing over the victim's head.'

Fleming rubbed his chin. 'Not that it makes a lot of difference to us, I suppose, but which blow do you think was the fatal one?'

'Without doubt, the one to the chest. The blade severed the anterior interventricular artery.'

'His heart, Naomi,' Logan explained with a smile.

'Thank you, Sarge,' Naomi quipped with a hint of sarcasm. 'I'd worked that one out.'

Kumar smiled. 'Exactly, Sergeant Logan. It's actually a branch of the left coronary artery.'

'And time of death?' Fleming asked.

Kumar shrugged. 'I estimate the time of death – that is to say the physiological time of death–'

Logan gave Anderson a knowing nudge and broke in, 'That's when the body, including vital organs, ceased to function.'

Kumar smiled. 'Thank you once again, Sergeant Logan. You're being most helpful,' he said with a hint of irony.

'Not at all, Doctor. Not at all. Just need to ensure rookies like Anderson here understand the jargon.'

Anderson glared at him and thumped his arm.

Kumar laughed and looked at Fleming. 'Do you have to put up with this banter all the time, Alex?'

Fleming smiled. 'They haven't been on my team very long, but I'm beginning to realise what I might have to put up with.'

'If I may continue,' Kumar said, stifling a laugh, 'I estimate the time of death to be around ten o'clock on the Friday night, the evening before he was found. However, I have to add a word of caution – this is an estimate and he could have died up to an hour either side of that.'

'Thanks, Nathan,' Fleming said. 'Anything else we should know?'

'Yes,' Kumar replied with a trace of excitement. 'I removed a sample of tissue from under the fingernails of the victim's right hand. It's skin. Could well be from his attacker if there was a violent struggle.'

'Thanks for that, Nathan,' Fleming said. 'I'll look forward to reading your full report.'

～

On the way back to Oxford in the car, Logan broke the silence. 'You thinking what I'm thinking, boss?' he asked Fleming.

'What are you thinking?' Fleming replied.

'Did you notice Mr Rainer's face when we saw him at the mortuary yesterday? He had some scratch marks down his left cheek.'

Fleming had wondered if anyone else had seen it. 'Yes, I did notice. Naomi, can you run a criminal record check on him? Be worth finding out if he has any previous convictions.'

'Today would be good, if you can find the time,' Logan teased, looking over his shoulder at Anderson.

Anderson thumped his arm with her newspaper. She'd been reading an article on the front page. It covered the mounting speculation that the prime minister might face a leadership challenge. The press tipped Charles Trenchard as a potential successor to Oliver Huxley despite Trenchard's protestations of continued support for the PM.

15

Sarah Nielson's house was on the outskirts of Marlow. It was a lovely two-bedroom period cottage within walking distance of the River Thames, only a mile from the town centre. Fleming had brought Anderson with him. He'd noticed how concerned she was for Mrs Nielson at the mortuary and thought it a good idea to bring her along.

'Lovely setting,' Anderson said as they walked up the path to the front door. It was in stark contrast to her rather dingy flat which sat above a shop near Oxford town centre.

Fleming nodded his agreement as he rang the doorbell.

There was a slight delay before Sarah Nielson appeared looking somewhat anxious. 'I'm so sorry to keep you waiting. I was on the phone... to my father. He's very sweet. He keeps asking if I'm all right. Wanted to come over this morning while you were here, but I said there was no need.'

Fleming told her not to worry. 'You've met DC Anderson.'

Sarah smiled. 'Yes... yes, of course. Come in.'

She led the way into a little sitting room. 'Do have a seat.' She indicated the settee behind a coffee table.

'Mrs Nielson,' Fleming began, 'thank you for seeing us so

soon. We don't want to take up too much of your time, but we do
need to ask you a few questions.'

'Yes... of course. Go ahead.'

Fleming watched Anderson get her notebook out and saw a
nervous glance from Sarah. 'We need to make notes,' Fleming
explained, 'if that's okay with you?'

Sarah smiled weakly. There was a slight hint of a Cockney
accent when she spoke. 'No problem. I ought to make more
notes. Memory's like a sieve at times.'

'When did you last see your ex-husband?' Fleming asked.

'I haven't seen him since the divorce.'

'When was that?'

'Oh, last June.'

'Have you spoken to him since then?'

'No, I had nothing more to do with him. There were no chil-
dren so there was no need to keep in touch on that score.'

'Can I ask why you divorced him?'

Sarah hesitated and brushed a strand of hair from her face
with a shaky hand. 'It was mostly because of the affairs he had.
He'd been unfaithful on at least three occasions that I knew
about–'

'Mostly?'

'He... he used to bully me. Not just mentally...' Sarah
hesitated.

'Go on,' Fleming prompted.

'He would lose his temper. Sometimes it was over nothing
and he could snap. That's when he would hit me.'

'Did you ever report it?'

'No. I daren't. But my dad knew. The first time I had bruises
on my face I told him I'd fallen and hit my head on a table. But
after two or three occurrences, I ran out of plausible excuses. I
eventually told him. He was mad. Wanted to go and confront

Ronnie. He said he'd sort him out. I pleaded with him not to. My life would have been a misery–'

'But wasn't it anyway?'

Sarah shrugged. 'I suppose so.'

Anderson looked up from her notebook in which she'd been scribbling furiously. 'It must have been very difficult for you, Mrs Nielson. But I understand your predicament. Unfortunately, there are lots of women who are in the same situation as you were.'

Fleming had been looking around the room. 'Do you have any photographs of him with friends or army colleagues?'

'God no, I burnt every one he was in.'

Fleming showed her the wedding photograph from Nielson's house in Bourne End. 'That's you, Ronnie and your father. Who's the other man?'

'Goodness, I'm surprised he still had that in the house. That's Eddie Slater. He was Ronnie's best man.'

'Were he and Ronnie still friends?'

'No, they were best mates, but Eddie was killed in Afghanistan in 2002.'

Fleming showed Sarah the army photograph from Nielson's house. 'Any idea who the other five men are in this photo?'

Sarah looked at it closely then pointed at Slater. 'That's Eddie Slater again. I've no idea who the others are.'

'Did you ever meet any of his army friends or colleagues?'

'Not really. We had the odd drink with people at parties and so on, but there were never any regular long-term friends as such that I knew of.'

'Did Ronnie keep in touch with old army colleagues when he left the army?'

'I don't think so.'

'Did he keep a diary or address book?'

'I never saw one. I think he kept everything like that on his laptop.'

'No regular visitors to the house?'

'Not really.'

'I gather he threw lots of parties at the house. Weren't any of the people he invited regulars?'

'Can't say they were. I think most of them were casual business acquaintances that he wanted to wine and dine. You know what it's like in the business world.'

Fleming didn't, but he could guess. 'So how was business in his club?'

'I've no idea. He kept all of that to himself. I never interfered or asked about his business dealings.'

'You didn't have a joint bank account?'

'Goodness, no. He'd never let me anywhere near his finances. He only gave me an allowance, but was very generous. He used to buy me new cars, lots of clothes and jewellery. I never wanted for anything, so I suppose his business must have been doing all right.'

'Mrs Nielson, I have to ask you this, were you interviewed by the police about ten years ago regarding suspicions that Ronnie was involved in drugs in some way?'

Sarah frowned and her eyes flickered furtively between Fleming and Anderson. 'I... yes I was. But what–'

Fleming quickly reassured her. 'Ronnie was never charged with any offences, but have you any idea of what it was about?'

'No and I told the police that at the time. I knew nothing about any drugs. Ronnie said that a business rival was trying to stitch him up and not to worry. He said he would get it all straightened out soon. The police never came back to see me again and Ronnie told me it had all been sorted out. That was the last we heard of it.'

'And then two years later there was a murder in Reading.

Ronnie was a suspect. The police must have come to see you about that.'

'They did but he was innocent. He was with me at home all night on the night of the murder. I never understood how he could have been a suspect.'

'Maybe the police thought he had a motive. Even if he wasn't directly involved, he could have paid someone else to kill the man.'

'The man charged with the killing tried to say that Ronnie had put him up to it. Ronnie reckoned he was just trying to get back at him because he thought Ronnie had given evidence against him. Ronnie was never charged with anything and the man's claims were never proved in court.'

'Mrs Nielson, have you any idea who might have wanted to see Ronnie dead? Did he have any serious arguments or long-term disputes with anyone?'

'Gosh, people were falling out with him all the time. It was the nature of his business, running a nightclub in London. But no, I can't say that anything was so serious that someone would want to kill him.'

'Do you know anyone by the name of Emma?'

Sarah frowned. 'Can't say I do. Why?'

'There was a postcard from her to Ronnie on the boat.'

Sarah shook her head. 'Never heard of her. Doesn't surprise me though if he had a girlfriend.'

Fleming changed tack. 'Your father didn't have any time for Ronnie, did he?'

Sarah's eyes flashed with concern. She hesitated. 'Not really. He was angry when he found out Ronnie had been hitting me. They never really did get on, I suppose. I think Dad was just being protective toward me.' She wrung her hands together. 'I know what you're thinking. He didn't like Ronnie, but would never do anything like that.'

Fleming smiled. 'I'm sure you're right, but we do need to check on everyone who could have had a reason to kill him.'

'Of course. I understand.'

Fleming rose to go. 'Mrs Nielson, you've been a great help. I'm sorry to have taken up so much of your time.'

~

On the way back to Oxford, Fleming looked across at Anderson who seemed to be examining her notes closely. 'What do you think of it all so far, Naomi?'

'There are a few leads to follow up on, I suppose. There's the woman called Emma. If it is Hayden's wife, he would have had the motive to kill Nielson. And he commits suicide soon after. Then there's the men in the army photograph, and Mr Rainer.' Anderson hesitated. 'By the way, I noticed something else about him.'

'Oh?'

'He's right-handed.'

~

As soon as Fleming and Anderson left, Sarah Nielson was on the phone. 'Dad. It's me, Sarah. DCI Fleming and DC Anderson have just been to see me...'

'Yes?'

'They asked about you. They know you didn't like Ronnie. They asked me if I'd reported him for domestic abuse. I told them I hadn't but that you knew. Dad, I hope I haven't said anything I shouldn't have–'

'Sarah, don't worry. It's fine. They already know I hated the man. As good as said so outside the mortuary. Listen, why don't I come over to see you tonight?'

16

Nielson's Cellar was aptly named. The club was in the basement of an old rundown-looking building in the middle of Soho. Fleming and Logan had left Oxford on an early morning train to Paddington. From there they took the Bakerloo Line to Piccadilly Circus. London was bustling with morning commuters. It was hot and oppressive as Fleming and Logan walked up into Soho. Air pollution levels were high.

'Couldn't do this every day,' Logan complained. 'Bloody nightmare.'

Fleming tended to agree. He'd spent eight years working in London as a detective with the Met. He had to admit it had been a nightmare most of the time. 'You won't be asking for a transfer to the Met then?' Fleming joked.

'Not on your life,' Logan agreed.

The door to Nielson's Cellar was open, leading into a cramped hallway with a small desk stuck in the corner. Worn stone steps led down into a cavernous room with a stone floor. It looked like an old wine cellar with brick arches dividing a seating area with circular tables from a small wooden-decked dance floor. At the back of the cellar was a long bar that stretched across most of the back wall. Against one of the side walls was a slightly raised wooden stage.

A short man wearing faded jeans and a grimy white vest was busy stacking chairs on the tables. He looked up as Fleming and Logan approached. 'We're closed,' he grumbled through cracked and blistered lips.

Fleming showed his warrant card. 'DCI Fleming and DS Logan. We're here to see the manager, Scottie McBain. He's expecting us.'

The man glowered at the two men. 'Is that so?' he drawled. 'Scottie didn't tell me he was expecting anyone.'

'You Scottie's personal assistant as well as the cleaner?' Logan asked. He didn't wait for an answer. 'Run along and get him, there's a good chap.'

The man glared and shuffled off to a door at the side of the bar.

After a minute, he returned. 'In there,' he muttered, nodding toward the door.

Fleming didn't bother knocking since their arrival had already been announced. McBain's office was in stark contrast to the rest of the club. A dark-green tartan carpet covered the floor. A large photograph of Glasgow Rangers hung on the wall behind a desk cluttered with papers and files. Two yellow canaries perched in a large wire cage hanging from the ceiling and a bright light hung over the desk McBain sat behind. He looked like a retired boxer. Powerful frame, bulging biceps, heavily tattooed arms. In his fifties, Fleming guessed. Grey stubble hid the heavy lines on McBain's face, but failed to disguise thin cruel lips. He wore a tasteless tartan waistcoat over a white T-shirt and his left ear sported a diamond ear stud.

'I guess you'll be here about Ronnie,' McBain announced in a gravelly voice. He made no move to get up from behind his desk to greet Fleming and Logan. Reclining back in his chair, he clasped his hands over the thin grey bristle that remained of his hair.

'That's right,' Fleming confirmed. 'Need to ask a few questions.'

McBain shrugged and peered at Fleming through narrowed eyes. 'Feel free, but I doubt I can be of much help.'

Logan indicated some chairs by the wall. 'Mind if we take a seat?'

'You thinking of staying long?' McBain retorted.

'As long as it takes,' Logan replied.

McBain glared at Logan. 'Don't expect tea and biscuits as well.'

'A few minutes of your time, Mr McBain,' Fleming said, 'then we'll leave you to get on with whatever you're doing.'

'I was about to let Bonnie and Clyde out for some exercise.'

Fleming frowned.

'The birds – my two pet canaries,' McBain explained, nodding towards the cage.

Fleming looked puzzled. 'Exercise?'

'They need to be let out of their cage regularly during the day... bit like prisoners in the nick.'

'You know all about that, do you?' Logan quipped.

'What the fuck is this?' McBain demanded. He glared at Logan. 'You trying to wind me up?'

Fleming ignored the heated exchange. 'What happens to the club now?'

McBain shrugged again. 'Don't rightly know. It won't go to

his ex-wife. Ronnie made sure of that after the divorce. She got everything out of him then that she's ever going to get.'

'I understand there's no other family?'

'That so? Don't know his personal details. He was the owner – I just manage the place. No doubt the vultures will decide what happens to it.'

'The vultures?'

McBain looked at Fleming as though he ought to have known. 'Bloody lawyers, that's who. By the time they've finished sorting out Ronnie's estate, fuck knows what'll be left after they've taken their cut.'

'How long did you know Mr Nielson?' Fleming asked.

'About ten years.'

'You happen to know any of his old army colleagues?'

'No.'

Fleming showed him the photograph. 'Ever seen any of these men?'

'Yep.'

'Which ones?'

'Ronnie.'

'Bit of a comedian, Scottie,' Logan quipped. 'Maybe you'll find it funny if we get forensic accountants down here to check through the books. Could tear the place apart if we had to. Might be easier if you answer DCI Fleming's questions.'

McBain lunged forwards in his seat and leaned with his arms across the desk. His dark eyes glared at Logan. Then he relaxed and smiled. 'Of course, I'd be very happy to help you with your enquiries.'

Fleming resumed where he'd left off. 'So, you don't know anyone else on the photo?'

'No.'

Fleming showed him the wedding photograph and pointed to Rainer. 'Know who he is?'

'No.'

'He's never been here?'

'Never seen him before.'

'When did you last see Mr Nielson?'

'Wednesday. Said he was going to Bourne End for a few days. He had things to do and was going to come back to the club on Saturday afternoon.'

'Did he say what it was he had to do?'

McBain grunted. 'I'm not his keeper–'

'Answer the questions, Scottie. Make life much easier,' Logan said.

McBain glowered darkly. 'No.'

Fleming continued. 'Did Mr Nielson have any enemies?'

McBain laughed. 'Who doesn't in this game?'

'What do you mean by that?'

'Stands to reason, doesn't it? Type of place, type of clientele. He's fallen out with more than one client, and more than one supplier, and competitors.'

'Anyone on that list he upset enough that they'd want to kill him?'

McBain shrugged a third time. 'Doubt it. But you never really know people, do you?'

'Where did Mr Nielson keep records of all his contacts?'

'On his laptop.'

'There must be some records here... I mean for you to access when he's not here?'

'Only suppliers and business contacts. All his personal stuff was on his laptop.'

'We'll need to see a copy of all the contacts you have.' Fleming handed over his business card. 'You can send it to me by email.'

McBain took the card and slipped it into his shirt pocket. 'I'll get someone on to it.'

Fleming asked, 'Did Mr Nielson ever bring Emma here?'

McBain frowned. 'Who?'

'Emma Hayden?' Fleming tried.

'Never heard of her.'

'Sure?'

'Quite sure.'

'Know a man called Potts?'

McBain stiffened. 'Why d'you want to know?'

Fleming ignored the question. 'You do know him?'

'Of course I do. He used to work for Ronnie.'

'What did he do?'

McBain was evasive. 'Oh, this and that. Bouncer, barman, running errands–'

'What kind of errands?'

'How the fuck should I know. You'd need to ask Ronnie.' Scottie paused for effect and smiled. 'Oh, but then you can't, can you?'

Logan glared at McBain. 'Smug bastard, aren't you?'

McBain narrowed his eyes and clenched his fists. 'Anyone else spoke to me like that and I'd–'

'Kill them?' Logan offered.

Fleming ignored the exchange between the two men. 'Was he anything to do with the drugs investigation some years back?'

'The Met were all over the place then. They hauled Ronnie in for questioning, and so was Potts. They never found anything and never brought any charges. We reckoned it was someone who had it in for Ronnie that was trying to get the club closed down.'

'Who do you think that might have been?'

McBain laughed. 'Any one of a hundred people. Take your pick.'

'Two years later, Mr Nielson was suspected of being behind what was thought to be a drugs-related killing. Potts pleaded guilty to manslaughter. Think that could have been anything to do with the previous drugs investigation?'

'Your lot went over all of that back then. Potts knifed the man when a fight broke out. That's all I know. Why don't you go and speak to Potts?'

'We will. Thanks for your time, Mr McBain,' Fleming said, rising to leave. 'You have my contact details if you think of anything else.'

'Hope Bonnie and Clyde enjoy their exercise,' Logan quipped as they left.

McBain glowered.

On the train journey back to Oxford, Logan quizzed Fleming, 'You think there's some sort of vendetta going on here, boss? Nielson gets even with someone who he believed tried to get his club shut down. Potts takes the rap. Then some unknown party takes out revenge on Nielson?'

'Possible,' Fleming agreed. 'But then we also have Anthony Hayden if it was his wife having an affair with Nielson, and Mr Rainer who didn't hide the fact that he hated the man.'

17

Scottie McBain drove down to Brixton soon after Fleming and Logan left the club. The manager of a betting shop there was an old friend of his and had a spare room above the shop. McBain had asked him if an ex-employee of Nielson's club just released from prison could stay for a short while. The manager had been hesitant at first, but eventually agreed when McBain said the man would be no trouble and it would only be for a short time.

McBain looked down on the scrawny frame of Damien Potts lounging on an old easy chair with springs that had long since collapsed. His right arm dangled casually over the arm of the chair and a beer can hung loosely from his hand. A half-smoked spliff occupied the other hand.

Potts frowned and looked up at McBain through dark lifeless eyes. 'What're you doing here, boss?' he mumbled.

McBain wondered if he had done the right thing helping Potts. He shook his head in disbelief at the state of the man. His shoulder-long brown hair was unkempt, unwashed, and thinning on top. The long pockmarked face with thin lips had an expressionless haunted look. Shallow cheeks on his unshaven face suggested a lack of food. He was wearing soiled jeans with rips in the knees and a grubby sweatshirt. A tattoo showing two crossed daggers was clearly visible on his neck.

'Fuck's sake, Damien, have you seen the state of yourself? If you're going to come back to work for me you're going to have to tidy up a bit.'

Potts tried to suppress a sudden surge of anger. He closed his eyes and imagined plunging a knife into McBain. When he opened them, McBain was leaning over him.

'Damien, you all right?'

'Hell, yes. Never been better.'

'The cops have been to the club snooping around. They were asking about Ronnie, the old drugs investigation, Joe Cobb, and you.'

'What the fuck for? The drugs investigation was dropped and I've served time for doing Cobb. What are they asking about me for?'

'Maybe they think you killed Ronnie–'

Potts sat upright in his chair. His legs went into an involuntary spasm and his heels drummed the floor. 'Fuck!'

'They'll want to speak to you.'

'Fuck! I need to disappear–'

'Don't be an idiot. If you go on the run, they'll sure as hell think you did it. Take a couple of days to get yourself tidied up and I'll send someone to bring you to the club. We'll sort something out. And stop smoking that fucking weed, you moron!'

18

L ogan and Anderson watched as a stern-looking Liz Temple strode into Fleming's office. She pulled the door closed behind her and the two detectives could see through the office window that an animated conversation ensued.

'I know I agreed you could go to see Emma Hayden,' Temple was saying, 'but the chief constable isn't happy. When he found out he flipped his lid.'

'How did he know I'd gone to see her?'

Temple held Fleming's gaze. 'Someone told him.'

'Who?

'I don't know, but if I find out who's passing information upstairs to Upson behind my back they'll be for the high jump. He's getting pressure from Cecil Daubney. You know the score with the police and the crime commissioner. Upson thinks he's out to make a name for himself. He wants quick results.'

'What does that have to do with me going to see Emma Hayden, ma'am?'

'He heard you went to see Mrs Hayden because you thought

she might be the woman who visited Nielson recently. Upson blew a gasket. The last thing he needs is even more grief from Daubney. He'll not be a happy man if the press gets hold of the fact that a retired detective, who's just committed suicide, and his wife are involved in a murder enquiry.'

Fleming held Temple's gaze. 'So to be clear, are you telling me for information, or are you trying to say I shouldn't pursue this line of enquiry?'

Temple said nothing.

'Ma'am, I can appreciate the chief constable's concern about the need to tread carefully, but I can't let internal politics get in the way of the investigation, can I?'

Temple shook her head.

'Anyway,' Fleming continued, 'I didn't interview her – I just told her that Anderson and I were there to say how sorry we all were in the office to hear about her sad loss. Something the chief constable maybe should have done if he wasn't preoccupied with watching his back.'

Temple held up her hands. 'I don't need reminding that you have to pursue all lines of enquiry, but be careful, all right? And mind what you say about the chief constable.'

Fleming shrugged.

'So, are you going to tell me how it went?' Temple asked.

'What?'

'The meeting with Mrs Hayden, for God's sake!'

Fleming hesitated. 'She wears the same perfume we found on Nielson's boat, and the look in her eyes when I told her that Nielson had been found dead was enough to convince me she did know him. How well, I don't know at this stage.'

'Great!'

'We managed to get a copy of a photograph of her without her knowing. I'll have to interview her if the cleaner identifies her as the woman she saw on Nielson's boat.'

Temple rolled her eyes. 'That's all we need.'

On the way to the briefing room, Logan asked Fleming, 'What was that all about with Liz Temple, boss?'

'Internal politics,' Fleming replied without elaborating.

The whiteboard in the briefing room had more information on it than Nielson's name. A hush fell over those present when Fleming and Logan arrived.

'All right everyone,' Fleming announced, 'let's get started. Feel free to chip in at any point if you have any thoughts.' He looked round the room. 'Anything from the SOCOs so far?'

One young DC spoke. 'Nothing to get too excited about, sir. They found a few fingerprints but no matches, except for Mrs Dobbs, the cleaner. Same with the blood samples. No matches on the DNA database. All the photographs taken at the scene are there on the noticeboard. Oh, and they've bagged some samples of mud taken off the deck and carpet in the saloon.'

'Thanks. What about door-to-door enquiries?'

This time it was Anderson. 'Nothing.'

'And people on other boats that were in the vicinity?'

Anderson shook her head.

'The local marina?'

'Likewise,' Anderson said. 'All drew a blank, sir. No suspicious sightings – nothing out of the ordinary spotted by anyone.'

'Anyone come forward as a result of the notice on the towpath?' Fleming asked.

'Nothing,' came the reply from another DC.

'What about local hospitals and medical centres? Did anyone turn up with suspicious injuries?'

'Negative,' reported one of the team.

'Frogmen completed a search of the river bed yet?' Fleming asked hopefully.

'They're still searching, boss,' Logan said. 'But they've found nothing so far apart from the odd bit of junk thrown overboard from passing boats. They're not confident they will find anything. If there is a knife down there it could be buried under inches of silt by now. Oh, and I haven't been able to trace the other men in Nielson's army photo yet.'

Fleming shook his head. 'Okay, we don't seem to have a great deal to go on so far. I've got the pathologists report and there isn't all that much there either. We know Nielson was hit on the head with a blunt instrument before being stabbed to death. Angle of entry of the knife suggests the murderer was right-handed—'

'That narrows it down a lot,' someone quipped from the back.

A ripple of laughter broke out.

'Trust DC Gosman to come out with something like that,' someone else commented.

More laughter.

'All right, there is a bit more,' Fleming said, trying to stifle a smile. 'The pathologist found some skin tissue under Nielson's fingernails and there are some promising lines of enquiry I want to pursue. I'm now pretty certain that Emma Hayden did know Nielson and had visited him on his boat. I have a copy of a photograph of her. I'm going to see the cleaner again who found Nielson's body. Hopefully she'll be able to positively identify Mrs Hayden.'

Fleming continued in a sombre voice. 'No doubt you will all have heard by now of the tragic death of her husband yesterday. We need to find out what the relationship was between Mrs Hayden and Nielson. Anthony Hayden would have had a motive to kill Nielson if his wife was having an affair with him. And, just after Nielson's murder, Hayden commits suicide.'

'Bloody hell!' one of the detective constables exclaimed. 'That's all we need.'

'I know,' Fleming said. 'And I believe the chief constable isn't entirely happy with this line of enquiry.'

Fleming noticed the anxious looks on the faces in front of him. 'Don't worry. It's down to me to take any flak on this. I've asked Dr Kumar to check whether there are any scratch marks on Hayden's face and to take his fingerprints so we can check if they match anything on Nielson's boat. He's also taking a DNA sample so we can check it against the skin found under Nielson's fingernails.' Fleming tapped Eric Rainer's name on the whiteboard. 'Which reminds me – this is Sarah Nielson's father. He knew Nielson had knocked his daughter about on more than one occasion, and he hated the man. He had scratch marks on his face–'

'So, we're scratching around looking for clues?' It was another witticism from DC Gosman.

'Oh, Lord,' someone groaned, 'please help us.'

Fleming looked up at the ceiling. 'Please do let us know when you have something useful to contribute to this discussion, DC Gosman,' Fleming said jovially.

Smiling faces turned towards Gosman whose face had reddened.

'There's one more thing,' Fleming added, 'the Met suspected Nielson was using his club to front a drugs operation about ten years ago. They couldn't prove anything and never brought any charges. The club manager reckons a rival set them up. Two years later, a man was stabbed to death in Reading. A man called Potts, who worked for Nielson, was charged with murder. At first, he claimed Nielson had put him up to it, but later retracted his statement. He eventually pleaded guilty to manslaughter. Nielson was off the hook again.'

'So, what's your thinking, sir?' someone asked.

'Maybe the man Potts killed was responsible for putting the Met onto Nielson and Nielson did get Potts to kill him when he found out. Then maybe someone killed Nielson in revenge–'

'Sir?' It was Gosman. 'If Nielson's murder was a vengeance killing, why would whoever did it wait all this time?'

'Good point. That's the most constructive observation you've made so far, DC Gosman.'

'Aye, good on you, Gosman,' someone shouted. 'You'll make DS one day!'

Fleming laughed. 'He has a point though. It's something we need to bear in mind, but it is still worth pursuing the line of enquiry.'

Later in his office, Fleming was going through everything in his head again. He had two suspects: Hayden and Rainer. Or maybe there was a third – an unknown assassin out for revenge.

19

DCI Watson stood in the empty briefing room. The smell of sweat and coffee still lingered in the air. He'd made sure all of Fleming's team, and Fleming, had gone home.

He was cursing under his breath when DI Jardine limped in to join him. 'You don't look exactly happy, boss,' he observed.

'You seen this?' Watson exploded, waving a hand at the whiteboard. 'Bloody Fleming!' Watson stabbed a podgy finger at Emma Hayden's name and then Anthony Hayden's. 'I don't know what the fuck Fleming's up to, but I'm going to put a stop to it.'

'How do you intend to do that, boss? It's not your case... and Temple seems to think Fleming's up to it.'

'Peer review, Frank. Temple asked me to do the peer review. I've just finished it. And I'd be careful what you say in here. You never know when she might be nearby. Works round the bloody clock.'

'Yeah, don't we all these days,' Jardine grumbled. 'What have you put in your review of Fleming's investigative strategy?'

Watson thumped a hand against the whiteboard. 'All this stuff about Hayden and his wife. It's crap. He seems determined to pin this on Anthony.' Watson's face reddened. 'And this! The last thing we need is Fleming raking over old ground on the Nielson cases.'

'But,' Jardine argued, 'if you want to steer Fleming away from Hayden you could point him in the direction of Potts. He's just been released on parole and had it in for Nielson.'

Watson thought for a minute. 'Yeah, that's true, but if Fleming speaks to Potts, he'll blab on about being persuaded to plead manslaughter in the Cobb case to avoid being charged for murder as he would have been if he'd stuck to his story that Nielson had put him up to it.'

'But Fleming will speak to Potts anyway,' Jardine persisted. 'And he'll reiterate what he said at the time. His original claim that Nielson got him to kill Cobb was never proven so why should that worry us?'

'True, but Fleming's already asking why there was never enough evidence to charge Nielson. Fleming might stumble across something that suggests Potts *was* acting on Nielson's orders. That would make us look rather fucking silly, wouldn't it, Frank?'

'How come?'

Watson grunted. 'Because if Fleming can prove Nielson did get Potts to kill Cobb it would come out that we should have done him for murder and not manslaughter. And that Nielson should have been charged as well. But you're right; Fleming will speak to Potts anyway. It's a chance we'll have to take.'

Jardine shrugged. 'Word is that Upson isn't exactly happy that Hayden's wife has been named in the Nielson investigation. Might score some points with Temple and him if you trash Fleming's thinking about Hayden and suggest he concentrates on Potts and Eric Rainer.' Jardine looked thoughtful for a moment. 'Any idea how Upson might have found out about Hayden's wife anyway?'

Watson looked at him and smiled.

~

A light was on in Temple's office. Good, she was still at work. Watson wanted to get this over. He knocked on the door and poked his head round. 'Working late again, ma'am?'

'Hello, Bill. Yes, afraid so. Wanted to tie up a few loose ends. What are you doing here so late?'

He waved a brown folder in his hand. 'Just finished the peer review on Fleming's strategy on the Nielson case. Saw you were still here, so thought I'd drop it in. Time for a quick word about it?'

Temple sat back in her chair and clasped her hands behind her head. She looked tired. 'Okay, Bill. But don't take too long. I could read it or is there something specific you want to bring to my attention?'

Watson put the folder on Temple's desk. 'It's a bit delicate, ma'am. I wanted to speak to you about it rather than put it in writing in the review.'

Temple sat forward with a puzzled look. 'All right, Bill, you have my attention. Go ahead.'

Watson cleared his throat. 'It's Fleming, I think he's going about this all the wrong way. He's got a bee in his bonnet about Anthony Hayden and his wife. He's got Anthony down as a bloody suspect, for fuck's sake. Sorry, excuse my French, ma'am. That aside, he seems to think it's worth digging into the old drugs and murder cases involving Ronnie Nielson. God knows why–'

'Maybe he thinks they're relevant in some way.'

'I doubt it very much.' Watson hesitated. 'Can I be honest with you, ma'am?'

Temple laughed. 'Since when were you anything other than frank, Bill? You always speak your mind. Go on, let's have it.'

'You know I was one of the investigating officers on the drugs investigation when I worked with the Met?'

'Yes.'

'And I was the SIO on the Reading murder case that Nielson was accused of being behind?'

'Yes.'

'I don't know why, but I'm sure Fleming is out to try to undermine me, and poor old Hayden, for that matter. Fleming seems to be questioning my integrity because we never found enough evidence to charge Nielson.'

Temple looked thoughtful. 'It's not like you to be paranoid, Bill. Why on earth would Fleming want to do that?'

'He knows what I think about young relatively inexperienced detectives getting promoted too soon. I think he's out to prove he's better than old hands like Hayden and me. Just to make a point...' Watson hesitated. 'The thing is, he's in danger of rocking the boat here and bringing the whole unit into disrepute. Frankly, I don't think he's up to the job, if you want my opinion.'

Temple sat forwards and folded her arms across her desk. 'Bill, I don't want personal feuds to get in the way of our work. You need to put your prejudices to one side and get on with it. Understand?'

Watson looked uncomfortable. 'Yes, ma'am. Only... we've heard that the chief constable isn't entirely happy with the Haydens' names being associated with the Nielson murder investigation. I think he would be happier if Fleming followed up on Damien Potts. He was released on parole two weeks ago, but I think he's a long shot. More to the point, there's Sarah Nielson's father, Eric Rainer. He hated Nielson. He's my bet.'

'Does Fleming know that Potts is out of prison?'

'Don't know. He hasn't seen my review yet.'

'All right, Bill. I'll look at it when I get home. But you'll let Fleming know that Potts is out and that he ought to pull him in for questioning?'

Watson hesitated. 'Sure, I think he intended to speak to him anyway, but his focus seems to be on Hayden.'

'But now that Potts is out of prison he's a potential suspect. You need to bury the hatchet with Fleming. Have a friendly chat with him. Tell him you've given me your review of the case and you've recommended he concentrates on Potts and Rainer.'

Watson agreed he would do just that. Maybe a friendly word would do the trick. But somehow Watson felt he had not finished crossing swords with Fleming.

20

The journey from Oxford to Bourne End took about forty-five minutes. Fleming was driving and Logan fiddled with the radio controls. He hit a news channel where a reporter was interviewing Charles Trenchard.

'Not more about a leadership challenge,' Logan groaned. He was about to continue scrolling through the channels but Fleming stopped him.

'Hang on, Harry. Let's listen to this for a minute.'

Logan looked across at him. 'You're not really interested in this stuff, are you?'

'You should pay attention to things like this, Harry. Could affect us, you know.'

'Really? How come, boss?'

'There are senior people in the cabinet who are upset about quite a few things. Europe, austerity measures, policing, immigration, you name it. They think they could lose the next general election.'

Logan frowned. 'So how does that affect us... if by us you mean the police?'

'I was coming to that,' Fleming laughed. 'The rebels think our budgets are being squeezed too much. They reckon there should be greater funding for the police.'

'I still don't see how that affects us minions,' Logan said. Then it struck him. 'Ah, we get a pay rise! Missus would be happy if we did.'

Fleming smiled. 'Maybe, maybe not. But we may get a few more resources. We're currently one DI short. If we get more funding, you could be in the running for promotion, Harry.'

Logan nodded thoughtfully. 'I think we should definitely listen to this, boss.'

They listened in silence to the rest of the Trenchard interview. The reporter was pressing him on whether he would stand for election if there was a leadership challenge. Trenchard evaded the question and simply said that he hoped to have a meeting with the PM in the next few days and that Oliver Huxley had his full support.

'Sounds like the kiss of death to me,' Logan said.

A few minutes later, they were pulling up outside the small terraced house in Bourne End where Peggy Dobbs lived. The living room was small but the log burner and wooden beams across the ceiling added character. The house was spotless. There wasn't much furniture to speak of and no clutter, just a few paintings on the walls.

'Would you like some tea?' Peggy asked.

'That's very kind of you, Mrs Dobbs, but no thanks. We don't want to take up too much of your time.' Fleming glanced around the room. 'Nice place you have here. You live on your own?'

'Oh, yes. Vince... my husband... he died five years ago.'

'I'm sorry, Mrs Dobbs.'

'That's all right. I'm used to being on my own now. I have Toby to keep me company.'

Logan looked at the black and white cat that had appeared from nowhere to circle round his legs. 'The cat?'

Peggy smiled. 'Yes. He's a bit of a character.'

Fleming cleared his throat. 'Did Mr Nielson talk to you much when you went to clean his house and boat?'

'A bit, but we didn't have long conversations if that's what you mean. He was a very busy man, you understand.'

'Yes, I'm sure he was. There was a photograph in the house with Mr Nielson and some army colleagues on it. I presume you saw it?'

'Yes. Always picking it up to dust the bookcase.'

'Did you ever see any of the men on the photo in Mr Nielson's house or on the boat with him?'

'No, I can't say that I did.'

'Did Mr Nielson ever talk to you about his army days?'

'No, never.'

'There was another photograph next to the army one. A wedding photo of Mr Nielson, his wife, the best man and Sarah Nielson's father, Eric Rainer. Did you ever see him with Mr Nielson?'

Peggy thought for a moment. 'Well now, that's a bit strange...' She frowned, deep in thought.

'How do you mean, strange?' Logan prompted.

'I can't say I ever saw Mr Rainer with Mr Nielson in all the time I cleaned for him, right up to the divorce last year. Mr Rainer did come to the house, but it always seemed to be when Mr Nielson wasn't there. I got the impression they didn't get on.'

Fleming took out the copy photograph of Emma Hayden and her husband and showed it to Peggy. 'Is that the woman you saw on the boat with Mr Nielson a couple of weeks ago? The woman you thought he called Emma?'

Peggy took the photograph and peered at it closely. 'Yes. Yes that's her.'

'You're sure, Mrs Dobbs?'

'Yes, absolutely. No doubt at all.'

21

Charles Trenchard was deep in thought as he sipped on a large gin and tonic. Dressed in slacks and short-sleeved shirt, he was lounging in a deckchair on the lawn of his grand old house in Henley-on-Thames. The river flowed by at the bottom of the garden and a couple drinking from champagne glasses waved at him from a passing river cruiser.

Trenchard smiled and raised his glass in salute before taking another drag on his cigar. He knew he would need to act soon. The prime minister was vulnerable and the opinion polls were not looking good.

Trenchard's thoughts were interrupted as his wife, Helen, shouted from the kitchen window, 'Leo's here, darling.'

'Hello, Charles!' Miller shouted as he made his way down the lawn with a gin and tonic in his hand. He was wearing light casual trousers, a white jacket, open-necked shirt and a Panama hat.

'Your wife is the perfect host,' Miller announced holding up his glass and thrusting a spare hand towards Trenchard.

Trenchard smiled and shook his hand. 'Come and have a seat and tell me what you've been up to.'

Miller wheezed as he settled into a spare deckchair. He took his hat off and stuck it over a knee. 'Well now, Charles, things are moving fast. The shit is hitting the fan again on all fronts, especially Europe. The PM's being attacked right, left and centre in the press and he's threatening a cabinet reshuffle. He says it's because he needs to freshen up the front bench, but we all know it's to deflect attention from his poor rating in the polls. And he wants to get rid of those he thinks are plotting against him.'

Trenchard narrowed his piercing brown eyes and blew cigar smoke into the air. 'I know all that, Leo, but how are you getting on with drumming up support?'

'We're almost there. Bit short of the number we need to force a confidence vote, but almost half the cabinet want a change. One or two of them think they would stand a chance in a ballot if Huxley lost a vote of confidence. They don't have the balls to come forward though. They're all waiting to see if you make a move. They'll only put themselves forward for nomination if you do.'

'Are you sure I'll get the support of the majority of the Party if I put myself forward as a candidate for the leadership?' There was a hint of menace in the question.

'Leave it to me, Charles. I'm working hard on it. I'm certain we can muster enough support. I think it's a foregone conclusion that Huxley won't get the majority he needs to stay in power–'

'Yes, but how sure are you that I'll win the subsequent ballot?'

Miller raised his glass. 'I'm sure, old chap... absolutely sure. We just need to work on a manifesto saying what you stand for.'

Trenchard stubbed out his cigar. 'I hope you're right, Leo. I'm not going to be a happy man if this goes wrong. I'm putting my trust in you. You'd better not let me down. Your future depends on this as well.'

Miller grinned, downed the rest of his gin and tonic and rose to leave. 'Don't worry, Charles, I'll let you know as soon as we're ready to start the ball rolling.'

Trenchard lit another cigar and blew smoke into the air after Miller had gone. He wondered how much trust he could place in him, and worried that the press might start delving into his own past. Things seemed to have a habit of coming back to haunt you...

22

The streets of Oxford were busy and it was hot. Men in short-sleeved shirts hurried on their way to where they worked. Women were dressed in summer clothes. Sweating students cycled up and down the streets, and shoppers looked as though they'd walked for miles. Some probably had.

Fleming had brought Logan and Anderson out for lunch. There were things he wanted to discuss out of the office. Logan had suggested a burger bar he knew in George Street. He'd ordered a double cheeseburger and large portion of chips with a Coke.

'How can you eat all that at lunchtime and in this heat?' Anderson asked with a smile.

'Boss is paying,' Logan quipped. 'You should have a bit more. Looks as though you need building up.'

'I need to look after my figure. Need to stay slim and fit for my football,' Anderson replied, thrusting her head forwards as though heading an invisible ball.

Logan was impressed. 'I didn't know you played football, Naomi.' He thought for a second then added, 'Bet you play left back... left back in the dressing room.' He laughed at his own joke.

Anderson thumped him on the arm. 'Very funny, Sarge!'

'Just a joke, Naomi.'

Fleming was shaking his head. 'If you two have finished messing about, can we talk about work please?' He'd asked Anderson to talk to the Met and check the old case files on Nielson, and Bill Watson's files on the Reading killing. 'Did you come up with anything with the Met, Naomi?'

'There's not a lot to add to what we already know, sir. Seems a man by the name of Doherty had it in for Nielson. He owned a rival club and claimed Nielson was using his club to front a drugs operation. In fact, the Met had already been watching Nielson. They suspected that Damien Potts was pushing drugs for him. DCI Watson was on the case as an inspector at the time. He pulled Nielson and Potts in for questioning and called in at the club regularly to keep Nielson on edge. He wasn't getting anywhere so he organised a raid on the club one night. They found nothing. The guy I spoke to at the Met reckoned someone had tipped Nielson off. Watson then filed a report saying that there was no real evidence to support Doherty's allegations. He said further investigation would be a waste of police time. The case was closed.'

'Doherty wasn't the man Potts killed two years later by any chance?' Logan asked while chewing on a mouthful of chips.

Anderson shook her head.

Logan shrugged and washed down his chips with Coke. 'Just a thought.'

Fleming had been listening intently to what Anderson was saying. 'Did you find out why this Doherty guy had it in for Nielson?'

Anderson nodded while trying to swallow a mouthful of salad. 'The Met reckoned Doherty thought Nielson was trying to put him out of business and accused him of having an affair with his wife.'

'We need to speak to Doherty,' Fleming said.

'Ah, I don't think that will do us any good, sir,' Anderson said. 'He sold his club and moved to America shortly after Watson shelved the case against Nielson. My contact in the Met reckoned Doherty was frightened Nielson would come after him so Doherty packed up and left–'

'After which,' Logan broke in, 'he finds a man who will kill Nielson for him. Only Potts gets to his man before he gets to Nielson.'

'Nice theory, Harry, but that was eight years ago. And two years after the drugs investigation,' Fleming reminded him.

'So, Doherty's first attempt to get even with Nielson failed. What's to stop him finding another killer to have one more go now?'

Fleming groaned. 'You have a point, Harry. We're back to the possibility that an assassin, hired by Doherty, is the killer. Temple's going to throw a fit if we have to go to America to see Doherty.'

'Doherty didn't hire anyone,' Anderson said. 'And we don't need to go to America.'

Fleming and Logan looked at her in surprise.

'Doherty was killed in a car crash in America three years ago,' she explained.

'Why didn't you say so?' Logan demanded.

'I was about to before you interrupted me.'

'Okay,' Fleming said, trying to restore peace. 'What about Watson's files on Potts and the Reading killing, Naomi? Come up with anything there?'

'Man called Joe Cobb. Bit of history with various convictions. Did time for manslaughter some years ago. The Met suspected him of being behind a protection racket and gangland killings in London since his release. They never got close enough to him to bring charges. Potts stabbed Cobb to death outside a nightclub in Reading. Watson was the SIO and did Potts for murder. At first, Potts claimed Nielson had put him up to it. He said Nielson had told him Cobb had attempted to extort protection money from him and he was going to burn Nielson's Cellar to the ground if he didn't pay up. Potts later changed his statement and said he was acting in self-defence when he realised the charge could be reduced to manslaughter. Nielson was never done for incitement to murder. Potts pleaded guilty to manslaughter and got ten years.'

Fleming was beginning to feel uneasy. Watson was one of the Met officers on the Nielson drugs investigation. Nielson was never charged. Two years later, Watson's the SIO for the murder case in Reading. Nielson was cleared of incitement to kill.

'You okay, boss?' Logan asked. 'You've gone a bit quiet.'

'Yeah, sure, just thinking. Temple told me Watson thought the Reading killing was drugs related. Why would he think that if Potts came out with this story about Cobb trying to extort protection money from Nielson?'

Logan shrugged. 'But Potts changed his statement, and if his plea of manslaughter was valid, the killing was nothing to do with drugs, vengeance killing, or extortion. Watson might have settled for a plea of manslaughter to get a conviction even though he still believed it to be drugs related.'

Fleming frowned. 'So why would Potts claim he was acting on Nielson's instructions at first?'

'Maybe,' Anderson offered, 'Potts wasn't lying. Maybe Nielson did get him to kill Cobb, and Potts thought Nielson had shopped him. Maybe he wanted to get even and bring Nielson down with him. He then thinks better of it to get a lesser sentence.'

'If that's the case,' Fleming said, 'we're not dealing with a drugs-related vendetta.'

'No,' Logan agreed, 'but Nielson's killer could still have been someone known to Cobb who believed Nielson was behind his death and wanted revenge.'

'After all this time?' Anderson queried.

'That,' Fleming said, 'remains a complete mystery.'

'Where does that get us, boss?' Logan asked.

'We need to speak to Potts. Changing the subject though, what about our Mr Rainer, Naomi? Any previous convictions?' Fleming asked wearily.

'He had a previous for assault but that was over twenty years ago, soon after he left the army. Bar room brawl got out of hand. He got a suspended sentence. Nothing since.'

'What does he do?' The question came from Logan before taking the last bite of his cheeseburger.

'When he left the army, Rainer went to work as a boxing instructor for a club in Maidenhead.'

'Told you!' Logan exclaimed. 'I win the bet.'

'We didn't bet,' Naomi reminded him. 'He's sixty-five but still working there. His wife died four years ago. Lives on his own in a terraced house in Maidenhead. That's about it.'

'Thanks for all of that, Naomi. Not sure it gets us any further forward though. We still can't discount the theory that an assassin killed Nielson for revenge for whatever reason. But we do know that, if it was a hired killer, he wasn't hired by Doherty.'

On the way back to the office, Anderson remembered something. 'Oh, DCI Watson came to see you this morning, sir. You were out at Mrs Dobbs's at the time. Said he would pop in this afternoon if you were around.'

'Thanks.' Fleming wondered what he wanted. His last meeting with Watson had been less than friendly. Maybe he wanted to apologise for his behaviour. Somehow Fleming doubted it. He knew Temple had asked Watson to do the first peer review of his investigative strategy. Fleming dreaded to think what might be in it.

23

Fleming's desk was covered in papers. He had rough notes to type up, interviews to record, and Logan kept reminding him to sign off the overtime claim forms. Freya had been on the phone reminding him of his four o'clock appointment. She wasn't taking any chances after he'd missed the last one.

Fleming was looking at the list of Ronnie Nielson's business contacts that McBain had emailed him when Anderson popped her head round the door to warn him. 'DCI Watson's on his way to see you now, sir.'

Fleming scooped up the list of contacts and thrust them towards Anderson. 'Do me a favour, Naomi, will you? Run a check on this lot and see if anyone on the list ever had a major fall out with Nielson or had an axe to grind with him. They'll all have to be interviewed I'm afraid. Get the team on to it. There's quite a few, sorry.'

Anderson smiled and took the list. 'No problem, sir. I'll split them between the lads. Might be getting a few more of those,' she added, pointing to the overtime forms.

Fleming moaned. How he could do with a nice large glass of his favourite single malt.

Watson knocked and came straight into Fleming's office. 'You look busy, Fleming. Hope the job's not getting on top of you.' It appeared to be a weak attempt at light-hearted banter.

Fleming looked up from the papers on his desk. 'What can I do for you, Bill?'

Watson picked up a chair from the other side of the office. 'Mind if I sit down?' He placed the chair with its back facing Fleming's desk.

'Help yourself.'

Watson sat heavily and folded his arms across the back of the chair.

'To what do I owe the pleasure?' Fleming enquired, thinking it was going to be anything but a pleasure if his last encounter with Watson was anything to go by.

'I think I can do you a favour, Fleming—'

'That a fact. I seem to remember the last time we spoke you weren't exactly in a helpful frame of mind.'

Watson grunted. 'Ah, caught me at a bad time, that's all. Don't take it personally. No hard feelings, eh?' He didn't wait for an answer. 'Though it doesn't alter the fact that I still think Jardine should have got Hayden's DCI post. It should be Jardine sitting behind your desk.' Watson shrugged and lifted his hands in the air as though in resignation. 'But hey, that's life. He didn't get the job and that's it. We're all entitled to our own opinions, aren't we?'

Fleming ignored the question. 'What's the favour?'

'I need to be frank with you, Fleming. I've done the peer review on your investigative strategy and I think you're in danger of going off in the wrong direction. I've spoken to Temple about it and she asked me to have a word with you—'

'Oh? What makes you think that? And did Temple ask you to have a word because she agrees?'

'She didn't say so as such, but I do know she's worried about how the chief constable views bringing an old colleague and his wife into the investigation. It could reflect badly on the whole unit if you get this wrong. Last thing he needs is adverse publicity with Cecil Daubney breathing down his neck. Know what I mean?'

Fleming wondered where this was leading. 'I do know what you mean, but as I said to Temple, I have to follow up on every lead. You know that as well as I do, Bill. Internal politics are not my concern.'

Watson glowered at Fleming. His face reddened.

Fleming noticed Watson's knuckles whiten as he gripped the back of his chair. He waited for a caustic response. But surprisingly, Watson kept control of his temper.

'The favour,' Watson said quietly, 'is to point you in the right direction and save you a lot of trouble.'

'Okay, so what's the right direction you somehow seem to know about?'

'You know you were asking about the murder investigation in Reading and I told you a man called Potts was convicted of manslaughter?'

'Yes.'

'What I didn't tell you at the time was that Potts thought Nielson had shopped him, so he claimed that Nielson had asked him to kill Cobb. But he later said he'd made it up and pleaded guilty to manslaughter to get a lighter sentence–'

'I'm aware of that. Anderson checked your case files. Anyway, Potts is in prison so can't be the killer. But I do need to speak to him. I need to get to the bottom of this Cobb case to see if there's a link to Nielson's murder.'

'I was about to add, forget the crap about what Potts claimed. The Cobb case was manslaughter, no doubt about that. What you need to find out is whether there's another reason why Potts would want to kill Nielson. Oh, and by the way, there's something you obviously don't know. Potts was released on parole two weeks ago.'

Fleming raised an eyebrow. 'How come nobody told me Potts was out of prison?'

'Your team obviously missed it so I'm telling you now. Potts could be a suspect, but my bet is on Eric Rainer.'

'So that's what's in your peer review?'

'That's about it. Forget about Hayden. Check Potts out, but forget about raking over old cases, you're wasting your time. Concentrate on Rainer. Do that and you might keep the chief constable happy.'

Fleming sat forwards in his chair and looked at Watson. 'One thing though. I now have a positive ID on Emma Hayden. She definitely knew Nielson and has been on his boat–'

Watson pushed himself up from his chair and leaned menacingly over Fleming's desk. 'For fuck's sake, Fleming, can't you let it go? Maybe Emma Hayden was having an affair with Nielson, but that doesn't make her husband a murderer. He might not even have known. But if he did, it might have tipped him over the edge to commit suicide. He was suffering from depression.'

'Okay, Bill, keep your hair on. You may well be right, but Emma Hayden saw Ronnie Nielson recently and I have to interview her about that, along with everyone else who had any contact with him.'

Anderson knocked and stuck her head round the door. 'Super wants to see you when you're finished, sir.'

'Bear in mind what I said,' Watson warned as he made to leave. 'But make sure you get this right for your own sake, Fleming.'

~

Fleming knocked on Temple's office door once and entered. 'You wanted to see me, ma'am?'

Temple was behind her desk, reading glasses perched on the end of her nose as she studied a file in front of her. 'Yes. I wanted to make sure Bill Watson has spoken to you about the Nielson case.'

'He has.'

'And?'

'He told me he'd seen you about his peer review and that you'd asked him to speak to me.'

Temple took off her glasses and fixed a steely stare on Fleming. 'What I'm asking, Alex, is what did he tell you?'

'He told me Damien Potts was out of prison and I should forget about Anthony Hayden.'

'And you agree Potts has to be a suspect?'

'Yes.'

Temple drummed her fingers on the desk in impatience. 'I take it you're going to question him?'

'Yes, ma'am.'

'And what about Emma Hayden, dare I ask?'

'I need to speak to her again. I've got a positive ID. She went to see Nielson recently.'

Temple put her head in her hands. 'Christ! Why is this turning into a fucking nightmare?'

Later, on his way to his appointment with Freya, Fleming wondered the same thing.

24

Fleming was on his way to see Freya Nash in Wolvercote on the northwest side of Oxford. She was a caring sympathetic woman, friendly and easy going. He felt at ease in her company. But he wasn't sure if counselling was doing him any good. The flashbacks of the day his mother was murdered could occur at any time. Nights were the worst. If he was too tired he would sometimes get a migraine. He'd have painkillers washed down with a few glasses of whisky. The pain would eventually ease and he'd fall into a disturbed sleep. Then the nightmares would come.

Freya practiced from home and as Fleming pulled up outside, he wondered if this was going to be of any benefit. He shrugged. *You never know*, he thought, *she might succeed where others had not*. Freya was of Danish parents who had moved to England when she was a child. In her late forties, she'd studied integrative psychology at university and had worked in a bereavement service for seven years while training as a counsellor. She was now an experienced psychotherapist.

The front door opened as Fleming approached and Freya,

tall, slim, with short blonde hair and a fair complexion, greeted him. 'Hello, Alex. I saw your car. Glad you could make it,' she said, offering a hand.

Fleming could see the friendly twinkle in her bright green eyes as he shook her hand. Her grip was firm and confident. 'Thanks. I managed to tear myself away from the office,' he replied with a smile. 'Sorry I missed the last appointment... bit of a panic. I was called out to an incident.'

'I see. Nothing too bad, I hope?'

Fleming shrugged. The nature of the job was that most incidents were bad. Some worse than others. The worst ones for him were the murders involving knives. 'Not really,' he lied.

Freya showed Fleming into a small room, off the hallway, that she used as an office and treatment room. Two easy chairs sat by the window either side of a coffee table. Her desk was clear of everything except for a computer screen, keyboard, and a closed file with Fleming's name on it.

Freya pointed to one of the easy chairs. 'Take a seat, Alex.' She sat opposite him in the other chair and leaned forwards attentively. 'So, Alex, how have you been?'

'Busy.'

Freya smiled patiently. 'I mean physically and mentally.'

'I've had a few bad nights. I sometimes have vivid nightmares.'

'Can you describe these nightmares?'

Fleming took a deep breath. 'I see my mother being stabbed. I'm running but my legs feel like lead. It's as though I'm running in slow motion. There's someone chasing me. I hear heavy breathing. Footsteps getting closer. Then I see bright lights. I feel pain. I wake up in hospital and someone is standing over me with a knife. I scream. It's always the same.'

'Always? Always the same nightmare?'

Fleming thought for a moment. 'More or less.'

'Do you take anything to help you sleep?'

Fleming nodded.

'Sleeping pills?'

'Whisky.'

'And do you think that's helping?'

'Doesn't help the nightmares, but it does help me to get to sleep.'

'It sounds like you know drinking whisky isn't going to solve anything.'

Fleming shrugged.

Freya was holding eye contact with Fleming. 'Do you think you might subconsciously be having the same nightmare because a part of you wants to relive the trauma, hoping for a different outcome?'

Fleming shrugged again. 'Interesting idea, but I don't really want to have those nightmares. And I know I can't change the outcome.'

'It sounds like you have accepted that you can't change *anything*. How does that make you feel?'

'Angry, frustrated, depressed...'

'Depressed?'

'I feel a bit low at times. I get tired at work.'

'Yes, that's understandable if you've had a bad night's sleep. And I suppose the nature of the job can be... shall we say, depressing at times.'

'I suppose so.'

'Your father was a detective, wasn't he?'

Fleming looked up sharply. *Why is she bringing that up now?* 'Yes.'

'I suppose you must have had an idea what it was like?'

Fleming raised an eyebrow.

'Being a detective, I mean,' Freya continued.

Fleming shrugged a third time. 'I was only ten when he died. I didn't really think about it.'

'An Edinburgh gangster shot him, didn't he?'

Fleming wondered where this was going. 'Yes.'

'Then you witnessed your mother being killed by an intruder two years later.'

'Yes, look...'

'You said you felt angry. Was it anger against criminals that prompted you to follow in your father's footsteps and become a detective?'

Fleming thought for a moment. 'Possibly,' he finally answered. 'It's a job.'

Freya pondered before asking her next question. 'Do you think it's the right job? It must be stressful at times. You must come across a lot of violence.'

Fleming looked vacantly out of the window. 'I suppose I do.'

'Maybe the nightmares aren't helped by that.'

Fleming frowned. 'Are you suggesting the nightmares might stop if I change jobs?'

'It's a possibility. Maybe you're consumed by anger. Do you ever feel you'd like to take that anger out on the man who killed your mother? Jimmy Calder, wasn't it?'

Fleming turned his head sharply from the window to face Freya. He stiffened at the mention of the name. 'Yes. I mean, yes it was Jimmy Calder,' Fleming added quickly.

'And taking your anger out on him?'

'He's still in prison, as far as I know.'

'But if he wasn't?'

'It would be very satisfying, I must admit.'

Freya seemed to notice a change in Fleming's demeanour. 'Tell me, how do you rid yourself of pent-up anger and frustration?'

'I go to the gym or for a run.'

'It sounds as though you know how to channel your pent-up emotions in a positive way.'

'I try to keep calm. Once you lose your temper you lose control of a situation. In my job you can't afford to do that.'

Freya nodded. 'You have no siblings?'

'No.'

'And you were left on your own at twelve?'

'Yes.'

'Who looked after you?'

'An aunt.'

'And your wife was pregnant when she died, wasn't she?'

Fleming shifted uncomfortably in his chair. 'Yes, she developed complications after contracting flu. She died from pneumonia five years ago.'

Freya put a hand on Fleming's. 'You've had a lot of suffering in your life, Alex.'

Fleming pulled his hand away. 'Thanks for reminding me,' he said drily. 'Some have had it worse. I cope.'

Freya seemed to sense Fleming's discomfort. 'I think maybe we should call it a day for today. It's good that you have at least accepted that you can't change the past. Acceptance can go a long way to removing feelings of helplessness and anger. Not sure about the whisky remedy, but as long as you only drink in moderation it's not a problem.'

Fleming rose to leave, thanked Freya for her time, and promised to make another appointment after checking his diary.

On the way back to the MCU, he reflected on what Freya had been saying. He was curious about the reference to Jimmy

Calder. Why had she wondered if he had ever had thoughts of taking his anger out against Calder?

What Fleming didn't know was that his past was soon about to catch up with him in a way he didn't expect.

25

The black Audi was on the driveway of Emma Hayden's house. A cluster of reporters stood outside, microphones and cameras at the ready, hoping to catch a quick interview with Emma, or anyone else who came to the house for that matter.

'Looks like police to me,' one reporter exclaimed as Fleming and Anderson climbed out of his car.

The man rushed across and thrust a microphone in front of Fleming. 'Any comment on the rumour that Mr Hayden was involved in an investigation into Ronnie Nielson some years ago?'

Fleming glared at the man. 'No.'

'You're police, aren't you?'

Fleming ignored the question and pushed his way past the man.

As they walked up the drive, Fleming noticed Emma looking furtively out of the window from behind the curtains. The front door opened before they could knock. He was surprised at how different Emma looked from when they saw her just a few days earlier. She looked stunning in a sleek black dress with a red and black striped cashmere cardigan worn over the top. Not a blonde hair out of place. Her mouth shone with glossy pink lipstick. Her eyes were no longer bloodshot.

'I've been expecting you. DC Anderson said on the phone you would be coming. Please come in,' Emma said in a shaky voice. 'I daren't go out with all these reporters outside,' she added, quickly closing the door behind them.

Emma was wringing her hands as she asked if they wanted anything to drink. Fleming told her not to go to any trouble. They wouldn't take up much of her time. Emma sat on the edge of a chair and leaned forwards clasping her hands round her knees as though to stop them trembling.

Anderson spoke first to break the ice. 'As I said over the phone, we wanted to ask you a few more questions...'

'I don't understand. I gave a statement to a uniformed officer about my husband. What–'

Fleming interrupted her. 'Mrs Hayden, I'm afraid certain things have come to light that we need to ask you about.'

'Oh, about Anthony, you mean?'

'What time did you leave to go to Bristol last Friday night, Mrs Hayden?'

Emma frowned. 'What's that got to do with Anthony's death?'

'Please answer DCI Fleming's questions, Mrs Hayden,' Anderson prompted.

'Yes, of course. I was curious. Let me see... I suppose it was about seven o'clock. I didn't want to get there too late.'

'And your husband was at home when you left?'

'He was.'

'I hate to ask you this, but was he dressed in the same clothes when you found him on Monday?'

Emma frowned. 'Er, yes, I think he was. I didn't really pay much attention to what he was wearing on Friday night, or on

Monday when I found him.' She shivered. 'Why is that important?'

'It may not be,' Fleming admitted. 'Just curious.'

Anderson cleared her throat. 'Mrs Hayden, can you give us the name and address of the friend you stayed with over the weekend?'

Emma was beginning to feel unsettled with the questions. She rose slowly to her feet and crossed the room to a bureau by the door. She opened a drawer and took out a letter. She passed it to Anderson with a shaky hand. 'Her name and address are at the top.'

Anderson took the letter and copied the name and address into her notebook.

Fleming knew he was about to stray into difficult territory with his next questions. Superintendent Temple and the chief constable were not going to be happy if he got this wrong and Emma complained. 'Mrs Hayden, when we saw you last, you said your husband never mentioned Ronnie Nielson to you...'

'No, he didn't.'

'And you had never met him yourself?'

'Of course not.'

'It's just that you seemed shocked when I told you he was found dead on his boat...'

'Did I?'

'Mrs Hayden, we found a postcard on Nielson's boat. It was from someone going to see him. It was signed Emma. Know anything about that?'

Emma's eyes shot from Fleming to Anderson and back. 'I don't... no, of course not.'

'We also found a toilet bag in one of the cabins. There was a bottle of perfume in it. Same perfume you wear, Mrs Hayden.'

'That's obviously just coincidence.' Emma's voice was shaking. 'There must be loads of women called Emma who wear Eternity.'

'But not all of them about your height and age with blonde hair...'

'I don't–'

'The thing is, Mrs Hayden, Mr Nielson's cleaner has positively identified you. You went to see him on his boat recently, didn't you?'

'Oh, God! I didn't think anyone would find out. Yes, I did go to see him.'

'Why?'

'I... he asked me to go. I didn't know why.'

'But the note you sent suggested you were looking forward to seeing him. You asked if he wanted you to bring anything and you told him to call you.'

Emma slumped in her chair and her shoulders heaved. 'We... we were having an affair,' she finally admitted, sobbing.

'Did your husband know?'

'Yes. Oh my God! It's all my fault, isn't it? That's why he committed suicide.'

'He didn't leave a note anywhere?'

'No.'

'Then we can only guess why he killed himself,' Fleming said.

Emma dabbed a tissue at her eyes and nodded.

'There was no one else with your husband when you left for Bristol?' Fleming asked.

'No.'

'He wasn't expecting anyone?'

'No.'

'No one can confirm he was at home that night?'

'Wait... are you trying to say you think he had something to do with Ronnie's death?'

'You said he knew about the affair. He failed to find enough evidence to charge Nielson years ago. He was hardly going to like the man. He had time after you left the house to get to Bourne End. Maybe he did kill him and then decided to kill himself.'

'No. No, he'd never do that! I don't believe it!' Emma was shouting.

Anderson put her arm round Emma's shoulders. 'Mrs Hayden, I know this is all very difficult for you. We're not saying your husband did kill Mr Nielson, but I'm afraid he is a suspect.'

Fleming sighed. 'I hate to press you, but it would help us if you would agree to our forensic team to come to the house to check for fingerprints, blood samples and so forth. It might help eliminate your husband from our enquiry.'

'Absolutely not. Not with all the press hovering outside like vultures. Anthony couldn't have had anything to do with it. He just couldn't!'

'We could get a warrant,' Fleming pressed.

Emma rubbed her aching forehead with a shaking hand. 'All right,' she whispered almost inaudibly.

Back in the offices of the MCU, Fleming was sitting behind his desk when his phone rang. It was Nathan Kumar.

'Hello, Nathan. Any news?'

'Yes. Your Anthony Hayden...'

'Yes?'

'There are no scratch marks on his face. There's no match of his fingerprints with any we found on Nielson's boat, and there's no DNA match with the skin I found under Nielson's fingernails.'

'Thanks, Nathan. That's very helpful.'

Fleming put the phone down. *Looks like Watson, Temple and the chief constable will be happier*, he thought. Though he wished he'd known what Nathan had told him before he went barging in on Emma Hayden.

He leaned through his office door and signalled to Anderson. 'Don't bother getting forensics over to Hayden's house. Looks like he's in the clear. Oh, and you ought to call Mrs Hayden. Let her know and put her mind at rest... if that's possible.'

That evening, back in his apartment, Fleming poured himself a large glass of whisky and settled down in his armchair, deep in thought. He went through the suspects in his head. Hayden was off the radar. That left Rainer, the assassin theory, and Potts. Fleming wasn't sure why, but he felt uneasy. Maybe there was more to this than revenge.

26

Fleming was silent in the passenger seat as Logan drove the pool car on the way down to Maidenhead. He was thinking about his session with Freya. Did she think he was suffering from depression? She obviously thought he was drinking too much. Maybe he should pay a visit to the doctor. But when would he find the time while he was working on the Nielson case? Then there was Freya's interesting reference to Jimmy Calder: *Do you ever feel you'd like to take that anger out on the man who killed your mother?*

'Penny for them,' Logan said, turning briefly to look at Fleming.

'Just thinking, Harry. Going over what we have so far.' Changing the subject, Fleming asked, 'How are you and Naomi getting on together? You're a new team... never worked together before. You both okay with that?'

'Sure. We like a bit of banter and we rib each other, but she's a bright young officer. Only joined CID a couple of years ago. I think she'll do well.' Logan flicked on the wipers as heavy spots of rain hit the windscreen. Thunder rumbled in the distance. 'What about you, boss? We're all new. You'd hardly got your feet through the door of the MCU and you're landed with a murder case with two new detectives.'

'I'm sure we'll make a good team,' Fleming answered. 'What's your take on this guy Rainer?'

'He hated Nielson, that's no secret. He has scratch marks on his face, and he works in a gym. Looks as though he could take care of himself as well.'

Fleming nodded. 'He definitely didn't like Nielson.'

Twenty minutes later, Logan pulled the car into the cramped car park of the Max Fitness Gym near the station. The building looked old and uncared for. Paint was flaking off the metal entrance door. Inside there was a small reception desk behind which sat a young girl busy filing her nails. She was chewing gum while speaking on a telephone wedged between her shoulder and head on account of her hands being fully occupied. The call was obviously not business. She quickly said she would have to call back when she saw Fleming flashing his warrant card in front of her face.

'I'm DCI Fleming and this is DS Logan. Is the manager in?'

The girl's eyes widened. 'Yes... yes he is,' she stammered. 'I'll ring through and let him know you're here. Is he expecting you?'

'No. Is Mr Rainer here as well?'

The eyes grew wider. 'Yes, he's here today. Shall I—'

'No need,' Fleming said. 'Just get the manager.'

Five minutes later, they were in the small dingy office of a wary-looking manager. He introduced himself as Max Dunn. 'What can I do for you?' he asked. 'I hope none of the lads are in trouble. They're a good bunch in Eric's boxing club.'

'We'd actually like a word in private with Mr Rainer, if we may. How well do you know him?'

'I know Eric very well. He's been with us now for over twenty years. Ex-army. He's a brilliant coach. We're lucky to have him.' Max looked worried. 'There's nothing wrong, is there? There hasn't been an accident or anything? It's just that Eric lost his wife four years ago. It's not his daughter, is it?'

Fleming reassured Max. 'No, nothing like that at all. We just need to speak to him about his daughter's ex-husband. To fill in some background details, that's all.'

'Oh, you mean Ronnie Nielson. Dreadful business that. Though I dare say Eric won't lose any sleep over it. He always said the man was no good for his daughter. I'll go and fetch him. You can use my office if you like.'

Fleming thanked him and Max hurried off to find Rainer.

Rainer arrived five minutes later in tracksuit bottoms and a white sweat-stained sports shirt. He was wiping sweat off his balding head with a small hand towel. He narrowed his grey eyes and glared at Fleming and Logan. 'You wanted to see me?'

Fleming pointed at the tattoos of daggers with eagle wings on Rainer's arms. 'From your army days?'

Rainer turned his arms to look at the tattoos. 'Yeah, that's right. What exactly do you want?'

'Just a few questions, Mr Rainer...' Fleming started to say.

Rainer shook his head. 'This had better be important. I'm at work, you know. Or hadn't you noticed?'

'We're at work as well, Mr Rainer,' Logan pointed out.

Rainer grunted and folded muscular arms across his broad chest. 'Okay, what do you want to know?'

'When we last met, you made it clear there was no love lost between you and Nielson. You said he had it coming to him,' Fleming reminded him. 'In fact, I recollect you saying that you would gladly have killed him.'

'Oh, I see. You think I killed the man because I hated him. Let me tell you something, the man was a bastard... a bully. There must be loads of people like me who despised the man.'

'He physically abused your daughter. She said you were mad when you found out. Said you wanted to see to him – in a manner of speaking.'

Rainer glared hard at Fleming. 'Yes, and she probably also told you that she persuaded me not to.'

'Peggy Dobbs, Nielson's cleaner, she reckoned you only came to the house to visit your daughter when Nielson wasn't there.'

'So? I didn't like the man. Are you accusing me or what?'

Logan looked up from his notebook. 'You're only helping us with enquiries. If you were a suspect we'd have arrested you and taken you in for questioning under caution.'

Rainer smiled. 'So, I could tell you to piss off and stop wasting my time?'

'You could,' Logan agreed, 'but that wouldn't be a very sensible thing to do. We could arrest you as a suspect... or, we could charge you with obstructing a police investigation.'

'So how may I be of assistance to you?' Rainer asked sarcastically.

Fleming showed Rainer the photograph of Nielson with his army colleagues. 'Do you know any of the men in this photograph, apart from Mr Nielson?'

Rainer took the photo and studied it closely through squinting eyes. 'No, can't say I do.' He hesitated, looked again, then pointed at Eddie Slater. 'Looks a bit older there, but that could be Eddie Slater. He was Nielson's best man at the wedding.'

'Have you seen any of them recently?' Fleming persisted.

'No.'

'Were you aware that Nielson was being investigated by the Met ten years ago?'

'Yes, what's that got to do with anything?'

'Just wondered if maybe someone involved in that had it in for Nielson. Maybe a long-standing feud that eventually resulted in Nielson being murdered.'

'I wouldn't know. All I know is Sarah told me someone had tried unsuccessfully to stitch Nielson up. It was all straightened out and no charges were brought. Though it wouldn't surprise me at all if someone from the past had it in for him.'

'Ever heard of a man called Potts?'

'Can't say I have.'

'He used to work for Nielson.'

'So? Look, I've already told you I had nothing to do with the man. How would I know people who worked for him?'

'Eight years ago there was another investigation involving Nielson. A man called Joe Cobb was stabbed to death outside a nightclub in Reading by Potts. Potts claimed that Nielson had put him up to killing Cobb, but later retracted his statement. Did Sarah ever mention an ongoing feud between Cobb and her husband?'

'No, she didn't. She knew I wasn't in the least bit interested in Nielson's business.'

Fleming changed tack abruptly. 'How did you get the scratches on your face, Mr Rainer?'

'I run a boxing club. Someone scratched me with the laces of their glove while we were sparring.'

'Who?' Fleming pressed.

Rainer snorted. 'Bloody hell! How should I know? The day it happened I was sparring with loads of the lads. I didn't even notice it until I was back in the changing room. It could have been anyone.'

Fleming nodded slowly. 'Where were you last Friday evening?'

Rainer held Fleming's stare. 'At home.'

'Anyone with you?'

'No.'

'What were you doing?'

'Watching TV,' Rainer snapped.

'What were you watching?' Fleming persisted.

'A film.'

'What was the film?'

'Christ! What is this? I was at home... on my own... watching a film on a DVD. Would you like me to tell you the story and who was in it, for fuck's sake?'

'That won't be necessary, Mr Rainer. That's all for now.'

'For now?'

'You've been very helpful, but we may need to speak to you again.'

Once outside the gym, Fleming looked at Logan. 'What do you think, Harry?'

'I think he's lying. Guilty as hell, I'd say.'

'Hmm, I'm not so sure. He hated Nielson, but it seems he wasn't the only one. He has scratch marks on his face, but he says he can explain that. You think he's lying, but we can't prove it.'

'Gut instinct, boss.'

'Never got a conviction,' Fleming pointed out. 'Get Naomi to pay a visit to his neighbours. See if anyone can verify he was at home.'

Later that night, Fleming was on his second large glass of whisky when his phone rang.

'That you, Alex? It's Gordon here.'

Gordon Aitken was an old friend of Fleming's, a detective inspector with Police Scotland, formerly Lothian and Borders Police.

'Hi, Gordon. How are you?'

'Fine, fine. Alex, I thought you'd want to know: Jimmy Calder's been released on parole.'

Fleming was silent for a moment while he took in the news.

'Alex... Alex, you still there?'

'Yes. I'm here. When?'

'Two weeks ago. He was released from Shotts Prison on a life licence.' There was a short pause. 'Listen, Alex, you didn't find this out from me, okay?'

———

27

'What do you think of DCI Fleming?' Logan was asking Anderson. The squad car he was driving was on the A14 approaching the outskirts of Bury St Edmunds.

Anderson shrugged. 'Haven't known him long. Seems okay. Quite young to get to DCI though.'

'Yeah, and I'm still a sergeant after more years than I can remember of hard slog. And, I may add, I'll be retired off in about ten years,' Logan grumbled.

Anderson nudged Logan's arm playfully. 'Time for one more step up the ladder yet, Sarge,' she joked.

'Oh yeah?'

Anderson noted the doubt in Logan's voice. 'Fleming seems to hold you in high regard, and people like him need people like you,' she said, sounding serious.

Logan grunted. 'Changing the subject, what do you think's going on between Fleming and Watson? Bit of friction there, don't you think?'

Anderson thought for a moment. 'They don't get on, that's clear. I think Watson's got a bee in his bonnet because Fleming's young and got the DCI post he thought his buddy DI

Jardine should have had. Thick as thieves those two if you ask me.'

'Yeah, I think you may be right. All very interesting,' Logan mused.

∼

A few minutes later, he saw the sign for Bury St Edmunds ahead. 'Nearly there.'

Logan had been to see Sarah Nielson again to see if she could throw more light on the army photograph Fleming had shown her. She'd told him it was taken in Afghanistan. Nielson had served there with The Royal Anglian Regiment in 2002. He'd been based in Kabul with C Company in the 1st Battalion.

It hadn't taken Logan long to find the address of the regimental headquarters. A quick call to the secretary and he'd arranged to meet the civilian records officer, Mrs Eva Lakes.

The headquarters building was a striking red brick building with castle turrets. The regimental flag flapped in a stiff breeze at the top of a white mast above the front entrance. Eva Lakes occupied a small office on the ground floor with a window overlooking a garden that looked every bit as neat and tidy as the office. In fact, the whole place had all the feel of military precision, cleanliness and order. It hardly came as a surprise that Lakes herself was well organised, neat and efficient. She had short black hair swept back into a tight bun and wore a crisp white blouse and black skirt.

Logan showed his warrant card. 'I'm DS Logan, and this is DC Anderson.'

Lakes smiled. 'I believe you wanted to ask me about some ex-service personnel?'

'Yes.' Logan showed her the photograph from Nielson's house. 'We believe this was taken in Afghanistan around 2002.

We wondered if it would be possible for you to identify the men on it for us.'

'Just from a photograph taken years ago? That's a bit of a tall order.'

'We have two of the names, if that would help,' Anderson said hopefully. 'Ronnie Nielson and Eddie Slater. We believe Slater was killed in Afghanistan later that year.'

Lakes gasped. 'Oh, that's why you're here. I read about Ronnie Nielson in the papers.'

'Can you do it?' Logan asked.

Lakes hesitated for a moment. 'I can check my computer records for the names of all the men who served in C Company around that time. I should be able to find Mr Nielson and Mr Slater, but I'm not sure how to identify the others just from your photograph.'

Logan and Anderson watched closely as the cursor danced around the screen. Lakes clicked on folder after folder until she found what she wanted. 'Here we are. C Company as at January 2002.'

There were about a hundred names on file in alphabetical order. She scrolled though the list until she came to Slater, then double clicked on his name. A new document opened with his personal details. The file confirmed he was killed in action in July 2002.

Lakes scrolled further down the list until she came to Nielson. Again, she double clicked on the name and his details sprang onto the screen. Logan noticed he was discharged at the end of March 2005. 'That's the details of two of the men you're looking for. I'm not sure how I'm going to put a name against your photograph for the others though.'

Anderson frowned. 'Would you have a photograph of the whole of C Company, by any chance?'

'Yes, yes, of course! There might have been one taken just

before they left for Afghanistan.' Lakes closed the Word documents and clicked on the photo gallery icon. She opened the regimental folder, then the C Company sub-folder. There were hundreds of photographs. She clicked on 2002 to narrow down the number of images shown. As she dragged the cursor slowly over each tiny print, a larger version sprang into view on the screen. As the cursor hovered over the last image, a company group photograph appeared. A double left click and the photograph filled the whole screen.

Lakes looked backwards and forwards between Nielson's photograph and the computer screen. She ran her finger along the screen and tapped as she found each of the men on Nielson's photograph. 'They're all here!' she exclaimed.

Logan shook his head in exasperation. 'But all we've got is another photograph of the same men. How's that going to help us?'

'Because,' Lakes answered, 'there are hard copies of every photograph in our archives, and there'll be a record of all the names of everyone on the photograph. All I have to do is take the computer image reference to the archives and pull the hard copy with the list of names.'

'Can you do that now?' Anderson asked.

'I'm afraid that'll take some time. The archives are in another part of the building and they're in a bit of a mess. Sorting them out isn't a high priority at the moment so I'll need to get some help to look through them to see if I can find this photograph. It's Saturday tomorrow. I don't normally work at the weekend, but I could come in to have a look for you. In the meantime, I can print off a copy of the list of names of the whole Company as at January 2002 for you to take away. I'll call you if I find the photograph with the list of names.'

'That would be great, Mrs Lakes,' Logan said. 'You're a gem. I can't thank you enough for your time. You've been a great help.'

On the way out to the car, Anderson offered a less than encouraging thought. 'If she can't link names from the whole list to the photograph we'll have to trace and question the whole Company.'

'Yeah, I suppose so,' Logan agreed. 'It'll be a hard slog, but I'm sure you'll manage,' he joked.

28

Fleming sat in an unmarked police car parked down a side street in Brixton near the tube station. He'd been watching the flat above a betting shop all morning, but there had been no sign of Damien Potts. He'd used the time to reflect on what he was going to do with the information Gordon Aitken had given him about Jimmy Calder. He'd come to the conclusion that he would pay a visit to Edinburgh at the weekend. He had unfinished business there.

As he was beginning to give up any hope of seeing Potts, the passenger door opened and Logan jumped in. 'Any sign of him, boss?'

Logan had spent the morning with DC Anderson in Bury St Edmunds at The Royal Anglian Regiment headquarters. After they'd finished there she'd dropped Logan off at the station before driving to Maidenhead to see if any of Rainer's neighbours could vouch that he was at home on the night of Nielson's murder. Logan had caught a train to Charing Cross then took the tube to Brixton after checking Fleming's current whereabouts on his mobile.

'Been here for hours and he hasn't shown face. Maybe he

was somewhere else last night, or he's staying at home,' Fleming grumbled.

'This is the address approved by his probation officer under his parole conditions I take it?' Logan queried.

Fleming looked at Logan. 'No, I wanted to see if he would turn up to place a bet,' he said sardonically. 'Of course it is!' he added with a laugh.

'So why don't we go and knock on the door?'

Fleming smiled at Logan's simple logic. 'I could have done, but I didn't want you to miss out on all the fun. Seriously though, I thought it might be a good idea to keep an eye on the place.' Fleming shrugged. 'You never know who might turn up.'

'Fair enough.'

'My patience is wearing thin though,' Fleming admitted.

He was about to act on Logan's suggestion when an old black Audi A3 pulled up outside the betting shop. Potts appeared from a door at the side of the shop, rushed across the pavement and jumped into the car which sped off in the opposite direction to the one Fleming's faced.

'Just my luck,' Fleming grumbled, throwing the car into a three-point turn with tyres squealing.

Up ahead he saw the Audi take a left turn. He followed at a discreet distance through more side streets then left onto the A203 heading north. Fleming kept as close as he could all the way to Vauxhall, across Vauxhall Bridge, then right up Millbank towards Westminster. The Audi carried on up past Trafalgar Square to Leicester Square, then left into the labyrinth of Soho streets.

'Well, well. What do we have here,' Fleming whispered as the Audi pulled up outside Nielson's Cellar and Potts jumped out.

'Park round the corner and stay with the car,' Fleming told

Logan. 'And run a check on the Audi registration. I'm going to pay our friendly Scottie McBain and Damien Potts a visit.'

Fleming entered the club and made his way down the worn stone steps.

A young man with blond hair swept into a ponytail at the back looked up in surprise from behind the bar. 'Don't open until six, mate.'

Fleming flashed his warrant card. 'DCI Fleming. I'd like a word with Scottie and the man who just came in here.'

Ponytail's eyes flashed in alarm. 'I'll–'

'Tell him I'm here,' Fleming finished the sentence for him.

The man knocked and disappeared into McBain's office. He'd left the door slightly ajar and Fleming could hear McBain's raised voice. 'What! What the fuck does he want now?'

'Dunno, boss. He said he wants a word.'

McBain came to the door and strode out to confront Fleming. He crossed his arms. 'What do you want, Fleming? I'm busy.'

'I'd like a quiet word with the man who came in here. Damien Potts, isn't it?'

'Christ! You guys never leave anyone alone, do you? You been following him? He's just out of prison and you want to interview him already.'

'It's not an interview. Not at this stage anyway. I only want to talk to the man. Clear a few things up.'

'Like what?'

'That's between me and Potts. I can have a quiet chat with him in your office, or I can take him to the local station. His choice.'

At that point, Potts appeared hesitantly at McBain's office

door. He wore faded jeans, torn at one knee, and a loose-fitting grey sweatshirt. The unshaven face, thin lips, vacant look and scrawny frame reminded Fleming of the many drug addicts he'd come across in his career. He noticed the tattoo with two crossed daggers on Potts's neck.

'I ain't done nothing! Why are you following me?' Potts shouted.

'Just want a few words in private, Damien. If you don't mind,' Fleming added.

Potts shrugged and hobbled back into McBain's office.

'Thanks,' Fleming said to McBain as he pushed past him to follow Potts.

Fleming closed the office door behind him and looked into Potts's dark lifeless eyes.

'What have you been doing with yourself since you got out, Damien?'

'This and that... nothing much.'

'You're staying in a room above a betting shop in Brixton, right?'

'Yeah, so what?'

'How did you find out about the place?'

'Mr McBain... he knows the manager. He had a spare room upstairs and he did me a favour.'

'Why would he do that?'

'Well, it wasn't so much him doing me a favour as Mr McBain. Look, I cleared this with my probation officer. He knows where I'm staying. He doesn't have a problem with it. What's the big deal?'

'No big deal. I'm trying to establish how you came about to find lodgings, that's all. You said you've been doing this and that for the past couple of weeks. What exactly would this and that be and was it here in London?'

'I'm trying to find work to get some cash. That's why I'm

here. Mr McBain has offered to give me a job.'

'Why is Mr McBain so keen to help you out? He finds you accommodation. He offers you a job. Why would he do that? Does he owe you for something? Maybe something you did for him?'

'I... I don't know what you mean. I used to work here before I went to prison. He's just looking out for me.'

'Why did you change your statement after you killed Joe Cobb? At first you claimed Ronnie Nielson had put you up to it. Then you said he didn't and you pleaded guilty to manslaughter. You claimed it was self-defence.'

'That was years ago. I served my time. Why are you bringing all this up again now?'

'If Ronnie Nielson had asked you to kill Cobb, it would have been premeditated murder, wouldn't it? And Ronnie Nielson would have been guilty of incitement to murder. But you got off a murder charge, and Nielson walked free. How did you feel about that?'

'I don't know what you mean. I made a mistake, that's all. I thought Ronnie had shopped me and I lashed out, trying to involve him. Then I realised it was a stupid thing to do for the reason you've just said.'

'Here's the thing, if Ronnie Nielson did drop you in it you would have had a pretty good reason to have a grudge against him–'

'Fuck. You're trying to pin Ronnie's murder on me! Oh no, you're not going to get away with that, you bastard. It was nothing to do with me!'

'What were you doing last Friday evening, Damien?'

'I was in the flat. I felt ill so I stayed in that night.'

'Anyone with you?'

'No.'

'Can anyone verify you were in the flat?'

'You bastard. Fucking coppers. You're all the same. Out to set anyone up to get a quick result. It wasn't me. I swear!'

Fleming knew he had no real evidence to arrest Potts. All he had was the fact that Potts could have had a grudge against Nielson and an alibi that could neither be proved nor disproved.

'All right, Damien. That's all for now.' Fleming made to leave. He turned and glared at Potts. 'Don't leave town. I may want to speak to you again.'

'I've told you I had nothing to do with it. You can't prove nothing!' Potts shouted, more confident.

Fleming left to glares from Ponytail and McBain. 'I'll let myself out,' Fleming said jovially.

'Well?' Logan asked on the way out of London in heavy traffic.

'Scary-looking character, I must say. And McBain was his usual friendly self. Potts claims he was in his room above the betting shop on the night of the murder. Says he only tried to implicate Nielson with Joe Cobb's murder when he thought Nielson had shopped him. Interestingly though, he said he changed his statement when he realised that he would have been found guilty of murder rather than manslaughter if he persisted in saying that Nielson had put him up to it. What he didn't say was how he found out that Nielson hadn't shopped him.'

'Which might suggest that he did. Maybe Potts did have a score to settle.'

'It would only take just over an hour to get from Brixton to Bourne End by car. The man in the Audi who gave Potts a lift to Nielson's Cellar could have picked him up, taken him there, and brought him back. We need to question him and check Potts's fingerprints for a match on Nielson's boat.'

29

MPs, peers and visitors milled about in the grand Central Lobby of the Palace of Westminster. People met and shook hands. Members of both Houses came and went through the large arches that led to the House of Commons and House of Lords. The sound of footsteps crossing the ornately tiled floor sent echoes round the hall.

Leo Miller had drawn Charles Trenchard to one side, well out of earshot of anyone who might overhear them. 'Huxley took another mauling at Prime Minister's Questions on Wednesday,' he whispered. 'He was made to look inept at best.'

Trenchard pulled a carefully folded white handkerchief out of his pocket and dabbed at the sweat forming above his top lip.

'This can't go on, Charles. He's destroying us. He has to go.'

Trenchard fastened his dark eyes on Miller. 'Yes, I know all that. I did have a quiet word with him.'

'And?'

'I said I was worried that the press was having a field day and that rumblings in the Party were increasing. I told him a large number of our MPs wanted to trigger a vote of no confidence.

He seemed concerned so I went on to tell him that it could be avoided if he stood down.'

Miller snorted. 'Let me guess. He said it was out of the question. We need to hold our nerve: stick together, and all that crap!'

Trenchard rubbed a hand over his neatly trimmed grey beard. 'Something like that. The man's deluded. He thinks he can ride the storm and still lead us to victory at the next election.'

Miller frowned. 'Fat chance. Listen, old chap, I think we have sufficient numbers to force a vote. Most of the cabinet say they will support you in a leadership ballot if the PM doesn't get enough votes.'

'You're ready to start the ball rolling?'

'Yes.'

Trenchard thought for a moment. 'Okay, but if I'm going to put myself forward as a candidate I can't be seen as the treacherous cabinet minister who brought about the demise of the PM. I need to appear to remain loyal to him. I can only put my name forward as a candidate to replace him if and when he loses the confidence vote–'

'If and when? My God, Charles, it's a foregone conclusion!'

Trenchard smiled. 'As you're so confident, you won't mind doing one more thing for me.'

'Of course, Charles. No problem. Anything you want.'

Trenchard's eyes bore into Miller's. 'We need to do something dramatic to undermine the PM even more. Something that will act as the final catalyst to trigger the confidence vote.'

Miller hesitated and looked furtively around him, checking no one was within earshot. 'What are you suggesting, Charles?'

'You need to resign. Then you follow it up with a resignation speech to the Commons. You can use this to explain the reasons for your resignation and cause maximum political damage to the PM.'

Miller gasped. 'I say, old chap. But what if he wins the majority needed to stay in power?'

'I thought you said there's no chance he'll win the vote,' Trenchard argued with a slight smirk on his lips.

Miller frowned again. 'You're asking me to put my neck on the line, Charles.'

'That's right,' Trenchard confirmed. 'But if all goes to plan, and I win the subsequent ballot, I'll make sure your loyalty is rewarded.'

There was a flicker of uncertainty in Miller's eyes.

'Don't worry, Leo. It's sure to work. You've already said you think there are enough people who want a confidence vote, and most of the cabinet is keen for a change of leadership. When the PM loses the vote, he'll have to resign. I'll say that I regret that he's had to step down, but that, after being encouraged to do so, I've decided to stand for election.'

Miller looked around again to make sure no one was paying any undue attention to them. 'I hope nobody has noticed us talking. It might lend credence to any conspiracy theories after I resign.'

Trenchard laughed. 'You worry too much, Leo. We were discussing the summer garden party I was hoping to arrange and whether you and your good lady would be able to attend.'

They parted company with Trenchard calling after Miller for good effect. 'Hope you can make it, Leo.'

Later, over a large gin and tonic, Trenchard was wondering if this was going to go to plan. So many things could go wrong. He worried again about the press scrutiny that would inevitably follow his announcement that he intended to stand for the leadership.

30

It had been another busy day and it was late evening. Fleming was tired. So were the team. A few sipped at the foul coffee from the vending machine, but most of the team was subdued and quiet.

Fleming glanced round the briefing room and wondered why the atmosphere was so gloomy. He dropped the heavy cardboard box he was carrying onto a desk. There were a few puzzled looks as Fleming slit it open. 'Anyone want a change from coffee?' he asked, pulling out cans of beer from the box. 'Drinks are on me.'

The atmosphere suddenly changed. There were smiles all round. 'I love briefing meetings,' one detective announced as he led the stampede to the desk to retrieve the beers. 'Cheers, boss,' one detective after another said as they lifted cans in salute to Fleming.

'Nice one, boss,' Logan added, then turned to face the team. 'All right, you lot, settle down. Let's get some work done then we can go home.'

The whiteboard was showing more names. Emma Hayden, her husband Anthony Hayden, Sarah Nielson, Eric Rainer, and

Damien Potts. Lines joined some of the names with scribbled notes showing the relationship between them. It was beginning to look like a mind map. An unnamed assassin was linked to Nielson as was the army photograph found in Nielson's house. There was a question mark above the photograph. All lines pointed to Ronnie Nielson in the centre. Logan had listed actions, questions and thoughts with his usual military precision.

Fleming took a swig of his beer and waved the can at the whiteboard. 'As you can see, we're starting to build up a picture. But we're making slow progress. We have potential suspects in Rainer and Potts. And there's the as-yet-unknown assassin theory–'

'You've now eliminated old DCI Hayden as a suspect, have you?' a young detective called Kevin asked. 'That wouldn't be to do with the fact that Bill Watson told you to, would it? Or because the chief constable wasn't happy with that line of enquiry?'

Fleming ignored the inference that internal politics might have been involved. 'No. Emma Hayden has admitted to having an affair with Nielson so her husband would have had a motive to kill him. But there's no DNA match with the skin samples found under Nielson's fingernails, there were no scratch marks on Hayden's face, and his fingerprints were nowhere on Nielson's boat.'

'Okay,' Kevin conceded, 'but Nielson could have scratched someone other than his killer, and Hayden would know how to ensure he didn't leave any fingerprints.'

'Christ, Kevin, give it a rest!' one of the older detectives exclaimed. 'What's this witch hunt against poor old Hayden all about, for fuck's sake? Do you seriously think he did it, or are you just shit stirring?'

Kevin was about to answer but Fleming held up a hand.

'Let's calm down, shall we? Kevin makes a valid point and we need to keep that in mind. I had thought of getting forensics round to Hayden's house to check it out but decided against it when I found out there was no forensic evidence on Nielson's boat to point to Hayden as the killer. Maybe I need to review that decision and get them to check if there's any trace of Nielson's blood on Hayden's clothes.'

'Bloody hell,' Kevin's detractor muttered. 'Bill Watson and the chief constable are really going to love you!'

'My problem,' Fleming said.

Kevin smirked behind his can of beer.

Fleming pointed at the whiteboard again. 'The assassin theory is a line of enquiry we need to investigate further, but at this stage it's only a theory. We need to do a bit more digging into Nielson's potential enemies, and particularly anyone connected to the drugs investigation involving Nielson and the murder in Reading eight years ago.'

Fleming looked at Logan and Anderson. 'Anything to add?'

'Still no luck finding the murder weapon,' Logan said. 'And we're waiting for a call from The Royal Anglian Regiment. They're searching their records to see if they can put names to the people on the army photograph found in Nielson's house.'

'You got anything, Naomi?' Fleming asked.

'Yes. Eric Rainer claims he was at home on the night of the murder, but a neighbour saw him leave in his car around eight. She didn't see him return.'

Fleming thought for a second and pointed at Rainer's name on the board. 'There was no love lost between him and Nielson, Rainer has scratch marks on his face, and now he's lying about where he was on the night Nielson was murdered. Naomi, can you check all the CCTV footage we have around Bourne End and the marina to see if Rainer's car shows up anywhere.'

'And we have our friend, Potts,' Logan added. 'Not long out

of prison, he could have had a grudge against Nielson, and his alibi can't be verified. I'm running a check on an Audi that picked Potts up from his flat to take him to Nielson's club.'

Fleming nodded. 'How are we getting on with the list of Nielson's business contacts, Naomi?'

'Still ploughing through them, but so far nothing to suggest anyone had a motive to kill Nielson.'

'Okay, keep at it. We need to make sure everyone who had any contact with Nielson is interviewed.'

'And make sure you keep the overtime claims under control, Naomi,' Logan joked.

Anderson stuck her tongue out at him playfully. 'Oh, by the way, we checked with Mrs Hayden's friend. She confirms Mrs Hayden stayed with her in Bristol over the weekend that Nielson was found.'

Fleming nodded. 'All right everyone, I think that about wraps it up for tonight. Thanks for all your efforts. Keep up the good work. Harry, can I have a quick word?'

The others had all drifted out, leaving Fleming alone with Logan. Fleming was stuffing some papers into his briefcase as he spoke. 'I need to go up to Edinburgh for the weekend, Harry. I have some business to attend to there. You're in charge until I get back.'

Logan looked puzzled. 'Sure, no problem, boss. When do you think you'll be back?'

Fleming heard Freya's voice in his head. *Do you ever feel you'd like to take that anger out on the man who killed your mother?*

Fleming shrugged. 'I'm not sure.'

31

The plane dropped below dark grey clouds and banked steeply to the left over the River Forth on its flight path to Edinburgh Airport. Fleming looked through his window and saw the rail and road bridges below. It was raining heavily and the plane shuddered as it hit pockets of turbulence. A storm was closing in fast.

The landing was bumpy and there were a few sighs of relief as the plane taxied to a halt. Fleming had used the seventy-minute flight from Luton to reflect on the phone call from Gordon Aitken. Fleming hadn't slept well for two nights since. He'd relived the night Jimmy Calder murdered his mother. The anger returned and he wanted to kill him. He didn't have a plan, but he had just known that he had to come to Edinburgh.

Fleming had travelled light with only hold baggage and was soon at the car hire office where he picked up a BMW X5. He took the A8 into the city centre, along Princes Street, then into the car park at Waverley Station where parking was available for guests staying at The Scotsman Hotel.

It was only a short walk to the hotel. Fleming checked in and took a shower before making his way down to the lounge where he'd arranged to meet Aitken. Fleming spoke briefly to the man behind the reception desk who wore a badge saying his name was Bruce. He confirmed he could serve coffee in the lounge when Fleming's friend arrived.

Aitken arrived twenty minutes later with a big smile. He was a well-built man, about the same age as Fleming. They'd met as students at Edinburgh University and had stayed in touch ever since. Fleming had always made a point of looking him up when he was in Edinburgh, though his visits had been less frequent recently.

Aitken strode across the room and gave Fleming a big hug. 'Alex, great to see you again. God, how long since you were last here?'

Fleming smiled. 'Too long, Gordon.'

The two men sat and reminisced briefly about their old student days. Aitken had stayed on in Edinburgh and joined the police. Fleming had worked in a solicitor's office for two years after getting his law degree, but soon decided civil law was not for him. He wanted to catch criminals and joined the Met.

'So how are you keeping?' Aitken asked. He looked awkward. 'I mean... you know. It must have brought things back to you when you found out that Calder was out of prison.'

Fleming shrugged. His friend didn't know he was still seeing a counsellor. 'Oh, I'm fine, really.' He changed the subject. 'Not long transferred from the Met on promotion. I'm now with the Major Crime Unit in Thames Valley Police.'

'Always knew you'd rise through the ranks quickly,' Aitken observed then hesitated. 'You're not only here because Jimmy Calder's out of prison, are you?'

Fleming knew he couldn't fool Aitken. 'It's great to see you,

Gordon, but I must admit something made me come here when you told me about Calder. I don't suppose you know where he's living?'

Aitken looked dubious. 'Alex, you're not going to do anything stupid.'

'Of course not. Thought I might just pay him a visit. Let him know he might have served his time, but that he hasn't been forgotten. I thought if I confronted him it might help put things to bed for good–'

'I hope by that you don't mean what I think you mean.'

'Relax, Gordon. Haven't you heard of the restorative justice process? You know... victims meet offenders. I get a chance to tell Calder what the impact of his crime was on me. He gets a chance to apologise and be held to account for what he did.'

'I'm not so sure I like that last bit,' Aitken said. 'Hasn't he already been held to account for his crime by serving over twenty years?'

'By the legal system maybe... but not by me.'

Aitken looked concerned. 'And how do you propose to hold him to account?'

'Like I said, he needs to show some regret for what he did, some remorse.'

Aitken shrugged and fished into his jacket pocket. He pulled out a folded newspaper cutting and passed it to Fleming. 'That was the story carried in the Edinburgh Evening News when he was released.'

Fleming unfolded the cutting. The headline read, MURDERER RELEASED ON LIFE LICENCE. He read the story quickly and felt his anger rise. 'Do you know where I can find him?'

Aitken reluctantly pulled the news cutting towards him, fished a pen out of his jacket pocket and scribbled above the headline.

Bruce arrived with the coffee. He glanced at the newspaper headline, but Aitken quickly folded the cutting and passed it back to Fleming.

Fleming waited until Bruce poured the coffee and had left before flicking the paper open to see the name and address of the hostel Aitken had scribbled down for him. 'Very grateful, Gordon, thanks.'

'You realise I could get into serious trouble over this, Alex.'

'Don't worry. No one will ever know you told me about Calder's release or where he's living.'

'Let's make sure it stays that way,' Aitken said. 'Listen, I'm afraid I'm on duty tonight; catch up for a pint tomorrow night?'

'Sure. I'll look forward to that.'

Later, in his room, Fleming was listening to the news on the radio. Leo Miller had resigned as chancellor. Fleming switched the radio off and went to close the window as a gust of cold air swept into the room. Lightning flashed over the city. Thunder rumbled and the first heavy drops of rain lashed onto the glass. He thought back to his last session with Freya. Revenge wasn't intended in the restorative justice process. But it was supposed to allow victims to decide what should be done to repair the harm, wasn't it? Though what he had in mind was hardly to be recommended. The following day he would pay a visit to the hostel.

Bruce couldn't believe his luck as he picked up the phone and dialled the number for Davy Purvis. He had an arrangement with the journalist to help supplement his income. He would let him know if anyone important checked into the hotel and would tip him off if he had any information that might lead to a good story. In return, Purvis would give him a few quid. The size of the payment depended on the story.

After a few rings, the familiar voice answered. 'Purvis.'

'Davy, it's me, Bruce. I've got something big for you.' He went on to explain what he'd seen and that Alex Fleming had checked into the hotel.

'Alex Fleming, the man whose mother was killed by Jimmy Calder?'

'That's him,' Bruce confirmed.

'Thanks, Bruce. Be in touch.' He rang off.

Purvis smiled. He saw the perfect opportunity to manufacture a story.

32

Davy Purvis watched Jimmy Calder leave the hostel off Ferry Road in Leith. Purvis recognised him straight away from the photograph in the paper. He couldn't mistake the scrawny stooped frame of the man who was probably in his sixties, straggly grey hair, thinning, and a creased face that wore a haunted vacant look.

Purvis left his car and followed Calder on foot.

After a ten-minute walk, Calder entered a dingy-looking pub near the Water of Leith. Purvis followed him into the bar after a couple of minutes. It was busy and noisy with loud chatter and bouts of raucous laughter. Purvis spotted Calder's old faded leather jacket and pushed his way to the bar beside him.

The barman was handing Calder a pint.

'Here, let me get that for you,' Purvis said. 'And the same for me,' he told the barman.

Calder looked at Purvis through dark cold eyes. 'Who the fuck are you?' he growled in a thick gravelly voice.

Purvis smiled. Now he was close to the man, he noticed the heavy bags under Calder's eyes, his thin unsmiling lips and his bulbous red nose. 'Thought I recognised you... Jimmy Calder, isn't it?'

'Who wants to know?' Calder demanded.

'A man who can do you a favour.'

Calder looked wary as he grasped his pint with a rough hand. His fingernails were chewed and dirty. 'Oh yeah, and how's that then? And how come you know my name?'

'Saw you in the paper a couple of weeks ago. I happen to have been on the wrong side of the law myself and heard something that should be of interest to you.' Purvis took his pint and nodded towards the front of the bar where there was a table and bench under a grimy window. 'Let's have a seat over there, shall we?'

Calder looked dubious, but he was clearly intrigued. He shrugged and made his way to the bench. Purvis eased his way in beside him.

'Who exactly are you, and why would you want to do me a favour?' Calder asked.

'Like I said, I've been on the wrong side of the law myself. Police – hate the bastards. People like you and me, they're always harassing us.'

Calder knew what he meant. 'What's this big favour then?'

Purvis leaned closer and whispered in Calder's ear. 'The woman you killed... Fleming was her name, wasn't it?'

Calder ignored the question and sipped at his pint. He frowned and glared at Purvis as he thumped his glass down on the table. 'What the fuck do you want?'

'Thing is, she had a son, didn't she? Alex Fl–'

'So what?' Calder interrupted. 'What the fuck has that got to do with anything?'

'Friend of mine, he works at The Scotsman Hotel. Guess who's checked in?'

Calder was getting impatient. 'Who?'

'Alex Fleming.'

Calder froze.

'He was talking to some guy – police, my friend reckoned. He was showing Fleming a cutting of the newspaper article that covered your release.'

'That so?' Calder whispered through clenched teeth.

'That's not all. He'd scribbled the address of your hostel on the paper.'

Purvis downed the rest of his pint and got up to go. 'Just thought I'd let you know, mate. He's obviously here to find you.'

Calder stared after Purvis as he left the pub. 'Fuck!' he cursed under his breath. He finished his pint and left the bar quickly.

Fleming had risen early. He'd gone for a run before breakfast. Afterwards he drove down to Leith and found the hostel where Jimmy Calder was staying. He parked down the street where he could keep an eye on the entrance. He daren't show his face in the hostel. To go inside looking for Calder would be asking for trouble. He decided to wait and keep an eye on the place, hoping to catch a sight of Calder.

A couple of hours passed but there was no sign of him. Either he'd gone out before Fleming arrived, or Calder was in for the day. Eventually Fleming took a chance and phoned the hostel from a payphone on the end of the street. The girl he spoke to wasn't much help. She'd only just come on duty and said Calder wasn't in his room. Fleming cursed. He'd missed him. He couldn't stay here all day and he was meeting Aitken for a drink later. Maybe he'd stay on for another day and try again.

He went back to his hotel room and felt troubled. Dark thoughts swirled round his head. *I'm a police officer*, he thought. *Why am I doing this? I could lose everything.* He suddenly felt the need to talk to Freya. His hands were shaking as he picked up the phone and dialled her number.

'Hello,' said the familiar voice.

'Freya?'

'Yes.'

'It's me, Alex Fleming.'

'Oh, hi Alex, how are you doing?'

There was a long pause before Fleming spoke. 'I'm in Edinburgh. Jimmy Calder's here. He's out of prison.'

'Alex, what are you doing there?'

'I'm... I'm not really sure.'

Freya hesitated, as if she sensed Fleming was in danger of doing something stupid. 'I think you should come home. Come and see me, promise?'

There was another long pause.

Maybe it wasn't a good idea to phone after all, Fleming thought.

'Alex?'

'Sure,' he said and rang off.

Later that evening, Fleming met Aitken in the hotel bar. He looked tense.

'You look like you need a drink, Gordon,' Fleming said.

'Too bloody right I do!'

Fleming ordered two pints and took them over to the seat

Aitken had found well out of earshot of anyone else. 'Bad day at the office?' Fleming joked.

Aitken stared hard at Fleming. 'Where have you been all day?'

Fleming sensed something was wrong. He couldn't lie to Aitken. He'd see through it straight away. 'I went to the hostel to see if I could see Calder. Waste of time. He was out. Seems I missed him.'

'Christ, Alex, what do you think you're doing? Are you mad?'

'It's okay, I didn't go in. I watched outside but there was no sign of him.'

'You absolutely sure you didn't see him, Alex?'

'No, I didn't. Why? What's wrong?'

'We could both be in deep shit, that's what's wrong. Calder's disappeared.'

33

Charles Trenchard sat on the front bench a few seats away from the prime minister. The atmosphere in the House of Commons was electric. The rows of green leather-clad benches had been virtually empty the day before. But today the House was packed. MPs on both sides waited with anticipation. They sensed a crisis. The hum of urgent chatter grew louder. The tension in the air was palpable. The PM's face was ashen. His eyes were tired and sunken with worry and sleepless nights. The press gallery was packed. Reporters looked down on the scene below like vultures. They knew the prime minister was in trouble.

At the north end of the chamber, the Speaker sat calmly in his green leather chair. He raised his right hand and called for order. The noise in the chamber failed to cease. He called again, more loudly, 'Order! Order!' He waited for a few seconds until the din died down. He cleared his throat and spoke. 'Before I ask the chancellor to offer his resignation speech, I must remind the House that it has to be heard in silence.' He looked across at Miller and nodded.

Miller rose slowly from his seat. The notes in his right hand shook. The speech he had prepared was short. His voice trembled slightly as he spoke. 'Thank you, Mr Speaker.' He paused and took a deep breath. 'I have addressed this House many times in the past, but today it is with great sadness that I speak to you to offer the reason for my resignation from the government. But first let me say this: it has been an honour and a privilege to serve my country, and my right honourable friend, the prime minister, for the past three years. I am proud of my achievements as chancellor and so it was with great sadness that it became necessary for me to resign. In short, my position had become untenable.'

Millar glanced down at his notes and paused to take breath. 'This came to be,' he went on, 'because I was unable to agree with certain policies. In particular, I could not agree with the prime minister's views on fiscal matters. We debated this at some length, but I regret to say that the prime minister failed to see or accept my point of view. This in itself is not unusual. People in high office often have differing views on a wide range of matters.

'However, what I could not accept was the prime minister undermining my authority. He did so by issuing statements in public on matters of policy he had not discussed with me. Matters for which I was responsible and with which I could not agree. I was torn between loyalty to the prime minister, and what I believed to be my duty to the nation. In the end, the only course of action for me was to resign.' He paused briefly and those present waited eagerly to hear what Miller was about to say next. 'Now I have returned to the back benches,' he continued, 'I am able to speak my mind freely.'

As if on cue, Trenchard looked across at the PM and covered a smile by raising a hand to his mouth as though to stifle a cough. The prime minister stared straight ahead with a resigned look. His face had drained of blood. He dabbed a handkerchief on his forehead and looked as though knew he faced the final act of betrayal.

Miller cleared his throat. 'I believe,' he continued, his voice booming, 'that the prime minister has lost the confidence of his Party, he has lost the confidence of this House, and he has lost the confidence of the nation. The time has come for change and I believe that the required number of Conservative MPs have submitted a written request for a confidence vote in the prime minister. There will therefore be an opportunity for others to decide whether he is the right person to continue as leader.'

Miller had said enough. He sat to pats on the back.

Gasps of shock came from the public gallery and there was an eruption of shouting and waving of papers by MPs on both sides of the House. Never had such scenes of uproar been witnessed in recent years.

Trenchard allowed himself a small smile.

The prime minister glared at Miller. He could not conceal the rage he felt at this final act of treachery as he rose shakily to his feet and walked from the buzzing chamber.

34

Fleming was deep in thought as he drove to the office. It was early, but traffic was already building up on his way out of Oxford. He remembered what Aitken had said. *We could both be in deep shit.* 'You could well be right,' Fleming muttered. He worried about the dark thoughts that had entered his mind in Edinburgh. Would he have killed Calder? Fleming shrugged the thought away. He'd discuss his mental state with Freya, but he'd need to be careful over what he said.

Logan and Anderson were already in the office, staring at flickering computer screens. 'Bloody system's on the blink again!' Logan cursed as Fleming arrived. Logan slapped the box under the screen to an amused glance from Anderson.

'You're in the wrong trade, Sarge,' she laughed. 'You should have been a computer technician.'

Logan scowled. 'And you should have been a comedian,' he muttered.

Fleming smiled and waved for Logan to join him in his

office. 'Take a break from that thing and come and give me a sitrep.'

Logan nodded and smiled at Anderson as he rose from his desk. 'Coffees would be nice,' he said over his shoulder as he made for Fleming's office.

Anderson stuck a tongue out at Logan's back. 'Right away, Sergeant Logan.'

'Do you two ever stop?' Fleming said, laughing as Logan came into his office.

'It's all in good fun, boss. We both like a bit of light-hearted banter. How was your trip to Edinburgh?'

'Fine. Now, what's the current state of play? Any developments while I've been away?'

'I held a briefing meeting yesterday. Just one or two things to report. Still no luck with Nielson's business contacts. Naomi and the lads have been working their way through them, but so far there's no reason to link any of them to the murder.'

Fleming sat on the corner of his desk. 'What else?'

Logan screwed up his face as though in pain. 'Super's on the warpath. She's had the chief constable breathing down her neck.'

'Oh?'

'We got a warrant to search Hayden's house. Bagged all his clothes and sent them off to forensics for examination. Upson blew a gasket when he found out. He told Temple there had better be a good reason for it. The last thing he needs is for Cecil Daubney to think that an ex-officer is suspected of murder. Temple will probably collar you as soon as she finds out you're back.' Logan hesitated for a moment. 'Oh, by the way, she wanted to know why you had to go to Edinburgh in the middle of a murder investigation. Thought you ought to know.'

'Thanks for the warning.'

'There's more bad news, I'm afraid...'

'Great.'

'I had a call from The Royal Anglian Regiment. They managed to identify the other five men in the photograph you found in Nielson's house. Two of them were killed in action in Afghanistan – Eddie Slater and Tim Banks. Both sergeants. The others were officers. They all left the army in September 2002 on return to England from Afghanistan. A guy called Martin Cook who emigrated to Australia in 2003, and a Giles Bonner. He now lives on the south coast – Lymington.'

'And the last man?'

Logan drew a sharp breath. 'You're not going to like this, boss. It's Charles Trenchard, of all people.'

Fleming took in a sharp breath and frowned.

'I take it you heard the news yesterday?' Logan continued. 'Leo Miller's resigned as chancellor and there's going to be a confidence vote in the prime minister. Trenchard is expected to stand for the leadership if the prime minister loses the vote. And we're going to have to question him in a murder investigation. Nice, eh?'

Fleming shrugged. 'He knew a man who was murdered, that's all. It's just routine questioning–'

'Routine! Bloody hell, boss, I wouldn't like to be in your shoes when Temple and the chief constable find out, and the press get a whiff of it.' The blood had drained from Logan's face.

Fleming acknowledged the problem. 'Matthew Upson will definitely be bouncing off the walls. Apart from political flack, he'll have Cecil Daubney on his back.'

'Never a dull moment,' Logan grumbled.

'Any joy with the Audi driver who took Potts to Nielson's club?' Fleming asked.

'I traced him and pulled him in for questioning. Name's Tommy Tyler. He's got previous. Burglary, assault, drove the getaway car in a jewellery shop raid. He's been in and out of prison. Has a bit of a short fuse.'

Fleming smiled. 'Seems like Nielson's club has some interesting employees.'

Logan laughed. 'Clearly, but he has a cast-iron alibi for the night of Nielson's murder.'

'Oh?'

'He was in a police cell all night after a drunken brawl outside the club.'

'So, he didn't take Potts to Bourne End – assuming of course that Potts was the killer. Any fingerprint matches with Potts at the scene?'

'None.'

'And Eric Rainer. Has Naomi found anything on CCTV footage yet?'

'Still going through them all. Nothing yet.'

Temple poked her head round Fleming's door. Her eyes blazed and there was a hard edge to her voice. 'My office, Alex – now!'

35

Fleming knew he was in trouble. He knocked on Temple's door and entered.

Temple was sitting behind her desk studying a copy of an email with a fixed stare. She pulled off her reading glasses, threw them onto the desk and looked hard at Fleming without saying a word.

'Ma'am?' Fleming prompted.

'Sit down, Alex.' She paused and took in a deep breath. 'I thought you'd concluded that Anthony Hayden was in the clear...'

'I had.'

'And?'

'I thought on reflection that I'd maybe been a little hasty–'

'Hasty?'

'There wasn't any forensic evidence to put Hayden on Nielson's boat, but I later realised that Hayden would know how to ensure there wasn't any trace–'

'And so you decided to cover up for your lack of foresight by having forensics tear his house apart looking for evidence.'

'With respect, ma'am, it was an afterthought, not lack of foresight.'

'And what exactly were you hoping to find there?'

'I wasn't hoping to find anything. I wanted to check if there were any traces of Nielson's blood on Hayden's clothes.'

'And was there?'

'Still waiting for forensics to get back to me.'

Temple groaned. 'I take it DS Logan has told you I've had Matthew Upson on my back?'

'He has.'

'He's furious you've decided to open up enquiries into Anthony Hayden again. You know what makes it worse, Alex?'

'What?'

Temple slammed a hand onto her desk. 'The fact you'd eliminated Hayden from your enquiries, then, when Upson's ire has abated, you decide to open it all up again!'

'Sorry.'

'Sorry! Alex, you've fucked up and you're sorry!' Temple breathed deeply as she put her reading glasses back on. 'You don't know how much you've fucked up, do you?'

'Ma'am?'

'You went to Edinburgh over the weekend. Why?'

'I had some business to attend to–'

'Business! What kind of business is more important than a murder investigation? An investigation, by the way, which seems to be going around in circles without any real progress. Upson thinks you're wasting your time investigating Hayden, and Cecil Daubney is on Upson's back over lack of progress on all the outstanding murder cases.'

'The others aren't my cases. The Nielson murder is my first case.'

'And at this rate, Alex, it may be your last.' Temple paused, and then spoke more softly. 'Would this business in Edinburgh be anything to do with this?' She pushed the email she had been reading across the desk.

It was a copy of an article written by Davy Purvis in an Edinburgh newspaper. Fleming tensed and drew a deep breath. Gordon Aitken's words rang in his ears again: *We could both be in deep shit.* The headline read, MURDERER RELEASED ON LIFE LICENCE GOES MISSING AFTER VICTIM'S SON TURNS UP IN EDINBURGH.

'I'm waiting for an explanation,' Temple said. She looked at Fleming with a steely glare over the top of her glasses.

'I witnessed my mother being murdered twenty-three years ago. I was twelve at the time. I found out that they released the man who did it on life licence a couple of weeks ago. I had a misguided notion that if I could speak to him, get some hint of remorse, I might be able to move on. Bit stupid really.'

Temple was more sympathetic. 'And did you see him?'

'No.'

'You're sure about that?'

'Sure.'

'So how come the press found out you were in Edinburgh?'

Fleming frowned. Then it came to him. 'In the hotel... I was being served coffee and the man serving me must have seen a newspaper cutting I was looking at. It was about Calder's release. I checked in under my own name. The waiter must have put two and two together and told the press.'

'So how come Calder knew you were there?'

Fleming shrugged. 'You know the press. My guess is that this reporter, Purvis, must have warned Calder, thinking he might run, and then he'd have a story.'

Temple frowned. 'You realise this looks bad. If Calder isn't found, you'll be a suspect.' She pulled the email back across her desk and slipped it into a top drawer. 'If this kicks off, you could find yourself suspended. You realise that?'

Fleming slumped back in his seat.

Temple looked hard at him. 'Is there any more bad news you want to give me while you're at it?'

'Only that we've identified the men who were in an army photograph I found in Nielson's house.'

'And why do I think this is going to be yet another problem?' An exasperated Temple moaned.

'One of the men is Charles Trenchard. I'll have to question him, I'm afraid.'

Temple held her head in her hands and groaned. 'Why is this turning into a fucking nightmare? Upson will do his nut.'

36

Damien Potts was worried. He'd been unsettled by Fleming's visit to Nielson's Cellar. He knew only too well what prison life was like and would do anything to make sure he didn't end up inside again. In a panic, all rational thought had left him. He'd contacted a man who he thought might be able to help him.

It was nine o'clock in the morning as the tube pulled into the station at Vauxhall. Brakes squealed as the train shuddered to a halt. Potts pushed his way through the crowds and headed off in the direction of Vauxhall Bridge. He half-skipped, half-ran across the road as he dodged the traffic. Sweating profusely under the glare of the sun, he took the steps that led down to the path that ran in front of the headquarters of MI6.

He looked up and down the walkway but could see no sign of Carl Yapp. He was late. Potts took out a half-finished cigarette, lit up and leaned over the wall. A long barge was steadily ploughing its way up the Thames against the fast-flowing current. Sirens went off across the river and Potts saw the blue lights of a police car speeding up Millbank heading towards

Westminster. He flicked the butt of his cigarette into the river and turned as he heard footsteps approaching him.

Yapp was a freelance journalist who had moved to London after a rather dubious career working for the press in Belfast. There had been threats on his life following several articles he'd written. He'd come across Potts some years ago when he was covering the Met enquiry into claims that Ronnie Nielson's club was involved in drugs. He'd seen him as a useful source of information in the underworld and was curious why Potts wanted to see him soon after his release on parole.

'Hi there, Damien. Sorry I'm a bit late. Things to do, people to see.'

Potts looked surprised. Yapp had put on some weight since he last saw him. Either that or he'd been working out at the gym. He was tall and his receding grey hair was clipped short. His crumpled suit jacket was slung over his shoulder.

'Hi, Carl. Got a fag?'

Yapp fished in his pocket and pulled a pack of twenty out. 'Help yourself.' He looked curiously at Potts, whose hands were trembling. 'Trouble?'

Potts took in a deep drag and blew smoke out over the wall as he turned to look over the river. 'I'm in deep shit,' he said, coughing violently.

'You should give these up, mate.'

Potts ignored the comment. 'You heard about Ronnie Nielson?'

Yapp frowned. 'Yes.'

'A cop came to see me. I think he's going to try to stitch me up for Ronnie's murder.'

Yapp raised an eyebrow. 'Did you kill him?'

'No, I fucking didn't!' Potts shouted, then lowered his voice when he realised people were looking at him. 'The cops think I had a grudge against Ronnie–'

'And you were released on parole just before he was killed...'

'That seems to be enough for them. Bastards!'

'Hold on, Damien. That's all they have on you?'

Potts shook his head and sucked deeply on his cigarette.

Yapp lit a cigarette for himself and blew smoke up in the air. 'So, what else?'

'I've got no fucking witnesses to verify where I was on the night of the murder!' Potts blurted. He raised a shaky hand to his mouth to take another deep drag of his cigarette. 'They're going to do me, Carl!'

Yapp looked closely at Potts. 'So where do I come into this? Your paranoia about the police being after you isn't exactly a story is it, Damien?'

Potts looked furtively around him. 'No, but what about corrupt cops?'

Yapp smiled. 'Go on.'

'There were some bent cops in the Met. They were on the take from Ronnie.'

'Hang on,' Yapp said, 'aren't Thames Valley Police dealing with Nielson's murder? How come you want to bring the Met into it?'

'Ronnie told me that the bent cops were with the Met, but they transferred to Thames Valley Police.'

Yapp was becoming more dubious by the minute. 'Sounds a bit far-fetched.'

Potts shrugged.

'Have you any proof?' Yapp pressed.

'Ronnie told me one day when he'd had a few drinks that he had some cops in his pocket.'

'Ronnie told you! That's it? Just his word? You ever see him handing a package to anyone? Meeting anyone?'

'No.'

'For fuck's sake, Damien, this gets thinner by the minute.'

Potts was suddenly unsure of himself. 'But... but Ronnie–'

'Damien, there's fuck all to go on other than your word.' Yapp shook his head and tossed his cigarette butt into the river. 'The police will laugh it off and say you're a deluded, angry man who's making this up because you think they have it in for you. You've got no evidence.'

Potts shrugged again.

Yapp was getting frustrated. 'What are the names of these officers?'

'Ronnie didn't say.'

Yapp drew a deep breath. 'Damien, you're not thinking straight. Lashing out at the police and accusing them of corruption is hardly likely to help you.'

'I... I thought it might take the heat off me if the top brass were preoccupied with corruption allegations and that their officers were accused of victimising me.'

Yapp was convinced that Potts was out of his mind. He had no evidence, and he didn't have names. 'I can't do anything about your claim that the police want to set you up for Nielson's murder.'

'Fuck! I thought you could get them off my back if you ran a story on police corruption.'

Yapp shook his head. 'Not a chance, mate. But there's

nothing to stop me stirring things up a bit – see what comes to the surface.'

'What are you going to do?'

'I'll get in touch with Thames Valley Police, say I've received allegations of corruption and ask for a statement. Best thing you can do is disappear until the dust settles.'

37

Watson was about to blow a gasket. He'd heard that Fleming had asked for a search of Hayden's house and that forensics were looking for traces of Nielson's blood on Hayden's clothes. He was about to storm off in the direction of Fleming's office when his phone rang. 'Watson!' he growled.

'Is that DCI Watson of the Major Crime Unit?' a cool voice asked.

Watson frowned. He didn't recognise the Scottish voice. 'Yes,' Watson replied guardedly. 'Who am I speaking to?'

'Chief Inspector Nichol, Lothian and Borders Police. Sorry... I should say Police Scotland. We now have a new title since all the local forces were merged a while back. Anyway, we have a bit of a problem you might be able to help us with.'

'Oh?'

'Yes, a guy by the name of Jimmy Calder was released on life licence from Shotts Prison a couple of weeks ago. He's breached his licence conditions by leaving his approved address at a hostel in Leith. He's disappeared.'

'So how can I help?'

'A friend of his at the hostel reckoned that Calder had a

contact in Reading... an old pal from prison who was released a year ago. Calder had spoken about maybe moving there. Thought his old pal might be able to get him some work, cleaning in a club where he worked.'

'You think he could be on our patch and you want us to keep an eye out for him?'

'That's about it. If you could let us know if he turns up, I'd be most grateful.'

'Sure, no problem, email his details and a photograph to me and I'll see what I can do.'

Nichol paused for a second then cleared his throat. 'Thing is... there's something else you should know. It's a bit delicate really.'

'Go on.'

'It concerns one of your colleagues, which is why I'm calling you.'

Watson was all ears. 'Oh?'

'This chap Calder, he murdered a woman in Edinburgh twenty-three years ago. The woman's son was twelve at the time and saw it happen. He's now a DCI working with you. Alex Fleming–'

'What!'

'The thing is, I wouldn't want a fellow detective to get into trouble.'

'Why would Fleming get into trouble?' Watson was confused, but very interested in what Nichol had to say.

'I went to the hostel to question the manager and residents. It seems that Calder met a stranger in a local pub the night before he disappeared. The man warned him that Fleming was in town looking for him. Next morning, Calder was gone.'

'Well, well,' Watson muttered. He hadn't known that Fleming had gone to Edinburgh, let alone why he would want to go there.

'You can see,' Nichol said, 'it's important Fleming doesn't find out that Calder may be on your patch. He's already up to his neck in it–'

'Just because Calder disappeared when he found out that Fleming was in Edinburgh?'

'It gets worse. One of the local papers ran an article about Calder's disappearance after Fleming turned up in town... the inference being that Fleming may have been behind it. Usual press stirring things up, that's all. But you can see it doesn't look good.'

Watson whistled. He'd found the skeleton in the cupboard he was looking for. He couldn't believe his luck. 'No, it doesn't.'

'You should also know that your boss knows about it. My boss sent her a copy of the newspaper report this morning. What she doesn't know is that Calder may turn up in Reading. Wanted to let you know so you can watch your mate's back.'

'Yeah, sure, you can rely on me to make sure Fleming doesn't find out. And I'll be in touch if we find Calder.'

Watson rang off and smiled. Getting Fleming into trouble was exactly what he wanted.

Watson called in on Frank Jardine on his way out of the office. 'Popping out for a while, Frank.' Watson winked. 'I may have found a way to get Fleming off the Nielson case. In fact, we may get lucky and get rid of him altogether. We may get you promoted into the DCI post yet.' He left a bemused Jardine as he called over his shoulder, 'Skeletons in the cupboard... remember?'

Watson didn't want to risk being seen in Long Hanborough so he drove down to Witney to find a public payphone. He dialled a number in London. The phone was picked up after a few rings. 'Yeah?'

'Bill Watson here, put me on to your boss.'

There was a few seconds' delay before a familiar voice answered. 'Bill, to what do I owe the pleasure?'

'I need a favour...'

'Sure, how can I help?'

'I need to find a man by the name of Calder... Jimmy Calder. He's on the run from Scotland and word has it that he may be heading for Reading to hook up with an old mate of his to work in a club. You've got contacts in the clubs around there. Any chance you could put feelers out and let me know if he turns up?'

'What's he done?'

'Nothing... He's been released from prison on a life licence and he's disappeared from his authorised address.'

'Okay, leave it to me.'

'If you do find him, don't call the office. Send me an email at home with the address. It's important nobody else knows about this, know what I mean?'

'Got you. Be in touch.'

38

Eric Rainer sat in interview room one with his solicitor. He watched as Logan broke the seal on a new pack of two audio cassettes and plugged them into the recorder.

Fleming was looking through the papers on the table in front of him.

Logan whispered, 'All ready, boss.'

Fleming pressed the record button and spoke. 'This interview is being recorded. This is an interview with...' Fleming looked at Rainer. 'State your full name, address and date of birth please.'

Rainer's eyes were fixed on the table top as he answered in a quiet voice.

Fleming continued, 'I'm DCI Fleming. Also present is DS Logan and...' He looked across the table at Rainer's solicitor who needed no prompting.

'Christopher Grimes, solicitor.'

Fleming concluded the introductions. 'There are no other persons present.' He then gave the date, time the interview started, and location. He looked at Rainer and said, 'You do not have to say anything, but it may harm your defence if you do not mention when questioned, something which you later rely on in court. Anything you do say may be given in evidence.'

Before Fleming could continue, Grimes interrupted. 'Just for the record, my client has not been arrested and is attending here voluntarily to help with your enquiries. He is therefore free to leave at any time unless you do arrest him.'

'That's correct,' Fleming confirmed. 'I was about to say so and thank Mr Rainer for his co-operation.'

Rainer sat impassively, arms folded tightly across his chest.

'Mr Rainer,' Fleming began, 'you work as a boxing instructor, don't you?'

'Yes.'

'For how long?'

'Twenty-one years.'

'How did you get into that?'

'I boxed in the army. Saw an opportunity when I was demobbed and took it.'

'Would you say you have to be an aggressive man to be a boxer?'

'What's the point of this line of questioning?' Grimes interrupted. 'It's surely irrelevant to the case you're investigating.'

'Trying to establish some background about your client.' Fleming continued, 'You have a previous conviction for assault–'

'Look here,' Grimes objected, 'that was twenty years ago. That has nothing to do with why he's here today... voluntarily, I may remind you. If this ridiculous line of questioning continues I will advise my client to leave.'

Fleming looked from Grimes to Rainer who was smirking. 'I believe you never visited your daughter at the house when Nielson was at home. Was there a reason for that?'

'We didn't get on.'

'When we last met, you described him as a bastard. You said he had it coming to him. You said you'd gladly have killed him...'

Rainer glanced nervously at Grimes who nodded imperceptibly. 'I was angry with him, that's all. He bullied Sarah. He hit
her if he got angry. Who wouldn't want to see a man dead who
abused his daughter? Doesn't mean I did it.'

'Can you remind me how you got the scratches on your face,
Mr Rainer?'

'I told you. It was from the laces of someone's boxing glove
when we were sparring.'

'And you couldn't say who?'

Rainer shook his head. 'How many times do I have to tell
you? I was sparring with loads of the lads. I didn't even notice
until I got back into the changing room.'

'You said you were at home the night Mr Nielson was
murdered. Is that correct?'

'Yes.'

'You absolutely sure about that?'

'Yes.'

'So how can you explain the fact that a neighbour saw you
leave your house at around eight p.m. and didn't see you return?'

Rainer shrugged. 'They probably got the wrong date.'

'There's no question about the date. I think you're lying, Mr
Rainer.'

'This is preposterous!' Grimes exclaimed. 'My client is here
to help with your enquiries. He is not under arrest!'

Fleming was unperturbed. 'It would help if we knew where
your client really was...'

Grimes looked hard at Fleming. 'I take it you have a statement from this neighbour?'

'We do.'

'I'd like to see it please.'

Fleming slid a folder across the table. 'For the purposes of
the tape, I'm presenting Mr Rainer's solicitor with document
number five. This is a statement provided by a neighbour on

the whereabouts of Mr Rainer on the night of Mr Nielson's murder.'

Grimes put on some reading glasses and read in silence. He pushed the folder back to Fleming after a few minutes.

'So where were you, Mr Rainer?' Fleming persisted.

Rainer looked at Grimes for guidance. There was an imperceptible shake of the head.

'No comment,' Rainer said.

'We're currently checking the CCTV cameras around Bourne End. Any chance we might find your car turning up there?' Fleming prompted.

'No comment.'

Grimes cleared his throat. 'Are you arresting my client on suspicion of murder?' he asked quietly.

'Not at this stage. But that situation may change if we do find anything on CCTV footage to put Mr Rainer at or near to the scene of the crime.'

Grimes gathered up his papers and stuffed them into a folder. 'In that case we will leave.'

Fleming nodded. 'You are free to go.' He looked at his watch. 'Interview terminated at ten thirty-five.'

Watson knocked once on Temple's open office door and looked in. 'Got a minute, ma'am?'

Temple looked up from the file she was reading and took off her glasses. 'Sure, come in, Bill.'

Watson thought she looked tired. 'I gather you had an email yesterday... about Alex Fleming and Jimmy Calder...'

'How do you know?'

'I've been speaking to a DCI in Police Scotland... They're

worried Fleming might do something stupid if he finds Calder. Thought you ought to know because...' Watson hesitated.

'Yes?' Temple prompted.

'I think this business about Jimmy Calder is a distraction for Fleming. He takes off to Edinburgh in the middle of a murder investigation and could end up under suspicion if Calder isn't found. Frank Jardine and I could take on the Nielson case.'

'I hear what you say, Bill, but I don't like changing SIOs midtrack. Let's see what happens before we make any hasty decisions.'

Watson shrugged. 'Fine,' he said, making to leave. 'But I think you're making a big mistake keeping him on the case. Thought I'd let you know that Frank and I are willing to take over.'

'I'll bear that in mind, Bill,' Temple said, indicating for him to sit. 'There's something else I need to discuss with you. I've just had a reporter on the phone...'

39

It had been a hot day and Fleming fancied a drink after the trip to Maidenhead to interview Rainer. He'd surprised Logan and Anderson by suggesting they packed up for the evening and went to The Trout Inn at Wolvercote. Both had agreed with raised eyebrows. Fleming had not appeared to be much of a socialiser.

Thirty minutes later, they were sitting outside on the pub terrace looking over the Thames. 'Quite famous, this place,' Anderson suddenly announced after taking a sip of her beer.

'Oh... yeah, Bill Clinton came here when his daughter graduated,' Logan said. 'Some years ago.' He clinked glasses with Anderson. 'Impressed with my grasp of local general knowledge?'

Anderson smiled. 'I didn't mean because of him. I was referring to something closer to our line of work.'

Logan frowned. 'What?'

'Bit of a gap in your general knowledge, Sarge?' Anderson teased.

Logan glared at Anderson. 'Go on then, enlighten us.'

Fleming knew what Anderson was about to say but left it to her.

'Colin Dexter... Inspector Morse!'

Logan looked baffled. 'What's that got to do with anything?'

Anderson was enthusiastic. 'They say that Colin Dexter was a regular here and the pub features in some of his Inspector Morse novels.'

Logan raised his eyebrows. 'That a fact?'

Anderson laughed. 'Don't you know anything, Sarge?'

'I know who's going to be getting the next round in,' Logan retorted.

Fleming shook his head. It never ceased to amaze him how quickly Logan and Anderson had warmed to one another. You would think they'd known each other for years the way they joked together with light-hearted banter. It was good to see that they did get on together. He could hardly say the same about his relationship with Bill Watson.

'You're a bit quiet, boss. Everything okay?' Logan asked.

'Yeah, sure... fine. Just enjoying the entertainment.'

Logan took a sip of his beer. 'So, was Temple more upset about you going to Edinburgh than because we searched Hayden's house?'

Fleming shrugged. 'About the same.'

'But you wouldn't have gone to Edinburgh if it wasn't important, would you, sir?' Anderson asked in defence. 'She must have known why you went.'

'She does now,' Fleming said.

Logan changed the subject. 'And Hayden?'

'She'll get over it. She knows it had to be done. I told her we were still waiting for forensics to get back to us. She's just upset because Matthew Upson is on her back.'

'Anyone for another?' Anderson queried.

'Thought you'd never ask,' Logan said, handing over his empty glass.

Anderson pointed at Fleming's glass. 'Sir?'

'Thanks, Naomi, don't mind if I do.'

Anderson disappeared inside to get the drinks and Logan took the opportunity to quiz Fleming. 'This business about Edinburgh, boss... I take it that it's nothing Naomi and I should know about? I mean if it's personal... it's personal. But it's nothing to do with the case, is it?'

'No, Harry. It's nothing to do with the case.'

'Okay, wanted to make sure, that's all.'

Anderson returned with a tray of drinks and some nuts. 'Everything okay?'

'Good timing,' Fleming said. 'About to go through our suspect list.'

Logan grabbed a bag of nuts and opened them. 'Well done, Naomi. I was feeling a bit peckish.'

'Should have brought you a plate of chips,' Anderson teased.

Fleming laughed. 'Can we discuss the case for a minute?'

Logan shrugged and helped himself to some nuts.

'It seems,' Fleming said, 'we have three potential suspects so far. There's Anthony Hayden. He had a motive and was left on his own on the night of the murder so he could have gone to Bourne End to kill Nielson–'

'But there's no forensic evidence to put him at the scene of the crime,' Anderson reminded him.

'No,' Logan agreed, 'but we're still waiting to see if there are any bloodstains on the clothes we took from his house.'

Fleming continued. 'If there isn't, I think we have to cross him off the list. Then we have Damien Potts. He had a possible motive, he can't verify his whereabouts on the night of the murder, but we have no hard evidence... and there were none of his prints at the scene–'

'Which brings us to Eric Rainer,' Logan broke in, 'always said he was our man. He had a motive. He hated Nielson. He had previous for assault. He's ex-army and a boxing instructor... knows how to handle himself. Then there's the scratches on his face.' Logan waited for effect then whispered slowly, 'And he lied about his alibi.'

Fleming nodded. 'He certainly seems like our best bet at the moment, but there's something niggling away at me. Can't quite put my finger on it. Call it gut instinct, but I feel like it all seems a bit too simple somehow.'

'Gut instinct never got a conviction,' Logan reminded Fleming.

'It'll be interesting if we find anything on CCTV that puts him near to the scene of the crime,' Fleming said.

There was a lull in the conversation. Logan took another handful of nuts. Fleming sipped quietly on his beer. Then Anderson appeared to remember something. 'Oh, by the way, I meant to tell you, I saw Bill Watson in Temple's office while you two were interviewing Eric Rainer. Her office door was open and I overheard a bit of what she was saying...'

'Do tell,' Logan said eagerly.

'She was saying she had a phone call from some reporter. Seems he'd heard allegations of police corruption and he's asked her for a statement.'

'No way!' Logan exclaimed.

'That's what I heard.'

Fleming frowned. 'No doubt Temple will tell me about it tomorrow. She's already upset over me bringing Hayden back into the frame. She hauled me over the coals because I went to Edinburgh, and she's not exactly jumping with joy over the prospect that I need to speak to Charles Trenchard. Now we have allegations of police corruption. Great!'

40

Fleming was not looking forward to the meeting. A young WPC was taking him up in the lift to the chief constable's office. He'd called the meeting to discuss the press request for a statement on allegations of corruption in the MCU.

Fleming hadn't yet met Matthew Upson and wasn't sure what kind of reception he would get. Fleming knew he wasn't exactly in his good books over Anthony Hayden, and he'd heard that Upson was a hard taskmaster. By all accounts he was a strict man who didn't suffer fools gladly.

The WPC showed him into a small meeting room next to Upson's office. Liz Temple and Bill Watson were already there. Upson sat stiffly at the top end of a table. He had short grey hair, neatly groomed, and the badge of rank on the black epaulettes of his spotless white shirt added to the air of authority the man carried.

Upson was in a foul mood. Angry brown eyes glared at Fleming as he entered. 'Glad you could finally make it, Fleming,' he snapped. 'Grab a coffee if you want one,' he added tersely. 'But be quick, I have a meeting with Cecil Daubney in half an hour. And I can tell you he's after heads if this business brings Thames Valley Police into disrepute.'

Fleming thought he recognised the accent: from Glasgow, he guessed. 'Sorry I'm late, sir. Road accident and a bit of a traffic jam.'

'Leave earlier next time,' Upson growled.

Fleming skipped the coffee. He thought it wouldn't be a good idea to hold things up any longer than necessary. He sat and waited for Upson to speak.

'Before we get on to the main reason for this meeting,' Upson said, 'I want to make one thing clear: I do not want the reputation of this force dragged through the mud. The last thing I need is for one of my ex-officers to be a suspect in a murder investigation.' He stared at Fleming. 'You had better be sure of what you're doing with regard to Anthony Hayden. I do not want this to blow up in my face. Do I make myself clear, Fleming?'

'Yes, sir, very clear.'

Upson turned to Temple. 'I've got Cecil Daubney on my back over unsolved murder cases. Fleming here seems to suspect an ex-colleague of murder. And now we have this!' He threw a newspaper into the middle of the table. The headline read: THAMES VALLEY POLICE ASKED FOR A STATEMENT OVER ALLEGATIONS OF CORRUPTION. 'What's this all about, Liz?'

Temple was calm and spoke with her usual confidence. 'A freelance journalist by the name of Carl Yapp phoned me yesterday, sir. He claimed he had a reliable source who told him there were corrupt detectives on the force–'

'Names?' Upson cut in abruptly.

'No names.'

'Who is this source?'

'He wouldn't say.'

'Did he say he has evidence to support this claim?'

'No, he just told me his source was reliable, but he wouldn't elaborate. He said that would all come out later. He asked if we were prepared to make a statement denying it–'

Upson slammed a hand on the table. 'This is ridiculous! The man can't justify what he's saying, he has no evidence, and he has no names. Unbelievable! How can he get away with writing such a story? It's libellous!'

'Not quite, sir. He was very careful not to say anything defamatory. He doesn't make any claims of corruption in his story. The story is simply that he's asked for a statement in response to allegations made to him by an anonymous source–'

'Well, Liz, you'd better issue a statement without delay, hadn't you? And make sure the denial is emphatic.'

'It's not a big deal really,' Watson chipped in. 'We get this all the time. People on the wrong side of the law make all sorts of complaints and claims against us. We should ridicule the whole thing... and the reporter for being gullible enough to go into print without a shred of evidence. Want me to pay the man a visit, ma'am?' he asked, looking at Temple.

'Christ, no!' Upson exclaimed. 'The last thing we need is him running another story claiming he's being harassed by the police. Issue a firm denial... and make sure we get the point across that there is no evidence to substantiate it.'

'I'll get a statement out today, sir,' Temple confirmed.

'Two more things,' Upson said. He looked at Fleming who had stayed quiet throughout the meeting. 'You'd better put this Hayden business to bed quickly, Fleming. And this nonsense about having to speak to Charles Trenchard, is it really necessary? We don't need any adverse political publicity on that front right now.'

'He knew Nielson,' Fleming said. 'That's all. We need to speak to everyone who had any contact with Nielson to help build up a picture. It shouldn't be a problem; he'll only be providing background information. No reason why there should be any adverse publicity.'

'Hmm, make sure there isn't,' Upson warned.

Later, back in his own office, Fleming was thinking over the claim about police corruption. He had a sneaking suspicion he knew who the source might have been.

41

Fleming was at home watching the reporter Hugh Bell on a news programme. It had been a long day at the office. He'd poured his second large glass of whisky and was about to take a sip when he heard the name. 'We're now going over to Westminster where Irving Baker is talking to Charles Trenchard,' Bell was saying.

Baker appeared on-screen holding an earpiece to his ear. There was a short delay before he spoke. 'Hugh, it's only a few days now before the much-awaited confidence vote. A vote which many say the prime minister is almost certain to lose. With me is Charles Trenchard who is widely tipped to be the next prime minister.' He turned to Trenchard. 'Thank you for joining us. You've had a fairly rapid rise in politics, haven't you?'

Trenchard shrugged. 'It's not so much a matter of how much time one has spent in politics. It's more to do with ability, hard work and commitment. And, I may add, loyalty and a willingness to serve your country. That is what is important.'

'Yes, before becoming an MP, you served for twelve years as an army officer. I guess that's where the ethos of service and loyalty springs from?'

'I think there's some merit in what you say.'

'You were appointed as foreign secretary only five years after being elected. That's quite a remarkable achievement. Do you think you will be the next prime minister?'

Trenchard's lips curled into a smarmy smile. 'Let me be absolutely clear about this. I mentioned loyalty as a desirable trait. I remain loyal to the prime minister. He has had, and continues to receive, my full support. I have no intention of getting into a hypothetical debate over what might or might not happen following next week's vote.'

'You are a front runner, are you not?' Baker persisted.

'There is inevitably a great deal of speculation over this. That's human nature. Of course it is just that, idle speculation. I have never said that I will stand for the leadership at any time.'

'Surely you must have given some thought to your position?'

'I've already made my position quite clear. Something you appear to have failed to grasp. The prime minister continues to receive my full support. What I'm considering is how to deal with the very important and pressing foreign issues that we currently face.'

'Okay, I understand your reluctance to be drawn on the leadership issue so let's turn to foreign affairs for a minute. You served in Iraq and Afghanistan. Do you think that getting into such armed conflicts has made our country a safer place?'

'We made significant progress in that regard–'

'Progress isn't exactly success, is it?' Baker broke in quickly.

'This whole question of how to deal with terrorism is not going to be solved easily. It's an ongoing problem that we have to deal with, I'm afraid. Let's be absolutely clear: we will leave no stone unturned in our efforts to protect our country.'

Baker shuffled some papers and read from one of them. 'One of our retired senior military men has questioned whether our involvement in Iraq and Afghanistan was a success. In fact, he argues we are more at risk now because of our actions. What do you say to that?'

'I don't accept that at all. As you rightly point out, he is retired. People are entitled to their own views on such matters. It's not a view I subscribe to.'

'Maybe, though, there are some who do agree–'

It was Trenchard's turn to interrupt. 'It's never an easy decision to go to war, but that's what we had to do. This Government is not afraid to make difficult decisions and we will continue to do so for the good of the country.'

'Okay, I think that's clear enough. You will not shirk from going to war again if you are the next prime minister?'

'I don't know how many times I have to say this: I have not declared any intention to stand for the leadership–'

'The question people are asking is whether you will–'

'It would not be the right thing to do to say in advance whether I will stand for election should the prime minister lose the vote. If I did so it would be seen as an act of disloyalty and could undermine his position.'

'Okay. You could end the speculation by confirming that you will not put your name forward,' Baker suggested.

'You are trying very hard to put words into my mouth, but I will not be drawn into making premature statements. I have said all I am prepared to say on this matter.'

'This is a major constitutional issue and I'm sure our viewers would like to know where you stand–'

Trenchard's eyes narrowed and his answer was curt. 'They know exactly where I stand as I have repeated to you several times.'

'With respect, foreign secretary, it's a perfectly legitimate question to ask whether you do intend to stand should the prime minister lose the vote. It is something you must have considered, is it not?'

'I've already told you what I'm currently considering.'

'Okay, one final point. I understand your reluctance to get into a debate about the prime minister's position, but you know very well that the majority of Tory MPs, and indeed the majority of the cabinet, have lost confidence in him. All the polls point to him losing the vote. It'll be a miracle if he wins, and even if he does, he will be a lame duck prime minister with no real authority.'

'Let's wait and see, shall we?'

Baker took a final glance at his notes and removed his glasses with a flourish. 'We have to leave it there. Foreign Secretary, Charles Trenchard, thank you for joining me.'

Fleming switched off the TV and poured another glass of whisky. He prayed that his meeting with Trenchard the following day would be easier and would not attract press attention.

At Nielson's Cellar, Scottie McBain sat back in his chair with his feet up on the desk. He looked across at the sorry figure in front of him. Damien Potts was a mess. He hadn't slept and his eyes had the haunted look of a desperate man. His long hair was unwashed and tangled.

'Scottie, you need to help me,' Potts pleaded.

'What exactly has Fleming got on you?' McBain asked.

'He knows I can't prove I was at home. I should have thought of a better alibi.' His feet were tapping on the floor and his eyes twitched nervously.

'And that's it?'

'I think so.'

'And you think disappearing will help? It smells of guilt, for fuck's sake. You go on the run and as sure as hell, they'll nail you.'

'If they catch me. You've got contacts, Scottie, people who owe you a favour. London's a big place. I could disappear here for a few months then sneak out of the country.'

McBain thought for a moment, swung his feet back onto the floor, and leaned across the desk. 'Okay, I think I can help, but I'll need some of that drugs money you've got stashed away. These things don't come cheap.'

Potts did know exactly what he meant, but parting with a few thousand was better than life in prison.

42

Fleming had told Logan he would go to see Charles Trenchard on his own. He thought a visit by two detectives might seem a bit heavy-handed, bearing in mind how sensitive a visit from the police would be. And it was only to ask a few routine questions to see if Trenchard could throw any light on Nielson's army career.

Fleming had decided to drive to Henley-on-Thames straight from home in the old Porsche because he had another appointment with Freya at lunchtime and he didn't want Logan to know where he was. Fleming had told him he would be back in the office in the afternoon. Although he'd arranged to see Freya, he wasn't sure exactly what he was going to tell her.

The sun glared in a clear blue sky as Fleming swung the Porsche through the open iron gates into the driveway. The tyres crunched on the gravel as he cruised to a halt in front of the house.

Trenchard's wife must have seen or heard the car approach.

She opened the front door as Fleming went to ring the bell. 'Hello, Chief Inspector... Fleming, isn't it?'

'Yes, ma'am.' He offered a hand. Her hand was small and smooth. No evidence of manual work, Fleming noted. She had neatly manicured bright-red fingernails. The handshake was limp.

'I'm Helen, Charles's wife. He's sitting out on the lawn at the back enjoying the sun... and a cigar. I don't let him smoke in the house. Do come through. Can I get you a drink?'

'Water would be fine, thank you.'

Helen led Fleming down a hallway, through a large kitchen and out the back door.

Trenchard rose from his seat when the door opened and he strode up the lawn towards Fleming, hand outstretched. Trenchard's casual trousers and colourful short-sleeved shirt were in stark contrast to the smart grey suit he'd worn the previous evening on TV. 'Hello, Chief Inspector. Thank you for agreeing to meet me here in private. Don't want tongues wagging, do we? Particularly at the moment.'

'Quite,' Fleming agreed as he shook hands. Trenchard's grip was powerful and confident. 'It must be a busy, if not stressful, time. I saw you on television last night. I guess all the reporters want to ask you about at the moment is the confidence vote and whether you will stand for election.'

'Yes, I'm afraid so. Do come and have a seat, won't you? Has Helen asked if you want a drink?'

'Yes, thank you.'

On cue, Helen came out with a large glass of iced water.

'Thanks,' Fleming said and took a seat beside Trenchard. 'Lovely view,' Fleming remarked waving his glass towards the river.

'Yes, I like to spend as much time as I can out here when I'm at home. It's a nice quiet place to think. So... what can I do for you, Chief Inspector? You said on the phone it was to ask me about an old army colleague.'

Fleming realised why no one had recognised Trenchard in Nielson's army photograph. He'd changed dramatically in appearance over the years. Much older, his hair was thinner and grey. A neatly trimmed grey beard and moustache replaced the clean-shaven look of his army days. 'Yes, it's a case of speaking to everyone who knew him... to build a picture... get some background.'

'Knew? You mean as a past colleague... or has something happened to him?'

'Sorry, I should have said.' Fleming took a sip of his water and continued. 'The man I'm interested in is Ronnie Nielson... he was murdered two weeks a–'

'Oh my God! How awful. Yes, I remember reading about it.'

'Did you know him well?'

'My dear chap, I'm afraid you've had a wasted journey... I didn't know him at all.'

Fleming fished Nielson's army photograph out of his pocket. 'You're in this photograph with him and four other men. It was taken in Afghanistan in 2002. You served there with The Royal Anglian Regiment in Kabul.'

Trenchard hesitated before saying, 'Yes, yes of course I did. But that was years ago. We regularly posed for photographs. I never knew half the time who the others in the photos were.'

Fleming pointed out Nielson. 'You didn't know him at all?'

'I'm afraid not.'

'What about the others in the picture?'

Trenchard reached across and took the photograph from Fleming. He peered at it closely for a minute before handing it back. 'I'm afraid not. In fact, I can't even remember that being taken... sorry.'

'Two of them were killed in action later in the year. Eddie Slater and Tim Banks. Remember the names?'

'Afraid not.'

'Another man, Martin Cook, emigrated to Australia in 2003.'

Trenchard shook his head. 'Name doesn't ring a bell.'

'And this chap, Giles Bonner?'

Trenchard took a moment then shook his head again. 'Can't say I remember the name, sorry.'

Fleming slipped the photograph back into his pocket. 'It was a long time ago. You must have come across hundreds of people in the army. You wouldn't remember them unless they were fairly close, I suppose.'

'Yes, quite. I didn't even keep in touch with men from the same company after I left. I'm sorry I haven't been able to help.'

'You left the army soon after your tour in Afghanistan, didn't you?'

Trenchard frowned. 'I did, yes. I don't want to appear rude, but I do have some work I need to get on with, if you'll excuse me.' He rose to signify that the meeting was at an end. He held out his hand. 'I'm sorry, again, I was unable to be of any help.'

Fleming shook his hand. 'Don't worry. I didn't really think you would. It was a slim chance that you might have been able to throw some light on Nielson's army background. Sometimes the slightest clue from someone's past is enough to steer an investigation in another direction.'

Trenchard nodded. 'Well, good luck.'

On his way to see Freya, Fleming reflected on his meeting with Trenchard. He had a feeling the man was holding something back. And he seemed anxious to avoid talking about why he'd left the army.

43

Fleming hadn't really expected to get much from Charles Trenchard. Following up on an old army photograph was a bit of a slim lead. Still, the meeting had been interesting. Was he imagining it, or had Trenchard been a little too quick to say he didn't know Nielson? Was there a slight hesitation when he saw the photograph, and when he'd pointed out Giles Bonner? Fleming shook his head. *Maybe my imagination is getting the better of me.* He pushed the thoughts out of his mind and tried to think of what he was going to say to Freya as he pulled up outside her house.

A few minutes later, he was seated in an easy chair in the room Freya used as her office. She sat opposite him and closed the file on her knees. 'It's only just over a week since I last saw you, Alex. How have you been since then?' Her voice was soft and comforting.

Fleming shrugged. He still didn't know what to say. 'Any

strong coffee on the go?' he asked, glancing towards the pot on the coffee table.

Freya looked into Fleming's bloodshot eyes. 'One too many last night?'

Fleming nodded.

Freya took a deep breath. 'I told you that you should only drink in moderation,' she reminded him as she poured two cups.

She waited until Fleming helped himself to sugar before speaking. 'Alex, when you rang a few days ago you sounded distressed... strange. What happened?'

'Jimmy Calder... he's out of prison.'

'Yes, you told me. You said you weren't sure why you'd gone to Edinburgh. Was it to see him?'

'A friend rang me to tell me that Calder was there.'

'And?'

'I wanted to confront him...'

'What happened?'

Fleming shrugged. 'I didn't see him.'

'So, nothing happened?'

'Not directly... except...'

'Go on.'

'I think a reporter told Calder I was in Edinburgh and the next day he disappeared.'

'You went to Edinburgh to confront Calder and he disappears.' Freya hesitated before continuing. 'This doesn't look good, Alex, does it?' she whispered gently. 'You told me last time we met that it would be very satisfying to take your anger out on him. Are you sure you didn't see him?'

'No, I didn't,' Fleming said wearily. He knew what Freya was thinking.

'Okay, Alex. You didn't see him and he's disappeared. Why did you ring me?'

'I didn't really know what I was going to do if I did see him. I went to stake out the hostel where he was staying. I kept watch for hours but there was no sign of him. I rang the hostel eventually and they told me he wasn't there. I went back to my hotel. I was worried about the thoughts going through my head. I began to wonder if I would have killed him. A part of me wanted to.'

'But you didn't, Alex, did you. Sometimes we all have irrational thoughts. We say things we don't really mean. You were angry. How many times have you heard the relatives of murder victims say they'd like to see the killer shot or hanged? Do they really mean it? It's actually part of the human condition to act and think irrationally at times. Particularly when tired, stressed, or angry.'

'I suppose you're right. It was an irrational thing to do to go to Edinburgh in the first place.' Fleming hesitated. 'The thing is, the reporter I think tipped Calder off wrote an article saying he'd disappeared just after I arrived in town. A copy was sent to my boss.'

'What did he say?'

'It's a she.'

Freya smiled. 'Okay, what did she say?'

'She wasn't best pleased and told me she might end up having to suspend me if Calder isn't found.'

'What will you do, Alex?'

'Carry on with the investigation I'm working on and see if I can find Calder to prove he's safe.'

'Is that wise? I mean... if people knew you were looking for him?'

'They won't.'

Bill Watson had heard Fleming was out for the morning so he decided to do a bit of stirring. He sauntered along to where

Logan and Anderson were sitting at their desks. He nodded at Logan. 'Got a minute, Harry?'

～

Logan was taken aback. Watson didn't usually spend the time of day with Fleming's team. 'Yeah, sure.'

Watson wandered off in the direction of the coffee machine. Logan rose from his desk to follow, shrugged and raised his eyebrows in surprise at Anderson.

'How are you getting on with young Fleming?' Watson asked when Logan had joined him.

Logan wondered what this was about. 'Fine... just fine.'

'Keep you informed of everything going on?'

'Sure.'

'Did he tell you why he went to Edinburgh?'

'Some business he had to attend to... personal, he said.'

'Did he tell you about his background?'

Logan shrugged. 'No, why should he?'

'Turns out he witnessed his mother being murdered twenty-three years ago. A guy called Jimmy Calder. Did he mention him to you?'

Logan's eyes were wide open in surprise. 'No.'

'I had a call from Police Scotland. Calder was released on life licence a couple of weeks ago. He was staying in a hostel in Edinburgh and disappeared the day after Fleming turned up there.'

Logan wasn't sure what to say. 'So why are you telling me this?' he eventually asked.

'Seems your boss doesn't tell you everything,' Watson said tapping the side of his nose with his forefinger.

Logan frowned. 'Why did Police Scotland ring you with this information?'

'They think Calder may turn up on our patch... possibly

Reading. Thought you ought to know,' Watson drawled as he walked away with a smirk.

'What was all that about?' Anderson asked when Logan returned to his desk looking serious.

'Oh, nothing,' Logan replied. 'Just a bit of information.'

Anderson appeared far from convinced.

44

Fleming tried ringing Logan and Anderson but both phones were engaged. He drove straight home from Freya's instead of going to the office, then took a taxi to the station in Oxford.

He tried Logan's number again while he was waiting for his train. This time Logan picked up. 'Major Crime Unit, Logan speaking.'

'Hi, Harry. Listen, I've had a change of plan and won't be in until early evening now. Can you do the briefing meeting? I'll catch up with you when I get back.'

'Sure. Where are you off to?'

'Popping into London to see someone.'

'This to do with the case, boss?'

Fleming hesitated. 'Sort of... I mean it might have a bearing on it. I'll explain later. Might have a bit more information by then.'

There was a long pause before Logan spoke again. 'How did your meeting with Charles Trenchard go?'

'Bit of a waste of time. Says he didn't know Nielson at all.'

'Okay. See you later, boss.'

Fleming cut the call and was in London just over an hour later. He took the tube down to Westminster and squinted against the bright sunlight as he emerged from the underground. He waited for the traffic lights to change then strode across the road and down past the Houses of Parliament to the first entrance into Victoria Tower Gardens. Carl Yapp had agreed to meet him at three o'clock by the path that overlooked the River Thames. He'd be wearing a light grey suit.

Fleming spotted him a few yards down the path leading towards Lambeth Bridge. He was leaning over the wall looking out at some barges moving slowly down river. Smoke from his cigarette drifted lazily over his head in the still air.

'Mr Yapp?' Fleming asked as he approached.

Yapp turned slowly after flicking his cigarette butt into the river below. 'Chief Inspector Fleming I presume,' he drawled.

Fleming noticed he didn't offer a hand. 'Yes, I'd like to ask you a few questions about the claim you made about police corruption.'

'Hold on there, Fleming. Let's get this straight: I didn't claim there were bent cops. I simply told Superintendent Temple that my source had made the allegation. All I wanted was a statement.'

'Fine. Who is this source?'

Yapp looked thoughtful. He turned and leaned back over the wall as a police launch raced up river leaving a white wake behind it. 'You could be one of three things, Fleming.'

'I'm not with you.'

'You could be conducting enquiries into the claim. You could be the copper who's harassing my source over the Nielson murder. Or... you could be one of the bent cops who wants to find out who's spilling the beans on them. Maybe even do a deal. Which are you, Fleming?'

Fleming smiled. Yapp had narrowed down the field of

possible sources. *You could be the copper who's harassing my source over the Nielson murder. Eric Rainer or Damien Potts*, Fleming thought. 'I'm just a cop doing my job, which happens to be investigating a murder.'

'So why did you want to see me?'

'Because you are now of interest to me–'

'Really, how come?'

'Because I think I know who your source is, and he happens to be a suspect.' Fleming took a guess. 'So how was Damien Potts when you saw him?'

Yapp stiffened. 'Who?'

'Come on, Mr Yapp, you know full well who I'm talking about. Potts used to work for Nielson before doing a stretch for killing a guy called Joe Cobb. Potts has recently been released on parole.'

'Yeah?'

'Nielson was killed shortly after. Potts might have had a motive. He's a pretty screwed-up guy with a serious chip on his shoulder. I'm pretty sure he would own up to speaking to you if I pulled him in for questioning and told him you'd pointed me in his direction.'

Yapp lit another cigarette and took a deep drag. Smoke drifted from his mouth when he next spoke. 'What if I did see him?'

'I want to know what he told you.'

'Ask him.'

'I'm asking you, and you now appear to be connected to a possible suspect. You could talk to me here, or I could take you in for questioning.'

Yapp sneered. 'I'm not legally obliged to answer your questions.'

'You are if I arrest you.'

'Oh yeah? On what grounds?'

'Obstructing a police officer in the course of his duty.'

'How do you make that out?'

'Refusing to answer my questions could be seen as hindering my investigation.'

'Are you serious?'

'Or how about wasting police time?'

Yapp appeared suddenly less sure of himself. 'I'm not wasting police time. Look, all Potts said was that Ronnie Nielson had told him there were some bent cops in the Met on the take from him. Potts reckoned they were now working for Thames Valley Police. He didn't have any names.'

'And you believed all that crap? No evidence? No names? Just say so? I can't believe you were taken in by that.'

Yapp shrugged. 'I thought I'd stir the pot a bit and see if anything came to the surface.'

'That's wasting police time,' Fleming reminded him.

'I was very careful not to make any claims of corruption. I simply said someone else had made the allegations and asked for a response.'

'Shit stirring based on a known criminal's word alone. Is that how you make a living, Mr Yapp?'

'Okay... it was a bad idea, I know. But, for what it's worth, Potts was adamant he didn't kill Nielson.'

Fleming shook his head in disbelief. 'He was hardly likely to tell you he did, was he.'

Yapp shrugged and tossed his cigarette butt over the wall into the river. 'We done then?'

'For now. A word of warning though, I'd think very carefully before you run any more unfounded stories.'

'Are you threatening me?'

'Not at all, just giving you some friendly advice.'

Yapp waited until Fleming was out of sight and pulled out his mobile phone. He didn't like being threatened. If nothing else, he'd drop the bastard in it. He tapped in the numbers for Superintendent Temple.

45

Logan was still at his desk when Fleming returned from London. It had been a long day. Anderson had gone home. The office was quiet and empty. Fleming fetched two coffees from the coffee machine and sat at Anderson's desk opposite Logan who was tapping away on his keyboard.

'Coffee, Harry?' Fleming asked, pushing a cup across the desk.

Logan stopped typing and reached for the drink. 'Thanks. How was your day?'

'Tiring. How about you?'

'Interesting.'

'So how did the briefing meeting go?'

'Chief constable's been on the warpath again. He's worried about this corruption publicity and the fact we seem to be making slow progress on the Nielson case.'

'Nothing new to report?'

'Yes, but the first bit of news doesn't help us.'

'Oh?'

Logan stretched his legs under his desk and leaned back in his chair. 'Forensics got back to us. There was no trace of Nielson's blood on Hayden's clothes. So there's no forensic evidence either on Nielson's boat or in Hayden's house to link him to the crime. I guess that rules him out as a suspect.'

Fleming frowned. 'Most likely. But we need to keep an open mind. He had a motive, and the opportunity...' Fleming's voice trailed off as he suddenly realised they had missed something.

'What?'

'We haven't checked whether his car turns up anywhere near Bourne End. And we didn't check with neighbours to see if anyone saw him leave the house on the night of the murder. How could we have overlooked that?'

'Because it seemed pretty obvious he wasn't in the frame?' Logan offered.

'There's that, but the lack of forensic evidence isn't entirely conclusive. Best get Naomi to check out CCTV footage and Hayden's neighbours. In fact, we ought to have done this before. Get her to list all the car registrations picked up near Bourne End on the night of the murder. Run a check to find the owners and get them all interviewed.'

'Bloody hell, boss, just when we think we can cross Hayden off the list of suspects, you think of another angle that puts him back on it. Temple and the chief constable will be ecstatic. They're going to think you have a one-track mind and that you're hell-bent on nailing Hayden.'

Fleming shrugged. 'Being thorough, that's all.'

'Oh, by the way, talking about CCTV footage, the second piece of news is a bit more encouraging. We have a result.'

Fleming leaned across the desk. 'And?'

'Guess what? Eric Rainer's car was spotted in a public car park in Bourne End on the night of the murder. He's seen getting out of the car and walking off in the direction of the river.'

'Time?'

'Half past eight.'

'Well I'll be–'

'That's not all,' Logan continued, 'Naomi had a hunch and went to see Mrs Dobbs again. She wanted to check if she had seen Rainer that night. Turns out that Mrs Dobbs got into a bit of a flap. She admitted receiving a phone call from Rainer on the night of the murder. He asked her if she knew if Nielson was at home or on his boat. She hadn't mentioned it before because she didn't want to get Rainer into any trouble. She was sure he couldn't have had anything to do with Nielson's murder.'

'Good for Naomi,' Fleming whispered. 'We'll pull Rainer in first thing. In the meantime, get someone to keep an eye on him in case Mrs Dobbs thinks she's doing him a favour by warning him. Looks like we could have our man. Good news for Temple and the chief constable. But still get Naomi to run the other checks, just in case.'

'Shouldn't we pull him in now?' Logan asked.

'No, best wait until the morning. Once we arrest him and take him into custody the clock will start ticking. We'll only have twenty-four hours to either charge him or let him go. I don't want his smart-arse solicitor wasting time claiming it's too late for him to be interviewed tonight.'

'Good shout, boss.'

Logan took a last sip of his coffee, crushed the plastic cup and threw it in the waste bin by his desk. 'You were going to tell me about your trip to London,' he said tentatively.

'Oh, yes. I had a hunch I knew who might be behind the allegations about bent cops. I went to see the reporter who phoned Temple. My hunch was right. It's Potts. He doesn't really have anything. No evidence, no names. The reporter's just engaged in a bit of malicious mischief making.'

'So how come Potts made the allegation?'

'He reckons Nielson had told him he had bent cops in his

pocket, and that's it. He also thinks we're trying to stitch him up over Nielson's murder–'

Logan held up a hand to cut Fleming off when his phone rang shrilly. He picked it up and looked at his watch. 'Half an hour,' he said and put the phone down. 'Missus wanting to know when I'm going home.'

Fleming smiled. 'I'd best let you get off then.'

Logan shifted uncomfortably in his seat. 'There's one other thing, boss.'

'Yes?'

Logan cleared his throat. 'Tell me to mind my own business if you want, but can I say something personal?'

Fleming frowned, wondering what was coming. 'Of course, Harry. Spit it out.'

'Bill Watson came to see me this morning...'

'And?'

'He said you weren't telling me everything.'

'Oh, how's that then?'

'He knew why you went to Edinburgh. He told me what happened to you when you were a child, how you saw your mother being killed.'

Fleming froze. 'How does he know that, and what the fuck's it got to do with him?'

Logan looked distinctly uncomfortable. 'The thing is, boss, he says he had a call from Police Scotland. They told him that the guy you went to Edinburgh to find has disappeared and that he could be heading for Reading. I thought you ought to know that Watson knows. That's all.'

'Sure?'

Logan shifted awkwardly in his seat. 'When you rang to say there was a change in plan and that you were going to London to see someone, I thought maybe you'd found out where this Jimmy Calder was. Thought maybe you were going after him...'

'And thought I might do something stupid?'

'Boss, I know this has nothing to do with me but I was worried about you. It's personal, I know, but I felt obliged to let you know what Watson told me. Not sure why, but it seemed the right thing to do. Wanted to clear the air, so to speak.' Logan lifted his hands as though in submission.

Fleming smiled. Logan was a good cop, and he was loyal. Fleming appreciated that. 'No problem, Harry. I'm glad you told me. But you can relax. You now know I did go to London–'

'Ah,' Logan broke in, 'that reminds me, I was going to say before my phone rang, Potts has disappeared.'

46

A violent thunderstorm had blown in suddenly from the west. The sky was dark and forked lightning flashed over Maidenhead. Thunder rumbled loudly and pedestrians sheltered as best as they could from the torrential rain. Two police cars sped through the wet streets, blue lights flashing and sirens blaring to warn the morning rush-hour traffic to clear the road. Four uniformed police were in the squad car in front. Fleming and Logan followed with two more uniforms in the second car.

The cars headed west, then south towards the station. They took a sharp turn to the right before reaching the station and weaved through a maze of streets heading for Eric Rainer's terraced house. Tyres screamed as they swerved into the street that ran adjacent to the railway line.

Rainer was about to climb into his car when he heard the wail of sirens. He looked up the street and saw the police cars careering round the corner, throwing up sprays of rainwater. Without thinking, he turned and ran across the road towards a warehouse on the other side. There was a gap in a corrugated iron fence. He squeezed through into a car park stacked with wooden pallets and heard the squeal of tyres as the two police cars screeched to a halt.

Doors were flung open and the uniformed police sped across the road after Rainer. Fleming and Logan followed.

Rainer dashed to the far side of the yard and was climbing a low fence that separated the yard from the railway line. A goods train was approaching slowly. Rainer ran across the lines in front of it and leapt over another small fence into a small copse.

One of the uniforms had seen what he was doing and was on the radio to get squad cars to block the roads on the other side of the railway line. The other uniforms with Fleming and Logan cursed as they waited for the goods train to pass. After what seemed an eternity, the last carriage went by. They raced across the railway line, their clothes wet through. There was no sign of Rainer.

Rainer emerged from the copse and sprinted across a footpath into a housing estate. If he was lucky he would find someone about to get into their car, grab it and make his escape. But as he made his way through the estate, he could hear the sound of sirens nearby. He turned a corner and saw a squad car crawl past the junction at the end of the road. Had they seen him? His answer came as the car screeched into reverse past the junction then swerved into his street with tyres screaming. He turned to run but another squad car came from the other direction. The game was up. There was nowhere to go.

Five minutes later, Fleming and Logan stood in front of the handcuffed Rainer. Fleming fished out his warrant card and held it in front of Rainer's sweating face. 'Mr Rainer, I'm DCI Fleming and this is Sergeant Lo–'

'I know who the fuck you are,' Rainer hissed.

Fleming continued. 'I'm arresting you for the murder of Ronnie Nielson. You do not have to say anything, but it may harm your defence if you do not mention when questioned, something which you later rely on in court. Anything you do say may be given in evidence. Do you understand the caution, Mr Rainer?'

Rainer nodded.

Fleming spoke to the uniforms who had caught Rainer. 'Take him to the station. I'll catch up shortly.'

Rainer and his solicitor, Christopher Grimes, sat behind the table in one of the interview rooms at Maidenhead Police Station. The duty sergeant had kitted Rainer out with a white boiler suit while his clothes dried. They'd taken his fingerprints and DNA samples. Fleming and Logan had changed out of their wet clothes into black police overalls.

Fleming pressed the record button on the tape recorder and went through the usual formalities stating who was being inter-viewed and identifying those present. He reminded Rainer that he was still under caution and read out his rights once more.

Rainer sat impassively with his arms folded across his chest, eyes fixed on Fleming's.

Fleming met his stare. 'Mr Rainer, you previously main-tained you were at home on the night Ronnie Nielson was murdered. You lied about that. When confronted with the fact a neighbour saw you leaving the house, you chose to make no comment. Would you now like to tell us where you were going?'

'I went to see a female friend.'

'Why didn't you tell us that before?'

'She's married. I didn't want to bring her into it.'

'Where did you go to meet her?'

'Slough.'

Fleming lifted a laptop onto the table and switched it on. He swivelled it round so that Rainer and Grimes could see the screen. Fleming spoke into the recorder. 'For the purposes of the tape, I'm showing Mr Rainer an extract from CCTV footage taken on the night Ronnie Nielson was murdered.'

After a few seconds, footage copied from the CCTV camera opened on the screen. 'Recognise this car?' Fleming asked.

Rainer stared ahead. 'No comment.'

Grimes looked anxiously at his client.

'Recognise who this is?' Fleming continued as Rainer emerged from the car. Fleming froze the frame and zoomed in on Rainer's face looking furtively over his shoulder.

'It's me,' Rainer whispered.

'Can you explain why you appear in Bourne End at half past eight on the night of the murder when you say you were visiting a female friend in Slough?' Fleming pressed.

'No comment.'

'And,' Fleming continued, 'can you tell us why you rang Mrs Dobbs that night to enquire if she knew if Ronnie Nielson was at home or on his boat?'

'No comment.'

'Why did you try to escape?'

Rainer was sweating.

'Know what I think,' Fleming went on relentlessly. 'I think things had come to a head, for some reason. You were consumed with your hatred for Nielson. You checked to see where he was that night. You drove to Bourne End and parked your car. You went to confront Nielson on his boat. You had to have something out with him. You didn't intend to kill him, did you. He got angry. A fight broke out. It all happened so fast. You didn't plan to kill him. You stabbed him with a knife from the galley. You panicked and ran. That's what happened, isn't it, Mr Rainer.'

Grimes spoke before Rainer could say anything. 'I would like to have a private consultation with my client before he answers any more questions or responds to what you have just said.'

Fleming nodded. 'Interview terminated at eleven twenty-two.'

Fleming and Logan left the interview room and stood outside. 'What do you think, Harry?' Fleming asked.

'Even more sure than I was before. The man's guilty as hell.'

'Hmm. We'll take him to court and apply to keep him in custody for three days so we can carry on interviewing him while we're waiting for fingerprints and forensics to get back to us. The evidence against him is compelling, but we need to get his prints and DNA checked. At the moment all we have is that he hated Nielson, has scratch marks on his face, lied over his alibi, and we can put him in Bourne End, but crucially, not at the scene of the crime. I don't think we have enough to charge him just yet.'

'Bloody hell, boss, how much do you want?'

'Enough to get a conviction, Harry.' Fleming frowned. 'I don't know why, but something tells me this is not as clear-cut as it seems to be.'

47

The previous day's thunderstorm had passed. A few white clouds drifted across the clear blue sky as Fleming drove south towards Lymington on his way to see Giles Bonner. He wondered if Logan was right. He'd said it was a waste of time following up on a lead on Nielson's army days. Logan was convinced they didn't have to look any further than Eric Rainer. But something was still nagging away at the back of Fleming's mind.

He'd rather enjoyed the drive down. It had given him time to reflect. He had to admit that things hadn't gone exactly smoothly on his first case in the MCU. The chief constable and Temple were not happy that he was treating a retired officer as a suspect, and they were nervous about him going to see Charles Trenchard. Then Temple had warned him that he could be suspended if the Calder affair turned nasty. And now he knew that Calder might have gone to Reading. He'd told Freya he would try to find him, but she wasn't convinced that it was a good idea. Would he still look though? Then there was the obvious tension between himself and Bill Watson because of his promotion over Frank Jardine. Fleming was beginning to wonder if there wasn't more to it than that.

He put his thoughts behind him as he turned into the car park on the quayside at Lymington. Parking the car, Fleming made his way up the street to Giles Bonner's whitewashed terraced house. Bonner was a tall thin man, tanned and fit looking. He still carried a military aura about him. His handshake was firm as he greeted Fleming.

'I live here on my own now,' Bonner said, showing Fleming up some open wooden stairs that led to the first floor. He showed the way through from the landing to a small balcony that had views out over the harbour. 'Thought you might like to sit out here since it's a lovely day. Now, can I get you a drink? Tea, coffee, something a little stronger perhaps?'

'A glass of water would be fine,' Fleming replied. He looked out over the harbour and took in the array of boats at their moorings while Bonner went to fetch his water.

Bonner returned a few minutes later with a glass of iced water in one hand and a beer in the other. 'Decided to have something a bit stronger myself,' he said with a smile. 'Now, Chief Inspector, how may I be of help to you? You said on the phone you wanted to check on some old army colleagues.'

'Yes, it's actually to do with a murder investigation–'

'How awful. May I ask who?'

Fleming pulled Nielson's photograph out of his pocket and pointed at Ronnie Nielson. 'Remember him?'

'Yes, I do. Much younger then, but I still recognise him. It's Ronnie Nielson.' Bonner paused for a second before it dawned on him. 'Of course, I read about him in the papers. Dreadful business.'

Fleming tapped the photograph. 'I found this in Nielson's house. I'm following up on anyone who knew him, to see if something in his past might throw up any new leads.'

'Oh, I see.'

'You're on the photo with him here. I wondered if you knew him well.'

'Actually, no, I didn't. He was in a different platoon.'

'You recognise the other men in the photograph?'

'Yes, yes I do. We all served with C Company.' He pointed to the other men one by one. 'That's Eddie Slater, Tim Banks, Martin Cook, Charles Trenchard, and, of course, me.'

'How well did you know the others?'

'We weren't best mates, if that's what you mean. We had three platoons in C Company, you see. Eddie Slater, Tim Banks and Ronnie Nielson were sergeants in different platoons. Martin Cook, Charles Trenchard and I were the three platoon commanders.'

'Who was the commander of Nielson's platoon?'

'That would be Charles Trenchard. Eddie Slater was in mine. Tim Banks was in Martin Cook's outfit.'

'So you probably knew Eddie Slater more so than any of the others?'

'Yes, decent chap. I knew he was best friends with Nielson. He was one of the few who were.'

'Oh?'

'Nielson was a bit of a fiery character, by all accounts. Bit of conflict between him and his platoon commander apparently. They didn't get on at all.'

'Trenchard?'

'Yes. But then I gather Ronnie Nielson didn't see eye to eye with any officers.'

'But you never had any trouble with him?'

'Certainly not...' Bonner paused as though deep in thought.

'But?'

'I can understand why he didn't get on well with Charles. Trenchard was a man who had a reputation for having a short fuse. I shouldn't really say this, but he had a ruthless streak, an obvious disregard for other people. I'm not surprised he's being tipped as a potential successor to the prime minister.'

'Trenchard was not everyone's favourite officer?'

'I suppose you could say that. He was driven by ambition and no man was going to get in his way.' Bonner downed the rest of his beer and looked at his empty glass. 'Another?'

'No, I'm fine. What about Martin Cook? Know much about him?'

'Not much. I heard he went to Australia to live soon after he left the army. A year after we returned from Afghanistan I believe.' Bonner shook his head sadly. 'And poor old Slater and Banks were killed in action. Soon after that photograph was taken. Tragic.'

Fleming put the photograph back in his pocket and rose to leave. 'Mr Bonner, thank you so much for your time. You've been most helpful. Thank you.'

'No problem. I'm pleased to have been of some assistance, though I fear I haven't been that much help.'

Fleming passed him a card. 'If you do think of anything else, give me a call.'

Bonner hesitated and scratched his head. 'It may be nothing...'

'Yes?'

'I don't want to speak out of turn, but...'

'Go on,' Fleming prompted.

'I'm not sure if something happened in Afghanistan. Trenchard and a few of the men went out drinking one night and, well, after that Trenchard seemed to be different somehow.'

'What do you mean?'

'He was... more subdued. Almost as though he had the weight of the world on his shoulders. But I shouldn't read too much into that. We all changed after a tour in Afghanistan.'

Fleming nodded. 'I think I can understand that.' He shook Bonner's hand and left, thanking him again.

On the drive back to Oxford, Fleming was not certain his visit had been wasted after all. Something may have happened in Afghanistan... Trenchard had seemed anxious to avoid talking about why he left the army. Very interesting. And Trenchard had said he didn't know Nielson at all, but he was Nielson's platoon commander. Why had he lied?

48

Fleming was in the office first thing. Logan and Anderson hadn't arrived yet. Liz Temple stuck her head round his office door. 'Got a minute, Alex?' She didn't wait for an answer, but turned and strode off back to her office.

Fleming knew from the serious look on Temple's face that something was wrong. He rose from his desk to follow her.

Temple's door was open but Fleming knocked anyway before entering. 'Yes, ma'am?'

'Come in, Alex, close the door and take a seat.'

Fleming noticed Temple had chosen to sit behind her desk and not at the coffee table. This was going to be formal, whatever it was.

Temple closed the file she had in front of her and looked hard at Fleming. 'Alex, I know you have a job to do and it's not easy at the best of times, but you do know how to make things difficult for yourself, don't you?'

'Ma'am?'

'You seem to have a bee in your bonnet over Anthony Hayden. I believe you've asked for further enquiries to be made despite the fact there is no forensic evidence to link him to the murder.' It was a statement, but Fleming knew from the tone of voice that it demanded a response.

'I'm running a check on all the CCTV footage we have. I want to trace and interview all the owners of cars that appear in Bourne End on the night of the murder. I'm hoping that will exclude Hayden. I've also asked DC Anderson to check with his neighbours to make sure he didn't leave the house that night. I want to be able to rule him out completely, that's all.'

'The chief constable isn't going to be happy.'

'He said he wanted me to put the Hayden business to bed quickly. That's what I'm trying to do.'

Temple didn't look impressed. She put her hands flat on the desk in front of her and spoke slowly and quietly. 'Do I have to remind you that he also said he didn't want anyone going to see Carl Yapp, the reporter? He said the last thing we need is him claiming he's being harassed by the police, did he not? And what do you do? You go and see him!' Temple clenched a fist and slammed it on the desk.

'I was–'

'Adding to the problem!' Temple was losing her usual calm composure for once. She took a deep breath and carried on. 'He phoned me after I'd issued a statement categorically denying the allegations of corruption. Know what he told me?'

'What?'

'He said a detective by the name of Fleming had gone to see him and had threatened him. That true?'

'Not exactly. I–'

'Not exactly!' Temple's face had reddened. 'What *exactly* did you say?'

'I simply said he should be careful about running any more unfounded stories, that's all. By the way, he had no evidence whatsoever. It was Damien Potts who made the allegation. He reckoned Nielson had told him he had bent coppers in his pocket, that's it. Potts is just trying to have a dig at the police. And now he's done a runner.'

'Great. Has he done a runner because he knows we'll be after him for making false accusations, or because he killed Nielson?'

'Probably the former. I was going to come and see you anyway this morning. I've arrested Eric Rainer for Nielson's murder. He's in custody. We applied to court to detain him for another three days so we can carry on interviewing him while we're waiting for fingerprint and DNA results. It's no secret he hated Nielson, he lied over his alibi, we have CCTV footage of him near the scene of the crime, and he tried to evade capture.'

'So why haven't you charged him?'

'We have no evidence to put him at the actual crime scene. I'm waiting for forensics to get back to me. If that proves conclusive, I'll charge him.'

Temple seemed to relax and a glimmer of a smile crossed her face. 'So, we could have a result by the end of the day. That will cheer the chief constable up. He'll be glad to get Cecil Daubney off his back.'

Fleming cleared his throat. 'Let's wait and see. I have a sneaking suspicion this isn't going to be as clear-cut as I thought.'

Temple's face had stiffened again. She glared at Fleming. 'What's the problem? You've just said you'll charge him if the forensic results are positive.'

'The problem is that I somehow suspect that the results may not be conclusive–'

'Hang on, Alex. You arrest the man. You take his fingerprints and DNA. Are you now saying you're not convinced he is the murderer?'

'I'm saying I doubt we'll have enough evidence to secure a conviction in court if the forensic evidence isn't conclusive.' Fleming hesitated, unsure if Temple could take more bad news.

'There is something else. Something I found out after arresting Rainer...'

Temple frowned. 'Why do I think I don't want to hear this?'

'The thing is... I went to see someone yesterday: a man who served in the army with Nielson in Afghanistan years ago. He's one of the men in the photograph I found in Nielson's house. It turns out Charles Trenchard lied to me about knowing Nielson. Said he couldn't remember the name.'

'So?'

'He was Ronnie Nielson's platoon commander... and apparently they didn't see eye to eye.'

Temple threw her hands up in the air in despair. 'Oh, fuck! Don't tell me you have him down as a suspect now, just because he forgot someone's name. That's all we need. First, you suspect a former colleague. Then we get allegations of corruption, a reporter making a complaint against us, you chasing after Jimmy Calder, and now you've got your eyes on a man who may be the next prime minister! You certainly know how to attract trouble, Alex. Tell me you're not seriously going to follow this up. Matthew Upson will go ballistic.'

'I'm afraid I have to, ma'am. When I spoke to him, I had a feeling Trenchard was being guarded about something. He seemed anxious to avoid any discussion about his army career. The man I saw yesterday was sure something happened in Afghanistan involving Trenchard: something that seemed to change him.'

'Alex, that was years ago. Can you remember everyone you met years ago? And don't you think you would have changed if you'd served with the army in Afghanistan?'

Fleming shrugged. 'I hadn't intended going to see him again... unless I don't have enough to charge Rainer—'

Temple drew a deep breath. 'Alex, you will not go to see

Trenchard again, full stop. Not until I've cleared it with Matthew Upson. Understand?'

'Yes, ma'am.'

'And, you will not go near Carl Yapp again. That is finished, gone. Understood?'

Fleming nodded. 'Was there anything else, ma'am?'

'Get this investigation wrapped up, but with no more hiccups. My patience is running out. Close the door as you leave.'

Fleming headed back to his own office. Logan and Anderson had arrived.

Logan looked at Fleming's dark face. 'Everything all right, boss?'

Fleming nodded. 'Everything's fine, Harry. Absolutely fine.'

Fleming went into his office, closed the door and didn't believe for a minute that it was.

49

The atmosphere in the interview room was tense. Rainer sat forwards in his chair with his arms folded on the table in front of him. Fleming had read him his rights again and the tape recorder was running. His solicitor sat next to him looking pensive. Logan was drumming his fingers on the table while fixing a stare across the table at Rainer.

Fleming was looking at an open folder. He tapped a pen on the table and remained silent.

Rainer and Grimes waited expectantly.

Fleming finally drew in a deep breath before speaking. 'Mr Rainer, you previously claimed you were at home on the night Ronnie Nielson was murdered. Then, when confronted with evidence that proved you were not at home, you said you went to see a female friend in Slough. You also lied about that. I showed you a copy of CCTV footage showing a man getting out of a car at Bourne End. You confirmed it was you. Is that correct?'

Rainer glanced nervously at Grimes. The solicitor nodded. Rainer ran his tongue over his bottom lip. Sweat ran down his forehead into his eyes. He blinked. His voice was barely a whisper. 'Yes.'

Fleming looked hard at him. 'Can you speak up for the tape please?'

'Yes!' Rainer shouted in exasperation.

'I asked you to explain what you were doing in Bourne End and you remained silent. Your solicitor, who is also present today, asked for time to have a private consultation with you and I terminated the interv–'

'Your point being?' Grimes interrupted.

Fleming ignored him. 'Have you now had time to reflect on your position, Mr Rainer? Would you now like to tell me what you were doing there on the night Ronnie Nielson was murdered?'

Grimes spoke quickly before Rainer could answer. 'Chief Inspector, your question verges on suggesting that my client was at the scene of the murder. The fact that he was coincidently in the same area proves nothing.'

Fleming remained silent and stared at Grimes. The solicitor shifted uncomfortably in his chair.

Rainer looked at Grimes as though for help. Grimes shook his head slowly. The movement was hardly noticeable.

Rainer glared at Fleming. 'No comment.'

Fleming persisted. 'Mr Rainer, you phoned Mrs Dobbs that night to enquire if she knew whether Ronnie Nielson was at home or on his boat. We found your fingerprints on Nielson's boat. You *were* at the scene of the murder. Perhaps you can explain that?'

Grimes gasped and shot a glance at Rainer.

Rainer breathed in deeply. 'All right... I was there. But it's not what you think. I lied about where I was because you knew I hated Nielson. I thought if you knew I'd been to see him you would sure as hell have me down as the murderer.'

'What were you doing on his boat if you didn't kill him?'

'He was dragging his feet over the divorce settlement. He'd

agreed to sell the house so Sarah could get half the proceeds, but hadn't even put it on the market. Nielson also owed her money from other assets, like the boat for instance. He'd made no attempt to pay her what she was due, the bastard! Sarah's solicitor had warned him that she would take him back to court, but Sarah was reluctant to go down that route. The divorce had been acrimonious enough.'

Fleming nodded. 'So, you decided to go and see him. Things got out of hand and you killed him. Is that it?'

Rainer put his head in his hands and slumped over the table. 'No, no, no!' he sobbed. 'That's not what happened!'

'Tell me what did happen,' Fleming coaxed.

Rainer looked at Grimes who gave him a resigned nod. 'I did go to have it out with him. I got to the boat. The cabin door was open. There was no sound from inside. I felt instinctively that something was wrong. I went down below and that's when I saw him. He was on the floor in the galley, lying face down in a pool of blood. It was obvious he was dead. I panicked and left. That's the truth. I swear. You have to believe me! I only lied to you because I knew things would look bad for me if I told the truth.'

Fleming looked at Logan who sat expressionless.

Grimes broke the silence. 'Are you going to charge my client, Chief Inspector?' His voice was calm, subdued. 'If not, you will have to release him.'

Fleming made a decision. 'Your client is free to go for now. Interview terminated at ten forty-five.'

After Rainer had left with Grimes, Logan was having a coffee with Fleming. 'Are you stark raving mad, boss? He had a motive, the opportunity, and the means. His fingerprints are all over the murder scene, and he lied. What more do you want?'

'Something's missing, Harry. The DNA from the skin tissue found under Nielson's fingernails doesn't match Rainer's. And something tells me he may now be telling the truth.'

'Bloody clairvoyant now are you, boss?' Logan shook his head. 'So, what do we do now?'

Fleming pondered for a second. 'I'm not a hundred percent convinced we could get a conviction in court on what we have. A good defence lawyer could argue a convincing case. An innocent man in the wrong place at the wrong time. There are other leads. Let's follow them up and in the meantime, keep Rainer under surveillance. You never know, the murder weapon may yet turn up with his fingerprints on it. We can easily re-arrest Rainer.'

'Some hope of finding the murder weapon after all this time,' Logan grumbled.

Bill Watson was at home looking through his emails when he suddenly spotted the one he was waiting for. His heart was beating faster than usual as he opened it. 'Yes!' he exclaimed out loud. In front of him was the name and address of a club in Reading where his contact had found Jimmy Calder.

50

Fleming was getting out of his Porsche in the MCU car park when Bill Watson's Ford swept in with a screech of tyres. He pulled in beside Fleming and slid his passenger window down.

'Hang on there a minute, Fleming,' Watson panted. 'Want a quick word before we go into the office.'

Fleming frowned. Had Watson heard he was making further checks on Hayden? Fleming waited while Watson pulled his ample frame out of his car. A dark blue tie hung loosely round his neck and he'd undone the top button of his white shirt. He pulled his jacket out of the car and slung it over his shoulder. 'Nice day, eh? Bit hot for me though.'

Fleming was sure Watson hadn't stopped him to exchange pleasantries. 'You wanted a word?'

Watson stood in front of Fleming. Beads of sweat were already forming on his forehead. He fished into a jacket pocket and pulled out a pack of cigarettes. He lit one up and sucked in as though it was his last breath. 'First one today,' he said, exhaling smoke from his mouth as he spoke.

Fleming doubted it. He waited.

Watson took the cigarette out of his mouth and examined it through screwed-up eyes. 'I hear you arrested someone for the Nielson murder, but then let him go.'

'That's right.'

'Why?'

'Why do you want to know?' Fleming wondered where this was leading.

'Oh, just curious that's all.'

Fleming shrugged. 'Not quite enough to secure a conviction. Convincing but not conclusive.'

Watson took another deep drag of his cigarette and exhaled a lungful of smoke up into the air. 'What happened to the Damien Potts lead?'

'There wasn't any trace of his fingerprints at the murder scene, but he did a runner after making allegations of police corruption.'

'That so?' Watson said thoughtfully.

'Finding him is a priority.'

Watson peered closely at Fleming through squinted eyes. 'I also hear you've asked for further checks on Anthony Hayden.'

'You've heard correctly. I want to be able to eliminate him from the enquiry if that makes you happy.' Fleming was getting impatient. 'Why the sudden interest in my case?'

Watson shifted his feet. 'Just making conversation.' He hesitated. 'Look, there's some information you may be interested in. It's a bit sensitive.'

'Go on.'

'Did Logan tell you I had a call from Police Scotland?'

Fleming stiffened. 'He did.'

Watson screwed up his face as though in pain. 'The thing is... well, I know we haven't exactly got on since you joined us, but as fellow police officers, we need to stick up for each other, right? I was shocked when they told me what happened to you.'

'It was a long time ago.'

'Yeah, but I bet you wish you could get your hands on that bastard Calder. Am I right?'

'He's served his time.'

Watson looked up slyly at Fleming after stubbing out his cigarette butt under his foot. 'Logan tell you they thought he might turn up in Reading?'

Fleming frowned. 'He did.'

Watson nodded slowly. 'I know where you might find him.'

'Oh?'

'Police Scotland asked us to let them know if he did turn up on our patch. I got some of my snouts to keep their eyes and ears open, and one of them came up trumps.'

'So why are you telling me and not Police Scotland?'

Watson belched. 'Do I have to fucking spell it out for you, Fleming? I thought maybe you'd want to know first, know what I mean? If Police Scotland catch him, the powers that be will revoke his licence and recall him to prison. I thought I'd do you a favour and give you a chance to get to him first.'

Fleming was about to speak, but Watson thrust a piece of paper into his hand, turned and walked off in the direction of the building's front entrance. Fleming couldn't see the smirk on Watson's face as he called out over his shoulder. 'Good luck!'

Fleming unfolded the paper and looked at Watson's scribbled note. It was the name and address of a club in Reading.

Later that night at home, Watson was on the phone to his contact in London. 'Thanks for the email. Very grateful.' He paused for a second. 'There's something else I'd like you to do for me.'

51

Fleming was having another nightmare. The fourth large glass of whisky before he came to bed hadn't helped. It wasn't the usual recurring nightmare. Watson had handed him a knife. Fleming took it without speaking. Calder was laughing. Fleming raised his knife hand and was about to plunge it into Calder's chest when he heard a loud ringing in his ears. He woke suddenly and the alarm clock crashed to the floor as he tried to switch it off. His head was pounding as he crept out of bed and made his way to the bathroom where he promptly threw up.

After a hot shower, two cups of black coffee, some painkillers and a quick breakfast he felt just about able to face the day. He was due to meet Logan in an hour so took a taxi to the station.

Logan was already there. 'Morning, boss,' he said, looking curiously at Fleming. 'You okay? You look a bit rough.'

Fleming hadn't had time to shave and his eyes were red. 'Bad night. Time for a coffee before our train?'

They were at Paddington just over an hour later. Fleming looked at his watch. 'We could save some time if we split up. You get yourself down to Brixton and have a chat with the bookie who owns the flat where Potts was staying. See if he has any idea where he might have gone. Ask around local shops and pubs as well. Oh, and see if you can find Tommy Tyler, the chap who took Potts to Nielson's Cellar a couple of weeks ago. You never know, he might have taken him somewhere. I'll go to Nielson's Cellar and speak to McBain. I'll meet you back here later. Say, in a couple of hours?'

'Sure. See you later. Good luck with McBain.'

Fleming took the tube to Piccadilly Circus and made his way into Soho on foot. On the way, he found himself wondering why Watson had told him where he could find Calder. Maybe there was a decent side to him after all. Was he really trying to help Fleming out? Or did he have some ulterior motive? Fleming remembered telling Freya that no one would know he was looking for Calder, but now Watson knew Fleming knew where Calder was. Fleming pushed his thoughts to one side as he approached Nielson's Cellar.

The young man with blond hair and the ponytail that he saw last time he visited the club was there again pulling chairs off tables. He looked warily at Fleming. 'Boss is in his office. Want me to tell him you're here?'

'Good idea. Before you do though, you might be able to help me.'

'Oh? How?' Ponytail's left eye twitched nervously.

'Did you know Damien Potts well?'

'Not really. I've only been here a couple of years. I knew he worked here for Ronnie Nielson before he went to prison. He came back to work for Scottie when he got out a few weeks ago.'

'What did he do?'

'He killed a man.'

Fleming smiled. 'No, I mean what did he do here? What was his job?'

Ponytail frowned. 'Now you mention it, I haven't a clue. He doesn't actually work regularly in the club, pops in from time to time to see Scottie.'

Fleming nodded. 'So when did you last see him?'

Ponytail thought for a second. 'Be about a week ago. He came to see Scottie. That was the last time I saw him.'

'Any idea where he might be?'

'No, no I haven't.'

McBain came out of his office. He froze momentarily when he saw Fleming talking to Ponytail, then smiled. 'Chief Inspector Fleming, what brings you here again?' He glared at Ponytail. 'Get on with the tables,' McBain growled. 'I'll see to this.' Standing to one side, he waved an arm theatrically, indicating for Fleming to go into his office.

'Take a seat,' McBain said as he walked over to a filing cabinet. He pulled out two glasses in the fingers of one hand and a bottle of whisky in the other. He lifted the two glasses and waved them towards Fleming with a questioning look.

'No, thanks,' Fleming said. 'Too early for me.'

McBain put one glass back, poured a good measure into the other one and slouched into the chair behind his desk. 'What can I do for you, Chief Inspector?'

'When did you last see Damien Potts before he did a runner?'

McBain feigned surprise. 'He's done a runner?'

'Come off it, McBain. You know he's gone into hiding. He's left the flat and breached his parole conditions.'

'I'd no idea.'

'He works for you, doesn't he?'

'On and off, you might say.'

'So when did you last see him?' Fleming repeated.

'Now let me see... yes, that would be a couple of weeks ago when you were last here.'

'Ponytail outside reckons Potts came to see you about a week ago.'

'Oh, yes... I forgot. So he did.'

'Why did he come to see you?'

'He wanted more work. Reckoned he needed money.'

'And?'

McBain took a large gulp of his whisky. 'I didn't have anything I could give him right now.'

'And what sort of work was he doing?'

'Like I said, he wasn't what you would call a regular employee. He ran errands, posted ads for club events, does a bit of stocktaking, collects emergency stocks, that sort of thing.'

'Where might he have gone?'

McBain shrugged. 'Haven't the faintest.'

'You don't seem unduly concerned.'

'I've already told you, he isn't a regular employee. He's not exactly a best mate.'

'Why did you give him some work when he got out of prison?'

McBain glared at Fleming. 'What's that got to do with him going missing? And why has he disappeared anyway?'

'He made a serious allegation against the police to a reporter. Know about that?'

'How the fuck would I know what he's done?'

'That's probably why he's done a runner.'

'Or because he thinks you want to stitch him up for Ronnie's murder.' McBain clearly suddenly realised he'd said too much and fell quiet. He sipped at his whisky and looked over the glass at Fleming.

'He told you that?'

McBain shrugged again. 'Something he said. He's paranoid. Thinks everyone is out to get him.'

'Is that why he really came to see you?' Fleming persisted.

McBain glared hard. 'I told you why he came to see me. I wasn't able to help.'

'So that brings me back to my question about giving him some work. Why did you want to help him?'

McBain downed the last of his whisky and thumped the empty glass on his desk. 'I don't know why you're asking me all these questions. How is knowing why I helped him going to help you find him, for fuck's sake?'

'Getting some background,' Fleming said. 'So why did you?'

'He worked for Ronnie for three years before he went to prison so I decided to give him a chance. Who else would?'

'Any friends you know of?'

McBain laughed. 'You're joking, right?'

'Any relatives?'

McBain shrugged.

Fleming was sure McBain was being evasive. Fleming suspected he knew more than he was prepared to say.

'Thank you for your time, Mr McBain.' Fleming rose to go and turned at the door. 'By the way, if I find out later that you've lied to me, I might just charge you with obstructing an investigation, or assisting a person to evade arrest. Take your pick.'

'Fuck you, Fleming!'

'I'll see myself out, shall I?'

~

Two hours later, Logan was tucking into a burger and chips when Fleming met him at Paddington. 'Hi, boss. Any luck with McBain?' he mumbled through a full mouth.

'Not really. But I think he knows more than he's letting on. I could tell he was lying through his teeth. You get any joy?'

'I managed to find Tyler who claims he has no idea where Potts is. Says he didn't even know he'd done a runner. No joy with local shops or pubs, but the bookie told me that Potts had rattled on about some friend he had in prison who was due for release soon and that he might need temporary accommodation until he finds something more permanent.'

'This guy have a name?'

'Madlock... Benny Madlock. He's in Wandsworth.'

'I think you should go and see him tomorrow. Check if he can throw any light on where Potts might have gone.'

'Where will you be?' Logan asked.

'I've got a migraine coming on. I think I'll take the weekend off.'

Logan nodded. 'Okay. Catch up with you on Monday.' He was worried about Fleming who didn't seem quite himself since he'd heard that Jimmy Calder might turn up in Reading.

Fleming was on his second glass of whisky. The evening news had announced that the prime minister had lost the confidence vote and elections were to take place for a new leader. Charles Trenchard had announced his intention to stand for election. Fleming cursed. That was all he needed. He looked again at the slip of paper Watson had given him with the address of the club in Reading where he might find Calder. Taking a large gulp of whisky, Fleming stared at the ceiling and wondered what he was going to do with the information.

52

The gate at HMP Wandsworth slammed shut behind Logan and Anderson with an echoing clang. Anderson felt a little uneasy. She'd never set foot inside a prison before. There was something about being behind locked doors.

After going through some security checks, a prison officer escorted them across a small open yard whistling nonchalantly and swinging his keys at the end of a long chain attached to his belt. He took them through another locked steel door and along a maze of corridors to a room they used for legal visits. There was a small table in the middle of the room with one chair on one side and two chairs on the other.

'It's Madlock you're seeing, isn't it?' the officer asked.

'That's right,' Logan replied.

'He'll be along shortly.'

'Why'd you ask me to come with you, Sarge?' Anderson asked.

Logan smiled. 'Thought you'd enjoy the experience.' Anderson's expression changed. 'Only kidding. A second officer has to be present at all prison interviews,' he said, more seriously. 'That's right, isn't it?' he asked the guard.

'Absolutely. You can't interview a prisoner on your own. You also have to have an officer within sight. That's me. Name's Keith... Keith Hunt, by the way.'

The door opened and a uniformed officer looked in. 'Benny Madlock for you,' he announced.

'Come in, Madlock,' Hunt said. He pulled the single chair away from the table and motioned for him to sit.

Madlock shuffled in, looking apprehensively at Logan and Anderson. He was of medium height, balding, and wore regulation prison clothing. Sitting down with a sullen look on his face, he rubbed at the greying stubble on his chin before resting his arms on the table.

Logan and Anderson settled into the two chairs opposite him. Logan got straight to the point. 'I'm DS Logan and this is DC Anderson. We want to ask you a few questions.'

Madlock said nothing.

'Benny... can I call you Benny?' Logan asked.

Madlock stared at him before replying. 'Call me what you like.' His steady gaze shifted from Logan to Anderson and back. 'Questions about what?'

'It's to do with Damien Potts. You became friendly with him, that right?'

Madlock frowned, instantly on guard. 'What's this about? Been a naughty boy already, has he?'

Logan put his hands on the table. 'Let's just say he's annoyed a few people... people he's frightened of. He's done a runner and we need to find him before they do.'

'Oh yeah? Who's he running from?'

'No one you'll know.'

Madlock sneered. 'That's crap. He's on the run from you, isn't he? You think he killed Ronnie Nielson, don't you? Potts is just out of prison and you lot want to pin Nielson's murder on him.' Madlock suddenly pushed his chair back from the table and turned to face Hunt. 'I'm done here. I don't have to talk to no cops.'

Anderson was impressed with Logan's slight twisting of the facts and decided a further distorting of the truth might help. 'Benny, it's not that at all...' She glanced at Logan who nodded agreement for her to continue. 'The thing is, we did question Damien about Nielson's murder. But we know he didn't do it. We've arrested someone for that–'

'Oh yeah?' Madlock retorted.

Anderson continued with the lie. 'Damien pointed the finger at him and the man we've arrested has friends. Damien is a witness. We need to find him.'

Madlock sat and frowned. 'So why should I help you?'

Logan seemed glad of Anderson's intervention. He held Madlock's defiant gaze. 'Two reasons. One he's your friend, and two, he was going to help you get temporary accommodation when you're released. He can't do that if he's on the run.'

Madlock's eyes darted suspiciously between Logan and Anderson. 'I don't see how I can help you,' he said guardedly.

'Have you any idea where Damien might be hiding out?' Logan persisted.

'Haven't a clue.'

'He never spoke about any other friends he had, any relatives?'

'No, can't say he did.'

'Never mentioned where he might go on release?'

'Said he would probably stay in London, see if he could get some work at Nielson's Cellar.'

'And if he couldn't?'

Madlock shrugged.

'Did he ever speak about where else he'd lived, maybe would like to go?' Anderson pressed.

Madlock shook his head.

'Did he say where he might find you temporary accommodation?' Logan added hopefully. He thought he knew the answer but it was worth a try.

'In London. Said a guy called McBain knew someone who had a flat above a betting shop in Brixton.'

Logan frowned. This was going nowhere. He sat back in his chair as though to signify that he had no more questions and looked at Anderson.

She shook her head.

'Okay, thanks for speaking to us, Benny,' Logan said.

'Can't see how I've helped,' Madlock replied, more relaxed. 'I hope you do find Damien before anyone else does.' He leaned back in his chair. 'Looks like my release accommodation's fucked, doesn't it?' He shot a glance in Anderson's direction. 'Sorry, miss. Excuse my French.'

Anderson smiled. 'I hear worse in the office.'

Logan looked across at Hunt. 'We're all done here.'

Later, on the way back to Oxford, the pair were quiet. Anderson finally broke the silence. 'Complete waste of time that was, wasn't it, Sarge?'

Logan tilted his head. 'Had to be followed up though.'

'Suppose so,' Anderson admitted. 'Why didn't the boss come?'

'Reckoned he had a migraine coming on and was going to take the weekend off,' Logan replied. He looked thoughtful before adding, 'He's acting a bit strange at the moment, doesn't seem quite himself...'

'Oh?'

Logan pulled a face. He wasn't about to tell Anderson what he knew about Fleming's past. Nor that Fleming had found out that Jimmy Calder might be in Reading...

53

A black transit van pulled into a side street and parked near the Lyons Den nightclub in Reading. The driver dowsed the lights and turned to the two men beside him. 'You know what we have to do. As soon as he leaves the club you call me on the mobile and tell me which way he's heading. Got it?'

'Sure thing, boss,' one of the men confirmed.

'Okay, get yourselves in there... and stay inconspicuous. One drink and that's all.'

The two men left the van and walked to the club. A sign above the door showed that Des Lyons was the proprietor. It was a rundown looking place from the outside. Inside was dingy to say the least. Worn stone steps led to a basement where loud music throbbed and reverberated around brick walls. A green strip light flickered underneath the full length of the bar counter. Rowdy customers sat around tables beside a small wooden dance floor, paying attention to the female singer. Loud raucous voices and laughter drowned out her voice. The three-man band behind her looked suitably bored. No one was on the dance floor.

The two men picked a couple of high stools by the bar and

ordered beer from a morose-looking barman. They sat making idle conversation while checking for sight of the man they were looking for. The singer gave up and left the stage to no applause. The band continued playing, but no one was listening.

One of the men suddenly nudged the other. 'That's him,' he said, nodding towards a man who had come out of a side door by the bar.

The man they were looking at was a rough unhealthy looking character who shuffled across the floor and started collecting empty glasses from the tables. They couldn't help but recognise him from the detailed description they'd been given. He had long straggly grey hair, unkempt and thinning. He looked emaciated and had a large bulbous nose. There was no doubt it was Jimmy Calder.

Calder spoke to no one as he collected the empties and deposited them on the bar counter without a word. He didn't notice the two men watching him as he went behind the bar to rinse them.

'Keeping you busy?' one of the men asked.

Calder stared at him with a cold vacant look in his eyes and shrugged. 'It's a job,' he growled in a hoarse voice as he carried on cleaning glasses.

'Must be a bit boring; collecting and washing glasses,' the same man said. 'What time do you normally work to?'

Calder looked up again, wondering why all the interest. 'Varies. Why?'

'Being sociable, that's all. Here, let me buy you a drink. You look as though you could do with one.'

Calder looked furtively around to make sure Des Lyons wasn't in sight. Calder nodded imperceptibly. 'Don't mind if I do. Whisky would be good. Double if you're feeling generous.'

Six sneakily downed doubles later at one o'clock in the morning, Calder left the club. He swayed against the walls on the way up the steps to the street above, unaware of the two men slipping off their stools to follow him. One of the men pulled out his mobile when they reached the street and spoke briefly into it.

Seconds later, the black van was coasting along the street behind them.

Calder turned into a quiet side street. He didn't realise he was being followed, but then heard the crunch of gravel behind him and looked back over his shoulder in alarm. The two men from the club were closing in on him fast. He turned and ran.

It was too late. He felt a heavy blow to the back of his head and went down. The black van pulled up beside him with a screech of tyres. Hands grabbed his legs and shoulders. The back doors of the van flew open. The two men threw Calder in and jumped in after him. The van drove off at high speed in a northerly direction.

After a few minutes, the van pulled up at the metal gates of an old scrapyard. One of the men in the back of the van jumped out and opened the gates. The van pulled in and drove across the yard to the front of a large garage. The scrapyard gates clanged shut behind. The driver jumped down and pushed the sliding doors of the garage open with a loud screech. He climbed back into the cab and drove inside. Tyres squealed on the smooth concrete floor as he spun the van round to face the doors and braked to a halt. Dust settled round the van as overhead lights clicked on.

The two men from the club pulled Calder out of the van. He collapsed onto the floor and looked up at his assailants, eyes wide open in fear. He tried to get up but a kick caught him on the side of the head. One of the men leaned over him. 'We know what you did, Calder. And a friend wants you to pay for it.' A fist slammed into Calder's face and blood spurted from his broken nose.

The man spoke again. 'Remember the name Fleming?' Another blow caught Calder on the side of his head. The man whispered in Calder's ear. 'He's coming for you, Calder. This is a taste of what's to come.' A kick landed in his groin and Calder groaned. Another foot caught his mouth. Blood trickled between his stained teeth.

Calder tried to speak. 'Pl... please. I'm an old man. I served my t–'

Another blow landed on his face. He groaned and spat out two front teeth.

'Okay, that's enough,' the driver said. He looked closely at Calder. 'Better get him to hospital. Fleming doesn't want him dead... at least not yet.'

Ten minutes later, they threw Calder's bruised and bloodied body out the back of the van by the entrance to the Royal Berkshire Hospital.

It was Sunday evening when Liz Temple took the call from the duty sergeant. 'I think you'd better come in, ma'am. Something's happened you should know about.'

54

Fleming sensed the solemn atmosphere as soon as he walked into the office. Logan and Anderson were at their desks looking somewhat subdued. There was none of the usual banter.

'Something up?' Fleming asked.

It was Logan who spoke. 'Seems like it. Super's in a foul mood. Came stomping in here, demanding to know why you weren't in yet. She wants to see you straight away... in the interview room.'

Fleming frowned. 'Who's there?'

'Her and two CID guys from Reading,' Logan answered.

The frown on Fleming's face deepened. 'Oh, something interesting happen over the weekend?'

Logan shrugged. 'She didn't say. But by the look on her face, I'd say something pretty serious is going on. Think you'd better get yourself in there, boss.'

'Okay, I'll catch up with you later.'

Fleming made his way to the interview room, knocked and entered without waiting.

Temple was sitting on the edge of the table, talking to the

two men. The conversation stopped as soon as Fleming entered. 'Come in, Alex.' Temple's tone was formal. Her face was unsmiling. 'This is DS Crowe and DC Valdez from Reading CID.'

Fleming offered a hand to the two men. 'Pleased to meet you.' He looked at Temple and raised an eyebrow.

'Take a seat.' Temple indicated her single chair behind the table. She, Crowe and Valdez settled into the three opposite.

'Alex,' Temple continued, 'DS Crowe and DC Valdez want to ask you some questions.'

'Sure, fire away.'

'Under caution,' Temple added.

'What on earth for?'

Temple ignored the query. 'Are you happy to stay and answer their questions voluntarily?'

Fleming shifted in his chair. 'Yes, of course.'

Temple nodded and looked at Crowe. 'Okay, let's get this over with.'

Crowe took the wrapping off two new tapes and plugged them into the portable tape machine. He pushed the start button. 'This interview is being recorded. This is an interview with DCI Alex Fleming. I am DS Crowe. Also present are DC Valdez and Superintendent Temple. There are no other people present.' He then confirmed the date, time and location of the interview. 'DCI Fleming, you do not have to say anything. But it may harm your defence if you do not mention when questioned, something which you later rely on in court. Anything you do say may be given in evidence.' He paused to take breath. 'You've agreed to be interviewed voluntarily under caution and as such you are free to leave at any point. Do you understand?'

'Yes,' Fleming replied in a resigned voice.

Crowe looked at Temple who tipped her head imperceptibly. 'Can you confirm what your relationship is with Jimmy Calder?'

Fleming froze. *So this is what this is all about.* 'There's no relationship. He killed my mother twenty-three years ago.'

'You knew he was released from Shotts Prison recently?'

'Yes.'

'How did you find out?'

Fleming had to think fast. He didn't want to get his old friend Gordon Aitken from Police Scotland into trouble. Recalling the newspaper article Temple had shown him covering Calder's disappearance when he'd gone to Edinburgh, Fleming assumed there would have been an earlier article covering Calder's release. 'I saw it in the papers.'

Crowe looked dubious. 'I don't recollect it being in the national press.'

'It was an Edinburgh newspaper.'

'You read them regularly, do you?' Crowe pressed.

'An old friend sent it to me,' Fleming lied quickly.

Crowe's lips tightened as if Fleming's answer was too glib. 'Can you tell me why you went to Edinburgh when you found out?'

'I'd read up about restorative justice and thought I could move on if I could speak to the man. Maybe he would say he was sorry... show some remorse.'

'You don't deny you were looking for Calder?'

'No, I was, but I didn't see him. I realise it was a stupid idea and I've given up on it.'

Crowe looked sideways at Temple.

She nodded. 'Tell him.'

'Jimmy Calder was abducted by three men from a club in Reading last night. They beat him to within an inch of his life. Know anything about that?'

Fleming paused before answering. 'No... no I don't.'

'Interesting thing is, they chucked him out of the back of a van in front of the Royal Berkshire Hospital afterwards. Why do you think people would beat a man up and then take him to hospital?'

Fleming shook his head. 'No idea. Seems a strange thing to do.'

'There is a plausible explanation,' Crowe said.

'Oh?'

'Calder said he overheard one of his assailants saying they'd better take him to hospital because you didn't want him dead... yet.'

'What!'

'He told us that you put them up to it. One of the men told him that the beating was a taste of what was to come–'

'This is ridiculous.'

'You didn't deny you had been looking for him,' Crowe said.

'Not after I'd been to Edinburgh,' Fleming reminded him. 'You're not really buying his story, are you? Why would I get people to beat him up and advertise the fact I'd sent them?'

Crowe shrugged. 'Does seem a bit ill advised, but maybe you wanted him to know it was you. You would deny any involvement anyway. He has no proof.' Crowe paused. 'Unless we find the three men.'

Fleming said nothing.

Temple intervened. 'Alex?'

Fleming shook his head in disbelief. 'I don't know anything about this.'

Crowe clearly wasn't about to give up. 'How did you find out where he was?'

Fleming paused for a second. This was getting awkward. He knew it could come out that Police Scotland had phoned Watson to say that Calder might be heading for Reading. But he didn't want to get Logan in trouble for telling him, nor did he want to snitch on Watson for giving him the address, despite his dislike for the man. Watson wouldn't admit to it anyway. 'No one told me. I had no idea.'

Crowe switched the line of questioning. 'How come you were off work over the weekend?'

'I had a migraine.'

'Go anywhere? See anyone?'

'No, I stayed at home.'

'Speak to anyone?'

'No.'

'It would help us if you agreed to let us have your mobile phone and computer for forensic examination to check for recent contacts. Are you content to hand them over to us?'

Fleming hesitated. 'Yes, fine. Do what you have to do.'

Crowe nodded. 'Thanks. I think that's all for now. Interview terminated at nine forty-three a.m.'

55

Later, back in Temple's office, she asked Fleming to sit down. 'Alex, I told you before what could happen if this all blew up in our faces. You are under suspicion of involvement in this. Under the circumstances, the chief constable has ordered me to suspend you from duty with immediate effect, pending further enquiries. You need to go and clear your desk. Go home. And tell Logan and Anderson to come and see me straight away. I'm handing the Nielson case over to Bill Watson. They'll be working for him with immediate effect. Any questions?'

Fleming shook his head. 'No, ma'am.'

'You can leave your mobile phone with me now. DS Crowe will be round to your home later to collect your computer. That's all.'

'Fine.' Fleming closed Temple's door behind him and made his way back to his office. He signalled for Logan to follow him.

'You look serious, boss,' Logan said. 'Everything okay?'

Fleming shook his head as he emptied his personal effects from his desk. 'No, everything is not okay. I've been suspend–'

'What! What for?'

'Jimmy Calder's been assaulted. He told Reading CID that the men who assaulted him said I'd sent them to do him over.'

'Fuck! How can they believe that, for Christ's sake! Why would you advertise the fact that you sent them? It's bollocks!'

'That's what I told them, Harry. But they're not convinced.'

'Bloody hell!'

'Temple wants you and Naomi to go and see her. Bill Watson's taking over the Nielson case and the pair of you will be working with him for now.'

'Great,' Logan groaned. 'Is there anything I can do?'

Fleming put the last of his things into his briefcase. 'Yes, there is. You can keep me up to speed on what's happening on the case, and with what Bill Watson is doing.'

An hour later, Fleming was at home waiting for Crowe to collect his computer. He mulled over the Calder business. Had Calder used a random assault to make up a story about him, hoping to get him into trouble? Or was something more sinister going on? Who would tell Calder he'd sent them, and why?

Watson had told him where to find Calder. He'd made it clear from the start he didn't agree with the way Fleming was handling the Nielson case. And Watson had wanted Frank Jardine to get the DCI post. The chief constable didn't want Anthony Hayden treated as a suspect, and he had told Temple to suspend him. They both had an interest in getting him off the case.

Yes, Fleming thought, *I need to have a little chat with Bill Watson...*

56

Logan couldn't believe what Fleming had told him. He filled Anderson in as they made their way to Temple's office. Anderson couldn't believe it either. Neither of them relished the prospect of having Bill Watson as their boss.

Logan knocked on Temple's door. Logan could hear voices inside. They waited.

'Come in!' Temple shouted. She was sitting at the head of her office's conference table. Watson sat next to her. He glared coldly at Logan and Anderson as they entered.

'Take a seat,' Temple said. 'I take it DCI Fleming has told you what's happened.'

'Yes, he has,' Logan confirmed, sitting down next to Anderson.

Temple looked deep in thought. After a brief pause, she updated them. 'I want you to know why I had to suspend your boss. It's not something I wanted to do, but I had no choice. He's accused of being behind a serious assault and will remain suspended from duty, pending enquiries.'

Logan and Anderson looked straight ahead and said nothing.

'I'm putting DCI Watson in charge of the Nielson case for now,' Temple continued. She looked at Watson. 'Bill?'

'Let's get one thing straight from the start,' Watson said. 'It's no secret that I didn't see eye to eye with Fleming. I always knew he was the wrong man to fill the vacant DCI post. What's happened here has vindicated my view. He's cocked up big time.' Watson's steady gaze shifted from Logan to Anderson. 'I don't want any divided loyalties on my team. If either of you have any problems with working for me, say so now.'

Neither spoke.

Watson stared at them both. 'I take it silence means you don't have any problems?'

'No,' Logan said.

'No... *sir*,' Watson prompted.

Logan held Watson's steady gaze. 'No, sir.'

Watson looked at Anderson with raised eyebrows.

'No, sir.'

'Good. Let's have an update on exactly where you're at with the investigation.'

It was Logan who spoke. 'We were due to have a full team briefing meeting this morning. We wanted to bring DCI Fleming up to date with a few things after his absence over the weekend. Maybe–'

'Forget the full team briefing,' Watson cut in, 'this is the briefing meeting.'

Anderson looked at Logan with a frown.

Logan saw the look but knew it was pointless challenging Watson. 'Okay, where do you want to start... sir?'

Watson looked at the ceiling. 'How about suspects and enquiries being followed up, for starters?'

Logan studied his notes. 'We ran further checks on Anthony Hayden to see if there was any CCTV footage of his car at

Bourne End and whether any neighbours saw him leave the house the night that Nielson–'

Watson thumped a fist onto the table. 'If I hear another fucking word about Anthony Hayden...' He breathed heavily through his nose. 'We know Fleming had a bee in his bonnet about him for some reason, but he arrested someone else. Why on earth are you still running checks on Hayden?'

'DCI Fleming wanted to eliminate him as a suspect,' Anderson pointed out. 'That's one of the things I wanted to update him on. Hayden's car doesn't appear on CCTV footage at Bourne End and none of his neighbours saw him leave his house that night. Neither was there any forensic evidence so he's in the clear–'

'Thank fuck for that,' Watson snapped.

'Also,' Anderson continued, 'DCI Fleming asked me to trace and interview all the car owners whose cars appeared on CCTV around Bourne End on the night of the murder–'

'Why?' Watson demanded. 'What's the point when he's already arrested someone?'

Logan came to Anderson's rescue. 'Just following up on everything, sir. Making sure there's no loose ends, that's all. Also, he decided to release Rain–'

'Another example of Fleming's lack of judgement,' Watson muttered. 'And why, may I ask, did he decide to release him?'

Logan shifted uneasily in his chair. He'd had his own doubts about that. 'He had a feeling Rainer might have been telling the truth when he said he had nothing to do with Nielson's murder.'

'A feeling!' Watson exploded. 'Give me bloody strength!'

'He felt there was a lot of circumstantial evidence,' Logan continued, 'but maybe not quite enough to secure a conviction. And the DNA from the skin tissue found under Nielson's finger-nails didn't match.'

'So what are you doing about him?'

'We're keeping him under surveillance...'

'And what good will that do?'

Logan shrugged.

'Maybe DCI Fleming wanted to make sure he didn't do a runner,' Anderson offered hopefully.

'Hmm.' Watson didn't sound convinced. 'We need to step up the search for the murder weapon. If we can find it, there may still be enough of a fingerprint trace on it to link it to Rainer. Get on to that as a priority, Naomi.'

'Yes, sir.' She glanced at her notebook. 'I was also running a check on all of Nielson's business contacts. Do you want me to carry on with that if we're concentrating on Rainer?'

Watson shook his head. 'Waste of time. Put it on hold.'

Temple had been sitting quietly, listening intently. 'There was another line of enquiry DCI Fleming wanted to pursue. One I told him to do nothing about until I cleared it with Matthew Upson.'

Watson raised an eyebrow. 'Oh?'

'He wanted to question Charles Trenchard again. Reckons he lied about knowing Nielson. He was his platoon commander in Afghanistan, but he told Fleming he didn't know him–'

'Or couldn't remember him,' Watson suggested with a sigh. 'Bloody hell, ma'am, Fleming certainly knows how to stir the shit. Trenchard could be the next prime minister!'

'Exactly.'

'And presumably the chief constable hasn't sanctioned this?'

'I haven't mentioned it to him yet and, under the circumstances, I don't think I will. My decision: there's to be no further questioning of Charles Trenchard unless all other leads draw a blank.'

'Understood, ma'am,' Watson agreed. 'Very sensible.'

Logan coughed. 'That leaves just one other name in the frame...'

Watson nodded. 'Damien Potts. I told Fleming right at the start he was a prime suspect.'

'Only thing is,' Logan said, 'there's no trace of his fingerprints at the murder scene.'

'Means nothing. Old hand like Potts knows how to make sure he doesn't leave any prints. And he's done a runner, has he not?'

Logan nodded.

'So we need to find him, don't we?'

'Yes, sir.'

'There was one other line of enquiry,' Anderson said.

'Another one of Fleming's ideas, I suppose,' Watson scoffed.

Anderson reddened. 'He thought we might get too tied up looking at a limited number of potential suspects. He didn't want to leave any stone unturned...'

'And?' Watson waited.

'He thought there was a possibility that Nielson's murder might have been a revenge attack. Something to do with a drugs investigation years ago... and a later killing in Reading. The one Potts was convicted for.'

'Forget it,' Watson snapped. 'It's either Rainer or Potts. Let's concentrate on those two.'

Temple looked at Logan and Anderson. 'That it then?'

'Yes, ma'am,' Logan said.

Anderson nodded agreement.

'All right, let's try to forget about the unfortunate business with DCI Fleming and get on with wrapping up this case.'

Back in his own office, Watson put a call through to Police Scotland. 'Chief Inspector Nichol please. DCI Watson from Thames Valley Police speaking.'

He didn't have to wait long before Nichol picked up. 'Chief Inspector Nichol.'

'Hello,' Watson said, 'I promised to get in touch if we found Jimmy Calder for you. I'm ringing to let you know there's been a development.'

57

Fleming had been at home for barely an hour before Crowe and Valdez arrived. They hadn't wasted any time, he thought. He didn't bear any grudges towards them though. They were only doing their job.

They didn't stay long. He offered coffee, which they declined. They took his computer and left, saying he could have it back in a few days. They already had his mobile and he wondered how long it would be before they checked with BT to get a record of incoming and outgoing calls on his landline. He decided to call Gordon Aitken to warn him.

A recorded message told him he wasn't in the office. Fleming tried his mobile.

'DI Aitken,' the familiar voice said after a few rings.

'Hi, Gordon, it's Alex. Listen, I'm afraid the shit has hit the fan over Jimmy Calder.'

'Oh?'

'He was found in Reading. Unfortunately, not in one piece. Three men assaulted him outside a nightclub. They told him I'd sent them.'

'Bloody hell, Alex...' Gordon's voice tailed off as though he wasn't sure what to say next. 'You didn't though... did you?'

Fleming knew Aitken had to ask the question. 'Don't worry. I had nothing to do with it.'

'Thank God for that! But you're in trouble, right?'

Fleming hesitated. He wasn't sure quite how to put this to his friend. 'That's why I'm ringing. Reading CID are buying Calder's story and I've been suspended.'

'Fuck! This is bad, Alex... I mean really bad.'

'The thing is they've taken my mobile and computer. They'll probably get a log of all my calls on the landline as well to check who all my recent contacts were.'

'Shit!' Aitken exclaimed.

'Don't worry, I told them I found out Calder was out of prison from a newspaper article that an old school friend had sent me. If they ask me why you called me, I'll say you wanted to find out how I was getting on in my new job. Stick to the same story if you get asked.'

'Okay, but what about this call if they do check your landline?'

'Say I was ringing to let you know I'd been suspended.'

Aitken let out a deep sigh. 'Thanks for the warning, Alex.'

'No problem, and listen... I'm sorry about all this.'

'Don't worry. You take care, okay? And let me know how things work out.'

'Sure.' Fleming rang off.

He stared at the phone for a minute, then picked it up again. Freya was at home.

'Hello, Freya Nash.'

'It's me, Alex. I don't suppose you're free this afternoon?'

'As it happens, I have a cancellation. I could see you at three. Is everything all right?'

'Not really, I've been suspended...'

'Oh, Alex. What's... Never mind. Tell me when you see me.' She rang off.

Having phoned Freya, Fleming wasn't exactly sure what he was going to say to her. Neither was he sure how she could help him. The phone call had been a knee-jerk reaction.

He made himself a coffee and settled into a chair to reflect on matters. The Nielson case had looked all done and dusted with Rainer's arrest, but then Fleming had decided to release him. Logan had doubted his judgement. Now he was beginning to doubt himself. Was he being too cautious? Should he have charged him and left it to the courts to decide whether he was guilty or not? But what would it look like if he failed to get a conviction on his first case for the MCU? What if he'd got it hopelessly wrong and Watson tied the whole thing up?

Thinking of Watson turned Fleming's thoughts to his present plight. He was angry with himself for going to Edinburgh to look for Calder and couldn't believe how stupid that had been. It had landed him in a right old mess. And was it purely a coincidence that Calder's assault took place a few days after Watson had told Fleming where to find him? Had Watson arranged it hoping to get him suspended and off the case? *Maybe I'm getting paranoid*, he thought.

He tried to take his mind off things and switched on the TV. Charles Trenchard was opening a new wing for a hospital. A reporter had thrust a microphone in front of him.

'When you were recently interviewed by Irving Baker, you were understandably evasive about whether you would stand for the leadership if the prime minister lost the confidence vote. He did, and you have now decided to stand for election. What are your chances of winning?'

'Firstly, let me say how sorry I am that the prime minister has had to resign. But we are where we are, and I believe, as do many others, that I am the best person to take over.'

'But do you think you will win?'

'Yes, I do.'

'You've been in politics for eight years and have held only one ministerial position. Some say you don't have enough experience.'

'I will have a strong team of experienced colleagues around me. What I have to offer is leadership and a vision for the future. I will be working closely with others to transform that vision into a strategy, and put in place the means and the people who can deliver that strategy.'

'What's the vision?' another reporter shouted out.

Trenchard smiled. 'A fairer, just, and affluent society. One where hard work and endeavour is rewarded, where more is spent here in the UK on rebuilding our infrastructure, and less on foreign wars and intervention abroad.' He waved away further questions. Two aides ushered him into a waiting car and he was gone.

Fleming wondered why he didn't trust the man. Was it because he was a politician and he generally didn't trust what they said? Or was it because he lied about knowing Nielson?

Swirling the dregs round in his coffee cup, Fleming stared into space thinking about Trenchard. He'd told Temple he hadn't intended seeing him again unless he didn't have enough to charge Rainer. He hadn't charged Rainer and would have followed up on Trenchard, but Temple had warned him not to. He couldn't anyway now Temple had suspended him.

Fleming was sitting in Freya's treatment room having second thoughts.

'Tell me, Alex, what's happened?' Freya asked.

'Listen, maybe I shouldn't have come. You're supposed be

counselling me over a childhood trauma, not over work.' Fleming made to get up from his chair.

Freya put a gentle restraining hand on his arm and smiled. 'Please, sit down, Alex.' She took in a deep breath. 'What's been happening at work is connected to the past, isn't it? You told me last time that your boss wasn't happy with you going to Edinburgh to find Jimmy Calder. Is that why you've been suspended?'

Fleming sank back into his chair. 'There's a bit more to it than that.'

Freya waited without saying anything.

Fleming rubbed a hand over his chin, deep in thought.

'You carried on looking for Calder and your boss found out. Is that it?' Freya prompted.

'No. Someone else found him. He was assaulted and told Reading CID that I was behind it.'

'But you weren't?'

'No, I wasn't.'

'But your boss suspended you anyway.'

'I suppose she had no choice really. Someone makes an accusation. It has to be investigated...'

'By Reading CID?'

'That's about it.'

'What happens next?'

'I could be charged with encouraging or assisting a crime if they find sufficient evidence.'

'But they can't if you didn't do it, can they?'

'Only if people lie under oath and swear I told them to do it.'

'But the police would need to find the actual assailants first.'

'Yes.'

'And what sentence would you get if they, whoever they are, manage to stitch you up?'

'Depends on what happens to Calder.'

Freya frowned. 'Apart from your current predicament, how are you coping generally?'

'Fine,' Fleming lied.

'And the nightmares?'

Fleming shrugged. 'Get them from time to time.'

'Still feel anger towards Calder?'

'I'll never forgive him, that's for sure... and yes, I am still angry with him.'

'I get that, but would you hurt him if you could?'

'You think that maybe I did have someone assault him... is that it?'

'No, I'm trying to understand the depth of your anger.'

Fleming ran a hand through his hair. 'I need to find a way to get closure on this. I want to be able to move on without this continual reminder of what Jimmy Calder did to my mother.'

Freya put a hand over Fleming's. 'You'll never forget it, Alex. But you will learn to live with it.'

Fleming shrugged again. He still wasn't sure how.

Freya withdrew her hand. 'You said the extent of the trouble you might be in depends on what happens to Calder. What are you going to do?'

Fleming frowned. 'I need to find out who's behind this and prove I didn't have anything to do with Calder's assault. And I may know where to start.'

58

'They're going to The White House pub after work,' Logan was saying to Fleming over the phone. 'Bill Watson asked if Naomi and I wanted to join him and Frank Jardine, but we declined.' Logan hesitated. 'Why don't we meet up with you somewhere for a drink? I could do with one after today, and I guess you could too.'

Fleming knew what he wanted to do when he heard where Watson would be. 'I've got things to do. How about tomorrow night?'

'Okay,' Logan agreed. 'I'll give you a call.' He rang off.

Later that evening, Fleming sat in his car in the pub car park. Watson's car was there. Fleming fiddled with the radio controls while he waited for Watson to come out. There was what seemed to be never-ending reports on the state of play on the leadership election and Charles Trenchard's chances of winning. The stock markets were getting jittery with the uncertainty. There were calls for a general election. Fleming found a music channel, listened for a minute, and then switched off the radio.

He was suddenly alert as the pub door opened throwing a shaft of light across the car park. A young couple came out and made their way to their car. The man seemed to whisper something in the woman's ear and she laughed loudly.

Fleming looked at his watch. Ten o'clock. He settled back in his seat and waited.

Ten minutes later, the door opened again. Watson came out, fished in his jacket pocket and pulled out a pack of cigarettes. He lit up and stood by the door, blowing smoke up into the night air.

Fleming took a deep breath, eased himself out of his car and walked across to Watson. 'Hello, Bill. Mind if we have a chat?'

Watson's eyes darted back towards the door as though looking for an escape route. He threw his cigarette onto the ground by Fleming's feet. 'I was about to go back in for my drink. Frank's getting them in. Care to join us?'

Fleming shook his head. 'I only want a word.'

'Better be quick, it's getting a bit cool out here.'

'I was wondering why you told me where to find Jimmy Calder.'

Watson breathed in deeply. 'I might have guessed that's what this is about. Listen, you didn't find out from me, understood? You're already in the shit. No sense in bringing me into it is there?'

'Don't worry, I had no intention of telling anyone you told me. I told the guys from Reading CID I had no idea where Calder was and had nothing to do with the assault.'

'Come off it, Fleming. Why do you think I told you? We

might not get on, but I wanted to give you a chance to get even with Calder. Looking after our own kind.'

'That was very thoughtful of you, Bill,' Fleming retorted sarcastically. 'But your idea of looking out for me hasn't exactly been helpful, has it?'

'How was I to know you'd get three buffoons to do the job for you and that one of them would blab your name?'

'You're not listening to me. I had nothing to do with it.'

Watson grunted. 'You finished, Fleming? My drink's waiting for me.'

'Actually, no, I'm not. You see, you made it clear from the start you didn't want me in this job. You had an interest in getting me suspended. I think you told me where to find Calder and you arranged the assault, knowing that's exactly what would happen–'

'Fuck you, Fleming. Why would I tell you where to find him if I intended to get him done over myself?'

'I was wondering that,' Fleming said. 'Maybe you thought I would actually go after him, and when I didn't, you decided to do it for me.'

'You're paranoid, know that?'

Fleming raised an eyebrow. 'It makes sense though. And, if you had to, you might even eventually own up to letting it slip where he was, to make the case against me even stronger.'

'What? And get myself into trouble?'

'You could say you promised to let Police Scotland know if Calder turned up and that I may have overheard you talking to them.'

'Got it all worked out, haven't you, Fleming? Let me tell you, coincidences happen. Have you thought someone else may have it in for you? Maybe Damien Potts for instance.'

Fleming frowned. 'How would he know about Calder and me?'

Watson shrugged. 'You tell me. MCU leaks like a sieve at times. Logan knew, Temple knew. Maybe one of them spoke to someone else. Maybe the Scottish reporter who ran the story about Calder and you has contacts in England. Maybe even with the reporter Potts spoke to. Who knows?'

'But even if Potts found out about Calder, how would he know where he was?'

'Calder was working in a club. Potts worked in a club. Maybe word got out. How the fuck should I know?' He turned to push the pub door open. 'Think about it, Fleming,' Watson said over his shoulder as he went back inside.

Fleming stood for a moment and did think about it before returning to his car.

On the way home, something Watson had said suddenly struck him. How did he know that it was three men who'd assaulted Calder?

59

'What was the score on Sunday?' Logan asked with a wicked smile.

Anderson glowered at him. 'You've asked me that three times since yesterday. Memory starts to fade when you get older, I suppose.'

Logan laughed. 'I just like to hear you reminding me that you lost by six goals. Getting my own back for you gloating about my team being relegated.'

'I'd change allegiance if I were you,' Anderson quipped. 'Anyway, we may have lost by six goals, but I scored three. And it was only a friendly.'

'No such thing as a friendly football match. Teams still want to win.'

'You're so cynical, Sarge.'

Fleming arrived with some drinks. 'At it again, you two?'

'Naomi's a bit sensitive after losing at football over the weekend.' He lifted his arms over his head playfully as Anderson raised a hand as though to thump him.

The banter continued for a few minutes more as they enjoyed the sun and made small talk on the terrace of The

Trout Inn, the events of the previous day temporarily forgotten.

'What did Temple have to say about things after I left?' Fleming finally asked.

It was Logan who spoke. 'Bill Watson was there–'

'He's a nasty piece of work!' Anderson suddenly exclaimed. 'He's rude, uncouth, arrogant... He's... he's–'

'A bastard?' Logan offered.

'Yes.'

'The working relationship is off to a good start then,' Fleming observed with a smile.

'The super didn't say much about you,' Logan said. 'She confirmed you'd been suspended and that we'd be working for Watson with immediate effect. He wanted to know where we were at with the investigation.'

'And?'

'He blew his top when I mentioned that Naomi was following up on Anthony Hayden, but calmed down when she told him there was nothing on CCTV and that none of the neighbours saw him leave his house on the night of Nielson's murder.'

'He told me to stop work on tracing the owners of all the cars that did turn up on CCTV at Bourne End, and all of Nielson's business contacts. Said it was a waste of time since we'd arrested Rainer,' Anderson added.

Logan took a swig of his beer and put his glass down carefully on the table. 'He seems to have already decided it was a mistake to release Rainer, and Watson's asked for the search for the murder weapon to be stepped up.'

'And,' Anderson added, 'he scoffed at the idea that Nielson's murder might have been a revenge attack related to the old drugs investigation or the murder in Reading that Potts was convicted for.'

'He's decided it's either Rainer or Potts,' Logan chipped in. 'All other leads are on hold. Watson wants the whole investigation focused on finding the murder weapon and Potts. Speaking of which, we had no joy with Benny Madlock in Wandsworth. He'd no idea where Potts might have gone.' Logan sniffed the air and looked enviously towards a barman bringing out a plate of fish and chips to one of the nearby tables.

'No mention of Charles Trenchard then?' Fleming asked.

'The super said you wanted to question him again because you thought he lied about knowing Nielson.'

'And?'

Logan shrugged. 'She was adamant he wasn't to be questioned again.'

Fleming glanced across the terrace as raucous laughter suddenly broke out at a table at the far end near the river. A man had fallen backwards over his chair as he tried to push it to stand up. The man's face reddened as he realised he had become the focus of attention. He grinned sheepishly, murmured something and made off towards the toilets in a line that was somewhat less than straight.

'Hope he's not driving,' Logan said with a smile.

Fleming returned the conversation to Trenchard. 'You can't switch the TV or radio on these days without hearing something about Charles Trenchard.' He frowned. 'There's something... something that happened in Afghanistan that I wanted to talk to him about. And why he lied about Nielson...'

'He may not have lied,' Logan pointed out. 'Maybe he just couldn't remember him. Anyway, you needn't worry about him anymore, boss. Thankfully, neither need we. Orders are orders. Speaking of which...' Logan raised an empty glass. 'Who's for another?'

'My turn,' Anderson offered. She took the empty glasses and disappeared into the pub.

Fleming looked at Logan. 'I went to see Bill Watson last night at The White House pub.'

Logan frowned. 'I didn't know you socialised with him, boss.'

'It wasn't a social call.'

'Oh?'

Fleming leaned forwards in his chair. 'Harry, you didn't tell anyone else about what Watson had told you... I mean about Calder?'

Logan gasped. 'Of course not. Why?'

'Someone set me up for the assault on him. I think it might have been Watson–'

'What! You're joking, right?'

Fleming shook his head. 'I confronted him with it: told him I thought he was behind it. He denied it of course. Said it could have been Potts.'

'How did he make that out? Potts couldn't have known about you and Calder.'

'Watson couldn't answer that. He said it could have leaked out somehow. But he said it was obvious that Potts wanted me off the Nielson case because I was treating him as a suspect. Getting me suspended would have suited him just fine.'

'But you're not buying that?'

'No, I'm not. Watson also wanted me off the case because I was following up on the lead regarding his old mate, Anthony Hayden. He's also made it pretty obvious he thinks Frank Jardine should have got my job.'

'Bloody hell, boss. What are you going to do?'

'Did Temple, by any chance, mention how many men were involved in Calder's assault in the meeting with you, Naomi and Watson?'

Logan frowned. 'No, why?'

'Watson knew it was three men. How would he know that?'

Logan repeated himself. 'Bloody hell!'

'The thing is, I can't understand why he would go to such lengths to get me suspended. The whole thing's a bit risky, to say the least.'

Logan looked over Fleming's shoulder. 'Naomi's taking her time. How long does it take to get some–'

She came out with a tray of drinks and a plate of chips. 'Thought you might like something to eat,' she said, looking at Logan. 'I noticed you licking your lips when you saw some fish and chips coming out earlier.'

'Naomi, you're a star!' Logan beamed, helping himself to a chip. 'No ketchup?'

Anderson fished into a pocket and threw three sachets at Logan. 'Miss anything interesting?'

Logan ripped open a corner of one of the sachets and squeezed tomato sauce onto the side of the plate. 'The boss was telling me about a conspiracy theory.'

'About the Nielson murder?' Anderson asked.

Fleming helped himself to a chip. 'I think you and Harry need to be very careful with Watson. He's up to something. I was telling Harry that I think he set me up to get me suspended.'

'What! Why?'

'That's what I'm not sure about. I think he's trying to hide something... something he thought I might stumble across while investigating the Nielson case. I thought it was to do with the fact that I was treating his old mate Anthony Hayden as a possible suspect but I'm beginning to think there's more to it than that. He took a big risk if he was behind Calder's assault to get me off the case.'

Anderson suddenly looked worried and glanced from Logan to Fleming. 'What do we do?'

'You keep all of this to yourselves for now. Get on with the investigation, but keep me informed. I want to know Watson's every move.'

'You've got it, boss,' Logan confirmed.

'Speak to DS Crowe in Reading CID. Ask him to let you know if they make any progress in tracking down Calder's assailants.'

Logan's mobile rang. 'Better get this,' he said, fishing it out of his jacket pocket. He put his hand over the mouthpiece. 'DS Crowe,' he whispered. He listened intently, then exclaimed, 'What! Okay, well thanks for letting me know.' Logan snapped his phone shut, slipped it back into his pocket and looked gravely at Fleming.

'Well?' Fleming asked.

'Calder's had a heart attack. He's in intensive care.'

60

Damien Potts pulled grimy net curtains apart and peered nervously out of the window to the street below. McBain had moved him from the flat to a room above a pub in Brixton where the landlord owed him a favour. It was only a temporary hiding place McBain had told Potts, who was waiting for Tommy Tyler to pick him up in the black Audi that had driven him to the club a couple of weeks earlier.

Tyler was late. McBain had said that he would pick him up at eleven that night. 'Where the fuck are you?' Potts muttered.

There was little traffic on the street, but as Potts let the net curtains drop back into place the Audi pulled up at the end of the road. The lights flashed three times before Tyler dowsed them.

Potts grabbed his bag containing the few possessions he had and hurried down the stairs and out of the pub. A few seconds later, he pulled the passenger door of the car open. 'Took your fucking time, Tommy,' he grumbled as he threw his bag onto the back seat and jumped in.

Tyler shrugged. 'Traffic. You bring the money?'

McBain had told Potts to bring two grand in cash. He'd told

him that an old friend up in Glasgow wanted money up front for hiding a fugitive: especially one who was a suspect in a murder case. Potts nodded. 'Who's this guy McBain knows in Glasgow?'

Tyler turned the ignition on and slipped the car into gear. 'Fucked if I know. I just drive.' Tyler eased the car forwards and headed north.

'So where are we going?' Potts asked.

'Somewhere near Vauxhall. There's an old empty ware-house. McBain will be waiting there with the friend who'll drive you up to Glasgow. That's all I know.'

Potts grunted and stared ahead. Neither man spoke again.

A few minutes later, Tyler took a right hand turn down a narrow side street, then turned left into a potholed road that ran down the side of an old building with boarded-up windows. He turned at the far end of the building and drove through open doors into a large empty area with a concrete floor. Rows of rusting steel joists supported the roof. The car screeched to a halt and clouds of dust settled round the car as Tyler extinguished the lights.

Potts heard the roller doors sliding down with a grating of steel as he got out of the car. A large flashlight suddenly switched on by the door of an office. He couldn't make out the dark figure from behind the light. He narrowed his eyes against the glare. 'That you, Scottie?'

'Sure. Come and join me in the office,' McBain said. The flashlight turned inwards to show a small empty room apart from one chair. McBain hung the flashlight on a hook on the wall and motioned towards the chair. 'Take a seat, Damien.'

Potts approached cautiously and looked nervously around him. Something wasn't right about this. 'Where's your Glaswegian friend?' he asked anxiously.

'He'll be here presently,' McBain said. 'I just want to have a little chat while we're waiting.' He tapped the chair with his foot. 'Sit down.'

Potts knew something was wrong. He turned around but Tyler was blocking the open door, arms folded. 'What's the matter, Scottie? What do you want to talk about? I've brought the money if that's it. It's in the bag in the car. I'll go and get it for–'

McBain grabbed Potts by his coat lapels and shoved him down onto the chair.

'Fuck, Scottie. What is this? What's wrong?' Potts asked, sweat breaking out on his forehead.

McBain thrust his face in front of Potts. 'I was doing you a favour, you fucking idiot! I found somewhere for you to stay when you got out of prison. I gave you some work. And what do you do to repay me? You screw everything up!'

'I... I don't know what you mean, Scottie. What have I done?'

'You thought this detective guy, DCI Fleming, was going to nail you for Ronnie's murder, right?'

'Yes. I'm sure he thinks I did it.'

'And I agreed to help you out yet again, right?'

'Yes, but–'

'Fleming came to see me, looking for you. I covered up for you. Said I didn't have a clue where you were.' McBain glared at Potts who was cowering in the chair. 'Then I find out you went to the press making all sorts of claims about police corruption–'

'I... I can explain that,' Potts started to say, but McBain didn't wait for the explanation.

'You told the reporter that you didn't have any names, right?'

Potts was panicking. 'No... no I don't–'

'You sure about that?' McBain's voice had lowered to a threatening whisper.

'No. I haven't. But why are you bothered about that? I'd have thought anything against the police would be music to your ears.'

'Is that so? Shall I tell you how you've fucked up, you drugged-up moron? The cops that Ronnie had in his pocket are now looking after me in return for a few favours and backhanders. Where do you think I get all my inside information from and how we manage to keep them off our backs at the club?'

'Oh, shit! I'm sorry, Scottie. I didn't know... honest! I'll keep quiet. I won't speak to the press again.'

'Damned right you won't!'

Potts was confused. 'Hang on, why did you have to cover up for me when Fleming came to see you if he's on the take?'

'You're not getting it, Damien, are you? Fleming isn't one of them. He's after you because you're a suspect. But you've now put the bent cops into a difficult position.'

'How... how do you mean?'

'They don't want you to be found. It's too risky. They might think you know who they are. See what I mean?'

'Oh, God! I swear I won't say anything!'

McBain shrugged. 'Too late, Damien. They want me to make sure. I need to keep them on my side so–'

Potts jumped out of the chair and kicked it into McBain. He pulled a flick knife out of his jeans back pocket, pressed a button on the side of the handle and a short silver blade shot out. He turned and lunged at Tyler standing by the door. The blade sliced across his face as he staggered backwards.

Potts raced past him, making for the roller doors. He dropped the knife and used both hands to try and open them. He heard the Audi engine roar into life and turned to see Tyler behind the wheel. The car lurched forward with tyres squealing. The headlights flicked on and shone at Potts. He froze for a second. Putting an arm up against the glare, he tried to run from the car bearing down on him but slipped and fell. He groaned and pulled himself to his feet, but it was too late. Tyler slammed the car into Potts and pinned him against a wall. Potts screamed in agony as Tyler revved the engine and eased the car forwards until Potts's broken body slumped over the bonnet. Tyler got out of the car and picked up the knife Potts had dropped on the floor. He stood over Potts. Blood was trickling from the corner of his mouth.

Potts tried to speak, but his voice was barely a whisper. 'Please...'

Tyler grinned and plunged the blade into Potts's back.

'Think that just about does it, boss,' Tyler said to McBain, standing beside him. 'He won't be saying anything to anyone.'

McBain looked at Potts's lifeless body. 'Guess not.'

Tyler dabbed at the cut on his face with a handkerchief before reversing the car away from Potts, whose lifeless body slid to the ground. Tyler looked at the front of the car. 'Not much damage.'

'Get the tarpaulin out of the boot,' McBain ordered tersely, 'and make sure the money's in the bag.'

The two men wrapped Potts up in the tarpaulin and tied it securely with rope.

Five minutes later, they were heading towards the river. Turning into a small road with a row of warehouses on one side and the Thames on the other, they checked no one was in sight before getting out of the car and dragging the tarpaulin out of the boot. They tipped it over the wall into the Thames, jumped back into the car and accelerated away with a screech of tyres.

Doug Harper, managing director of Harper Haulage, had been working late into the night. He left his office and crossed the warehouse yard to his car. He was about to get in when he heard a loud splash. Walking to the entrance of the yard, he saw two men jump into an Audi and speed off. Curious, Doug crossed the road and looked over the wall. The river was flowing fast at high tide. He could just make out a half-submerged object drifting up the river.

61

'You're looking pensive, darling. Is everything all right?' Charles Trenchard's wife Helen asked, handing him a gin and tonic.

He was sitting in his back garden, enjoying the evening sun in his favourite place on the lawn overlooking the Thames. A laptop computer was open in front of him on a small circular white table. He was working on a speech he was to make the next day at the Conservative Club in Henley. He knew he would be on home ground, but reporters would be there so he needed to be prepared for any awkward questions and how to deal with them.

'Fine. Working on my speech for tomorrow. I need to choose every word carefully. The press are good at putting words into your mouth.'

'I'm sure you'll be fine, darling. You always give a good speech.'

Trenchard smiled. 'What time's dinner?'

'I'll put it on in an hour. DCI Fleming won't stay with you too long, will he?'

'No, I'm sure he'll only be a few minutes. I told him to be here for six.'

Helen went back inside and Trenchard returned to his thoughts as he watched a passenger boat coast by. Loud music and laughter suggested it was a party cruise. Some people looked across and waved. Waving back, Trenchard took a sip of his gin and wondered why Fleming wanted to speak to him again. He'd seemed to accept that he couldn't remember the other men on the photograph he'd shown him.

Helen calling from the house interrupted his thoughts. 'DCI Fleming's here, darling.'

On his drive down to Henley-On-Thames, Fleming was going over things in his mind. Calder's heart attack was bad news. He had no desire for the man to live other than the fact that it would make his situation much worse if he died. Maybe Logan will have managed to find out from DS Crowe if he'd made any progress in finding the men who had assaulted Calder. Watson was behind it. Of that Fleming was sure. But if he was, he was taking a massive risk. Why?

Then there was the big risk he was taking himself, having arranged to meet Charles Trenchard again despite Temple warning him off. And he had no authority since she'd suspended him. His whole career could be at stake, but his gut instinct told him it was a risk worth taking. From what Logan had told him, no one else was going to go anywhere near the man.

Fleming put his thoughts to one side as he parked his Porsche on the gravel driveway in front of Trenchard's house. His wife showed Fleming through the house to the lawn at the back where he could see Trenchard sitting looking out towards the river. She shouted to him to let him know his visitor had arrived.

Trenchard rose from his seat and turned to face Fleming. He offered a hand and smiled. 'Chief Inspector Fleming, how nice to see you again. Do come and have a seat. Enjoy the view.'

Fleming shook hands and joined Trenchard at his table.

Trenchard lifted his gin and tonic. 'Can I get Helen to get you one? Or perhaps something without alcohol?'

'That's very kind, but no thanks. I won't take up much of your time.' He nodded at the open laptop. 'I can see you're busy.'

Trenchard smiled. 'Afraid so. Preparing a speech for tomorrow.' He tilted his head. 'I must say I was somewhat surprised you wanted to speak to me again. I wasn't able to help you with the people on your photograph and don't see how I can be of further assistance.'

Fleming chose his words carefully. 'I went to see Giles Bonner...'

'Who?' Trenchard asked innocently without taking his eyes off Fleming.

'He was one of the men in the photograph I showed you a couple of weeks ago.'

'Ah, yes, of course he was. Sorry, I forgot. Name doesn't mean anything to me.'

'No worries.' Fleming hesitated before speaking again. 'The only thing is... he remembers you.'

Trenchard's eyes narrowed and he met Fleming's steady gaze. 'Really? I'm sorry, I still don't–'

'From your army service in Afghanistan,' Fleming prompted.

'Yes, quite, you've just reminded me he was in the photograph. But as I explained to you before, I don't remember him. Nor could I possibly remember the names of all the other people in Afghanistan who appear in photographs with me. I didn't know half of them very well. This chap... Bonner, you say... must have a better memory than me.'

Fleming kept his gaze on Trenchard. 'Yes, he was sure of his facts. He told me that all of the men in the photograph I showed you served in C Company and that there were three platoons. You were one of the platoon commanders. Ronnie Nielson was your sergeant. You also told me you didn't remember him...'

'That's correct. Look–'

'Beginning to ring any bells now?'

Trenchard took a slow sip of his drink before answering. 'I was an army officer for twelve years, Chief Inspector. I don't remember all of the sergeants who served under me, I'm afraid.'

Fleming shrugged. 'I'm sure, but Afghanistan was your last posting with the army, wasn't it? Surely you can remember the last sergeant to serve under you? Especially somewhere as memorable as Afghanistan,' Fleming pressed.

'Maybe he was only with me a short time. Personnel changed. Sometimes quite quickly, you may appreciate.' Trenchard looked duly solicitous. 'I'm sorry you seem to have had another wasted trip. Are you sure I can't get you something before you go?' he said with a smile.

Fleming noted the hint that it was time for him to leave, but he wasn't ready yet. 'Eddie Slater, one of the other men in the photograph, served under Bonner. He was one of Nielson's best friends apparently–'

'Chief Inspector, I don't mean to be rude, but I'm not sure where you're going with this and I do need to get on with my speech.'

'He told Bonner that Nielson didn't see eye to eye with you...' Fleming persisted.

'This is childish tittle-tattle. I'm sure there were many men who didn't like me. My job was to manage and lead, not make friends.'

'Yes, I get that, only–'

'Chief Inspector, may I be frank with you and save you beating about the bush. For some reason you seem to be trying to establish that I knew this chap Nielson well. Let me reassure you that I did not. And, for the record, I had a meeting with Leo Miller in London on the night that Nielson was killed.'

Fleming was taken aback by Trenchard's sudden outburst. 'I'm sorry. I hope I didn't give the impression that I was treating you as a suspect. I was merely trying to get some background on whether Nielson was a particularly volatile character.' He rose to leave. 'I'm sorry to have troubled you again. Thank you for your time.'

Trenchard got out of his chair smiling and offered a hand to Fleming. 'Not at all, my dear chap. Not at all. Helen will see you out.'

'Thank you. Sorry once again to bother you. Good luck with the speech, by the way, and the leadership election.'

Charles Trenchard waited for Fleming to leave and picked up his mobile. He needed to get Chief Inspector Fleming off his back. The last thing Trenchard needed was the press looking for a story with him involved in a police investigation.

Later that evening, Fleming phoned Logan. 'Can you check with Leo Miller's secretary to see if he had a meeting with Charles Trenchard on the night of Ronnie Nielson's murder?'

'Oh, shit, boss. Please don't tell me you've been to see Trenchard.'

'Don't worry. No one will know. It was just an informal chat to clear a few things up. Check, but don't let Watson or Temple know. Okay?'

'Bloody hell, boss, that makes him the fifth suspect, that is if you want to include Watson.'

'Watson?'

'Just saying.'

Fleming shook his head and ignored what Logan had said.

62

'What if DCI Watson asks where you are?' Anderson asked Logan.

'Tell him I've gone to check on the surveillance on Rainer and, if I've got enough time, see if I can get any leads from staff at Nielson's club on where Potts might have disappeared to.'

Anderson raised her eyebrows. 'I hope you know what you're doing, Sarge.'

'Don't worry.' Logan pulled his jacket off the back of his chair and made for the door. 'See you later,' he called over his shoulder.

Logan headed for Oxford, took the A34 south, then headed east on the M4 towards Reading. He was worried about Fleming. First, there was the Calder business. He had left himself wide open by going to Edinburgh, and now he was suspended pending enquiries into the assault. To make matters worse, Calder was still in intensive care after suffering another heart attack. Fleming had told Logan he thought Bill Watson was behind the assault. Why would he do that? Then Fleming had gone to see Charles Trenchard while suspended. Things didn't look good.

Logan put his thoughts to one side as he wove through the streets of Reading towards the police station. He parked the car and made his way to the reception desk where he told the duty sergeant he was there to see DS Crowe.

Five minutes later, Crowe was showing him into the CID office where DC Valdez was staring into a computer screen.

'Budget doesn't run to tea and biscuits for meetings with police staff, I'm afraid,' Crowe told him. 'There's a vending machine over there if you want a drink.' He pointed across the office.

Logan wasn't that desperate. 'I'll give that a miss, I think.'

'You wanted to talk about Jimmy Calder, said something on the phone about his assault maybe being linked to a case you're working on. What case is that?'

Logan decided that total openness was the best way to get Crowe's co-operation. 'A murder. A guy called Ronnie Nielson. Owned a club in London. He was found dead on his boat near Bourne End Marina.'

Crowe nodded. 'Yeah, I heard about that. What's the connection?'

Logan rubbed his chin. 'We're not certain there is one, but we think it's possible one of the suspects may have tried to set DCI Fleming up to get him off the case. A guy called Potts. Incidentally, he's gone missing.'

Crowe frowned. 'And you think Potts arranged the assault on Calder and got the assailants to tell him that DCI Fleming had sent them?'

'That's about it.'

'I don't get it,' Crowe said, shaking his head. 'For one thing, how would Potts have known about Jimmy Calder? Secondly, what would be the point of getting Fleming suspended? Potts would still be a suspect in the Nielson case, wouldn't he?'

Logan was about to answer, but Crowe continued. 'And I have to say, there's some pretty damning evidence against Fleming. He knew Calder was out of prison. He went to Edinburgh looking for him, and he suddenly took ill over the weekend when Calder was assaulted.'

'You make it sound convincing. We don't know how Potts could have known about Calder. That's anyone's guess. I take your second point, but Potts isn't exactly the brightest gem in the box, and he's a man who bears grudges. As to the evidence against DCI Fleming, have you found anything on his phone or computer to link him to the assailants?'

'No, we haven't.'

'So there you are. There's no hard evidence. Just the word of a man who's a known criminal.'

Crowe nodded slowly. 'What we have so far is CCTV footage from the bar at the club where Calder was working and of a van passing outside around the time he left. The same van appears later at the Royal Berkshire Hospital where his body was thrown out.'

'You've traced the owner of the van?'

'Afraid not. They were using fake number plates.'

'Are there any other leads you're following?'

'A barman at the club saw Calder talking to two men. They bought him a drink and were seen leaving at the same time as Calder. The barman reckons he'd never seen them there before.' He motioned towards Valdez. 'Come and have a look at this.'

Logan followed Crowe across the room to where Valdez was sitting at his computer. He watched as Valdez flashed the cursor across the screen and clicked on files rapidly. Suddenly, the CCTV footage appeared with the black van passing the club. Then, after a few more clicks, the same van appeared dumping a body in front of the hospital before driving off at speed.

'What about the men at the bar?' Logan asked.

Crowe nodded at Valdez. 'Show him.'

The cursor flashed quickly round the screen again. Two clicks of the mouse and the bar sprang onto the screen. Crowe pointed out the two men the barman had told him about, but their backs were to the camera. Then one of the men turned and gazed around the club floor.

'Freeze it there!' Logan exclaimed.

'Recognise him?' Crowe asked hopefully.

'Yes,' Logan confirmed. 'A guy called Tommy Tyler. He drives an Audi for Scottie McBain, the manager of Nielson's club.'

Liz Temple slammed her phone down after the chief constable had rung off. She cursed and wondered how far Fleming was going to test her patience. Charles Trenchard had lodged a complaint against Fleming with the chief constable. He'd claimed that Fleming was harassing him. Upson wanted blood.

63

Word had spread round the MCU that Temple had sent for Fleming. He received a few awkward glances as he made his way to her office.

He knocked on the door and waited.

There was an edge in Temple's voice. 'Yes!'

Fleming entered uneasily and saw the stern look.

'Close the door,' Temple said curtly, looking up from the file on her desk. 'Sit down, Alex.'

Fleming sat on the chair placed in front of Temple's desk.

She glared at him, face still stony. 'I gather you've decided you do not want to be accompanied by a police friend at this meeting. Is that correct?'

'Yes, ma'am.'

Temple leaned forwards and folded her arms over her desk. 'I take it I don't need to remind you of the seriousness of your position.'

'No, ma'am.'

'You know why I've sent for you?'

'I think I can guess.'

Temple glowered at Fleming. 'Despite being under suspension, and despite me giving you explicit instructions not to, you went to see Charles Trenchard again.'

Fleming shifted uncomfortably in his chair and remained silent.

Temple sighed. 'The chief constable hauled me over the coals. He'd had a call from Trenchard who's made a formal complaint against you. He claims you're harassing him. Upson is livid.'

'Sorry,' was all Fleming could think of saying.

'Sorry! You bet your arse you will be!' Temple exploded. 'It's bad enough disobeying orders, but to carry on with an investigation while suspended is bloody irresponsible!'

'Yes, ma'am.'

'Christ, Alex, is that all you can say? What on earth possessed you?'

'There was something about Trenchard when I first spoke to him. I was sure he was being evasive. Then I found out that he'd lied to me about knowing Ronnie Nielson–'

'You told me that, and I said it wasn't unreasonable for someone to forget a name, did I not?'

'You did, yes.'

'And I told you not to see him again. Is that correct?'

'Yes, ma'am.'

Temple placed her hands on the edge of her desk. 'I'm afraid you've gone too far this time, Alex. Upson has asked me to instigate misconduct proceedings against you for breach of the Standards of Professional Behaviour. This is in relation to the accusations made against you regarding Jimmy Calder, for disobeying a direct order while under suspension, and due to the complaint of harassment made against you by Charles Trenchard. There will be a disciplinary hearing following a full enquiry into the circumstances. You will get confirmation of this in writing. Do you understand?'

'Yes, ma'am.'

'Christ, Alex, at best you could be demoted to constable and put in uniform back on the beat. You could even face dismissal, depending on the outcome of the enquiry. What were you thinking of?'

Fleming shrugged. 'I had nothing to do with Calder's assault. I was set up. And I went to see Trenchard because I believed it to be necessary. I knew no one else would. I'm sure my name will be cleared on the Calder business and that my actions regarding Charles Trenchard will be justified.'

'If you were set up over Calder, as you claim, you're going to have to be able to prove it. And I don't see how your actions relating to Trenchard will be vindicated. You messed up big time. Your judgement is questionable, to say the least.'

Fleming said nothing.

Temple looked down at the file she'd been reading when Fleming arrived. 'That's all, DCI Fleming. Close the door behind you,' she said without looking up again.

Fleming left.

He didn't bother to call in on Logan and Anderson on his way out. He noted that Temple had reverted to calling him by rank and surname rather than Alex.

As he drove home, he could see the end of his short career in the MCU looming fast.

64

The atmosphere in interview room two was tense. It was hot and stuffy. Sweat had broken out on Tommy Tyler's forehead. A solicitor sat grimly beside him. On the other side of the table, DS Crowe was looking at a note the duty sergeant had just passed to him. Logan was there looking across the table at Tyler. Logan had asked if he could be present.

Tyler was worried. Crowe had arrested him in connection with the assault on Calder. But he wondered if he knew anything about Potts. Surely not, he thought. It had only been two days since he and McBain had tossed him into the Thames. And there hadn't been anything on the news to say a body had been found. No, he assured himself, this was just to do with the Calder guy.

Crowe pressed the record button. 'Interview recommenced at eleven a.m.' He slipped the note under the folder in front of him. 'Mr Tyler, you said you didn't know Jimmy Calder and had never been to the Lyons Den nightclub in Reading.'

'Yeah, that's right,' Tyler spat.

'Where were you on the night of the tenth of July?'

Tyler sneered. 'At Nielson's Cellar in London.'

'Can anyone vouch for you?'

'Yeah, sure. The boss, Scottie McBain. He was at the club.'

Crowe took a photograph from the folder in front of him. He slid it across the table for Tyler to see. 'For the purposes of the tape, I'm presenting Mr Tyler with photograph reference P671007X. This is a still taken from CCTV footage at the Lyons Den nightclub on the night of tenth of July. The night that Jimmy Calder was assaulted. Do you recognise this man?'

Tyler glanced at his solicitor who simply nodded. 'It's me,' Tyler admitted resignedly.

'So why did you lie and claim you'd never been there?' Crowe pressed.

'All right, I was there, but I don't know nothing about this guy Calder, honest. I lied because I didn't know you had photos and didn't want to get mixed up in something I didn't do.'

Crowe took the photograph back and slipped it into the folder.

Tyler's eyes shot shiftily from Crowe to Logan and back to Crowe. Tyler licked his lips nervously.

'You still claim you didn't know Calder, or of him?' Crowe asked.

'No, I didn't!' Tyler burst out.

'So why buy a man a drink you didn't know?'

'I didn't!'

'Come on, Tommy. We have a witness. The barman remembers seeing you buying him a drink,' Crowe persisted.

'I had nothing to do with this! I felt sorry for the man, that's all. He was working hard clearing glasses.' More confident, he added with a smirk, 'Too generous by half, that's me.'

Crowe changed tack. 'Who was the man with you at the bar?'

Tyler's eyes averted Crowe's steady gaze. He stared at the wall then slouched back in his chair and stretched. 'Haven't got a clue, he sat beside me. Never seen him before.'

'Barman says the two of you were deep in conversation. Do you normally start up conversations with complete strangers?'

Tyler sneered at Crowe. 'I'm friendly as well as generous.'

Crowe glared at Tyler. 'The barman says you and your stranger friend left the club at the same time just behind Calder. Shortly after that, CCTV footage outside the club picked up a black van crawling by.'

'So?'

Crowe continued. 'The same van was picked up again, speeding away from the Royal Berkshire Hospital after dumping Calder's body outside.'

Tyler shrugged. 'Don't remember seeing a black van.'

'How did you get the cut on your face?' Crowe asked.

'Bit of an accident at the club. Some guy was drunk and lunged at me with a glass. It's nothing.'

'Did you report it?'

'Hell no. He was drunk... didn't know what he was doing. As I said, it was nothing.'

Crowe scowled at Tyler and drew the note out he'd placed under his folder. He looked hard at it then glanced sharply up at Tyler. 'Okay, Tommy, here's the thing. We have enough to charge you with assault, but I've been told that Jimmy Calder has taken a turn for the worse. The charge becomes a murder charge. You could be heading for life inside unless you co-operate and start talking.'

The blood had drained from Tyler's face, sweat running freely down his forehead. He looked pleadingly at his solicitor.

'It's best to tell the truth now,' the solicitor said. 'They might be more lenient on you if you do. Isn't that right, DS Crowe?'

Crowe shrugged. 'A judge will always take into consideration the extent to which someone helps the police with their enquiries.'

Tyler slumped across the table and sobbed.

Crowe looked toward the recorder. 'For the purposes of the tape, the suspect is crying.'

Tyler looked up and wiped his eyes. 'I only had to follow him out of the club and help get him in the back of the van,' he whispered.

'Can you speak up for the tape,' Crowe prompted.

'I was only to follow him out of the club and help get him in the back of the van!' Tyler shouted.

'Who else was involved?' Crowe asked gently.

There was a look of terror in Tyler's eyes. 'Oh, God! They'll kill me!'

'Who?'

'Scottie... Scottie McBain. He was driving the van. He's the manager of a club in London, Nielson's Cellar.'

'And the other man with you at the bar? The man with blond hair and the ponytail?'

'Eckhard... Paddy Eckhard. He works at Nielson's Cellar.'

'Okay, Tommy. You'll be charged with assault and bailed to appear in court. But if Calder dies you'll be facing a murder charge. Interview terminated at eleven-twenty.'

Tyler's eyes widened. 'But... but Scottie and Paddy will kill me if they find out I shopped them.'

'Don't worry, we'll be pulling them in as well.'

Tyler put his head in his hands. 'I'm a dead man.'

65

F leming's mobile phone was ringing and vibrating on the coffee table beside him. He cursed and wished DS Crowe hadn't been so prompt in returning it. Fleming opened his bloodshot eyes and peered at the screen: *Logan*.

'Harry?'

'Hi, boss. Are you at home?'

'Yes.'

'Okay for me to come round to see you after work? Say seven? I have a bit of news.'

'Fine, I'll be here. See you later.' Fleming cut the call and went to make himself a strong coffee.

He'd had a bad night after drinking too much whisky, then woke up with a dreadful hangover. He wasn't sure if his mental state was due to anxiety over his future in the MCU, his past trauma, or both. Overall, things did not look too rosy.

A couple of hours later and after several cups of coffee, Fleming's door buzzer sounded.

Logan frowned when he saw an unshaven bloodshot-eyed Fleming. 'You look a bit rough, if you don't mind me saying so, boss. I haven't eaten since breakfast and I've brought some fish and chips. Got two lots, in case you hadn't eaten either.'

Fleming forced a smile. Good old Harry. He'd grown fond of his sergeant. Always reliable, dependable, and a damned good detective. 'Thanks, Harry. Very thoughtful of you. I haven't eaten. Bit too much whisky last night I'm afraid. Been on coffee all day.'

'There you are then. Just what you need, a nice fish and chip supper. Not too greasy either,' he added quickly at the grimace on Fleming's face. 'Plates or out of the paper?' he asked jovially.

'Plates, I think,' Fleming said. 'Coffee?'

'Don't suppose you have any beer in the fridge?'

Fleming disappeared into the kitchen and came back with plates and two cans of beer. 'Might as well join you,' he said, passing a can to Logan.

They ate in silence for a few minutes before Fleming asked, 'So, what's this news?'

Logan swallowed a mouthful of chips and took a swig of his beer. 'I went to see DS Crowe in Reading. He had some CCTV footage of the club where Calder was working on the night he was assaulted and guess what? Tommy Tyler, the Audi driver who works for Scottie McBain, appears large as life at the bar with another man. One of the barmen saw them buying drinks for Calder and they left the club right behind him. Crowe pulled Tyler in for questioning this morning...'

Fleming raised an eyebrow. 'And?'

'Crowe told him that Calder had taken a turn for the worse

and Tyler could be facing a murder charge. Said he could be heading for life unless he started talking. Anyway, he finally admitted that Scottie McBain and a guy called Paddy Eckhard were the other two men involved.'

Fleming frowned. 'Paddy Eckhard?'

'Works for McBain at Nielson's Cellar. Long blond hair... ponytail at the back.'

Fleming nodded. 'I've met him. He was at Nielson's club when I visited. Have McBain and Eckhard been arrested?'

'Warrant's out on them. I'll let you know.'

Fleming saw a glimmer of hope. 'Maybe DS Crowe will get them to say who put them up to the assault.'

Logan forked a piece of fish into his mouth and chewed on it. He looked thoughtful. 'What if McBain claims it was you?'

Fleming shook his head. 'He would have to prove it, and he can't.'

Logan washed the fish down with a swig of beer and nodded. 'DS Crowe did confirm that there was nothing on your mobile or computer to incriminate you.'

'It's Watson. I'm sure of it.'

Logan chewed another mouthful of chips. 'What did the super want you for?' he asked eventually.

Fleming sighed. 'Temple isn't a happy bunny. The chief constable's been on her back. Charles Trenchard phoned him to complain I was harassing him.'

'Oh, shit!' Logan exclaimed, choking on a mouthful of beer.

'He's asked Temple to start misconduct proceedings against me... breach of the Standards of Professional Behaviour.'

'What, because of a bloody toffee-nosed politician?'

'That's part of it. There's also the Calder incident, ignoring an order not to speak to Trenchard again, and doing so while suspended.'

Logan grimaced. 'You don't do things by half, I'll grant you that, boss.'

'Talking about Trenchard, did you manage to check with Leo Miller's private office to see if he did have a meeting with him the night Nielson was murdered?'

'Yes, I did, but there seems to be some confusion. I spoke to a civil servant who said Miller's diary had been free that evening and there was no record of a meeting with Trenchard. The assistant thought that strange because the chancellor was always meticulous in insisting that all his engagements were in the diary.'

'Now I'm even more convinced that Trenchard was lying to me.'

'Could have been an informal, personal meeting,' Logan offered.

'Maybe, but it wouldn't be wise to investigate that further at this stage bearing in mind Trenchard's complaint about being harassed. You need to steer clear of him for now.'

'Definitely.'

'Any other progress on the Nielson case?'

'Nope, still haven't been able to find the murder weapon, or Potts for that matter. Rainer's still under surveillance but it doesn't look like he's about to do a runner.'

'Okay. Thanks for the fish and chips, Harry. Keep in touch, yeah?'

'Sure thing, boss.'

Logan's mobile phone rang as he was getting up to leave. The incoming call was from Anderson. 'Hello, Naomi, what's new?'

Logan listened intently for a few seconds and his eyes widened.

Fleming could hear the sound of Anderson's voice, but couldn't make out what she was saying.

Logan cut the call and looked at Fleming in shock.

'What's up?' Fleming asked.

'Naomi's just taken a call from the Met. Potts is dead. A jogger found his body washed up on the shore of the Thames.'

66

DS Crowe had arranged with the Met for Scottie McBain and Paddy Eckhard to be held in separate interview rooms at West End Central Police Station. Logan was with him in interview room four where Crowe was questioning McBain.

Logan stared at McBain who was looking nonchalantly up at the ceiling while drumming his fingers on the table. They were waiting for an answer.

'Well?' Crowe prompted.

'No comment,' McBain grunted.

'Refusing to answer questions is not doing much for your position,' Crowe pointed out.

'Go fuck yourself,' McBain spat, arms folded defiantly.

'We have Tommy Tyler and Paddy Eckhard both on CCTV at the Lyons Den nightclub in Reading on the night Jimmy Calder was assaulted.'

McBain said nothing.

'Do you still deny being involved in the assault on Calder?' Crowe persisted.

McBain glared at Crowe. 'I had nothing to do with it,' he said, lounging back in his chair.

'Tyler and Eckhard bought Calder drinks.'

'Did they?'

'Tyler told us you drove the van.'

McBain shrugged. 'He's getting mixed up with another day.'

'Paddy Eckhard confirmed you were the driver.'

McBain leaned across the table. 'He got the wrong day as well then, didn't he?'

Crowe glared at McBain. 'I don't think so. You, Tyler and Eckhard could be facing a murder charge. Calder's in a bad way. Had a massive heart attack. He's still in intensive care.'

McBain smirked. 'So now you want to pin someone's heart attack on me! You're having a laugh.'

'Your mates panicked and want to do a deal. They'll admit to the assault and plead guilty in return for leniency. We'd be prepared to consider a charge of manslaughter rather than murder if Calder dies. After all, you did take him to hospital... in a manner of speaking. Hardly the actions of someone intent on murder.'

McBain's eyes narrowed and he sucked in air through his teeth.

Crowe continued. 'Your two mates have signed statements confirming you were in charge.'

McBain lurched to his feet. 'Bastards! I'll get them for this!'

Crowe was unruffled. 'Please sit down, Mr McBain.'

Logan had pushed himself up from his chair. He was ready to restrain McBain in case he tried to launch himself across the interview table at Crowe. He put a hand on McBain's shoulder and gently pushed him back onto his seat. McBain slumped into the chair without resistance. The smug demeanour had deserted him.

Logan wondered if McBain would say who it was who had put him up to the assault and why. Fleming was sure it was Watson. But what possible link could there be between McBain and Watson?

Crowe must have read Logan's thoughts. 'You could make things easier on yourself if you co-operate, Mr McBain. Tell us who was behind this. Who asked you to assault Calder?'

McBain said nothing.

'Whoever it was must be laughing now,' Crowe continued. 'They got what they wanted and they're off the hook. He's probably thinking to himself, *Scottie will take the wrap. Good man. He won't involve me.* If Calder dies, you could go down for murder. Maybe just manslaughter, if you play your cards right.'

McBain still said nothing.

Crowe continued. 'So, you go down and he walks free. Must be paying you well to keep him out of it. A person who intentionally encourages an offence to be committed can get the same sentence as you. Did you know that?'

McBain stayed silent.

'You want to take the wrap and let him go free? Think he would do the same for you?'

'You're saying you could go easy on me if I tell you?'

'That's right,' Crowe lied.

'And if I give you a bit extra, how do I stand?' McBain blurted.

Crowe shrugged nonchalantly. 'Like what?'

Logan sat impassively, but he too was wondering what McBain thought he had to offer.

McBain licked his lips. 'I'll need protection... a safeguard...'

Crowe frowned. 'It can be arranged if necessary. Go on.'

'There's this detective. A DCI. He was behind it. A guy called Watson. He used to work for the Met but he's with Thames Valley CID now...'

Crowe glanced at Logan, then back at McBain. 'So why did DCI Watson ask you to assault Calder and tell him that DCI Fleming was behind it?'

McBain shook his head. 'No idea. We just did what he asked us to do.'

Logan chipped in. 'How come you and DCI Watson knew each other? Is it to do with the extra information you were talking about?'

McBain nodded submissively. 'When DCI Watson worked for the Met, he was on the take from Ronnie Nielson. There were three of them: DCI Watson, DCI Hayden, and DI Jardine. They kept Ronnie and the club out of trouble in return for a few favours and backhanders. When Ronnie was killed, Watson wanted to carry on the arrangement. Said he had friends in the Met and he could still look after us.'

Crowe looked at Logan and said, 'I think we need to take a break here. Interview terminated at eleven-thirty.'

Logan was in shock. This had turned into something entirely more serious. No wonder Watson wanted Fleming off the Nielson case. There was always the risk he might find out that Watson, Hayden and Jardine were corrupt. Christ, what a mess! But at least Fleming was in the clear over Calder.

On his way back to Long Hanborough, Logan wondered how they would prove what McBain had claimed. After all, they only had his word.

Liz Temple took the call from DS Crowe just before noon. She frowned as she put the phone down. He wanted to come and see her straight away, and no, he couldn't say over the phone what it was about. It was far too sensitive.

67

I t was early on Saturday morning. Thunder was rumbling in the distance and the first spots of rain began to pelt against the window. Bill Watson had been about to leave the house for the office. He was in a bad mood having fallen behind with his paperwork during the week and had to go in on what should have been a day off. He cursed and was on his way to fetch his raincoat when his phone rang. Snatching it out of its cradle, he growled into the mouthpiece. 'Watson!'

'You all right, boss?' Frank Jardine asked. 'You sound a bit harassed.'

'Too fucking right I am. Bloody weather... and I have to come in today to catch up on paperwork. Anyway, what do you want?'

'Thought you ought to know... Scottie McBain, Tommy Tyler and Paddy Eckhard have been arrested for the assault on Jimmy Calder.'

Watson drew in a sharp intake of breath. This was the last thing he needed to hear.

'Boss? You still there?'

'I'm still here. Listen, keep me informed. I've just realised something. Change of plan. I'll not be coming into the office after all. You can sort out the overtime forms for me. I'll be back in on Monday.'

'Okay, boss. Whatever you say.' Jardine rang off.

Watson put the phone down slowly, deep in thought. Would McBain involve him in the Calder business, or would he stay quiet? How the fuck did they get caught anyway? More worryingly, he felt the noose tightening on the police corruption. He was within a whisker of being exposed. *If McBain squeals, I'll have to front it out*, he thought. *Deny it of course. Say there's no proof.*

It was only McBain's word about Calder. And as far as corruption was concerned, Watson could say that McBain had had it in for him ever since he was investigating Nielson's club while with the Met. Bit thin, but that would have to do.

There was a loud clap of thunder and the house seemed to shake. Watson went back into the living room, poured himself a whisky and slumped into his armchair. If McBain did talk, they would suspend Watson pending a full enquiry. If they found proof, Temple would reinstate Fleming and Watson would be off the force. He needed to think straight. He hadn't known about Emma Hayden's affair with Nielson until bloody Fleming found out. Would Nielson have told her that he, her husband and Frank Jardine were on the take? Did she know anything? Watson stared blankly at the rain running down the window. He really was in trouble if Emma knew they were bent cops. Watson made up his mind. He would pay her a visit.

❧

Emma's house was on the other side of Woodstock. Watson would have taken the car even if it were two streets away due to the torrential rain. He'd phoned to make sure she was at home. He eased his car onto Emma's driveway and parked behind her

Audi. She must have heard his car arrive because she was at the front door holding it open for him, dressed casually for once in jeans and a white blouse. 'Hello, Bill. What brings you here?'

'Just a social call,' Watson lied. 'Bloody weather,' he moaned as he squeezed his large frame through the front door.

They went into the living room and Emma offered a drink. Watson took a seat and wondered how he was going to play this while Emma was in the kitchen putting the kettle on.

She soon returned with two coffees, handing one to Watson, and settled into an armchair, waiting for Watson to speak.

Watson took a sip of his coffee. 'Need a nice hot drink on a day like today. Wouldn't think it was summer, would you?'

Emma smiled.

'So how are you doing, Emma? I mean... are you coping all right?'

Emma sniffed and pulled a handkerchief out of her sleeve. She dabbed at her eyes theatrically. 'I guess so. It's... well, hard to come to terms with.'

'I came to make sure you were okay,' Watson lied again. 'See if there was anything I could do for you.'

'That's very kind, thanks. But no, I'm fine really.'

'Oh, by the way, did anyone get back to you after your house was searched? I'm afraid that was bad judgement on DCI Fleming's part.'

'No, I haven't heard a thing.'

Watson took another sip of his coffee. 'You needn't worry on that front any more. I'm in charge of the Nielson murder enquiry now and Anthony is no longer a suspect.'

Emma sighed with relief. 'Thank goodness for that.' But then she frowned. 'So how come you're in charge of the investigation?'

'Oh, Fleming's been suspended.'

'Really? Why?'

'He's been a bad boy. Out of his depth. I always knew he wasn't the right person to fill Anthony's shoes.'

'What did he do?'

'It's a long story, but he had a skeleton in the cupboard that came back to haunt him. He arranged for someone from his past to be beaten up.'

Emma's eyes widened in horror.

'Then he disobeyed a direct order and went to interview someone who's in the public eye and they complained about police harassment. Very embarrassing.'

'Gosh. Still... I'm glad you're in charge.'

Watson cleared his throat. 'The thing is...'

'Yes?'

'I hate to bring this up... You had an affair with Ronnie, right?'

A tear rolled down Emma's cheek. 'Yes, DCI Fleming found out.' She looked anxiously at Watson. 'This isn't a social call is it, Bill?'

Watson put his cup down and leaned forwards in his chair. 'Of course it is,' he said earnestly. 'It's just that Anthony knew, didn't he?'

'Yes,' Emma whispered.

'The main thing is that Anthony's name is in the clear. I wondered if Ronnie ever talked about things...'

'What things?'

'Oh, about what he did as well as running a club? You presumably knew that Anthony and I were heading a drugs investigation involving him way back when we worked for the Met?'

'Yes, but what...'

'Then he was suspected of being behind a murder in Reading two years later. Anthony and I were on that case as well after we'd transferred to Thames Valley CID.'

'He was cleared on both counts though, wasn't he?'

'Yes, he was. Insufficient evidence. Did he ever talk about it?'

'No, not really.'

'He never spoke to you about me and Anthony being involved in the investigations?'

'Oh, goodness, no he didn't. He never mentioned you or Anthony. Why would he?'

Watson relaxed and smiled. 'No reason at all, Emma. Curious, that's all. Listen, I don't want to take up any more of your time. Just wanted to make sure you were okay.'

Emma showed Watson out. The storm had passed over and the sun was shining. A rainbow shone in the watery light over Blenheim Palace.

After Watson had gone, Emma felt a twinge of alarm. She thought she had managed to convince Watson that Nielson had never spoken to her about him or Anthony, but she knew all about their little secret.

68

The Trout Inn at Wolvercote was becoming a regular place for out-of-office meetings. Fleming had received a call from Logan to ask if he could meet Fleming there. He'd said he had some news and that Fleming wouldn't believe his ears. It was hot stuff, but Logan had explained he couldn't talk over the phone.

The previous day's storm had passed and now the sun shone in a clear blue sky as the two men sat by a table on the pub terrace with their pints of beer. Fleming raised his glass in the air. 'Cheers, Harry. So what's this news?'

Logan smiled. 'Nice day, nice pint, and even better news. You won't believe this, boss.'

'Try me,' Fleming said, laughing at Logan's enthusiasm.

Logan put his pint down after taking a long swig. 'DS Crowe arrested McBain and Eckhard yesterday. I was with him when he interviewed McBain.'

'And?'

'At first, McBain denied he had anything to do with the assault on Calder, but when Crowe told him he might be facing a murder wrap and that his two mates had squealed, McBain

316

decided to talk. He wanted to do a deal in return for information.'

Fleming's heart skipped a beat. 'He told you who put him up to it?'

Logan leaned forwards in his chair and glanced furtively from side to side to make sure no one was within earshot. 'More than that. It's a bombshell, boss.'

'How much longer are you going to keep me in suspense, Harry? Spit it out.'

Logan wiped some froth from his mouth with the back of a hand. 'He said it was Watson who put them up to the assault on Calder.'

'I knew it!' Fleming exclaimed, slapping his hand on the table. 'Did he say why?'

Logan shook his head. 'Didn't have a clue. They just did as they were told.'

Fleming frowned. 'Why did you think I wouldn't believe my ears, Harry? It confirms what I suspected. And how come Watson knew McBain and company?'

'That's the bombshell.' Logan grinned. 'McBain accused Watson of being in Nielson's pocket. McBain said that Watson, Hayden and Jardine were on the take.'

Fleming whistled. 'So Potts wasn't bullshitting after all about police corruption.'

'No, and McBain said that Watson wanted to carry on the arrangement with him after Nielson was murdered. He told McBain he still had friends in the Met and that he could look after him in return for a few favours and backhanders.'

'Well, well. That really is hot news. Does Liz Temple know about this?'

'Yes. DS Crowe rang her and went to see her yesterday afternoon.'

'Have Watson and Jardine been pulled in for questioning?'

'Jardine has. He's been suspended. Watson was due in the office but Jardine told the super that he wouldn't be in until Monday.'

'Didn't she send someone to bring him in straight away?'

'Yes, but he's not answering his phone and he's not at home. No one knows where he is.'

Fleming frowned. 'You know what he's doing, don't you?'

'What?'

'He's disappeared to give himself time to think. He'll be working out a story on where he's been over the weekend and how to answer McBain's allegations. He'll probably claim that McBain is lying. Watson will laugh it off and ask what evidence there is. Probably come up with some story about McBain having it in for him ever since the drugs enquiry involving Nielson's club.'

'But I know that Watson knew about Calder, don't I? And so does the super. He took a call from Police Scotland about him. He can't deny that, can he?'

'Perhaps not. But knowing about him doesn't prove he was responsible for the assault. And there would need to be more than McBain's word over a corruption charge.'

'Does this get you off the hook though? Do you think the super will lift your suspension?'

Fleming shrugged. 'I'm not sure. It certainly muddies the water over the Calder business, but there's still the question of Charles Trenchard's complaint. I haven't received written confirmation of the misconduct proceedings yet, so who knows?'

'But the super will have to suspend Watson as well as Jardine, pending a full enquiry. She needs someone to head the Nielson murder enquiry so she's got to reinstate you.'

Fleming was about to speak when his mobile rang and vibrated urgently on the table. He picked it up and tapped on the green phone icon. 'Hello? DCI Fleming.'

There was a long pause.

'Hello?' Fleming repeated.

This time, the caller spoke hesitantly. 'Oh, hello. This is Emma Hayden. I wonder if I might come and see you. Something's happened and I'm scared...'

Fleming's eyes narrowed. 'Sure. Listen, if it's urgent you can see me now if you want. I'm at The Trout Inn at Wolvercote with DS Logan.'

'Oh, right. I'm actually in Oxford so I could be there in half an hour or so... if that's okay?'

'Sure. See you shortly.' Fleming cut the call.

Logan looked inquiringly at him. 'Trouble?'

Fleming looked thoughtful. 'Emma Hayden. Wants to come and see me. She says she's scared...'

69

Forty minutes later, Emma Hayden appeared. She spotted Fleming and Logan on the terrace and tottered over to join them in her red high-heel shoes. She wore a matching red dress and carried a red handbag over her shoulder. The only thing that wasn't red was the thin black leather belt she wore round her waist.

Fleming stood as she approached. 'Hello, Mrs Hayden. What can I get you to drink?'

'That's very kind of you. A large white wine please.'

'I'll get that,' Logan offered, 'if you have things to talk about.'

Emma sat. She looked uncomfortable. 'I believe you've been suspended, and Bill Watson has taken over the investigation into Ronnie's... Mr Nielson's murder.'

Fleming nodded. 'That's right. What can I do for you?'

'It was Bill who told me. He came to see me yesterday. He said you'd been suspended because you arranged for someone to be assaulted...'

'That's not true. I was suspended because I'd been accused of it, but I now have evidence to prove someone else was behind it.'

'He also said you'd been accused of police harassment.'

'That is true. But it wasn't harassment. I simply questioned someone that the powers that be didn't want to be questioned. Bit political, I'm afraid. But that's not why you wanted to see me is it, Mrs Hayden?'

Emma smiled weakly. 'No... of course not.'

'You said you were scared. What's scared you?'

'Bill... he...'

'Go on.'

'I don't quite know where to start, but he seemed strange. Worried maybe. I got the impression he was fishing for information about Ronnie and me.'

'What did he say?'

'He mentioned the drugs investigation he and Anthony worked on when they were working for the Met, and the Reading murder investigation they both worked on two years later.'

Logan returned with Emma's drink. She smiled and thanked him. She took a large sip before speaking again. 'He asked me about my affair with Ronnie and whether Ronnie ever talked about the investigations Bill and Anthony were involved in. Bill seemed anxious to find out if Ronnie ever mentioned them at all.'

Fleming looked at Emma. 'And did he?'

Emma took another large sip of wine. There was fear in her eyes. 'I don't know what to do,' she suddenly sobbed. She took a handkerchief out of her pocket and dabbed at her eyes.

'Take your time,' Fleming said gently.

'Oh, God, this is awful!'

'What is it, Mrs Hayden?' Fleming pressed.

'Ronnie... he told me one night when he was a bit drunk that he had some police in his pocket... corrupt detectives.'

'Go on,' Fleming prompted.

'It was Bill Watson, Anthony, and Frank Jardine,' Emma blurted. 'He said he would blow the whistle on them if they couldn't keep the Met off his back. I'm so frightened. If... if Bill knew what I know, he'd... oh, I don't know! What should I do?'

'What did you say to DCI Watson when he asked whether Ronnie ever talked about him?'

'I told him that Ronnie never mentioned him at all.'

'Have you any reason to think he didn't believe you?'

'I suppose not.'

'All right, Mrs Hayden. Don't do anything for now. We will need a statement from you though, I'm afraid. DS Logan can come and see you at home later, if that's okay?'

Emma nodded. 'Yes, that's fine.'

'Is there anyone you can go and visit for a few days? Someone DCI Watson doesn't know about?' Fleming asked.

'I have a friend in London. I could go and visit her, I suppose.' Emma dabbed at her eyes again. 'Do you think I could be in danger?'

'I'm sure not, Mrs Hayden. Just a precaution, and you'll be less worried. Let me have your contact details and I'll be in touch.'

Emma finished her wine, stood and made to leave. 'Things will be all right, won't they?'

'Yes, of course. You've no need to worry,' Fleming assured her.

After Emma had gone, Fleming looked at Logan. 'That's two independent allegations that Watson, Jardine and Hayden were bent.'

Logan nodded. 'Seems like Bill Watson and Frank Jardine have a lot of explaining to do.'

70

B ill Watson sat behind a small desk facing Matthew Upson and Liz Temple. A portable tape machine was running.

Upson spoke first. 'For the purposes of the tape, DCI Watson has not been arrested but is being interviewed under caution.' He looked at Watson. 'You understand that as you are not under arrest you are free to leave at any time.'

'I know that. Let's get on with it.'

'Serious allegations of misconduct have been made against you that will be subject to a full investigation. Criminal proceedings could follow. Do you understand?'

Watson unbuttoned his jacket and ran a finger under his shirt collar to pull it away from his neck. 'Yes, sir, but this is ridiculous. Allegations can be made mischievously by anyone. There's no proof to substantiate them.'

Upson ignored the protest. 'Liz?'

Temple opened a file on the table in front of her. 'Two allegations have been made against you. Firstly, Scottie McBain and two other men have been charged with an assault on Jimmy Calder. I have a written statement from McBain, claiming you asked him to find Calder for you and then carry out the assault on him. He says you told him to tell Calder that Fleming had sent them. Do you deny that?'

'Of course I do! How can you possibly take his word for it without any proof?'

'Did you know Calder had a heart attack after the assault? He's in intensive care. He could die.' Temple gazed steadily at Watson.

Watson sat impassively. He shook his head. 'I didn't, but why would I? His welfare is of no concern to me. I don't know the man.'

'His welfare will be of concern to you if McBain's claim is proven,' Temple said.

'It won't be. The man's a liar.'

Temple flicked through the file in front of her until she found what she wanted. 'A check of McBain's telephone records shows an incoming call from a public payphone in Witney soon after you left the office.'

'So?'

'Did you make that call?'

'No.'

'And then a check of your home phone records shows you made a call to Nielson's club a week later...' Temple continued.

'That would probably be to do with the Nielson murder enquiry,' Watson said glibly.

'But you weren't on the Nielson case then.'

Watson shrugged. 'Not officially, no.'

'So why did you call McBain?'

'I don't like telling tales, but I didn't think Fleming was making fast enough progress on the Nielson case. I heard that Damien Potts had done a runner. I was sure he was a key suspect and I thought I'd check whether DCI Fleming had made enquiries with Nielson's club.'

'You did know that Calder might have been in Reading though, didn't you? You told DCI Fleming. Why?'

Watson held up his hands in mock surrender. 'That I am guilty of, I admit. I knew he was looking for the man.'

'Fleming claims that you knew three men assaulted Calder...'

'Does he? I can't recall saying anything to him about that. He's trying to drop me in it. He resents the fact I was put in charge of the Nielson murder investigation.' Watson glanced from Temple to Upson and back. 'This is ridiculous. This whole thing is getting out of hand. All you have is the word of a criminal and a discredited detective. There's no hard evidence that I was instrumental in the attack on Calder. The fact you haven't arrested me proves my point.'

'Yes, I do appreciate that you have agreed to be questioned voluntarily. I'm just trying to establish the facts,' Temple explained.

Watson sat back in his chair. He was thinking fast. McBain hadn't stayed quiet about the Calder business. He thought he'd dealt with Temple's questions on that well enough though. They couldn't prove a thing. Any evidence they had was purely circumstantial. But Temple had said there were two allegations. He dreaded what was coming next.

Temple cleared her throat. 'I said there were two allegations against you. The second is far more serious...'

Watson looked straight ahead with unseeing eyes.

'Mr McBain has also made a statement to the effect that you were one of three corrupt detectives on the force.'

'Christ! You're not seriously going to believe that, are you?'

'DCI Hayden was the second and DI Jardine the third,' Temple continued.

Watson shook his head. 'No way! This is rubbish. I can't believe you're buying that crap!'

'He claims it started when all three of you worked for the Met.'

'Bollocks!'

Temple carried on. 'You were a DI at the time. You were in charge of a drugs investigation involving Nielson's club but you filed a report saying there was insufficient evidence to bring charges.'

'You've got that right for once. There wasn't. How does that prove I was on the take?'

Temple smiled. 'It doesn't. I'm just stating facts. Two years later you were the senior investigating officer in a murder case which Nielson was suspected of being behind. You dropped the case against him when Damien Potts confessed to the killing. He claimed it was self-defence and was convicted for manslaughter. No charges were brought against Nielson.'

'Right again. There was no evidence to prove Nielson put him up to it.' Watson glanced at Upson. 'I don't know where Superintendent Temple is going with this. She's making ridiculous assumptions based on two cases in which there was no evidence against Nielson... and the word of bloody Scottie McBain.'

'I was merely observing that it's a bit of a coincidence that you brought no charges against the same man Scottie McBain claims you were taking bribes from.'

Watson shook his head again and muttered, 'Unbelievable!'

'We also have the question of police corruption raised by a reporter at the behest of Damien Potts, who is now dead.'

'Don't tell me you're going to try to pin that on me as well!' Watson laughed.

Temple ignored the outburst. 'And we have a statement from Emma Hayden who claims Ronnie Nielson told her that you, DI Jardine and her late husband were in his pocket.'

Watson gasped. 'I don't believe you're taking this seriously. If you're so sure of your facts, why don't you arrest me?'

Temple changed tack. 'Mrs Hayden also claims that Nielson told her he would blow the whistle on you if you couldn't keep the Met off his back and he went down for something.'

'This is pure fantasy! Don't think I don't know where you're going with this. You're going to say I had a motive to have Nielson killed simply because of an alleged threat he was going to blow the whistle on me for something I'm not guilty of. Ridiculous!'

Temple stayed calm. 'Would you care to tell us where you were on the night Ronnie Nielson was killed?'

Watson laughed derisively and looked at Upson while pointing an accusing finger at Temple. 'She's totally out of order, sir. I've been a policeman for twenty-six years. I've served with distinction and never had a blot on my career. And now... now she's accusing me of arranging an assault, corruption, and possibly murder.'

Temple glared at Watson. 'I'm simply pointing out to you that we have statements that need to be fully investigated. The outcome of those enquiries could place you in a somewhat awkward position in relation to Damien Potts and Ronnie Nielson.' She raised an eyebrow. 'Look, Bill, you're not under arrest and so you don't have to answer my question, but it would help us if you did.'

Watson slumped in his chair, shaking his head. 'I don't believe this is happening,' he said, then added in a resigned voice, 'I was at home with Frank Jardine having a drink. He can confirm that.'

Temple glanced at Upson who nodded imperceptibly. 'All right, Bill, thank you. You do know that due to the seriousness of these allegations, I have to suspend you from duty with immediate effect. There will be a full enquiry of course. That's all.'

Watson drew a sharp breath. 'It'll be a complete waste of time, believe me.'

Later at home, Watson poured himself a large whisky. He took a big gulp and slumped into his armchair. His head was spinning. Christ, he really was in it up to his neck.

71

Fleming had received a call from Liz Temple requesting his attendance at a meeting with her and the chief constable at the new Kidlington South HQ. She hadn't said why. Just that he'd better be on time and on his best behaviour.

They were using the small meeting room next to Upson's office. Temple sat next to him. Fleming sat on the other side of the table. Upson closed the file in front of him and glowered at Fleming. 'I'm not at all happy with the way things are going,' Upson finally said. 'I had you suspended because you were suspected of being behind an assault on Jimmy Calder. You disobeyed a direct order by going to see Charles Trenchard again, and then I received a complaint of harassment from him.'

Fleming made to speak but Upson held up a hand to stop him. 'However, I now find myself in a position where I need to postpone the misconduct proceedings against you for the time being.'

Fleming sighed with relief. 'Thank you, sir.'

'This is not a reprieve, Fleming. It's just a temporary change of circumstances,' Upson warned.

'I understand, sir.'

Upson grunted. 'I've been a police officer for thirty-five years and I'm due to retire soon. I want to retire with my head held high. I'm proud of what I've achieved, but I now have Cecil Daubney on my back on an almost-daily basis. I do not need a situation where I have to answer to him for the lack of integrity in some of my officers. Do you understand, Fleming?'

'Yes, sir. I'm sorry–'

Upson cut him off before he could say any more. 'As regards the Calder issue, we have a statement from one of the assailants who claims it was DCI Watson who was behind the assault. I have therefore suspended him, pending a full enquiry. On top of that, I now have allegations that he was a bent cop.' Upson shook his head as though in disbelief. 'You and Watson have caused me a great deal of grief, Fleming.'

'I'm sorry, sir.'

Upson ignored the apology. 'The Charles Trenchard fiasco is now over, no thanks to you. I managed to placate him by offering a profuse apology and by promising him you'll not bother him again. Is that clear, Fleming?'

'Perfectly, sir.'

'Good. I want you to return to duty and take charge of the Nielson murder case again.'

'Thank you, sir.'

'But let's get this straight,' Upson continued, 'I do not want any more complaints from Charles Trenchard. Do you understand?'

'Yes, sir.'

'Think yourself lucky that you have a second chance, Fleming. Do not mess it up,' Upson warned. 'That's all.'

〜

On his way back to the office, Fleming wasn't convinced he was lucky. He somehow felt things were about to get worse.

72

The MCU was buzzing. DCI Fleming was back. Word had spread about Bill Watson and Frank Jardine's suspension. The chief constable had called a meeting with Liz Temple and Fleming. Rumour had it that Cecil Daubney was after Upson's blood. Press speculation over Upson's position was rife. There was a real sense of crisis in the air.

Fleming had received a warm welcome back and had held a briefing meeting to get up to speed on the Nielson case. There had been attempts by some to fish for information on what was going on, but Fleming kept things to himself. He'd said they would find out all in good time.

After the briefing meeting, Fleming asked Logan and Anderson to join him in his office. He motioned for them to find a chair as he sat on the edge of his desk. 'Okay, to recap: Anthony Hayden is off the radar, Potts is dead, and forensics found no prints or DNA to put him on Nielson's boat.'

'Running out of suspects,' Logan observed.

'We still have Rainer,' Anderson said.

'True,' Logan admitted. 'But we've had him under surveillance. There's no sign he's about to do a runner. And... we haven't found the murder weapon yet.'

'You were sure he was our man weren't you, Sarge?' Anderson said.

'I was,' Logan agreed, 'but the boss here isn't so sure, are you, boss?'

Fleming shook his head. 'You may well be right yet, Harry. We could charge him, but I feel there isn't enough to secure a conviction. Things could change if we find the murder weapon.'

'Looking a bit thin after all this time,' Logan pointed out.

'We do have two other possible suspects,' Fleming said.

'Oh no... please don't tell me one of them is Charles Trenchard,' Logan groaned.

Fleming smiled. 'I'm afraid we can't rule him out yet. He lied about knowing Ronnie Nielson. He also said he couldn't remember Giles Bonner, one of the men in Nielson's army photograph. But Bonner remembered him. Trenchard commanded Nielson's platoon in Afghanistan. Bonner reckoned they didn't see eye to eye with each other... and Trenchard seems to be very reluctant to talk about his time there. Bonner reckons something happened.'

'Not much on which to suspect the man of murder though, is it?' Logan argued.

'He also lied about where he was on the night Nielson was killed.'

'That could just have been a mix up in diary arrangements.'

'Maybe. But I can't go and quiz Leo Miller or Trenchard about what they were doing that night. The chief constable has warned me off. There'll need to be some pretty damning evidence before he'll agree to me speaking to either of them.'

'Has the leadership election been held yet?' Anderson asked.

'Not yet,' Fleming confirmed. 'I think it might be next week.'

Logan groaned again. 'That's all we need. Trenchard wins and becomes prime minister and then we might find evidence to incriminate him. Great!'

'You said there were two other possible suspects,' Anderson said. 'Who's the other one?'

Fleming pushed himself up from his desk and walked over to the window that looked out over the open-plan office outside. Everyone other than him, Logan and Anderson had gone. Fleming turned. 'This has to stay within these four walls. Understood?'

'Of course,' Anderson said.

Fleming took a deep breath. 'Bill Watson was suspended because he arranged for Jimmy Calder to be assaulted.'

'But what's that got to do with Ronnie Nielson?' Anderson asked, frowning.

'And,' Fleming continued, 'he and Frank Jardine are suspected of being bent cops. Anthony Hayden as well.'

'Bloody hell!' Anderson exclaimed, then quickly apologised. 'Oh... sorry, sir!'

Logan laughed. 'DC Anderson, you swore!'

Anderson smiled and gave a playful nudge against Logan's shoulder.

'The thing is,' Fleming went on, 'Emma Hayden claims that Ronnie Nielson had threatened to blow the whistle on Watson.'

Realisation dawned on Anderson's face. 'So, Watson could have killed him! Bloody hell!'

Logan tut-tutted and shook his head. 'This swearing is becoming a habit, Naomi.'

She stuck her tongue out at Logan.

'Liz Temple is the investigating officer for the allegations of corruption made against Watson and Jardine,' Fleming continued with a smile. 'She'll be getting their telephones, mobile accounts, computers and bank accounts checked. She'll also get their houses searched, and she'll need to question McBain over times and dates when Watson allegedly met Nielson. I'll leave all of that to her. The last thing I want to do is tread on her toes.'

'So, what's the plan, boss?' Logan asked.

'I want to have another look at Nielson's house. Maybe we missed something. We need to find out if there's anything that can link Watson to him. Maybe Nielson was blackmailing him.'

Logan looked at Anderson who seemed to be in shock. 'Never a dull moment, eh?'

73

'**B**ad idea,' Logan muttered. He was driving one of the unmarked cars from the MCU pool down the M40. It was early and the morning traffic heading towards London was heavy.

'We've got all day,' Fleming said. 'Relax.'

Logan grunted and concentrated on his driving.

Twenty minutes later, Logan left the crawling traffic on the motorway and headed south towards Marlow then east to Bourne End. 'Bill Watson is certainly in it up to his neck,' he said, breaking the silence.

'It could get much worse,' Fleming said. 'Calder's in a bad way. He could die.'

Logan nodded. 'Then Watson's really in the shit.'

Fleming looked thoughtful and stayed silent for a while, watching the first drops of rain hit the windscreen. Eventually he spoke. 'Damien Potts goes to the press, claiming there were corrupt detectives on the force, and then he turns up dead...'

Logan looked sharply across at Fleming. 'You think Watson and Jardine may have been behind that as well, boss?'

Fleming shrugged. 'Could be. Maybe they couldn't take the chance that Potts knew they were involved.'

'This is getting hard to believe. I mean, where does it all end?'

Fleming shrugged again. 'Badly for Bill Watson?'

Logan nodded. 'He could also be Nielson's killer, or he may have paid someone to do it for him. He could go down for being involved in three murders at this rate. And how far is Jardine involved in all this, I wonder?'

'Anybody's guess at this stage,' Fleming said as Logan pulled the car up outside Nielson's house. He switched off the screeching windscreen wipers, killed the engine and grabbed the house keys which they'd picked up from the police station at Marlow. He dashed to the front door to escape the rain.

Nielson's house felt cold even though it was mid-summer. It was pretty much as Fleming remembered it. 'You have a look down here. I'll look upstairs.'

'What exactly are we looking for, boss?'

'Any evidence that might link Watson to Nielson and, if we're lucky, something that suggests Nielson may have been black-mailing him.'

Logan nodded his understanding. 'Okay, let's make a start.'

Fleming made his way upstairs. He went into what appeared to be the master bedroom first. He knew the SOCOs would have been through everything, but he went through all the drawers and cupboards anyway. There were no wallets, papers or documents. There was an old leather briefcase tucked into the back of the built-in cupboards, but it was empty. Fleming found a suitcase under the bed, but it too was empty. He felt the lining to see if anything was concealed inside. Nothing.

There was a clatter of pans and a curse. Logan shouted upstairs. 'Sorry, boss. Little accident in the kitchen!'

Fleming smiled and carried on his search. He looked in the other two bedrooms, opening drawers and wardrobes but found nothing of interest.

Doors were slamming downstairs. He sensed Logan's frustration and was beginning to think this had been a waste of time. Why did he think they could possibly find something the SOCOs had missed? The bedroom Nielson had used as an office had to be the best bet.

The computer had gone. The SOCOs would have taken that away for forensic examination. There was nothing on the top of the antique desk apart from an old paper knife. Fleming opened the drawers one by one. The papers he'd looked at before were all still there: bills, bank statements, utility and insurance documents. He was sure the SOCOs would have been through them all, but he went through them again anyway. There was nothing to suggest a link to Watson.

Fleming heard footsteps on the stairs. Logan joined him and shrugged. 'Bugger all. How about you?'

'Nothing.'

'You pulled out all the drawers?' Logan nodded at the desk. 'Something may have fallen down the back,' he added hopefully.

'No... no, I didn't,' Fleming said thoughtfully as he pulled out one drawer. He took one side of the desk and Logan took the other. There was nothing.

'Oh well,' Logan said. 'Worth a try, eh?'

Fleming was pushing the last drawer back in place when he exclaimed, 'Hang on!'

Logan looked at him expectantly. 'What?'

'All these drawer fronts are the same size.'

Logan shrugged again. 'So?'

'So how come this bottom side drawer isn't as deep as the others?'

Logan looked over Fleming's shoulder. 'I see what you mean.'

Fleming pulled out the contents and threw them onto the top of the desk. He grabbed the paper knife and slipped the point of the blade into a small gap at the front of the base. It stuck for a moment, but then suddenly gave way, revealing a narrow space under a false bottom.

'Wow!' Logan exclaimed. 'Bet you're glad I came up here.'

Fleming smiled and pulled out an external hard drive from the hidden compartment. 'This could be promising,' he said, turning to Logan. 'Remember you found a laptop case on Nielson's boat, but there wasn't a laptop there or here in the house. Could be the killer took it.'

'What? Bit much to kill a man for a laptop.'

'No. I was thinking that the killer maybe took it because he thought there was something on it that might incriminate him. If there was, Nielson would certainly have kept a copy.' Fleming waved the device at Logan.

Logan nodded. 'Pity the desktop hasn't been returned. We could have checked it out here.'

'We'll do it back at the office,' Fleming said, pulling out an address book that had been under the external hard drive. He flicked open the pages and found the telephone numbers for Bill Watson, Frank Jardine, Anthony Hayden, Emma Hayden, and Charles Trenchard. A folded newspaper cutting was slotted in at the back of the book. Fleming took it out and carefully unfolded it.

'What is it?' Logan asked excitedly.

'An article about Charles Trenchard, would you believe,' Fleming said.

He showed it to Logan. The headline read:

WEALTHY FOREIGN SECRETARY RUMOURED TO BE PREPARING LEADERSHIP BID.

Nielson had circled a photograph of Trenchard with a red pen and had underlined the first word.

'I wonder why Nielson had that,' Logan said, 'and how come the SOCOs missed all this?'

Fleming shook his head. 'Not thorough enough, but I can make a decent guess why Nielson had this,' he said, waving the newspaper cutting.

Fleming was deep in thought on the way back to the office. He recalled his conversation with Bonner: *Something must have happened in Afghanistan. Trenchard was Nielson's platoon commander and they didn't get on...*

Back at Long Hanborough, Fleming plugged the external hard drive into his computer while Logan looked anxiously over Fleming's shoulder. Fleming clicked on the external drive icon and opened Word. There was nothing of note in the documents. At least nothing to suggest Nielson was blackmailing anyone.

Fleming clicked on the calendar and found the day Ronnie Nielson was killed.

Fleming whistled. 'Trenchard! He had a meeting with Trenchard!'

'It's him!' Logan exclaimed. 'It has to be!'

Fleming clicked on Videos and found a folder headed Kabul. He clicked again and the video started. The camera was shaky. A man in uniform sprang into view. The quality of the video wasn't brilliant, but there was no mistaking the man waving a pistol and shouting. The younger Charles Trenchard that Fleming had found in Nielson's old army photograph. He was swaying on his feet. Four Afghan civilians cowered in a quiet alleyway. Fleming turned up the volume.

'You're all Taliban. I know you are!' Trenchard was screaming hysterically.

'No... no!' the men shouted in unison. They held their hands up, pleading. 'We're just market traders... shopkeepers. We hate the Taliban!' The camera focused in on frightened faces, eyes wide open in terror as Trenchard waved the gun at them.

'Liars! You're all the same. You plant roadside bombs. You kill our soldiers–'

'No... no!' the men shouted.

'I've had enough, do you hear? Enough!' Trenchard pointed the gun at the first man and pulled the trigger.

Fleming and Logan flinched as the shot rang out. The man fell backwards against a wall and sank to the ground, smearing blood on the wall behind him.

Whoever was holding the camera shouted. 'Fuck, sir, let's get out of here!'

Trenchard laughed as he let off a stream of shots, mowing down the other three men. Blood was everywhere. Bodies twitched on the ground. The video swayed, and then the screen went blank.

Fleming and Logan sat in silence until Logan finally spoke in a whisper. 'Oh, shit. This is dynamite. The man could be the next prime minister, for God's sake! The powers that be are not going to be happy with this.'

'No,' Fleming agreed. 'That's why we don't tell them until after we've arrested him.'

'God help us.'

74

The sound of wailing sirens broke the early morning peace in Henley-on-Thames. Two police cars raced through the streets towards Charles Trenchard's house on the outskirts of the town. Fleming and Logan followed in an unmarked car.

'I hope you know what you're doing, sir,' Logan said as the car sped forwards. 'You know the super and Matthew Upson are going to go ballistic. They warned you not to speak to Trenchard again. But arresting him without even telling them is suicidal.'

Fleming shrugged. 'Internal politics can't get in the way of justice. You know what they say: no man is above the law.'

'No,' Logan agreed, 'but you could have told the super last night after we'd been to Nielson's house.'

'True, but I didn't want to risk her speaking to Upson and him calling us off. Let's get this done first. I'll tell her later. It's a pity about the delay, but I wanted to wait until this morning to arrest Trenchard. I didn't want to give his solicitor a chance to argue that it was too late last night to interview him and have the night eating into the time we have to question him before either charging or releasing him.'

'Even more reason why the super will say you had plenty of time to consult with her first,' Logan argued.

'She won't be happy, but there's enough evidence to show that Nielson was blackmailing Trenchard. Once he's under arrest, we'll get DNA samples and fingerprints. Forensics will clinch it.'

Logan shook his head. 'I hope you're right, boss. Because the fact that Nielson was blackmailing Trenchard doesn't prove he killed him, or had him killed.'

'Maybe, but there's also the matter of the shooting in Afghanistan. He's guilty of a war crime if nothing else.'

The two squad cars swung through the open iron gates and crunched to a halt on the gravel driveway. The unmarked car stopped behind them. The sirens were silent and the blue flashing lights reflected in the house windows.

Charles Trenchard appeared at the open front door in his dressing gown. 'What the hell's going on?' he demanded as Fleming and Logan strode towards him.

Fleming flashed his warrant card. 'Charles Trenchard, I'm arresting you for the murder of Ronnie Nielson. You do not have to say anything, but it may harm your defence if you do not mention when questioned, something which you later rely on in court. Anything you do say may be given in evidence. Do you understand the caution, Mr Trenchard?'

Trenchard was speechless for a moment. He glared at Fleming. 'You must be mad! I've already complained to the chief constable about you, and now this! You're making a very big mistake, Fleming. You'll be in serious trouble over this!'

Trenchard's wife had appeared at the door looking terrified. 'What's going on, Charles? Why are the police here?'

Trenchard turned to her and put a hand on her arm. 'It's all right, darling. Nothing to worry about. There's been a dreadful mistake, that's all.'

She didn't look convinced.

Trenchard had recovered his composure and turned to face Fleming. 'I'm perfectly happy to accompany you to a police station to answer any questions you–'

'You don't have any choice in the matter,' Fleming cut in. 'You're under arrest.'

'What!' Trenchard's wife exclaimed. 'Charles, what on earth for?'

'As I was saying,' Trenchard continued as though he hadn't grasped what Fleming had said, 'I am happy to help with your enquiries, but I will require my solicitor's presence.'

'Of course,' Fleming said.

'And,' Trenchard continued, 'I shall be speaking to the chief constable about this outrage.'

Fleming shrugged. 'Would you like to get dressed before we go?'

Trenchard sneered at Fleming and turned sharply to go inside.

Fleming signalled for two uniformed officers to follow him.

Ten minutes later, Trenchard appeared at the door dressed in smart casual clothes. 'I take it handcuffs will not be necessary?'

'Fine,' Fleming confirmed.

Trenchard's wife watched from the doorstep, wringing her hands as a uniformed officer held a hand over her husband's head while he ducked to get into the back seat of the front car.

Fleming and Logan followed the two squad cars as they left Henley heading towards Maidenhead Police Station.

On the way to the station, Fleming's mobile rang. He looked at the screen: *Liz Temple*. 'Hello, ma'am,' Fleming said in as calm a voice as he could muster.

Logan grimaced.

'What the fuck do you think you're doing, Alex!' Temple shouted down the phone.

Fleming held the phone away from his ear and shot an uncomfortable glance at Logan. 'I can explain–'

'Too fucking right you will. Matthew Upson will be furious. You were warned not to go near Trenchard again–'

'Yes, but–'

'But nothing,' Temple fumed. 'What part of "I do not want any more complaints from Charles Trenchard" did you not understand? Your career could be over. You do know that?'

Fleming decided to take a firm stance. 'Even if Trenchard is the killer? Ma'am, I'm perfectly aware of the politics and sensitivities around this, but I have concrete evidence to show that Charles Trenchard killed innocent civilians in cold blood in Afghanistan, and almost certainly killed Ronnie Nielson.'

There was a moment's silence before Temple spoke again. 'Where are you taking him?'

'Maidenhead.'

'I'll meet you there.' Temple cut the call.

Fleming looked at Logan. 'Looks like Trenchard's wife wasted no time.'

75

The atmosphere was tense. Liz Temple was leaning over the table where Fleming was sitting. The whites of her knuckles contrasted starkly with the red rising in her face.

Fleming waited for the onslaught.

'I don't know where to begin, Alex. I'm almost speechless at your tactless disregard of authority. Do you know what you've done?'

'I–'

Fleming didn't get any more words out before Temple launched into him again. 'You've fucked up big time. How many times did we warn you to back off from Trenchard?'

Fleming said nothing.

'You idiot! What do you do? You ignore all the warnings and go charging after him like a demented bull. Christ, give me strength! The man could be the next prime minister!'

Fleming knew it was pointless saying anything. He would have to wait for Temple to run out of steam.

'Matthew Upson nearly had a heart attack when I told him! He can't believe what you've done after what he said to you. Cecil Daubney will have him out of the door by the end of the day if we release Trenchard without charge. And, rest assured, we'll be just behind him!'

Fleming stared ahead waiting for more.

'Upson told you not to mess things up, but you ignore the warning and go and completely screw up! The consequences of your actions are... are immeasurable!' Temple spluttered. She finally did run out of steam and sat wearily with a resigned look on her face. 'So... are you going to tell me what possessed you to arrest Trenchard without checking with me first?'

Fleming took a deep breath. 'I'm sorry I acted without telling anyone what I was going to do, ma'am, but I knew if I told you about it you would be duty bound to report up to Matthew Upson. No disrespect, but I was sure he would stop me arresting Trenchard because of the politics involved and the flack he would take from Cecil Daubney.'

'Too bloody right he would!' Temple exploded. '*He* would want to make absolutely sure before he would allow such a thing. That's the responsibility that comes with high rank.'

Fleming nodded his understanding. 'I thought I could take that pressure off him, and you for that matter, by acting independently. If things go pear shaped, you can both claim I was a loose cannon acting without authority or permission. You knew nothing of my intentions and so were powerless to stop me.'

'That's very decent of you, Alex,' Temple said with more than a hint of sarcasm. 'You're so sure of yourself over this that you're prepared to fall on your sword and take all of the blame?'

'Yes, ma'am.'

'Okay, so what exactly have you got on him, apart from the fact he possibly lied to you about knowing Nielson?'

'He also lied over where he was on the night Nielson was killed.'

'And that's it? Please tell me you have more than that.'

'Yes, I have,' Fleming said, his eyes gleaming. 'Logan and I searched Nielson's house again. I thought maybe we could find something the SOCOs missed. Something that would prove Bill Watson was on the take and that Nielson was blackmailing him. If he was, Watson would have had a motive for killing him.'

'But you found something to incriminate Trenchard instead?'

'Yes. There was a false bottom in one of Nielson's computer desk drawers. There was an address book which had Trenchard's telephone number in it, and a newspaper clipping with a photograph of Trenchard.'

'Is that all?'

'Nielson also had the phone numbers for Bill Watson, Frank Jardine, Anthony Hayden, and Emma Hayden.'

'I mean on Trenchard,' Temple said irritably.

'No. There was an external hard drive. We found a video showing Trenchard shooting four unarmed civilians in Afghanistan. We also found a copy of Nielson's electronic calendar. He had a meeting arranged with Trenchard on the night he was killed.'

'You think Nielson was blackmailing him?'

'I'd bet my life on it.'

'Still doesn't prove Trenchard killed him, Alex. If you've got this wrong, your career will be over. I hope for all our sakes that you're right.'

76

Interview room one contained just a table and four chairs. It was hot, and beads of sweat were already forming on Trenchard's brow. He sat next to his solicitor, speaking in a quiet voice but fell silent when Fleming and Temple entered.

They sat across the table from Trenchard and his solicitor. Fleming broke the seal on a twin pack of audio cassettes and plugged them into the recording machine. The twenty-four-hour clock had started ticking. Liz Temple's words were still ringing in his ears: *If you've got this wrong, your career will be over.*

Fleming glanced at Temple who nodded. He pressed the record button. 'This is an interview with...' He looked towards Trenchard. 'State your full name, address, and date of birth please.'

Trenchard spoke quietly in a confident voice and glared defiantly at Fleming when he had finished speaking.

'Thank you,' Fleming said, then turned to face the recorder. 'I am DCI Fleming. Also present is Superintendent Temple and...' He looked across at Trenchard's solicitor, prompting him to speak.

The man was neatly dressed in a dark grey suit, white shirt

and blue tie. He had short blond hair and a thin pale face. Piercing blue eyes gazed at Fleming. The man spoke quietly. 'Silas Quigley, solicitor.'

'Thank you,' Fleming said. 'There are no other people present.' He noted the time, date and location and read Trenchard his rights again.

Trenchard put both hands face down on the table in front of him. 'I think you ought to know, Chief Inspector, that I've complained to the chief constable about your continued harassment. I also deny any involvement in the crime for which you have arrested me, but I am happy to help with your enquiries.'

Fleming ignored the menace in Trenchard's voice. 'When we first spoke, you claimed you didn't know Ronnie Nielson.'

'That's right. You showed me a photograph. You pointed out to me that one of the men in it was Ronnie Nielson, did you not?'

'Yes, I did. I also reminded you in a later meeting that you were Nielson's platoon commander in Afghanistan.'

'Yes, and if I remember correctly, I told you I couldn't possibly remember everyone I served with and that I couldn't remember the names of all the sergeants who served under me. Some of whom were only with me for a short period of time, I may add.'

'Do you tend to remember people you didn't get on with?'

Trenchard shook his head. 'I'm not sure what you're getting at.'

'One of your old officer colleagues, Giles Bonner, claims you didn't see eye to eye with Nielson.'

'There were many men I didn't *get on with*, as you put it. That was the nature of the job, I'm afraid. I don't remember all of the people I'd crossed swords with.'

'Mr Bonner also told me he thought something happened in Afghanistan when you went out drinking one night. He reckons you were a changed man after that night. What do you think he was referring to?'

'My dear chap, I haven't the faintest idea what you're talking about. We had lots of nights out when we could, and yes, I suppose a lot of us did change after a tour in Afghanistan. People we knew were dying, having limbs blown off. Bit difficult to stay unaffected, wouldn't you say?'

Fleming changed tack. 'You said you were with Leo Miller in London on the night Ronnie Nielson was killed. What was the meeting about?'

'Leo wanted to talk to me about the position of the prime minister and whether a no-confidence vote would be forced. He wanted me to stand for the leadership if the prime minister failed to get the support he would need to remain in office.'

'We checked with Mr Miller's private office. They had no record of any such meeting.'

'That doesn't surprise me. The nature of our meeting was hardly one we were going to document.'

'Mr Miller's private office told us he insisted all of his meetings were entered in his official diary. He could have asked them to log the meeting without being explicit over what it was about.'

'He obviously didn't, or his office forgot to enter it. Look, I've no idea why they didn't record the meeting. Why don't you check with Leo himself?'

'It seems he claimed that it was just a personal and private meeting that didn't need to be in the diary.'

'There you are then,' Trenchard said triumphantly.

'Mr Miller's wife claimed her husband was at home with her all that night,' Fleming said, fixing a steady gaze on Trenchard.

'She's mistaken,' Trenchard countered, shrugging. 'People can get days mixed up in their minds.'

'Can we have a short break?' Temple asked.

Fleming saw the look on her face and nodded. He spoke into the recorder. 'Interview suspended at eleven fifty-four.'

Trenchard and Quigley exchanged glances as Fleming and Temple left the room.

Once outside, Temple drew Fleming to one side out of earshot of anyone who might be in the vicinity. 'This is not going well, Alex. He's batting back your questions with the ease you'd expect of a politician. You need to put him under more pressure. Press him on the evidence you found in Nielson's house.'

'I was just about to get on to that. I wanted him to think he has the better of me. I'm hoping he might get careless and be thrown off guard when I hit him with the serious stuff.'

'Don't you think he'll be ready for that? Quigley has had primary disclosure. He's been told what evidence we have against Trenchard.'

'Yes, but I want Trenchard to sweat a little first.'

'Don't keep him sweating too much longer. He might do the opposite of what you think and gain in confidence. Bit like interviewing a candidate for a job and asking the simple questions first to put them at ease.'

'Okay,' Fleming agreed. 'I'll get tougher on him.'

77

Trenchard and Quigley were talking in urgent whispers when Fleming and Temple re-entered the interview room. Quigley was about to say something but fell silent. Fleming guessed he would have been reminding Trenchard of what was about to come.

Fleming sat and restarted the recorder. 'Interview resumed at eleven fifty-nine.' He stared hard into Trenchard's eyes. 'Is there any reason why Ronnie Nielson would have your telephone number?'

'No.'

'Can you explain why it was in an address book in his house?'

'No.'

'He also had a newspaper cutting. It was an article about you. He'd underlined the fact you were wealthy...'

'I'd no idea he wa a fan of mine,' Trenchard said nonchalantly.

'We also found an external drive for his computer.'

Trenchard laughed weakly. 'So?'

'There was a video on it. The one I think Ronnie Nielson showed you when he tried to blackmail you...'

'This is ridiculous! I have no idea what you're talking about, Chief Inspector.'

Fleming noticed the change in Trenchard's demeanour. There was uncertainty in his eyes. Panic even. 'You appear on the video shooting four unarmed Afghan civilians.'

'This is absurd!' Trenchard exclaimed. 'There has to be some mist–'

'There's no mistake,' Fleming cut in. 'That's what Giles Bonner was referring to, isn't it? That's what made you a changed man. You were living in fear of being found out.'

Trenchard laughed and shook his head.

'Or maybe it was remorse?' Fleming pressed.

'The video is obviously a fake.'

'A fake?' Fleming queried. He opened the laptop in front of him, tapped on the touchpad and turned it so that Trenchard and Quigley could see the screen. He spoke into the recording machine. 'For the purposes of the tape, I'm showing Mr Trenchard exhibit Voo1XB which is a copy of the video taken in Afghanistan.'

Trenchard and Quigley watched in silence.

'That *is* you holding a gun, isn't it?' Fleming pressed.

'Yes,' Trenchard admitted confidently. 'We did have guns in the army in Afghanistan you know. Someone clearly took that video of me and somehow managed to splice it together with another one... the one you see here of the shooting.'

'Why would someone do that?' Fleming pressed.

'I have no idea.'

Fleming turned the laptop round and closed it. 'Your name was in Ronnie Nielson's electronic calendar for the night he was killed. You weren't with Leo Miller that night, were you? You were meeting Nielson.'

'No, I was not.'

'You shot innocent civilians in Afghanistan. Someone captured it on video. Nielson somehow got hold of it and decided to keep it in case it came in handy one day.'

'No, this is all clearly a set-up.'

'He asked you to go and see him on his boat. Said he had something you might want to see. Something you might want to pay for.'

'This is ridiculous!' Trenchard protested.

'You went into a fit of rage when he showed you the video on his laptop. You didn't mean to kill him. You picked up a heavy glass ashtray and hit him on the head. He fought back. You thought your life was in danger. You grabbed a knife and you stabbed him. That's what happened, isn't it?'

'No,' Trenchard whispered, 'that's not... I mean no... it's not true! This is all a big mistake.'

'You left and took the laptop with y–'

'I'd like a private word with my client if I may,' Quigley broke in.

Fleming nodded. 'Okay. We will be going to court with an application to keep your client in custody for three days, pending further enquiries and forensic results. Interview terminated at twelve fifteen.'

Outside the interview room, Temple looked worried. 'I hope you're confident that his fingerprints and DNA samples will give you enough to charge him. Because so far he has answers to everything.'

Fleming's mobile rang as he was about to answer: *Logan*. 'Hello, Harry.'

Logan sounded breathless. 'Just had word from DS Crowe. Jimmy Calder's dead. Another heart attack.'

Fleming cut the call, took a deep breath and stared at the phone. He couldn't speak.

'Alex? You all right?' Temple asked.

Fleming looked at Temple with glazed eyes. 'I'm fine, just fine.'

78

Logan and Anderson had made a thorough search through the documents supplied by the banks. The work had been slow and painstaking, but they had found some interesting large payments made to both Watson and Jardine.

Fleming hadn't yet returned from the interview with Trenchard when the phone in Fleming's office rang. Logan picked up his handset and tapped on the group pick-up button to answer the call.

Anderson could hear the voice on the other end but couldn't make out what they were saying. She looked quizzically at Logan as his eyes opened wide in disbelief. 'What is it?' she mouthed softly.

Logan waved away the query, listening intently to what the caller was saying.

'Okay,' he finally said, 'I'll let him know as soon as he gets back from Maidenhead.' Logan put the phone down thoughtfully.

'Well?' Anderson asked.

Before he could answer, Fleming arrived.

'Everything all right?' Fleming asked, noticing the questioning look on Anderson's face.

'I need a word, boss. I've taken a call from the Met that came through on your extension. There's something you need to know.'

'Better come in then,' Fleming said, making towards his office door.

'There's been a bit of a breakthrough. Seems our friends McBain and Tyler have been up to more than doing over Jimmy Calder,' Logan said as Fleming came through the door.

'Oh?'

'They've been arrested for the murder of Damien Potts.'

'Really?' Fleming looked deep in thought.

'What are you thinking, boss?'

'I think there's a good chance that Watson got McBain to silence Potts. We now know that Watson and McBain were in cahoots with each other. Watson got him to do over Jimmy Calder making it look like I was behind it because he wanted me suspended and off the Nielson case. Reason being, he was worried I might stumble across something that proved he and Jardine were on the take. Then he can't take the chance that Potts knows the names of the bent cops so he has him killed.'

'So, Nielson's murder probably had nothing to do with bent cops,' Logan mused. 'Watson would have had a motive to kill him because Nielson had threatened to blow the whistle, but it looks like Trenchard did that for him.'

Fleming nodded. 'Did the Met say how they caught McBain and Tyler?'

'Simple policing in the end. There was a newspaper article about a body found washed up by the Thames. It turns out a man had seen something suspicious a few days earlier; a car speeding off with two men in it after hearing a loud splash so he went to have a look. There was a large object drifting up river with the tide which he put down to fly tipping at the time. He only went to the police when he saw the newspaper article. He remembered the car was an Audi and part of the registration number. The Met traced it to Tyler. It was the same Audi I checked out. They did the usual forensic checks on his car and the idiot hadn't even bothered to clean it up. They found traces of Potts's blood in the boot. Tyler panicked under questioning and named McBain as the other man.'

'All neat and tidy, eh?' Fleming observed. 'Looks like they're going down for two murders now that Jimmy Calder's dead. Changing the subject, how are you and Naomi getting on with the little task Liz Temple set you?'

'Painstaking work, but we've had some success. There are loads of unexplained payments into Watson and Jardine's bank accounts.'

'Probably not the news Temple and Upson would have wished for, especially Upson. The last thing he needs is proof that he had bent cops on his force,' Fleming said. He thought for a moment then asked, 'Have they both been arrested?'

'No. The super wants more evidence.'

'You're joking. It's in their bank accounts.'

'The payments didn't come directly from Nielson or McBain so we need to prove that someone else made the payments for them. We're still working on it.'

'They've not even been pulled in to explain how the payments got there?'

Logan shook his head. 'Not yet,' he said, making to leave Fleming's office. He turned by the door. 'Oh, by the way, almost forgot to tell you the other good news...'

'Which is?'

'They've found the Nielson murder weapon. It was buried in the silt at the bottom of the river a few yards away from Nielson's boat. Forensics think they might be able to recover partial prints.'

'That's great news,' Fleming said.

Later, alone in his office, Fleming was thinking things were becoming clearer, but something told him this was not quite over. He couldn't shake off the sense of foreboding that had come over him.

F leming, Temple, Trenchard and Silas Quigley were back in interview room one. Quigley glanced uneasily across the table at the two police officers and looked as though he wished he was somewhere else. Temple seemed calm. Trenchard drummed his fingers on the table in front of him as though bored.

Fleming gazed at Trenchard. 'I showed you a video yesterday. It shows you shooting unarmed civilians when you were serving with the army in Afghanistan. You claimed it was f–'

'Of course it is,' Trenchard cut in. 'That was not me shooting these people, I can assure you.'

'We've had the video examined by experts and it shows no signs of having been tampered with,' Fleming persisted.

'I'm afraid that proves nothing,' Quigley said. 'It's not easy to detect alterations when a recording is digitised and copied onto a computer. And it's not always possible to spot physical or electronically edited footage that has been recopied onto another video.'

Fleming knew a good defence lawyer could tear apart a major strand of his evidence and began to feel sick. Fleming tried to stay calm. 'But the fact remains that the video has been examined and there is no evidence to support your client's claim that it's a fake.'

'Do you have any eye witnesses to verify the validity of the video?' Quigley persisted.

'No,' Fleming admitted. 'We do not. However, we are satisfied the video is genuine.' He turned to Trenchard. 'Do you still deny meeting Ronnie Nielson on the night that he was killed?'

'Yes... yes, of course I do!' Trenchard spat out. 'I'd not set eyes on the man since Afghanistan.'

'Forensics went through your house with a toothcomb.' Fleming was talking fast. 'They found traces of mud in a shoe cupboard that matches mud samples taken off Nielson's boat.'

Trenchard glanced nervously at Quigley.

Fleming didn't relent. 'They also found minute traces of blood on one of your pullovers. DNA testing proves that it came from Nielson.'

'I... I...'

'You recently grew a beard. That was to hide scratches on your face, wasn't it?'

Trenchard shook his head.

'We found some skin tissue under Nielson's fingernails. It matches your DNA.'

There was panic in Trenchard's eyes as he looked pleadingly at Quigley who stared ahead with a blank look on his face.

Fleming was relentless. 'Wool fibres matching those from your pullover were found on Nielson's boat.'

The blood drained from Trenchard's face.

'Your fingerprints are on the boat, and on the glass ashtray you hit him with. Still deny you were there?'

'I... I...' Trenchard stammered.

Fleming completed the onslaught. 'We've found the murder weapon,' he said quietly. 'It has your prints on it.'

Trenchard slumped over the table and sobbed. 'I had to do it. He threatened to send the video to the press unless I paid him a hundred grand. God! I was so close. The result of the leadership election will be announced next week!' Trenchard was sobbing uncontrollably. 'He's destroyed me!'

'I think you've destroyed yourself.'

Logan took the call. It was from the Met again. McBain and Tyler had tried to do a plea-bargaining deal to get a reduced sentence. They'd admitted they wanted to frighten Potts into keeping quiet about police corruption, but claimed he'd pulled a knife on them and that they were acting in self-defence. They hadn't set out to kill him and claimed that Bill Watson had put them up to it.

Logan put the phone down. 'Is the boss in?' he asked Anderson.

'He left ten minutes ago.'

'Know where he went?'

'He said Frank Jardine phoned him and wanted to meet... something to do with information he had about Bill Watson.'

'Did he say where he was meeting him?'

'No, why?'

'Fuck!' Logan muttered.

'Problem?'

'I think the boss could be walking into a trap,' Logan said, reaching for the phone.

80

Heavy rain lashed against the windscreen of Fleming's Porsche as he made his way to the park and ride car park on the north side of Oxford. He was curious about the phone call from Jardine who had asked to meet, saying he had information about Bill Watson. Maybe Jardine thought the noose was tightening and wanted to do a deal before they were both arrested.

Still mulling things over in his mind, Fleming swung his car into the car park. The rain was easing slightly as he cruised round to where Jardine was parked and pulled into a space beside him. He switched the wipers off and killed the engine. Jardine waved and indicated for Fleming to join him. He was alone.

Fleming jumped out of his car and slid into the passenger seat next to Jardine. Fleming looked at him curiously. There was something wrong. Jardine appeared furtive, nervous.

The back door flew open and Watson appeared from nowhere. He dived into the back seat behind Fleming and pressed a knife against his neck. 'Good of you to come, Fleming,' he snarled. 'I wouldn't do anything stupid if I were you. I don't mind getting a bit of blood on your nice white shirt, but we don't really want blood squirting all over Frank's car, do we?'

Fleming could feel the blade pressing into the side of his neck. A trickle of blood ran down under his shirt collar. 'What's this about, Bill? Aren't you in enough trouble?'

'Shut the fuck up,' Watson said. 'We're going for a little ride.'

'Where to?'

Watson ignored the question. 'Drive,' he whispered urgently to Jardine.

Fleming was cursing himself for walking so easily into a trap. They headed north through Kidlington and carried on towards Banbury. Fleming wondered where they were taking him. After a while, Jardine took a sharp right-hand turn and then turned right again. They were on an old rutted road with grass growing up the middle. They carried on for a few hundred yards before Jardine stopped the car.

Watson had put the knife away and was pressing the barrel of a gun into Fleming's neck. 'Out of the car,' Watson ordered.

Fleming eased himself slowly out of the passenger seat and wondered if he would be able to disarm Watson by slamming the door against him as he got out.

Watson must have read his mind. He was pointing his gun at Fleming through the open rear window. 'Take a few steps away from the car, there's a good chap.'

Fleming obliged and watched as Watson and Jardine climbed out of the car.

Watson pointed up the track ahead that led to an old derelict building. 'Up there.'

Rubble, crumbling concrete and the remnants of rusty metal structures littered the whole site. Fleming walked slowly towards what remained of the building. A wooden door was hanging off rusty hinges. Traces of blistered blue paint hung stubbornly to the panels. All the windows were broken.

'Apologies for the state of the place.' Watson laughed. 'Not the most inviting place, I must admit.'

'Mind if I ask what this is about?' Fleming asked rather unnecessarily. The fact that Watson had brought him to some remote old industrial site and had a gun spoke for itself. It was obvious he intended to kill him. Fleming's mind was racing. He needed to play for time.

Watson pushed him hard in the back. 'In there.'

Fleming stood in the middle of what must at one time have been the site office. Rubble and broken glass littered the floor. He turned and faced Watson and Jardine. 'I think you're about to make a very big mistake. You're in the clear over Nielson's murder, you know.'

'That a fact. I could have told you that I had nothing to do with it,' Watson said. He frowned and added, 'So how come you've come to that conclusion?'

'You were in the frame when Mrs Hayden told us that Nielson was threatening to blow the whistle on you, but we've found new evidence.'

Watson was curious. 'Oh yeah, what would that be?'

'We searched Nielson's house again in case we'd missed anything. There was an address book. It had your number in it... and Anthony Hayden's.' Fleming looked at Jardine who was standing with his mouth half open. 'Yours was there too, Frank.'

'So how come you've concluded that I didn't kill Nielson?' Watson asked.

'There was something else... an external hard drive. It had enough evidence on it to confirm that Nielson was blackmailing Charles Trenchard.'

'Trenchard? You're joking, right?'

'No joke, Bill. So whatever you had in mind here isn't a good idea. They might be able to prove you are guilty of misconduct in public office, but you're in the clear for murder. Might even get away without a prison sentence, but at worst you're looking at two... maybe four years. You'd be out in a year to two years. Kill me and you get life.'

Watson sneered. 'A year... two years... it might as well be life. Know how many criminals I've put away in my time, Fleming? There's quite a few inside that'd make sure the only way I left prison was in a wooden box. I can't run the risk that I'll get a prison sentence.'

Fleming shrugged. 'More chance you'll die in prison if you kill a cop.'

Watson snorted. 'You're forgetting McBain's claim that I asked him to carry out the assault on Jimmy Calder. I'll be in a whole shitload of trouble if you can prove that now that Calder is dead.'

'All we have is McBain's word for that, and the fact you told me where to find Calder which could point to you trying to set me up. But it's all circumstantial, isn't it? Could be difficult to prove unless you confessed to it.'

'Fuck you, Fleming.' Watson raised the gun and pointed it at Fleming's head. Watson was breathing hard.

'He has a point,' Jardine blurted. 'All they have on us are the allegations that we're bent cops. We can't–'

'Shut the fuck up!' Watson screamed at Jardine, the gun shaking in Watson's hand.

'Please, boss,' Jardine pleaded, 'put the gun down, for God's sake!'

Watson glared at Jardine. 'You're weak, you know that? And stupid. They're going to try to pin Potts's murder on me as well. He went to the press with allegations of police corruption and now he's dead. They'll think I had him killed to keep him quiet.'

Jardine fell silent.

'As it happens, I did get McBain to kill Potts,' Watson continued. 'And now I'm going to kill our friend here and that's a fact. He's managed to ruin my career. He wants to see me go to prison and he's going to pay for that. I wanted to get him off the Nielson case before he found out too much. That's why I tried to set him up for the assault on Calder. But that backfired because bloody Tyler, McBain and Paddy Eckhard were careless. There's going to be no mistake this time though. You're a dead man, Fleming.'

Jardine turned to leave. 'I'm out of here. I don't want anything to do with this!'

'You stay right where you are, Frank,' Watson threatened.

Fleming's mind was racing. He had no doubt that Watson was going to shoot him. 'You'll never get away with this,' Fleming said calmly. 'Naomi Anderson knew I was coming to meet Frank. Someone will find my body...' His voice trailed off. Maybe they wouldn't. Maybe they intended to bury him. Oh, shit! He carried on, desperate. 'You're bound to be a prime suspect–'

Watson laughed. 'I couldn't care less whether they think I killed you or not. But I have allowed for that possibility.'

Fleming was desperately playing for time, but he couldn't see how he was going to get out of this. He looked at Jardine whose face had turned white. 'How about you, Frank? Want to spend the rest of your days inside?'

Jardine looked pleadingly at Watson and then at Fleming. 'It's... it's too late. We're already guilty of abduction and threatening you with a gun. We'll go down for that anyway.'

Fleming saw a glimmer of hope. 'As far as anyone else is concerned, I came to meet you because you said you had information about Bill. Turns out your information was to put him in the clear over the Calder business. We could walk out of here and forget this happened.'

Watson laughed. 'Think I'd fall for that, Fleming? Give me credit. No, I have a better plan. I asked Frank to call you asking for a meet so that only his name would be in the frame. He was acting on his own. He brings you here, shoots you and then shoots himself. Simple case of vengeance, then suicide.'

'What!' Jardine exclaimed, panic in his voice. 'What are you saying, boss? Surely you don't intend–'

'Oh yes I do. Sorry, but you've got to die too, Frank. No loose ends, you see.'

Sweat had broken out on Jardine's forehead. 'You can't–'

'Whether I end up as a suspect is neither here nor there, you see,' Watson broke in. 'I'm not going to prison, even for a year. I've got a flight to Spain in six hours, then an onwards flight out to sunny Australia. Melbourne is a nice city, they say. And Australia is a big country to get lost in.' Watson laughed. 'I may just have done enough to get away with murder.'

'You're forgetting something, Bill,' Fleming said.

'Oh? What's that?'

'The car. We all came here in Frank's car. If you take the car they'll wonder how Frank and I got here.'

'I thought of that. The car stays here. Just a short walk and I get a taxi. I pick my car up at the park and ride and it's off to Luton. Got my bags all packed ready.'

Fleming was running out of ideas. He was getting ready to lunge at Watson. It was his last chance. He looked at Jardine to see if he could detect any sign that he was prepared to rush Watson. There was none. Jardine had frozen.

'Enough of the talking,' Watson said, interrupting Fleming's thoughts. 'I have a plane to catch.' He turned and pointed the gun at Jardine as Fleming launched himself at Watson.

81

Three armed response vehicles were speeding out of Oxford heading north with sirens blaring. There were three firearms officers wearing black bulletproof vests in each vehicle. They all carried Glock 17 self-loading pistols and Heckler and Koch carbines. Logan sat in the back of the first vehicle.

Anderson was acting as a liaison point in the MCU, getting up-to-date reports on the position of Fleming's mobile phone through the GPS triangulation capability built into his handset. She was relaying the information to Logan who was tracking its location on the map on his smartphone. The latest report had shown that Fleming's phone had been stationary for the last half an hour.

Logan checked his map again. 'Got it!' He leaned forwards in his seat and spoke urgently to the driver. 'He's at an old cement works not far from here. Best cut the sirens now we're clear of the town. We don't want to advertise the fact that the cavalry's arriving.'

Logan reflected back for a moment on what Anderson had said. She'd questioned whether calling in the armed response unit was really necessary and had wondered if he ought not to have checked with the super first. She'd thought it was maybe a bit over the top. After all, they had no real reason to believe Fleming might be in serious trouble. Not that much trouble at any rate. But Logan was sure he'd done the right thing after the call he'd received from the Met. He was taking no chances.

A few minutes later, the armed response vehicles drew up silently to a halt behind Jardine's car. The armed officers spilled out of the vehicles leaving one officer behind to control the incident. They fanned out in a line, and made their way on foot towards the old building ahead, Heckler and Koch carbines held ready at shoulder height. Logan, who was unarmed, followed.

They approached stealthily and took up positions either side of the old door. One of the men peered cautiously through a broken window and signalled with his fingers to show that three men were inside. Then he held up one finger to warn that one man was armed.

Two shots rang out from inside the building. The lead officer burst through the door, followed by the other armed officers. He shouted at Watson. 'Drop the gun or I'll shoot!'

Fleming and Jardine were both on the floor.

Watson froze. It was more in shock than the command that made him freeze. 'Where the fuck did–?'

The Heckler and Koch carbines were all trained on Watson.

'Drop the gun!' the lead officer commanded again, more urgently this time.

Watson made as though to throw the gun down, but then hesitated.

One of the officers had gone to Jardine's side. He kneeled,

put a finger to the pulse in his neck, and shook his head. He went to Fleming. 'This one's still alive.'

'Is he?' Watson queried. 'Not for long.' He raised his gun.

'Drop it!' The command was loud and urgent.

Watson smiled and aimed the gun at Fleming.

'Fire!' the lead officer shouted.

Several shots rang out and the noise echoed round the room.

Watson was flung to the ground with the force of the bullets tearing into him. Blood seeped across the floor. He tried to say something. It was merely a whisper. The officer who had been attending to Fleming knelt over him to hear.

'What'd he say?' the lead officer asked.

'Not going to prison,' the man said. He felt for a pulse. 'He won't be.'

Logan pushed forwards and knelt down beside Fleming. Blood was oozing through the right side of his shirt. 'Ambulance!' Logan screamed.

'Already on its way,' one of the men said. 'We radioed in for one as soon as we knew where we were going. Just in case.'

Fleming grabbed at Logan's arm and tried to speak, but no words came.

'Hang on, boss. You'll be fine. Paramedics are on the way.'

Fleming looked up at Logan but couldn't make out what he was saying. There were dark figures all around. They dissolved into a haze. Everything went black.

82

B wing in Wormwood Scrubs housed nearly two hundred remand and sentenced prisoners.

The occupant of cell B175 held a man rather better known than the average occupant of B wing. Charles Trenchard had been remanded in custody there, awaiting trial for the murder of Ronnie Nielson. Further charges would follow for the atrocity carried out in Afghanistan.

Other remand prisoners had bullied and mocked Trenchard from the minute he'd arrived. They were a hardened bunch who did not hold politicians in high regard. Trenchard knew he could never last a full sentence. His life was in ruins. There was nothing left. He hadn't slept and had made up his mind. His cell-mate was in the segregation unit and he might not get a better opportunity.

At first light, before the call for breakfast, he got wearily out of his top bunk bed. His face was pale, his eyes red. He tore off a long length of sheet, twisted it into a tight rope and tied one end round the metal frame at the top of the bed. Tugging it hard to make sure it was secure he tied the other end in a noose around his neck. He checked there was only a short enough length for him not to reach the floor then knelt up on the bottom bunk and leaned forward slightly until he could feel the sheet was taut. Tucking his hands tightly into the back of his trousers, he took a deep breath and flung his body forwards. The noose tightened round his neck and his face reddened. His eyes bulged as the pressure in his head increased. He felt a buzzing in his ears and he struggled for breath. The cell became a blur. His body convulsed. Then there was darkness.

Prison officer Gary Nesbitt had been on duty all night. It was time to open the cell doors and let the inmates out onto the landing, ready to make their way down for breakfast. He tugged on the secure chain attached to his belt to pull the cell key from his pocket. Swinging it round while whistling loudly, he slipped his hand up the chain and grabbed the key. He pushed it into the lock of cell B175 and turned it with a loud echoing clank.

'All out for breakfast,' he called, pushing the door open. His mouth dropped open at the sight that met him. Trenchard's body was hanging limply over the side of the bunk bed. His bulging eyes stared lifelessly at Nesbitt. 'Bloody hell!' He called for help and rushed into the cell to lift Trenchard's body up while pulling at the knot securing the twisted sheet to the top of the bed. Trenchard sank to the floor as four other officers rushed into the cell.

'Sound the alarm!' one of them shouted. 'Get the doctor over here and ring for an ambulance.'

'Bit late for that,' Nesbitt said. 'He's dead.'

EPILOGUE

Fleming had his own room at the John Radcliffe Hospital in Oxford. He'd received surgery to remove a single bullet from his right shoulder. The bullet had fractured his collarbone on impact and he'd lost a lot of blood, but the doctors had said he would make a full recovery. He had various lines, drips and monitors attached to him, but bearing in mind what he'd been through, he didn't feel too bad. The painkillers probably had a lot to do with that.

Liz Temple and Matthew Upson had been to see him.

'I've dropped the misconduct procedures against you,' Upson had told Fleming. 'I accept you did the right thing with regard to Trenchard. Even though you ignored a direct order, you had no choice. I understand that.'

Temple had agreed and both she and Upson had praised him for his diligence, and for not allowing political pressures to interfere with his investigation.

'Cecil Daubney,' Upson had gone on to say, 'was not best pleased when he found out that Watson, Jardine and Hayden were bent cops. Neither is Daubney happy with the number of unsolved murder cases. Wants the number reduced.' Upson had drawn a deep breath. 'I'm seeing him later. Police corruption and unsolved cases all happened on my watch. I somehow think it's going to be an uncomfortable meeting.' Upson had smiled weakly and left.

Temple hadn't stayed much longer but had said she wanted Fleming to look at the cold cases as soon as he was back at work.

Freya had also been to see him. They'd had a long chat.

'I think I might finally have closure on the Jimmy Calder business,' Fleming told her. 'Maybe Watson did me a favour in a perverse sort of way.'

'We'll talk about that when you're out of hospital,' Freya said.

After the visits, Fleming was feeling tired. He was dozing off to sleep when he heard familiar voices outside.

'We won't be long,' Logan was saying to a nurse. 'Promise. Naomi here just wants to hand in these grapes and reassure the boss that I've got everything under control back at the office.'

'Huh!' Anderson retorted. 'He means I'm struggling to keep him under control, and the quicker the boss gets back to work the better.'

'Naomi,' Logan pleaded, 'how could you say such a thing?'

'Truth can often hurt,' Anderson quipped, smiling.

'All right,' the nurse agreed. 'But only a few minutes, mind you. He's already had too many visitors today.'

Fleming smiled. As usual, Logan and Anderson were good value for some light entertainment.

Seeing Fleming was awake, Logan went first. 'Ah, glad you're up and about, boss. Thought we'd pop in to see how you're doing.'

'He's hardly up and about,' Anderson remonstrated,

thumping Logan on the back and pushing him further into the room. She smiled. 'Ignore him, sir. How are you feeling?'

'Better already. Grab a chair.'

'You heard the news, boss?' Logan asked.

'What about?'

'Trenchard. He's dead. Managed to hang himself.'

Fleming groaned. 'He obviously knew he wouldn't be able to survive life in prison.'

'The leadership vote is in disarray,' Logan added. 'Looks like there might have to be a general election.'

Fleming grimaced in pain as he tried to haul himself up in bed. 'Watson and Jardine?'

'Both dead.'

'So, there'll be no corruption trial,' Anderson chipped in. 'All three suspects are dead.'

Fleming nodded. 'Upson will probably be relieved about that, though I doubt it'll save his bacon.'

Logan looked at the bunch of grapes Anderson had put on Fleming's bedside cabinet. 'Mind if I have some?' he asked Fleming.

'Sarge! I didn't bring them here for you. Don't you get fed at home?' Naomi protested.

'Making sure I get some of my five a day.' Logan laughed.

Fleming shook his head. 'Go ahead, help yourself. Has anyone been to see Eric Rainer?'

'Yes, sir,' Anderson confirmed. 'I went to see him to let him know he's in the clear. He'd already heard on the news about Trenchard.'

'And Emma Hayden?'

'Likewise,' Anderson confirmed. 'And she knows she has nothing more to fear from Bill Watson.'

'Talking of Trenchard,' Logan said, 'how did Ronnie Nielson get hold of the video?'

'From Eddie Slater,' Fleming explained. 'He was the one who filmed Trenchard. After confessing, Trenchard said that Nielson had told him that he'd taken the video camera from Eddie Slater's locker after he was killed, thinking it might come in useful one day.'

'Oh, by the way,' Logan said, 'Scottie McBain, Tommy Tyler, and Paddy Eckhard have been charged with Jimmy Calder's murder. And McBain and Tyler have been charged with Damien Potts's.'

Fleming nodded sleepily.

'Listen,' Logan said, 'I think we'd better go. We said we wouldn't be long and you're looking tired. We'll pop in again tomorrow, if that's okay?'

'Sure, fine,' Fleming whispered.

After Logan and Anderson left, Fleming was thinking about the cold cases Temple had mentioned. Fleming could see the pile of files landing on his desk, and as he fell asleep, he wondered if Bill Watson had worked on any of them.

THE END

CPSIA information can be obtained
at www.ICGtesting.com
Printed in the USA
LVHW111933160920
666192LV00005B/1014